ADVANCE PF

Bitter Magic

BITTER MAGIC

Also by
NANCY HAYES KILGORE

Wild Mountain

Sea Level

BITTER MAGIC

NANCY HAYES KILGORE

MILFORD
HOUSE

an imprint of Sunbury Press, Inc.
Mechanicsburg, PA USA

MILFORD HOUSE

an imprint of Sunbury Press, Inc.
Mechanicsburg, PA USA

For information about special discounts for bulk purchases, please contact Sunbury Press Orders Dept. at (855) 338-8359 or orders@sunburypress.com.

To request one of our authors for speaking engagements or book signings, please contact Sunbury Press Publicity Dept. at publicity@sunburypress.com.

FIRST MILFORD HOUSE PRESS EDITION: February 2021

Set in Adobe Garamond | Interior design by Crystal Devine | Cover by Sara Oliver | Edited by Lawrence Knorr.

Publisher's Cataloging-in-Publication Data
Names: Kilgore, Nancy Hayes, author.
Title: Bitter magic / Nancy Hayes Kilgore.
Description: First trade paperback edition. | Mechanicsburg, PA : Milford House Press, 2021.
Summary: TBA.
Identifiers: ISBN : 978-1-620068-42-7 (softcover). TBA
Subjects: TBA.

Product of the United States of America
0 1 1 2 3 5 8 13 21 34 55

Continue the Enlightenment!

For Shanti

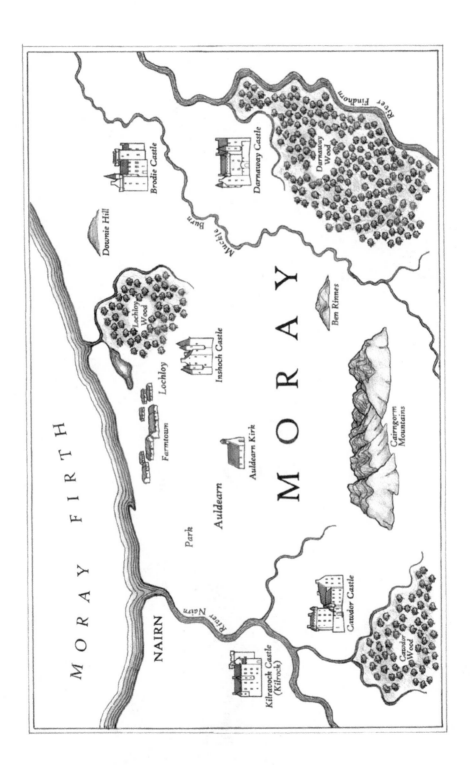

Margaret

Auldearn, Scotland, 1660

CHAPTER 1

The wind blustered, and Margaret pulled her cape tighter, walking briskly past the fields of flax, past the loch, and across the dunes.

She scrambled down the path, slipping on the scree as pebbles tumbled down the dune side. Landing on her feet, she walked toward the sea. *Alone in this wide land*, Margaret thought, except for the gulls that swooped and shrieked above.

And in the distance, a figure, gray and brown against the sandbar.

The woman's dress blew around her as she bent and raked. She was plucking cockles and placing them in a basket. Steady motions, bending and raking and plucking, in tune with the rhythm of the waves and the tide. Just a barefoot peasant, like generations before her and those to come after, people harvesting from the sea and blending with its melodies.

But there was something else about this woman.

A dignity. Or self-possession. An unusual stillness, as if she were a world in and of herself.

The sea churned, and two dark humps rose and fell in the green water. Dolphins. The gray-brown woman faced the sea and raised her arms as if beckoning to them.

Margaret hesitated, then walked across the sandbar as the woman straightened and looked back at her. The hood of her plaid flapped in the wind, hiding and then revealing light eyes in a pale face. Her look was both open and inscrutable. She stared at Margaret and nodded, almost as if she had been expecting her.

Suddenly Margaret stumbled, confused. Though she was just seventeen, the peasants usually bowed or curtsied when they saw her, but this woman did not. Perhaps she should have been insulted, but instead, she was curious. Who was this?

The woman lifted her arms, swinging them back and forth as if conducting an orchestra. The dolphins jumped and flipped in the air. Could they be following her commands? One had a scar on its cheek and the other a dark spot on the back. These were the two dolphins that were here so often, showing off and commanding attention like children. Margaret had always felt that they knew her. Did they know this woman, too?

Margaret clapped her hands—as she always did at their performance—so as not to let them down. "Excellent!" she shouted.

The woman peered at her again. She was younger than Margaret had thought, perhaps closer to thirty, and now she looked familiar . . . one of the farmtown women. Her face was marked by the pox, and her fixed stare shifted as the corners of her mouth curved up. Light seemed to shimmer around her body.

"Titania and Oberon," cried Margaret.

The woman furrowed her brows. "What say ye, mistress?"

"Those are the names I've given them. After the fairy queen and king." The dolphins jumped again and dived beneath the surface.

"The fairies, ye say?"

"Yes, in Mister Shakespeare's play." It had been something she wasn't supposed to read, but when she'd found the volume containing *A Midsummer Night's Dream* in Aunt Grissel's library, she'd begged and begged until she was allowed to read it. When Margaret opened the book, she found herself stepping into another world, a world where fairies danced and frolicked.

The dolphins came close, smiling and raising their soft snouts out of the water. They seemed to recognize Margaret, too, and she called their names again. "Oberon! Titania!" Now there were two or three more, and they cavorted and jumped in the water.

"Mister Shakespeare's been to Elfane," the woman said, "but ye need not travel to London to find it." It was as if she knew Margaret's thoughts and her longing to go to London, now that the ban on theater was lifted, to see a real play.

"Elfane?"

"The fairy kingdom."

The fairy kingdom. Mister Harry preached about this belief in fairies, this "superstition of the devil to keep the people ignorant and away from God."

The woman turned again, flicked her wrist, and called out a rhyme:

> *Go with the fisheries gone to sea*
> *and bring home mickle fish to me*
> *bring the mickle fish to me*
> *go out with the fisheries gone to sea.*
> *In the name of the Trinity three*
> *The Father, the Son and the Holy Ghost,*
> *In the name of St. Andrew and Trinity three,*
> *Bring the mickle fish to me.*

The dolphins dived and disappeared. Margaret gaped. "Did they understand you?"

"Aye, mistress, and they'll do my bidding. I'll have a good harvest when the boats come in."

"How did you learn to talk with the dolphins?"

The woman looked around and lowered her voice. "Nay, 'tis not to say."

The woman launched into Gaelic now. Though Margaret spoke it a little, this was too fast for her. There was one word she understood: *shin,* or *fairies.*

Was this magic? Margaret felt her legs shaking and looked around to make sure her family was not watching, even though she knew they were far away in the castle. If they could see her now, talking about fairies . . . or if, God forbid, Mister Harry, the minister, was about. She shuddered but forced herself to stand firm. "Have you seen the fairies?"

"I have *an da shealladh,* mistress."

"What?"

"The two sights."

Second sight.

"I see the other world, the place of the spirits, where be the fairies."

Margaret's eyes widened. "The other world?" According to Mister Harry, fairies were devils, and people who associated with them were evil. She had never heard about this *otherworld* here on Earth where fairies lived. What did it mean? Was it like in *A Midsummer Night's Dream?*

The woman bowed her head in assent. Veiled but piercing eyes looked up at Margaret. "And where be the dead."

The dead? Margaret shivered.

The wind had picked up, and the woman wrapped her plaid around her shoulders. "I mun go now."

"But—" Margaret wanted to ask, "How?" and "When?" but she was sore afraid, and the words stuck in her throat.

Without another word, the woman of second sight turned and started back along the strand. Margaret could only watch as she walked away, her body small and graceful beneath her garments.

As Margaret hastened home, the mist trailed across the *machair* in filaments—a bit like the fairies, beings of light and air who came and went. To her right sat the farmtown, a dreary place of peasant homes. A cluster of huts in a semicircle, gray humps that rose out of the earth like the dolphins from the sea, it was a familiar sight. But now it took on a different hue as it came to the foreground of her mind. Did that woman have a special place in this community?

Tiny columns of smoke rose from the huts and blended with the mist in a cloud of mystery.

The wind settled, and the air grew still and cold as darkness descended. Margaret walked faster, her boots sinking into the damp earth.

A rustling sound from a copse of oak made her start. Was it a fairy? A Royalist? A murder of crows rose and circled, screeching and squawking. Margaret ran, her heels sinking and pulling up from the mud with a sucking sound.

All of a sudden, something brushed across her face. A fluttering and croaking, and a mighty wing, black and shiny, flapping and rising. The crow carried the secrets of the spirits, messages from beyond. Was this a message for her? Margaret's shoulders tensed, and she ran faster. Only when the castle towers came into sight, lit by the last rays of sun from the west, did she slow down.

Inshoch Castle was her home. Situated on the highest point for miles, it had been built over a hundred years earlier by her ancestors, the Lairds of Park and Lochloy. It was her home, and she was proud of it—proud to be Lady Margaret of the ancient clan of Hay.

The land around it, so wide and vast, was her home even more so. The *machair*—that grassy plain where the cattle grazed—and the loch, the flax fields with feathery greens ruffling in the wind, and the sandy path to the castle . . . this was where she was most free. This was her Eden.

Eden. "Beware," Mister Harry had said. "Beware of Eden, beware of paradise, for it is here the snake doth lurk, it is here temptation lies in wait."

"Curiosity!" he'd shouted. "Like Eve, it is woman's sin." Yes, she was curious, especially about the woman she'd just met. In this world were so many things to discover, and so much she wanted to learn.

"Margaret! Where have you been?" Her mother, Elizabeth Brodie, Lady of Park and Lochloy, looked up from her seat. Tall and regal in her blue brocade gown, her expression was unreadable, a combination of disapproval and relief, perhaps.

"Just walking, Mother."

"By yourself? You know the danger. The Royalists!" Mother worried about the savage Catholics who swooped down in packs like wild dogs to steal cattle, horses, and even worse.

"But it wasn't dark yet, Mother. And the Royalists haven't raided us for two years."

"Fifteen months, to be exact. And your gown and boots! Covered in mud."

Margaret looked down. The hem of her woolen gown and her beloved red boots were wet and stained. She hadn't given them a thought until now.

Her father, puffing on his pipe, looked up from his accounts book. He frowned but said nothing.

Margaret's mother beckoned her to the carved oak table and sat down before a book that lay open in front of her. Candlelight illuminated the pages and flickered on the silken tapestry behind her. Hunters raced, herons soared, and a fox with a silver-embroidered eye glinted and winked at Margaret. She took the opposite chair, closest to the fireplace.

"I will read aloud from the Westminster Confession," Mother declared. "We all must learn its wisdom." Margaret's sister Lucy glanced up from her chair by the fire, but her face showed no expression, and she quickly lowered her head back down over her sampler. Lucy was not interested in religion or history, though she made a good show of it when necessary. She was fourteen, three years younger than Margaret, and she had recently been trying out her flirting techniques on unsuspecting stable lads. Margaret shook her head. *Her* interests were drawn to far more important things.

She settled in, warming her back and wet boots by the fire. "Mother," she said before the older woman started to read. "I want to visit London."

"London? What new notion is this?" Mother asked, glancing quickly at her husband at his desk in the back of the room.

"I could go with Aunt Grissel. She travels there often with Uncle Alexander." Grissel was her mother's cousin, Uncle Alexander, her father. He was the Laird of Brodie at Brodie Castle, a nearby estate much larger than the Hay's. "I could see Covent Garden and Bridewell Palace, the new fashions, the shops, and the great ships in the harbor. And a real play by Mister Shakespeare."

Lady Elizabeth gave Margaret a sympathetic look but shook her head. "London is dirty. Tis ridden with disease and varmints of all kinds, both animal and human."

"Och!" her father's voice came out of a haze of pipe smoke. "London is the devil's playground! Have you not heard Mister Harry speak of that place, with all its pompous papistry? And those plays are dens of iniquity where drunken knaves carouse and brawl." He lay down his fist with finality and bowed his head again over his book.

Margaret clenched her fists.

Father must have sensed her anger, for he raised his head and his voice, shaking his pipe. "And as for this roaming about, daughter, 'twill be the devil to pay."

Margaret knew what he meant, of course. She winced but set her jaw. Sometimes, her parents treated her like a china doll that might fall and break at any moment. Nothing untoward had ever befallen her in her "roaming."

Lady Elizabeth cleared her throat and read from the parchment before her. "They whom God has accepted in His Beloved, effectually called and sanctified by His Spirit, can neither totally nor finally fall away from the state of grace."

Lucy sank further in her seat.

This was about predestination, though, and Margaret *was* interested. It was fortunate that she had learned to read and had even been encouraged to think about theology. But she was feeling contrary now. "How do we know whom God has accepted?" she said. "If I'm in the elect, then I don't have to worry about grace. And if I'm not, I might as well give up."

There was a shocked silence. Lucy smirked, and Mother gave her a withering look. "No, we never give up on grace." She looked to her husband for help, who frowned, opened his mouth, then closed it again.

"Mister Harry will instruct you further, daughter," he said.

Margaret sighed. She would have to learn this Westminster Confession. She felt a flutter of fear in her heart at the thought of the kirk session, that austere gathering where she would have to profess her faith. She pursed her lips. While the English girls got a dance to introduce them to adulthood, she had to be tested by the kirk.

And now, with the light increasing to encompass the whole day and into the evening, wouldn't it be delightful to run along the strand and dig for cockles like the gray-brown woman? She turned her eyes to the light and imagined the fairies dancing with the dolphins.

Bessie Wilson came up from the kitchen, pushing back her head kerchief and wiping her hands on her apron. With her sunken cheeks and beady eyes, she reminded Margaret of a hawk. "Would ye be wanting anything else, m'lady?" she asked Mother as she picked up the tray. She smiled at Margaret, obliterating the image of the hawk—because, even though she had only one tooth showing, and a grayish one at that, her smile shone with warmth. Bessie had been with the Hays since before Margaret was born, and Margaret was her favorite of the children.

"No, thank you, Bessie," Mother replied, waving her hand. Bessie sailed back through the door and down the tower stairs. The kitchen was on the ground floor, off the tower stairway that also led to the outside door.

Of a sudden, Mother's shoulders sank, and she hunched over the book with a sigh. She struggled to her feet, huge in her voluminous layers of skirts. The baby was due soon, and the family was hoping for a boy this time . . . as, no doubt, everyone had hoped when both Lucy and Margaret were due. No one expected wee John, who was three, to live. If Father died when Lucy and Margaret were still unmarried, and there was not another boy child, the estate would revert to the Marquess of Huntly, also known as the Duke of Gordon, the ward holder for all the lands.

And then what would happen to us? Margaret thought. Would she be forced to marry one of the Brodie lads? Unlike their grandfather, the laird, Uncle Alexander, whose conscience and piety radiated all around him, Jack and William spent their time racing about the countryside, shouting and teasing the farm girls.

"I must see to wee John," Mother said, holding her back as she waddled to the staircase. "You may continue your study."

"May I sit with Bessie first, Mother?"

Her mother gave her a skeptical glance, as if talking were too much of a chore, but nodded and disappeared up the stone stairwell.

The kitchen smelled of fish and rosemary from supper, and Bessie's cup of tea sat on the big wooden table. Above the table hung ropes of onions and herbs. Bessie was pouring water into the firepot.

"Bessie," Margaret said, "I must ask you about the fairies."

Bessie flinched; her eyes fearful. She slumped onto the stool and indicated that Margaret should sit on the other one. "What is it you want to know, Maggie?"

Bessie had warned Margaret and Lucy about the fairies. "You must never go near a fairy mound," she'd said, "or they will grab you and take you to their home beneath the hill. They'll put a substitute child, a changeling, in your place, and your family will never know that you are gone." Margaret's mother, though, had said that these were all stories, superstitions, and that true Christians did not believe them.

"I met a woman who sees them and talks to them," Margaret said. "The fairies taught her to talk with the dolphins."

Bessie narrowed her eyes.

"It seems to me a wonderful thing," Margaret rushed on, though, in truth, she was not at all sure it was wonderful. "The fairies can help her, like the fairies in Mister Shakespeare's play."

Bessie's light eyes darted back and forth under black eyebrows, looking to the doors and back. She lowered her head and whispered, "You mun' not talk with that woman."

"But why? She seemed to do no harm."

"She may not seem to, but when you see the straws in the wind, these will be the fairies flying. And then you must sanctify yourself so the fairies and elves canna' shoot the arrows at you."

"I know; you have told me that. And I don't believe it." Margaret set her mouth with determination. "But I sanctify myself just in case." She made the sign of the cross on her forehead and chest, reciting, "In the name of the Father, the Son, and the Holy Ghost." Bessie had taught this to both Lucy and Margaret, though they couldn't let their mother and father know. To them, this was just another Catholic superstition. "But that woman," Margaret said, "is not a fairy."

"I know that woman. Her name is Isobel Gowdie. You must *never* talk to her, and you must *always* sanctify yourself when you see her."

"But Bessie, why?"

"I say no more."

CHAPTER 2

The next morning, Father finished his porridge and stood up from the table. "To the cellar, young lady."

Margaret had no choice. Though she was seventeen, her father treated her like a child, and she had to follow him down the tower stairs, past the kitchen, and to the last cellar room, or some harsher punishment would follow.

He lit one candle in the gloomy dungeon and pulled her over to the wall. "I am your father, and I must keep you safe," he said with some sorrow in his voice.

"But I am seventeen, Father. I know how to be safe."

He shook his head. "Daughter, you must learn to stay within our walls and not go roaming of an evening. Night is a time of danger. Great danger." The birch rod through her pantaloons came like a shock, a terrible sting. At least he no longer beat her on her bare skin.

This punishment hurt her, almost more in heart than in body. This father who loved her—she knew he did—to beat her so, how could he? She clenched her teeth. She would not cry out, but beneath the anger, silent tears flowed. She must try harder to be a good daughter. She would learn the catechism so perfectly that Father would smile with pride. And she would try to stay in the castle in the evening. She sighed. She knew the fields and paths, the Wood of Lochloy, the strand and the shore so well. She was sure that she could roam them without any light.

But now it was morning, with no need to hide. As soon as she could, she saddled Miranda, her bay roan, and leapt up, straddling her horse in a very unladylike seat. Oh, that sting on her bottom. But she ignored the pain and galloped under the gray sky towards the sea, the bog to her left, the fields of flax on the right. She would go to Henrietta. Henrietta Rose, her dearest friend, who would be as fascinated as Margaret herself with the fairy woman.

Skirting the bog, Margaret followed the path past the farmtown. Several people were about—a farmer dragging a sledge, two women carrying peat—but no Isobel Gowdie.

Margaret pulled off her cap as she flew past the loch, over the machair, and down to the strand. On horseback, this was the quickest way to Nairn. Henrietta was the one person she could confide in, the one who knew her best.

It was vulgar for a woman to straddle a horse as opposed to riding side-saddle, but Margaret could go so much faster when she pulled up her skirts and threw one leg over. Loose hair was another thing she could be punished for, because that meant a woman had loose morals, but hardly anyone was around to see her, and she loved to feel the wind in her hair.

Margaret leaned over and clung to Miranda as they galloped along the shoreline, the sea calm beside them, the air gray with mist, the strand deserted with the fishermen out at sea.

She stopped at the estuary, the mouth of the River Nairn. Rich smells of rotting life and oozing life, and little burns gushed through the pale marsh grass into shallow pools. The tide was low, and Miranda's hooves squished in the soggy peat as she splashed into the water and across.

A flock of Redshank pipers, their spindly legs bright orange against the deep brown of the peat, moved away as they approached. Farther down, two fishermen held a salmon net over one of the pools. They tipped their hats and bowed to Margaret.

On the other shore, Margaret pulled on her cap and lifted her leg back over to the side. Nairn was a busy village, and people would be about. She sat up, refined and graceful, and trotted along the King's Steps Road, past the wee thatched houses and to the stone manse beside the kirk where Henrietta's father, Mister Hugh, was the minister.

"Margaret!" Henrietta ran out the front door to greet her, pale red hair translucent in the sun. They embraced, and Henrietta led her into the parlor.

Like the castle, it was dark in the house, but there was something cheerful about the Rose house. Margaret didn't feel the oppression of Inshoch Castle. Perhaps it was because this was a more modern home, with windows and a garden on the same level. No tower stairs to bumble down in the gloom. But really, she thought, it was more because of Henrietta's mother, the Lady Anne. There was about Lady Anne a feeling of flowers, warm colors, and comfort.

Henrietta's freckled nose crinkled up as she smiled, and they went into the drawing room, all yellow and white with sun coming in through the windows. Henrietta, like Margaret, loved horses and riding, and they often met on the strand to gallop and wade. They had been friends since childhood and could talk about anything. Henrietta's father, Mister Hugh, was her tutor, and, like Margaret, she endeavored to be a pious Covenanter lady. But while Margaret was more passionate, Henrietta was thoughtful and practical.

Lady Anne, in a green satin gown, smiled at Margaret as she brought tea and oatcakes, then excused herself to see to the wee lads.

Hungry after her ride, Margaret took a big bite of oatcake as Henrietta sipped her tea. Margaret couldn't wait to tell her. "I met a woman," she burst out, her mouth full of cake, crumbs spilling down the front of her gown.

Henrietta laughed as Margaret brushed them off. "A woman?"

"A woman who sees the fairies and knows magic." Margaret tore off her cap and shook out her untamed curls. "Henrietta, she can talk with the dolphins and the fairies. She has the second sight."

Henrietta pushed back one strand of her fine hair. "Is she a witch?"

"No, no, she is a wise woman, I'm sure. She said a charm to talk to the dolphins, and she sent them out to bring fish to the fishermen. I will visit her and find out more."

"You know that magic is forbidden, and fairies are evil?" Henrietta's face looked skeptical, and Margaret pulled back. She'd thought her friend would be enthralled.

"Yes, I know 'tis what the kirk says, but not all fairies are evil. There really is a fairy kingdom, like in Shakespeare's plays, a world of delight and surprise. This woman knows it, and I would love to go there, too. I will visit her and ask how." Her excitement was so great that Henrietta was now smiling and nodding.

Margaret hesitated. "You won't tell, will you?"

"No, of course not, Margaret. But come with me." Henrietta stood up and went to the door, where she put on her cloak.

She led Margaret out, and they walked, turning right, away from the kirk and into the market square. Here, the fishwives stood with their salmon, trout, and eels in baskets, and farmers prodded cows and goats through the crowds of people talking, watching, or buying. Smells of fish, cow dung, and men's sweat mingled with the sea air.

"Look," Henrietta said, pointing across the square. She indicated the tollbooth, a bleak stone building that housed the jail and the sheriff. In front of it stood the gibbet, a high L-shaped wooden frame with a frayed rope dangling and swaying as if the ghost of a hanged man hovered around it. Beside it was a stake surrounded with charred black rubble and ashes. "'Tis where Jane Dunlop was burned for witchcraft," Henrietta said. "Just last month."

Margaret gasped and clutched her throat. "You could not think that I am in this kind of danger?"

"Of course not, my dear."

A fisherman staggered into the square with a new load of salmon. People shouted and jostled as he called, "Step back. Step back."

The two young women stood in silence, staring at the blackened stake.

ISOBEL

CHAPTER 3

I glanced up toward the castle. Who was this lass, this Lady Margaret with the dark curls and eyes like a deep ale, and why was she questioning me?

I shook my head. Not to think on this when there was work to do. I called the cows, *ooheeee*, like a keening or a chant. One by one, they turned and followed as I walked. I swung my distaff, twirled it round and round, pulled the flax from the ball of lint, and spun it into linen thread with one arm.

Sunlight reflected off the waters of the firth, to the white clouds above and back to the land, where the flax waved its pale flowers, a soft swelling of blue. The fairies were busy today, dancing and skittering in the sun.

Mistress Gowdie, came a voice—a singing voice, like wind on the sea or a rustle of grass. *Good Tidings!*

Tidings? I asked without speaking. *What tidings?*

She was there: the Queen of Fairy, radiant in white and lemon.

I could see beyond sight and hear beneath hearing. Others would have wished for this gift. Others were envious. But this was *my* power, and mine alone.

What tidings? I asked again.

But the queen had vanished, as the fairies did, so unpredictable and capricious.

I shrugged and sang to myself, in rhythm with the walking and the swinging, the waves on the distant side of the dune. My voice was low like the rhythm of earth, the undertone of the day:

Come, Brendan, from the ocean,
Come, Ternan, most potent of men,
Come, Michael valiant down
Bring favor to my cows.

The cows were treasure and sustenance, constant companions and the substance of all life in this land that bordered the sea. A land of darkness in winter and light in summer; and now, in the spring, it was a place of radiant skies over open plains.

I stopped and gazed past the cows. What did the Queen of Fairy mean?

The cattle followed me across the machair, the open grassland where they grazed. Calves jumped and ran back and forth beside them as the cows lowed and moaned. They were thin, like so many in this land—animals and people both.

There was the tree. The rowan tree. Wider than tall, with a thick trunk and spreading branches full of leaves, the tree bore clusters of red berries that burst like fiery suns upon it. The rowan was the threshold between the worlds, the numinous place where life met life, the place I came to sit and spin while the cows settled and fed.

My voice went down to earth and belly, and my song lifted into the song of Thomas:

True Thomas lay over yon grassy bank and beheld a lady gay,
a lady that was brisk and bold, riding over the fernie brae.

I swung my distaff, swaying and humming. The wind frolicked and whistled, and a man appeared.

I stopped. Where a moment ago there had been just a tree, a man was now standing before it. A man in green, from cap to waistcoat to pantaloons. Over six feet tall, with yellow hair and yellow beard, wild and tangled, and a merry smile. He was humming, too. He smiled and sang out the next line in a hefty bass:

Her skirt was of the grass-green silk, her mantle of velvet fine,
and at each tuft of her horse's mane hung silver bells, fifty and nine.

The man paused his song, bowed, and reached out his hand. "Come here, my lady," he said—like a gentleman or a king as if I really were a lady, not the rough and barefoot wife who sat on the dirt in her hut.

I straightened and beamed. The promise of goodness and abundance was present in his face and in his every move. Good tidings.

Yes, I *was* a lady, full of sunshine and good food, plump, and dressed in velvet and gold. I took a step, for I would go to him. Who would not?

But sudden-like, I halted. I lowered my head and glared at him through my lashes. Was this a trick? Some English soldier come to attack me, like in the battle time, when a man had sprung from behind the hedgerow?

Dressed all in red, with a wicked smile and sweat running down his face, the man reached out. In his open hand was a beautiful pastry topped with a sugar violet. I took it, of course . . . to my everlasting regret.

I looked back at the skinny cows, but when I turned again, the green man was gone.

At the fireside that night, with Elspeth Nychie and John Taylor and the rest, I sat with my distaff, spinning still, and sang the ballad again:

> *True Thomas he took off his hat,*
> *And bowed him low to his knee:*
> *All hail, though mighty Queen of Heaven.*
> *Your peer on Earth I ne'er did see.*

The eyes around the fire shone in excitement and suspense, though they had heard the story many times. People were sitting on the dirt floor around the peat fire, with smoke pervading the room and only a thin thread wending up and through the roof hole. Immersed in smoky darkness, here were Lilias Dunlop with her knitting, Elspeth Nychie carding, her daughter Ann teazing the wool into strands, little lads perched sleepily on bags of grain, and little girls snuggled between their fathers' knees. At the end of the room in the byre, the cows rustled and grunted, and the goats snorted and jumped, knocking their hooves against the wooden stall. The strong smell of animals mingled with that of human sweat, unwashed wool, and peat smoke, all as familiar as breathing.

I looked with a dreamy head back into the afternoon. "In truth, I saw Thomas this day."

Thomas the Rhymer was a name everyone knew, and everyone knew that Thomas, though a legend, was still present in the land.

Elspeth pulled a strand of gray hair away from her face and looked up sharply. "And would this be at the rowan tree?"

"Aye, and he was dressed all in green from his head to his toes. I was singing his song, and the cows were with me, and there he was."

"Like to take you into his bed, I'll wager," John Taylor bellowed, and the others laughed.

"A bed of green, green heaven," Agnes Pierson sighed. She stood up and yanked at her low bodice. The men stared at her plump breasts as she poured the last of the precious ale into upheld cups around the circle.

"There's no man like the fairy man for anything a lass desires," Lilias shouted, and the roaring commenced.

John Taylor plucked the fiddle, his wife Elspeth Nychie picked up her pipe, and everyone joined the song:

> *For forty days and forty nights,*
> *He wade thro red blood to the knee.*
> *And he saw neither sun nor moon*
> *But heard the roaring sea . . .*

The little lads got up to dance as Agnes put down her carding and joined them in a jig. The singing grew louder and louder:

> *O, they rode on, and further on,*
> *'Till they came to a garden green.*
> *Light down, light down, ye lady free,*
> *Some of that fruit let me pull to thee.*

We sang and shouted Thomas and the fairy queen through the garden till she bade him stop. The music slowed, and the voices quieted. This was the place in the story where Thomas had to make his choice: the road to hell that looked so fair, the road to heaven, with its briars and thorns, or the road to fair Elfane, where lived the fairy queen.

All but unnoticed, my husband, Hugh Gilbert, passed quietly in through the low door, hunching down his tall form and bringing a new kind of darkness into the darkened room. He unwrapped his plaid—the woolen blanket that everyone used as cloak—lay it down, and sat, fading into the dark corner.

And now the music rose again as Thomas made his choice: He would go with the fairy queen to fair Elfane. He is given:

A coat of the even cloth,
and a pair of shoes of velvet green
And till seven years were past and gone
True Thomas on earth was never seen.

I sighed into the quiet that followed the song. "Ah, were I but to go with Thomas to fair Elfane."

Elspeth looked up from her knitting with a mysterious smile. "But you can, my dear. You can."

From the corner came a *harrumph,* loud and ominous.

CHAPTER 4

In the morning, I fed Hugh first before the bairns who were whinging and crying for theirs. He ate his porridge quickly, made to go outside, but stopped at the door and turned around. "We'll leave for kirk directly when I return."

I avoided his eyes, looking down at the linen thread in my lap. "I mun' spin and finish today."

"Nay, ye'll come with me," he boomed. "I'll not have my wife in the tollbooth again."

The last time I'd tried to stay away from kirk, the searcher came 'round. It was the law of the land that everyone attend kirk. We were a land of the pious, the searcher said, a Covenanting land and all must hear the word of the Lord.

I won't go, I said, but he dragged me off. On the way, though, I pulled loose from his grip and ran, but then three others chased me, took me to the tollbooth, and locked me up in that clammy stone crypt.

I sighed and gathered the bairns. We tramped across the machair, a white gold light slipping between gunmetal clouds and Hugh's tall darkness casting long shadows.

The Auldearn Kirk sat high and wide on its hill above the town, an edifice of stone upon stone, stark in the morning mist. The few small windows, low and crude, gaped like empty eye sockets from the dark interior, and the wooden door was so low that Hugh had to stoop to get through it.

At the top of the hill, we stopped in front of the kirk. To the left of the door a head and hands protruded from the stocks, her hair all a-tangle, her head drooping down. Jonet Fraser, this tall and proud woman, usually so loud and boisterous, moaned to herself.

"What ha' ye done, Jonet Fraser?" I asked.

Jonet moaned again.

"That woman has committed adultery with Robert Cumming," Hugh Gilbert snarled, and he tugged at my arm. I quickly snatched it away and knelt with Jonet. But the strong smell of urine came at me, and I stood up again. The punishment for adultery was to sit here in the stocks all the day long, every Sunday for a month.

"We'll remember Mister Harry for this, Jonet," I said and turned to follow Hugh into the kirk.

We sat in the back, the coldest section of that cold kirk. Most of the other peasants and farm folk stood barefoot on the stone floor, but they always saved a seat for me, Isobel, the Cunning Woman.

In came one-eyed Jack the Smith, smelling of stale ale and horse sweat, and sat down beside Hugh Gilbert. And now Angus Watson, limping on his crutch, his severed leg swinging, followed by his bonny wife Abigail Murray. Around the room, at least half the men had scars or missing limbs, these survivors of the Battle of Auldearn just a few years ago, these victims of the bloodthirsty English. After the battle, they were chased down and chopped up, and those who came back came defaced and disfigured. Those who didn't come back, the dead, still roamed and flitted and sometimes even came to kirk. There sat Alexander Murray with half a head, beside Abigail, his sister, and on the end of the pew old James Glasach with no arms at all, who had been the first to die. I nodded to old James, though I knew the others couldn't see him.

At kirk, Margaret saw *her* again.

Margaret sat between her mother and her sister Lucy and sang the psalm at the top of her voice. She was wearing the new gown that her mother had made in Edinburgh. Though she would have preferred satin, the gown was cotton, in a lovely pale green color and with an embroidered collar in white. Mother had convinced Father that this was a modest style befitting a Covenanter woman. The Covenanters, Margaret's people, had formed the foundation of the Scottish Reformation, and their Kirk was now, she reflected, the most pure and earnest expression of Christianity. They believed that women should never flout fancy dress and jewelry or dwell on outward appearance. Margaret admitted, though, that she did enjoy being noticed in her new gown by an English soldier in town. In his bonny red coat with the shiny buttons, he looked so handsome and merry. He'd smiled at her, and she couldn't help a smile in response until she noticed her father glaring at her, and she lowered her eyes. This father who hated the English, the "bloody red devils" who occupied his land, the land of the Scots.

Mister Gordon, the precentor, a short man with a long beak of a nose, was leading a hymn, and Margaret sang out:

> *Give to the Lord ye potentates,*
> *Ye rulers of the world;*
> *Give ye all praise honor and strength,*
> *Unto the living Lord.*
> *Give glory to His holy name.*

Everyone said she had a lovely voice, clear and high, and it was true that she loved to sing. This was her favorite part of the kirk service. Beside her Lucy, who, with her dark wavy hair looked very much like her sister, raised her eyebrows with a frown, as if to say *be quiet,* but Margaret took a deep breath and sang louder:

> *Worship him in his majestie,*
> *Within his holy throne!*

Another frown shot at her from her father. She knew what he was thinking. Singing was a way to worship God, but one should focus only on God, not on the enjoyment of the music. She adjusted her visage to look more somber, though in truth she continued to feel the pleasure of it.

Shouts and rowdy voices arose from the back of the sanctuary. The peasants were jostling and laughing, not still and proper like the gentry in the front, and of course they weren't singing, as they couldn't read the words. Margaret sang louder again to drown them out, but not before glancing back to see if *she* was there. Everyone had to go to kirk, it was the law, but she didn't see Isobel Gowdie.

And the peasants *did* sing. One day Margaret had heard music from the farmtown. She'd ventured near, seen the people dancing and singing, and longed to join them, but Bessie had pulled her away. "Ungodly ways," she'd declared.

Margaret peeked back again, but her mother pulled at her sleeve, admonishing her to turn around.

The minister stood up, raised his arms, and the kirk fell silent. Mister Harry was tall and thin, with a pointed nose and wiry ginger hair that was never combed. "We are like naughty worms," he proclaimed, his voice shrill and strident, "digging in the filth of our minds and deeds. Our thoughts lead us into sin and evil, and when we see our wicked selves, we shrink in shame and despair."

There were squirming and rustlings from the back of the church, and Margaret hunched up her shoulders. What horrible words. But then she straightened up and glowered. She was not a naughty worm with filthy thoughts.

"So how, the believer asks, can saving work go on in the heart of one so unworthy and fickle?" He paused and wiped his pale hair back from his face, making it poke out like straw on top of his head. He looked up to heaven, then gave a satisfied smile. "Nothing," he shouted, "is too hard for the Lord. God's covenant is written on our hearts in a place much deeper than our own wickedness. Everything will perish, sun, sea, heaven, and earth, but not the Lord's people."

Margaret sighed at the beauty of his words, and on the other side of the kirk, her tutor, Mistress Collace, smiled with a look of rapture. Mister Harry noticed Mistress and smiled back, but she puckered her brows and patted her cap as if to straighten her already perfectly coifed blonde hair.

Mister Harry lifted one arm and pointed to the back of the room. "The devil is in our thoughts and also in the world, lurking in the ditches and glens, disguising himself as a fairy or an elf, and ready to trick you at any opportunity. When you see a fairy, pass on by. Do not give him opportunity, for he will lead you away from the Lord your God."

At the back of the kirk, the scoffing and murmurs grew louder, and the people moved about restlessly. Margaret's hand sprang to her mouth. The peasants all believed in the fairies.

She craned her neck. There she was, Isobel Gowdie, in the very back between Hugh Gilbert, the black-bearded farmer, and two children. She sat still and stern-faced amidst the restless and murmuring peasants, her icy eyes glaring up at Mister Harry.

What was Isobel thinking?

The murmurs and protests grew louder. This was common in the kirk, where the people chafed at having to attend and often argued with the minister—but now the ruckus escalated. Two men stood up, raised their fists at Mister Harry, and shouted something in Gaelic. They started to rush at him, but two other men held them back.

Then a woman threw a shoe.

A shoe! It hit Mister Harry in the stomach.

The kirk fell silent.

Mister Harry's face flushed pink and twisted into a puzzled grimace.

Protest was customary here, and people often stood up and argued with the minister, but never to this extent.

Mister Gordon scurried down the aisle and prodded the shoe-throwing woman with a mace. Mister Harry bowed his head as if in humility, then went right on preaching. Was everyone supposed to ignore this occurrence? Margaret glanced around the room, and everyone, even the peasants in the rear, looked as astonished as she felt.

After church, Mistress Collace and Mister Harry stood in the kirkyard off to the side, deep in conversation. He talked and gestured, his face erupting into florid smiles, his hands waving wildly as Mistress nodded and answered in her measured manner. Only her eyes, widening, narrowing, and changing expression with each word and sentence, reflected her brilliant mind. Mistress Collace's father was a minister somewhere near Edinburgh, and she was well-versed in theology. Margaret's mother admired her considerably and said that Mistress Collace's steady hand was greatly needed in this volatile country. But what were they talking about so intently? It looked as though Mister Harry was protesting something.

Margaret turned to stare at the woman in the stocks. Adultery, Bessie had said.

The woman sat on the ground just beside the door, a filthy heap, her head and hands in the stocks, her hair a tangle of wild snarls. She smelled like a waste hole. A couple of lads taunted her, shouting, "Scurvy whore!"

She spat and cursed back at them, "Rapscallions! Venomous toads!" Some of the peasant men gathered and laughed, enjoying the spectacle. The shoe woman would no doubt be the next captive here.

Isobel Gowdie came out of the kirk with her husband and stopped as if to say something to the woman, but her husband tugged her arm and pulled her away. She and her little family walked silently down the hill toward the farmtown.

MARGARET

CHAPTER 5

The family was sitting in the drawing room after supper. Evening sun shone through the windows, making bright patches on the worn carpet, everything converging into stillness and serenity. Father sat at his desk, Mother was reading the Bible, Lucy working a sampler, and Margaret bowed over her assigned reading, the Westminster Confession, the crowning document of the Presbyterian faith. She smiled to herself. She and Henrietta had agreed to meet at the estuary tonight.

A sudden bang startled them as Father pounded on the desk. "We were struck down at Inverness!"

Margaret looked up. "Another battle?" She shuddered as images of bloodshed and death arose in her mind.

Father shook his head. "'Twas but a skirmish, and the Royalists had us outnumbered. But we'll round up our lads and rout them out."

Margaret sighed. "Why couldn't we live in a place where reason reigns? Where battles cease, where brothers can study and not fight?"

Father laughed. "If you find that place, pray tell me. But I doubt 'twill be on this Earth."

"But now that our true king is coming home, we *will* have peace!" Mother proclaimed. The Lady of Park and Lochloy sat straight and dignified, her dark eyes shining with patriotism. "'God alone is Lord of the conscience,'" she quoted from the Westminster Confession, "and King Charles understands this."

Under the king's father, Charles I, all of Scotland, England, and Ireland had been Presbyterian. But when King Charles I died, Oliver Cromwell became the Regent, and Charles II was forced into exile. Cromwell, who had at first sided with the Covenanters, turned tail and fought *against* the Covenanters, joining with the Royalists to demolish them at Auldearn.

But now that Cromwell was dead, the tables had turned again, and Charles II was coming back to Scotland. He had promised to restore the Covenanters to power.

"And now," Margaret declared in a surge of zeal, "we will be free to worship the true God!"

Her mother smiled at her.

Margaret's father, surrounded by a cloud of pipe smoke, frowned and shook his head but said nothing.

Thankfully, Margaret had not inherited her father's skepticism or sour disposition. According to her mother, this angry father had once been happy and enthusiastic—until Malcolm, his firstborn, had been killed at the Battle of Auldearn.

Margaret looked up from the Confession. "And may Oliver Cromwell feel the fiery scourge of Hell!" She shouted in a burst of loyalty.

"Nay, Margaret," her mother said with gentle firmness. "We must not wish that even upon our enemies. Rather, let us pray that his misguided soul be redeemed in the end."

"Is it true, what they say?" Margaret asked. "About Cromwell's body?"

Father looked up sharply, and Mother spoke quickly. "What did you hear about that?"

Margaret shrank from her mother's stern face.

Lucy stood up and shouted, "That they dug up his body from the grave and cut off his head!"

Margaret wrinkled up her nose. "And stuck it on top of a pike for all to see."

"None too harsh a punishment for that one," Father growled. "The one whose hypocrisy lured us to his cause, then deceived us and turned his back on the true kirk." He jabbed the air with his pipe. "The one who made a pact with the devil."

"But, John," Mother said, "we must not become the savage beasts that our enemies are." She turned to Margaret and Lucy with sadness in her eyes. "This brutal practice of piking heads exists on both sides. But our Lord instructs us not to return hate for hate. Though we live in such trying times as these, we must adhere to the Word for guidance."

Father's voice rose in ire. "The devil cannot be dealt with like a man!"

Margaret bowed her head then looked up quickly from the Confession. "It says here that the Pope is the Antichrist! Doesn't that mean *he* is the devil?"

Father smiled and nodded. "He is indeed. And it gladdens me to hear you are learning your Confession, Margaret."

"But Father, how can the pope be the Antichrist, when, according to Aunt Grissel, the Catholics believe that he is *for* Christ, and that *they* are worshipping the true God? She says we just have a different way of understanding."

Mother and Father exchanged a look, and Father pursed his lips, a sign of his rising anger.

He adjusted his plaid around his shoulders. "Grissel Brodie, like her father, the laird, is too friendly with the Catholics."

"Aye, Father," called Lucy, who was walking around the room lighting candles in the wall sconces, even though the sun was still bright. She held the taper high and stole a triumphant look at her sister. Margaret knew that she was favored by Aunt Grissel while Lucy was not and aligning with Father against Margaret was Lucy's way of getting back at her.

"But don't forget, John," Mother said, staring at him above her spectacles, "that Uncle Alexander is, at this moment, escorting Charles back to Scotland."

Father lifted his shaggy eyebrows. "May God speed the Laird and the King. But—"

As Mother and Father launched into a heated discussion about Uncle Alexander, who was one of the dignitaries bringing the king back from exile, Margaret quietly left the room, noticed only by Lucy with a questioning look.

It was the perfect moment to steal away. The tide would be going out, so Henrietta could cross the estuary, and the sun would be up until nine o'clock. Margaret could be back before dark.

Henrietta, on her steed, was already waiting at the strand. The lasses pulled off their caps and let their hair fly loose, laughing and straddling their horses like men. Margaret thought suddenly of the woman in the stocks and shivered. They could be punished for loose hair in public. She let this thought fly away in the wind as they raced back and forth on the sand and into the water, where the horses waded and splashed.

"Someone threw a shoe at Mister Harry in kirk!" she shouted, putting on a look of distress, as was proper.

"And what did Mister Harry do?" Henrietta called over the wind, her pale hair whipping across her face in wispy strands.

"He just kept talking!" Margaret replied, and they both burst out laughing.

The pair slowed their horses to a walk and became more contemplative. This was the place where they shared their innermost thoughts.

"What of the fairy woman?" Henrietta asked. "Do you still want to visit her?"

A sudden image of the gibbet and the burning place made Margaret wince, but she stuck up her chin. "Yes. I want to hear about the fairies and see them myself."

"Did you know that Mister Harry was a commissioner in the execution of Jane Dunlop?"

"Oh, no." Margaret clutched her heart.

"If you associate with that woman, you might be suspect, too."

Margaret stopped Miranda and glared at her friend. "Enough, Henrietta! I am not an ignorant peasant. I am a Covenanter woman striving for piety. No one can condemn me for talking to her."

Henrietta raised an eyebrow but said nothing, and they led their horses back onto the strand.

"We have always been in such accord, Henrietta," Margaret said. "And I thought you would be as keen as I about this. Tis a whole other world to be discovered."

Henrietta reached out and touched her arm. "Tis only that I care for you, dear friend. And perhaps I admire you, too. You dare to explore what frightens me."

The two clasped hands, and Margaret felt the peace return between them. The sky darkened suddenly as a cloud passed over. "Oh, I see the sun sinking. I must get back, or twill be the devil to pay."

"But 'tis such a beautiful evening." Henrietta had dismounted and was stooping down to pick up a shell. "Shall we not stroll in the sunset?" She lifted her hand and gave the shell to Margaret, who put it in her pocket as she reined in Miranda and turned back to the path.

"You can stay here, but I must go," Margaret called over her shoulder as she spurred her horse into a gallop.

She had almost reached the Wood of Lochloy when there came a thundering of hooves and a shouting of voices behind her. Stomping and neighing, and the clanging metal of swords. Battle cries. Was it an invasion? The Royalists again? Margaret turned Miranda toward the wood, and they trotted faster than ever through an opening in the trees. With twilight upon them, the wood was in shade. Margaret led the horse to a place where the trees were thicker, dismounted, tied the reins to a tree, and stole up to where she could see out.

The shouts and noise grew louder. Now she could see them: a mob of mounted Highlanders with plaids flapping, wild hair flying every which way, swords and pistols waving. They howled and grimaced, their faces smeared black and horrible.

They were headed toward Inshoch Castle.

Miranda began to whinny and prance about on her tether, and Margaret hastily went to calm her down. "There, there, my love," she cooed, "we are safe here." But were they? She cowered and shrank back, crouching behind a fallen log. And what of the castle? Out there were close to twenty mounted men.

Now she heard a sound that terrified her most of all. A shriek. That voice. She knew it.

And there she was—Henrietta—crying and struggling, forcibly held on horseback by a villain with dirty blond hair and a mangy brown beard. He laughed as he crushed both Henrietta and the reins against himself with one arm, waving his sword with the other. The horse stomped and reared.

"Henrietta!" Margaret cried, and started to run out to stop them. Then stopped herself. They would only capture her, she realized, and turned back before she revealed herself. All she could do was crouch behind the log, shaking and sobbing as her dearest friend was taken away.

After they were gone and all was quiet, Margaret tore off her cap, pulled at her hair, and cried again. This was her fault. She should have insisted that Henrietta go home straight away, or that she come with her. She should never have left her on the strand by herself.

And now what was she to do? She couldn't go home. They were heading straight for Inshoch. Would they take over Inshoch Castle and harm her family? Would they use those pistols? Margaret's father hated the Royalists so. Would he do something dangerous and get himself shot?

Miranda had quieted down and was nibbling at something on the ground. Margaret needed to think. When she stopped trembling, she decided to steal through the wood to the other side, where she could see the castle from a closer spot.

She took the reins in her hands and walked as quietly as she could. The villains were gone, but still, she had to stay hushed. She knew there was a path through here, and she stumbled along, taking several different ways; but the wood was so dark, she couldn't find it. She'd known this wood since she was a child, but everything looked different in the night. An owl hooted overhead, and something squawked and fluttered away as branches snapped underfoot.

When Margaret came out into the twilight, she was on the west side, looking in the direction of Nairn instead of south toward the castle. No one was in sight, so she walked Miranda around to the south, where she could see the castle. There it stood in the last light of day, rising on the hilltop with its keep and towers, a majestic silhouette against a rose-tinged sky.

What should she do? As she gazed at her home, the castle that was now under siege, Margaret hugged Miranda, as much to comfort herself as to soothe the horse. Her home was so far away. Suddenly, the sounds came again—pounding of hooves, rattling of wheels, and shouts of men's voices. Now, from the direction of the castle, the noises were less frantic and more subdued. Into her sight rolled the wagons and carts pulled by oxen, all piled high with sacks. A herd of cattle plodded behind.

Margaret yanked at a strand of hair that had come loose from her cap and jumped from one foot to the other. *Those are our cattle. Our oxen. And that is our grain in the carts.* As the men came alongside, she shrank back into the trees. Where was Henrietta? There she was, still held on the horse by the blond-haired villain; but now, her head was bowed in despair. *Ah, woe.* Margaret buried her face in Miranda's mane and sobbed. If only she could take back the last few hours.

Margaret watched and listened as this horrible cavalcade headed toward Nairn—where, no doubt, they would take the road to the south and the mountains. When all was quiet, she mounted Miranda, and they trudged home in the deepening dark. The wind had died down, and all was still but for the lonely lass and the horse moving slowly across the land. Margaret put her hand in her pocket and pulled out the shell Henrietta had given her. Round and conical, with radiating ridges from the tip of the cone to the edge, the shell was a chalky white, and just fit in her palm. A limpet shell. She put it back in her pocket, running her fingers over the rough ridges. Where would they take Henrietta?

"Margaret. Margaret!" Mother, Bessie, and Lucy all ran up to her when she came into the Great Hall. Mother enfolded her in her arms as the three of them wept. "I thought you were gone," she wailed.

Margaret lay her weary head on her mother's shoulder. All of her tears had been spent. She was emptied out, a hollow shell of herself.

"We thought you were captured," Lucy shouted as Bessie wrung her hands. "They stole our oats and hay, and twenty head of cattle."

"I saw them," Margaret said, and sank down into the nearest chair. She wanted to tell them about Henrietta, but the words wouldn't come. It was as if saying it out loud would make it true, and it didn't seem true. It *couldn't* be true.

No one mentioned that Margaret had broken the rule again and stayed out after dark. After this catastrophe, that would be far from her father's mind.

He stood at the window, his face a furious red, and didn't even look at her. "MacDonalds," he growled, and his hand gripped the pistol at his side as if he would like to go out and chase the villains. "Those stinking papists."

Finally, Margaret managed to speak. "They took Henrietta."

"What?" her mother cried. "Henrietta? Where was she?"

"She was with me on the strand, Mother. But I left to come home while it was still daylight. They came from the west, and when I heard them, I hid in the wood. But Henrietta stayed on the strand, and they captured her." Her head fell down in desolation.

Her father placed his gun on the table beside the fireplace. The silver pistol, with its carved designs and curved hammer, had always made Margaret think of a seahorse. It was the gun he had captured from a Royalist in the Battle of Newburn. And as much as he hated the Royalists, this gun was John Hay's most treasured possession. Gleaming in the firelight, the pistol lay on the oak table beside the Bible.

The family remained in a stunned silence until Father picked up the Bible and gestured for all to gather round.

"I will lift up mine eyes to the hills, from whence cometh my help," he read, standing tall before the fire. *"My help cometh from the Lord, who made Heaven and Earth."*

He read the whole Psalm, and they bowed their heads, murmuring, "Amen."

"But the Lord did not protect Henrietta tonight," Margaret whispered to Lucy, who looked up, startled. Father frowned at her, but he hadn't heard, and Lucy poked Margaret with an elbow.

"Tis time for bed, lassies," Mother said.

"But I can't go up the stairs!" Margaret implored, looking towards the stone stairway. It was so dark and gloomy that even on a normal night, she imagined ghosts and demons that might jump out at her. "You must sleep with me tonight, Bessie!" she sobbed, and Bessie looked at Mother, who nodded.

"I must sleep with Margaret, too!" Lucy pleaded, and Mother consented again.

Margaret took her candle and started to mount the stairs, then turned around. "But Father," she wailed, "what if they come back?"

"They won't," he assured her. "They have their plunder, their ill-gotten gains."

Reluctantly, Margaret climbed the ominous stairwell, followed by Lucy and Bessie.

As Bessie unhooked her stays and Lucy huddled in bed, Margaret began to weep again. "What will they do with Henrietta?"

Bessie's eyes filled, and she bowed her head. "I don't know, dearie. We can only trust in the Lord."

CHAPTER 6

Over the next few days, the castle felt even gloomier than usual. Everyone walked about in silence, glancing sideways at the laird, whose misery accompanied him like a sickly vapor. When he spoke, it was only to curse the MacDonalds and moan about his losses. "I am ruined!" he cried. "Ruined!" When Margaret interrupted these tirades to plead for Henrietta's rescue, he told her not to worry. He'd sent word to the English army in Nairn for assistance. As the governing body in Moray-shire, the English were obligated to search out the marauders. Would they find her? Perhaps there was something Margaret could do.

After dinner she and Lucy sat at their sewing in the drawing room. "You mustn't go out roving again, Margaret," said Lucy, as if she knew that her sister was scheming about something. Lucy had a way of raising her eyebrows in the center, so that she looked innocent and vulnerable while she was scolding. "You know how much it burdens Mother." Margaret loved to rove and ramble, as Lucy was well aware, while she distinguished herself by being proper and good.

Margaret sighed. "But I can't help thinking of Henrietta, sister. She *must* be rescued!"

"But if no one knows where she is?"

"Father saw the MacDonalds, so surely there is a way. Someone must know—"

A scream resounded through the castle.

"John! John! Come quick!" Lady Elizabeth's cry carried from her chamber in the northwest tower. Margaret and Lucy jumped up, picked up their skirts, and ran through the Great Hall and up the tower to their mother's chamber.

Mother was standing at the open window as they rushed in, their father close behind. She was pointing out the window, and they all crowded in to look. On a distant rise marched a line of horsemen with a blazing fire leading them on. The fire was rising from a cross—a burning cross held high, screaming red, yellow, and white flames into the blackness of night. Behind it, the troops paraded in silhouette like a procession of devils.

"Who are they?" Margaret cried.

"Let me see!" Lucy pushed her aside to look through the narrow window, and Margaret pushed her back.

"The fiery cross," The laird said with reverence. "'Tis our men. The Covenanters."

Mother's face was angry. "Why are they carrying the fiery cross like that?"

"'Tis a call to battle."

"But there is no battle now!" shouted Margaret. "The battle was over when I was two!"

Lucy clung to her mother's skirts. "What does it mean?"

Their father stroked his beard and spoke in a thoughtful tone. "They are heading to Inverness to stop the Royalists." He smiled grimly. "Our men have learned of our losses, and they will avenge us."

"But they will frighten the plain folk," Mother protested.

"That is the intent." Father stood taller and lifted his chest. "To remind the ignorant ones, those who care more about their bellies and their hearth, the next harvest and the next milking, than the light of God. To inspire the fear of God in them. They will see that the fire of Christ and Covenant is a power far greater than all papist hypocrisy." His manner was solemn, as though he were in church.

Silently now, they watched the movement of the burning cross. As the rider flew, the cross of fire streaked across the dark land through farmtown and village.

"Like the burning bush," Father said. "The voice of God calling them to join the cause."

As Margaret stared, her body grew still. Without warning, something else came into her view: more fires, on the hillside and in the town. Fires burning on the road, men marching. Throngs of men, barely human-looking creatures in scraps of clothing. They staggered and fell, their faces smeared with soot and blood. Their heads were wrapped in bloodied cloths. Some had no arms, and others were missing a leg. They lurched and stumbled into the night.

A log dropped in the fireplace, and a word escaped Margaret's lips. "Malcolm."

"What?" Mother turned, her wide with fear. "What about Malcolm?"

"I saw him. He was with the troops." Malcolm, her older brother, had died in the Battle of Auldearn when she was two; but now he was there, with the soldiers.

Mother broke into tears, and Father hit his fist against the wall. "Malcolm is dead!" he shouted. "And you need not bring these ghostly dreams into our home." His face shone red in the candlelight.

"But I *did* see him, Father. Perhaps he is dead, but I saw him."

"Are you well, Margaret?" Mother put a hand on her forehead, and Margaret realized that she was hot and feverish. "Your imagination is running amok again."

"Malcolm would go with them," Margaret continued in a dreamy voice, her words emerging unbidden. "He would don his cloak and scabbard and boots, and he would plead with Father to go with the troops, to fight in the battle."

Father's head fell as he leaned on the table. "That *is* what Malcolm did."

In her own chamber, Margaret cranked the window open and looked out at the night sky. No fiery cross. Only millions of stars . . . the lights God put into the night. She could see across the rolling fields and farmtown, almost to the sea, with Loch Loy a glimmering reflection in between.

She breathed in the night air, cold and fragrant with the faintest whiffs of the sea. She had been protected, shielded from the wars and battles which, even after the Battle of Auldearn—the biggest battle of all—continued in skirmishes, raids, and all manner of fighting between her people, the Catholics, and the English. But her father could not protect her from what she had seen tonight.

Bessie knocked on the door.

"Come in," Margaret answered. Bessie unhooked Margaret's stays, and Margaret donned her nightdress. "I had a vision, Bessie."

Bessie was hanging her gown in the wardrobe. "What kind of vision?"

"I saw the Battle of Auldearn. I saw Malcolm leaving the house, and then I saw the soldiers coming home. Bloodied and maimed, with the English after them, chopping and hacking them to pieces."

Bessie dropped down on the chair and looked up puzzled. "How—?" Then she sighed. "Ah, yes."

"And Father said it was true. That *is* what happened." Margaret wiped a tear of anger from her cheek. "But why did no one tell me?"

Bessie heaved a sigh. "No doubt you'd not remember, but you had a vision when you were a wee one." Her eyes went faraway and upward, as if to the heavens. She gave Margaret a kindly smile that let her know she was loved. "Thou hast the gift, Lady Margaret."

"The gift?" Margaret punched the bed. "If this be a gift, I do not want it! To see such horrible things. I will give it back!"

"Indeed. Tis a dangerous gift." Bessie sighed again and shook her head. "Yet you may find it of use some day." She stood up and went to fetch her blankets from the great hall, where she usually slept near the fireplace with the other servants.

Of use? How could these awful visions be of use?

CHAPTER 7

When the English soldiers arrived, Margaret was sitting with Mistress Collace, tatting a collar. On the table before them lay linen thread, bobbins, and a pink satin pillow, all aglow in the afternoon sunlight streaming through the high window.

How could she continue with her usual chores, tatting and spinning, and Scripture lessons, when Henrietta had been captured? Where was her dearest friend? In some dingy dungeon below a MacDonald castle? Lying on cold stone, hungry, thirsty, or worse? Was Henrietta even alive?

Margaret forced those thoughts away and stuck pins in the pillow to hold the thread tight. When she'd started it, she had pictured herself at a ball or an elegant castle in London, wearing a red velvet dress topped by this very collar; but her mother declared that this would be a collar for her trousseau. And red would be unsuitable for a Covenanter lass, she'd said. "We don't want to look like the courtesans in London, those shameless women with no modesty at all."

Margaret squeezed the lace in her hand. She and Henrietta had often talked of balls and gowns, but her trousseau? She winced at the thought. To be beholden to a man, serving and birthing, carding and spinning and weaving, with hardly a moment to read . . .

She ran her fingers across the lace, feeling the bumps and smoothness of the tight pattern and allowed herself a brief moment of pleasure in her own creation. The lace was fine and white.

She held it up to show Mistress. "I believe 'tis more beautiful for its simplicity."

"As we should strive to be," Mistress Collace replied, "the way God made us, without richness or luxury." Mistress had lost a child and was always dressed in black. Her gowns were simple, but she still looked beautiful, with her thick blonde hair pulled back under a beaded cap. She raised her clear blue eyes to the light. "Lacemaking requires practice and discipline, just as the mind needs to 'pray without ceasing,' as the Apostle Paul tells us, so we can attune to God and the path of righteousness."

"I should aspire to such righteousness, I know, but my thoughts so often go in other directions."

"Ah, this is the human state," said Mistress with a sympathetic smile.

"And how can I pray without ceasing when so much killing and death comes into our lives? We prayed for my brother Malcolm, but he was killed by the English. And you, the most pious lady I know—your child was taken."

Mistress Collace's face turned cloudy and dark. "Aye, and it was more than one child of mine who died."

"More than one? But how many?"

Mistress hesitated, then spoke so softly that Margaret had to lean in to hear. "Nine."

"Nine?"

The erect body of her dignified mentor slumped, and a tremor shook her.

It was common for at least one infant in a family to die. One of Margaret's brothers had died in infancy, and it was the worst thing she had ever experienced. She had been eleven, and so excited about a new baby coming. But one day, when she saw him in his little bed coughing and wheezing, his wee body suddenly turning whiter and whiter, then blue, she had screamed for the nurse and her mother.

They had pushed Margaret out of the room. Then she heard her mother keening, and she knew. Little Alexander was gone. Margaret felt like she'd been sailing toward a beautiful horizon, but a storm had suddenly arisen, and now she was adrift at sea with no land in sight. She wailed and cried, more than Mother or anyone else. Bessie tried to comfort her, saying that this was just part of life, and it happened to every family. That did not console Margaret, though, because this had happened to *her* family.

She looked at Mistress Collace. "How could you bear the death of so many? All of your children! Nine?" Her eyelashes were wet with tears. "How could you go on after that?"

Mistress Collace was weeping now, too. "It is true that He has tested me almost beyond endurance."

Margaret touched the lace collar on the table in front of her. She lowered her head and whispered, "How did they die?"

"Ah, some to the pox, and one just stopped breathing. But the hardest test of all was my little Emilia. She the most recent, and I the least comprehending."

"How old was she?"

"Just four, but she was the wisest one of all, perhaps more so than I."

"Wise?"

"She knew that she would go to the Lord, and she told me His angels had come to her. 'They assure me that 'tis better to be with Him,' she said. Her sweetness stabbed my heart with love."

Margaret tugged at the thread with a jerk. "But you must curse the God who let that happen."

The eyes of her teacher radiated fierce blue fire like the edges of a flame. "Nay, child. Never speak such words."

Margaret shrank down in her chair. "But," she said in a low voice, "where did the children go? Do you believe that the dead are in some other place, and that we can see them sometimes?"

Mistress Collace looked Margaret in the eye for a long minute. "I believe the Lord allows us to sometimes glimpse our beloveds."

"I see my brother Malcolm. It's as if he is right here at home, and never left."

"Sometimes we see in the imagination, and then we are fooled into thinking they are there."

Margaret's shoulders dropped. She'd thought she could talk about her visions with Mistress, but now she sounded just like her father and mother, who blamed her "unbridled imagination."

"But I do see our Lord Jesus," Mistress continued.

"You mean that you really see him? What does He look like?"

"The most beautiful of men." Mistress's gaze lifted up to the light from the window. "He comes to me and sits with me. I touch his face and feel the wounds on his hands, and see his brown eyes so exquisitely filled with love for me, and then I know that my suffering is His, as well. He fills me with the utmost ecstasy and peace."

Ecstasy and peace. How odd that Margaret was now reminded of the woman on the strand. Isobel Gowdie had been dressed in a plain and threadbare skirt and a dirty plaid, her feet bare and her hair flying out of her hood, whereas Mistress Collace sat neat and elegant in her black gown and modest cap. But the expression on her face was so like that of Isobel Gowdie, as if she were in another world.

"Mistress Collace," Margaret said, "I met a peasant woman, and she spoke a charm for the boats to bring back fish."

Mistress's eyes transformed from fire to ice in a moment.

Margaret continued hurriedly. "I know Mister Harry preaches against charms and spells and such, but this was also a prayer, because she said it in the name of the Father, the Son, and Holy Ghost. And she was sure she would get many fish that night."

Mistress straightened her back. In her black gown and white collar, with her blonde hair under the black cap, she looked cross and stern.

"Perhaps," Margaret said in a small voice, uttering a thought that had just come to her, "I could ask Mistress Gowdie to say a charm for the safe return of Henrietta Rose?"

At the mention of Henrietta, Mistress Collace's face softened. "Aye, lass, your friend who was taken by the Royalists.

"But magic and charms are the works of the devil. These rhymes, though they invoke the Holy Trinity, are spoken not as prayer, but as magic. The peasants still hearken to the time of papacy, when they were told that if they repeated certain words, the words themselves would make something change; wounds to heal, a good harvest to come. They believe that there is something magical about the names of God, and do not see that the heart must be tuned, that the spirit in tune with God is what changes our lives, not magic words."

Margaret picked up her needle and lace again. Mistress Collace was so eloquent, so inspiring. *I will tune my heart to God, and then God will surely hear my prayers for Henrietta.*

Hoofbeats sounded from outside, and Margaret ran to the window.

In stark contrast with the Royalists, this troop of five English soldiers was orderly and quiet in line behind their commander, their red coats and white breeches dazzling in the sunshine, their gleaming horses standing disciplined and proud.

Bessie went to answer the door, Father close behind.

Sounds of huffing breaths and clanking arose from the tower steps, and Father, followed by two tall soldiers, came into the drawing room. Smells of leather and sweat invaded the room, overpowering the sharp, subtle scent of the flax and linen the women had been working on. Margaret fumbled and dropped her lace on the floor.

The commander, a tall, heavyset man with flowing black curls, and his adjutant, much younger and slimmer, stood at attention. Margaret and Mistress Collace, at the other end of the room, stood up and gathered up their tools and lace. Should they leave or stay? They stayed.

Though Cromwell was dead, the English still governed all of Moray from their headquarters in Nairn. Lady Elizabeth had said this was a good thing, as they could keep order and not let the Royalists prevail, but Margaret's father held his skepticism and resentment close, like a falcon on a chain. He didn't trust the English, and never would.

He eyed these English soldiers from beneath lowered lids. Margaret knew what he was thinking. Perhaps it was these very men who had killed Malcolm.

John Hay, Laird of Park and Lochloy, standing a full head shorter than the English commander, in his yellow doublet and brown breeches, took his place in front of the fireplace, fierce and dignified. Behind him, above the mantel, his grandfather Thomas, Laird of Park, stared down from his portrait as if to substantiate the Hay clan's moral superiority.

But Margaret knew that the English saw themselves as superior to the Scots. This commander no doubt regarded her family as country bumpkins. His immaculate red coat and blue breeches looked as if they had just come from under a hot iron, and his full lips spread into a florid smile as he peered down his long, fine nose at her father. "We come at your summons, my Laird," he proclaimed with pomp—and, perhaps, a touch of ridicule. "Major Walker at your command."

"You know of the raid?" Father asked.

The major nodded, and his adjutant, a lad of about Margaret's age, stepped back from the window where he'd been observing the horses. This lad couldn't have been more different than his commander. Tall and thin, he had a nonchalance in his manner and a hidden smile that seemed to suggest he was enjoying this escapade. His hair was straight and sandy-colored, not curled like the current fashion in the military, and this would have made him seem a bit rough, like the Highlanders themselves, if it hadn't been for his elegant manner. He wore his coat and breeches with ease, almost like an afterthought, as if he couldn't care less what he had on his body. His lanky steps were graceful and effortless as he walked back from the window. There was something familiar about him.

"We have heard tell of this cattle reiver by the name Callum Beg," the major said. "Would he be the villain we seek?"

"Nay," Father answered. "Callum Beg is the most notorious cattle thief in all of Moray, and we did suffer his raids here in former times. But Campbell pays him to leave off his lands, and that keeps him, we hope, from ours, as well." Father took a breath as if to control himself, then spat out, "Twere the Macdonalds! We saw them in our courtyard. With Angus at the lead, in all their brazenness, leading off our cattle and stealing our oats."

Why didn't Father speak of Henrietta? Was not one human life worth more than cattle and oats?

The lad stepped up; his interest piqued. "Would that be the MacDonalds of the mountains to the south?"

"Aye. They come from the Cairngorm." Father's face darkened. "Fifty head of cattle they carried away, along with several hundred sacks of oats and hay." He tensed, clutching the pistol at his side. "They raid and roam about, a party of several score—and if I knew where they were now, I would send my lads to buckle a torch with them."

Mistress Collace took Margaret's hand as if to restrain her, but Margaret couldn't help but step forward. "And Henrietta Rose!" she cried out. "What about her?"

Father gave her a look as if to admonish her for speaking out of turn, but the commander frowned and turned to her. "And who is this?"

"My dear friend Henrietta, of the Roses of Kilrock. We saw her carried away! Oh! Oh!" She wrung her hands, hopping from side to side with tears burning her cheeks.

"She is the daughter of Hugh Rose, Minister of Nairn," Father explained.

Now the young lad was attentive. His body poised and full of spirit, but he refrained from speaking. He smiled at Margaret.

Oh, she exclaimed inwardly. This was the soldier who had smiled at her in the village. She felt a blush she hoped was not visible and pulled at her gown—just an ordinary brown skirt with gray bodice, somber colors for a Covenanter lass. She wished she had on a prettier gown.

"We will do all we can to bring these villains to justice," the commander said as Father raised a suspicious eyebrow.

Margaret could see that the lad was eager to speak, but when he did, it was in a respectful tone. "Excuse me, sir, but I believe I can find them." Both Father and the commander started and turned towards him.

After a pause, the commander cleared his throat. "In that case, we will certainly bring her home soon." The lad moved over to the window and looked out at the horses.

"And for my losses, I will receive recompense, I trust?" Father asked.

The major shook his head. "This is not an easy thing, my Laird. These reivers make the cattle disappear, along with the other livestock and grain, and then they deny everything."

"Then I will petition the government for restitution, as the law provides."

"Ah, this may be just as difficult. There was only one case I recall in which restitution was granted."

"Thomas Dunlop of Grange," Father answered. "I know the case."

The commander bowed his head in agreement. "A lengthy court case, and rare: the plaintiff did win, but only after five years." Major Walker paused. "And I wonder if the law would even apply, in this case."

Father's face reddened. His mouth clamped shut, and his eyes were furious as the two soldiers left.

Margaret watched from the window. The lad sprang onto his horse, eager and confident. Though she had only seen him one other time, she had the sense that she knew him well: from a dream, perhaps, or from something else from long ago that she couldn't quite name.

Margaret walked back to Mistress Collace and the lace at the far end of the room, her shoulders sagging. The young man had smiled at her but turned away so quickly. To him, she was probably one of those ignorant Scots who'd never even heard of Shakespeare. He had a diffidence and a distance that belonged to some other world: a place of ease and knowledge, a place where people were free to enjoy theatre and art and music and didn't have to worry about being attacked by wild-haired Highlanders who stole their food and captured their friends. A peaceful English village, perhaps; a place where life was not focused on revenge.

But he would search for Henrietta.

As would she.

KATHARINE

❧

CHAPTER 8

Mistress Katharine Collace stepped out of the courtyard and set herself a brisk pace along the road to Auldearn. That expression on Margaret's face, the firm-set lips, the brown eyes intent on something in the distance. What had she been thinking? Hopefully, she wouldn't run off again, with these cattle reivers swooping about and ransacking Protestant farms.

Katharine was on her way to the manse. She squared her shoulders and smiled to herself. She and Mister Harry would continue the discussion they'd had after kirk. In his sermon he'd scolded the plain folk for adhering to the old ways, for calling upon the cunning women when they were sick instead of the one doctor to be found in all of Morayshire. As everyone knew, one doctor was insufficient for this population, and his practice of leeching and bleeding for almost every ailment was not popular. She had pointed out that the cunning women could often effect better cures, but then he only became more adamant in defense of the doctor.

He'd cited the doctrine of total depravity, quoting Titus: *unto them that are defiled and unbelieving nothing is pure.* These women, he said, need to be squashed underfoot before they contaminate others.

But weren't these women as capable of knowing God as everyone else?

Mister Harry was such a passionate preacher, but behind his burning eloquence, was there something missing? *No,* she thought, *Who am I to put myself above a minister of the Lord?* She needed to curb this sinful arrogance.

She had much to learn from this man, and, she modestly hoped, also much to contribute to him.

She looked behind her at Inshoch Castle, stark and bare on its hilltop. *How did I end up here?* This wild country of the Highlands was not an inviting place: flat plains of scrub and peat with occasional stands of gorse or heather, muddy roads and pools of standing water from frequent storms; constant wind and harsh stone mountains in the distance. The few clusters of mud huts comprising the villages were so dispiriting compared to the charming towns of England or even some of the communities around Edinburgh.

But today there was something different in the air. A clearing, an opening, and the beauty of the land was emerging like a shy and lovely maiden stepping out of some desolate hovel. The air was dry and sunny, warm for April. Wildflowers sprouted on the roadside, and in the distance, where the land spread down to the sea, sheep and cattle were scattered like toys on a green carpet.

She slowed down and picked up a stone the size of her palm. Such a simple piece of God's creation, with specks of quartz sparkling in points and crevices. Like the beauty of the Covenanters' theology, simple and solid, with so many facets that made it shine in brilliance.

The sky was a universe of billowing clouds, unfolding in a vastness of gray and white, arcing above her as she stood, small and solitary, on the flat land.

Katharine's dream, and that of the Covenanters, was of a new, pure Scotland, a moral government based upon love and justice. After all the decadence and corruption in the Catholic churches, John Knox had seen a new way, a new way of being Christian. His *Book of Discipline,* based upon St. Augustine's *Civitas Dei,* envisioned a society guided by the Presbyterian kirk, not the pope or the king. It would convert the Catholic Church's holdings, wealth amassed through corruption and greed, into alms for the poor. The new society would mirror the Kingdom of God.

Soon, she would introduce Knox's luminous text to Margaret: a girl with wide, brown eyes and a sturdy body, who loved theology as much as she loved riding her horse. Margaret was both earthy and ethereal, and Katharine thrilled to the endless questions that came out of that innocent child, though at times they brought her up short—like today, when the girl had asked Katharine about her children.

Katharine sighed. Her lost children. Perhaps she could bring these thoughts to Mister Harry, who, in spite of his shortcomings, was her spiritual guide here in Morayshire.

The manse was situated on the far side of the village of Auldearn, several miles yet, but the day was so clear, that the village was now in sight.

Ah, Edinburgh. She sighed. Another loss. That place of elevated discourse and interesting ideas. Her father, who believed in the education of women, had always affirmed her interest in theology and encouraged her desire to converse with the other ministers. One winter's day she'd sat beside the fire with a group of learned men as Thomas Hogg, the brilliant hero of the Covenanting cause, had spoken. His voice came deep and sonorous like the rolling thunder—like something inevitable, like the predestination he sought to explain. She had joined in the discussion, almost an equal with the men, and Thomas had praised the depth of her spirit. He had even thanked her for illuminating *him*.

Katharine smiled at the memory, and bent down to pick a delicate lavender flower, then looked out to sea, breathing in the salty breeze. On the distant road, a man was walking beside his horse and cart.

When she had been hired by the Lady of Park and Lochloy to teach needlework to her daughters, Katharine had harbored mixed feelings. Auldearn was isolated, far from the excitement and the heart of theological discourse, and she would miss the stimulating conversation and new ideas in Edinburgh. She'd prayed about the decision and then saw that the Lord was calling her to this place. She didn't know why, but there must be a reason.

Certainly, the girls were sympathetic charges, and she could see that they benefited from her scriptural teachings as well as the needlework. But what was her greater purpose here? Perhaps Mister Harry could shed light on the subject.

The clacking of wheels grew louder, and a farmer with his horse and cart appeared before her. He was a tall man with a long black beard, and his horse, thick and tall, was also black. The farmer's cart was piled high with green sheaves of spring barley. He doffed his cap and gave a slight bow. "Mistress," he murmured.

"Good afternoon," Katharine answered. "Twould appear a good harvest?"

"Yes, Mistress, the Lord has brought rain and sun for the corn." *Corn* was what the people here called any kind of grain. Oats, barley, wheat . . . it was all *corn*.

Such a polite man, Katharine thought. She had seen him in kirk.

As he clattered away, she continued her walk and her reflections. *Illumination* was the word Thomas Hogg had used. She had *illuminated* him. And why could she not bring that illumination here? Not only to the girls, but in dialogue with the minister, Harry Forbes? Was this why the Lord had called her to this bleak land?

On the hill to her right stood the Auldearn Kirk, a rough stone building with a few small windows along the side. The village, just ahead, was a tiny cluster of stone and wattle houses with steep thatched roofs overhanging the road. At the near edge of town a few people were gathered under the spreading branches of a giant oak.

Across from the little gathering, the alewife, Maggie Burnet, stood in her doorway. When she saw Katharine coming, she shouted at one of the women. "Jonet Fraser, ye drunken whore, quit yer bellowin'!" Katharine hadn't heard any bellowing; in fact, the people had been standing in a huddle and conferring in whispers.

Jonet Fraser. Wasn't she the one who had been in the stocks for adultery? Four sets of eyes glared as she walked by.

A thin stream of black smoke rose from the blacksmith's chimney, and as Katharine passed, she could see two men inside at the fiery forge. Next came the pottery, the dye house, and the seamstress's shop. Katharine liked to visit the seamstress, Lilias Dunlop, who also did spinning and weaving. Sometimes, she could find yarn or linen thread here for her needlework, but the wool and lace, she felt, were not of the quality she herself could make. Immediately upon that prideful thought, she begged the Lord's forgiveness. Pride was the devil in disguise, and she had to watch for his stealthy appearance.

After the seamstress's house came the manse—the only building in the village with a second story and two brick chimneys. Katharine approached the oaken door. Unpainted, it was scuffed and gouged, as if someone had taken a knife to it.

She walked up to the scarred door and knocked. Harry's wife, a short, broad woman, opened the door. Mistress Forbes, from beneath veiled lids, eyed Katharine up and down with an expression Katharine could only think of as spite. Why would this woman hold a grudge against her? Mistress Forbes scowled and shoved Katharine into the parlor, almost knocking her over.

Taken aback, Katharine righted herself. "I believe," she said, "we were supposed to meet in his study?"

"Ha!" The woman snorted. She pointed toward the hallway, then left the room.

As she recovered her bearings, Katharine observed her surroundings. Beneath the window, a table with one leg missing was propped against the wall, and beside it squatted a sofa, its horsehair worn away to the bare seat. On another table, a thick candle nub in a pool of melted wax looked as if it had been there for years. Dust lay deep on the furniture and windowsills, and a musty smell pervaded the room. That woman, with her imprudent manners and foul housekeeping, was a shocking travesty of a minister's wife. One must pity the minister, Katharine thought, to have made such a match.

She stepped into the hall and proceeded along the dark corridor. A child appeared out of the gloom, with a dirty face, bare feet, and nothing on but a thin shift that hardly covered its bottom. "Hello," Katharine said, but the child retreated back into a corner, silent and staring.

A sudden flurry arose, and a young serving woman of perhaps sixteen rushed past. Her hair was loose, and her cheeks flushed. She glanced at Katharine but didn't speak. *Who was she?* Katharine felt a tensing in her body, an uneasiness—not just about Mistress Forbes, but about this house.

At the end of the hall, a door opened, and Mister Harry, tall and gaunt, smiled broadly. "Mistress Collace. Please come in." He pushed back his sparse ginger hair, uncombed as usual, and ushered her into the room.

This was the first time Katharine had been to the manse, and the second time she had met with Mister Harry. After the kirk service, he'd invited her here to continue their "exalted discourse."

Katharine took a seat beside the fireplace, and Mister Harry sat opposite her. He beamed as he arranged his long limbs in the chair and sat at an angle. His clothing—the baggy, too-short trousers, stained white shirt under a jerkin, and crooked ruff—was in disarray, more so than usual.

Though extremely thin, Harry Forbes had a sensual face that seemed to shift and react with every passing breeze. Full lips over protruding teeth twitched and contracted as he spoke, and his smile emerged randomly, either to accentuate his speech or compensate for some inner pain.

Mister Harry's smile was lingering on her right now, and she clutched at the neckline of her gown, feeling somehow exposed. He was a man of the cloth and her spiritual advisor, she reminded herself. This was the place where she could open her heart.

"We were discussing," she said, taking her Bible out of her bag, "the doctrine of total depravity and these cunning women. And I have been pondering the meaning of Genesis I."

Mister Harry adjusted his ruff and opened the Bible on the table beside him.

Katharine took a breath. "God, it says, made man in his image. Male and female both, in the image of God. And if this is true, are not these poor women also made in God's image?"

Mister Harry dropped his Bible on the table with a bang and stared at her. He was speechless, something she'd never seen. He rubbed his hair and re-crossed his legs.

She waited.

Finally, he spoke. "Yes, you are correct. We are all made in God's image. But we are also all born in sin, and our task is to work toward goodness, something these wretches do not."

"I know we are born in sin," she said, "but how hard to believe, when I think of my children, so innocent." She bowed her head and shook it. "And after this latest death of my dear daughter. She who saw the angels."

That sweet child had been four years old—older than the others who had died. Katharine had loved her dearly, perhaps more than all the rest. Once, as Emilia had lain in her bed gazing up to heaven, Katharine asked if she would she take any meat. Emilia answered that she would come to Christ, and that his flesh was meat enough. "In Heaven, the Lord is there," she had said, "and the father of the Lord and all the holy angels and all the bonny things are there. And he will give me a new song to sing, *Hallelujah*." Katharine's tears came at the words, as if the child was already in Heaven. But then Emilia was gone. And again came the need to bury a child: a child of her body and soul. When they laid her in the ground, Katharine's arms reached out as if to hold, but found nothing . . . only emptiness. Now she was almost thirty and childless again.

"Ah," Mister Harry said. "We must endure such pain and suffering in this life, and these tests are given precisely to strengthen our faith."

They bowed and prayed, and Harry's words came clear and true. She felt a lifting of the weight as she sighed. "You have helped me remember," she said, "that in the loss of one thing the Lord gives something more, if only we can discern it. I find solace, and even ecstasy, in knowing that I, too, am the bride of Christ. He comes to me; I see and feel and hear him with all my senses, and he soothes my brow. He gives me such pleasure in his presence."

"Ah, yes." Mister Harry was sitting up now, more alert. "And what are the pleasures you find there, my dear?" Was that a leer? It couldn't be. To her own surprise, Katharine herself was now speechless. Had there been something unseemly in his question?

He looked away, his sharp nose affording him a rather dignified profile, then changed tack. "Sometimes, an earthly marriage is given to us as a trial, a continual chastisement, to remind us that our true loyalty and faithfulness, our true pleasure, should be in the Lord."

"Yes." Katharine sighed. "In my experience, rarely is marriage made in heaven. It is an earthly chore, sometimes entered into too hastily, but then we must pay the price for that haste." She knew too well the price. She'd been young, eighteen, and had not followed the advice of others in marrying John Ross.

Harry's smile widened. "And when one heart finds another, and minds are understood, as yours to mine, should we not rejoice, as well? And find solace therein?" He reached over and lay his hand on her knee.

Katharine started and stood up, wrapping her cape round her shoulders. She was confused. *Mister Harry is highly reputed for piety,* she thought. *But he took a liberty.* And she could never go in with that. She must examine her heart. Had she encouraged this liberty? Had she been backsliding? "Mister Forbes, I must go."

Mister Harry's smile faded, his eyebrows shot up, and his pale eyes looked almost tearful. "Ah, my dear, I, too, have a heaviness on my heart, and I had hoped I could confide in you, as well." He seemed unaware of her discomfort.

Perhaps she had misinterpreted his action. She sat back down.

"Such evil times we live in," he lamented. "With this belief in fairies and devils, and such a preponderance of witches."

She covered her mouth with her hand to hide the gaping. He'd steered the conversation back to his grievance.

"The simple people," she said. "Perhaps if they could read, lessons in scripture would advance their understanding."

He shook his head. "They need not read, but only listen to the Word, something they resist. They would rather believe in magic and endanger their eternal souls than attend to the Word of God. These witches, they rhyme and chant, and already, they have caused much harm—much evil in Auldearn."

"And you do speak against this evil in the pulpit," she replied. In fact, Mister Harry spoke against witches too often, in her opinion. She wished he would stick to the deeper questions of theology. Mister Harry could be eloquent when he wasn't focused on the witch controversy.

His shoulders sank, and he bowed his head. "The Lord has convicted me thrice over to *find* these maleficent women, to discern their deeds, and to root them out." He raised his head, his eyes shining. "This is why I warn and adjure the people to bring their names to me."

Bring their names to him. "Wasn't there a case in recent months?" Mister Harry, she knew, had been instrumental in bringing a case to trial.

"Ah, yes, Jane Dunlop. At first, she denied, but then gave a full confession."

It was common knowledge that Jane Dunlop had been pricked with pins and kept awake until she confessed. Katharine shuddered. "And she was burned at the stake."

Mister Harry bowed his head. "I know some objected, but I thank our Heavenly Father for showing us this evil incarnate. This was the only way to abolish it." He sighed. "But sadly, the power of Satan lives on in our parish."

"More witches?"

"Ah, too, too many." Mister Harry's eyebrows and lips went through several contortions, and his voice became whiny. "They have even come here, to my home, and caused me great harm: stomach pain and other sickness."

Katharine was silent.

"Exodus 22:18," he said. "*Do not suffer a witch to live.*" He paused. "And there is one here who yields much power and influence."

"A witch?"

"Aye. She is the leader of this group, I believe. Her name is Isobel Gowdie."

Katharine stared. This was the woman Margaret had met on the strand. The one Margaret had wanted to ask for a charm.

|SOBEL

CHAPTER 9

As the sun went down, I snuffed out the candle and bedded the bairns on the floor, their plaids wrapped round and round. Little Maria was demanding more milk, but the cow had not yet recovered from the winter, and there was no more, so I gave her a cup of ale I'd hidden behind the chest and a dram to the other two, as well. Immediately, the three bairns fell fast asleep. I banked the peat on the fire, peeled off some hay from the bale, threw it over the byre for the animals, and spread the extra plaids on the mat in the corner. And then Hugh Gilbert, who had been watching me in silence, grabbed me and pulled me down.

I submitted, as always. And as always, Hugh was fast and rough. This time, I felt some pleasure as I thought of Thomas the Rhymer, the man in green, and my body delighted as the warmth of Thomas came into me.

Hugh began to snore. I closed my eyes, and my body went still. Would I see him? Thomas, as full of sunshine and light as Hugh Gilbert was consumed in sullen darkness.

Would tonight be the night? Slowly, slowly, the familiar feeling came. My body became stiff, and now I was above it, with body beneath me. It was not my body now, but a stiff wooden thing: a broom, a besom, a twig tied with branches and straw. The besom would lie in the bed. And if Hugh awakened before I returned, he would think this piece of wood and straw to be his wife.

Now I was outside the hut, and here was Thomas, his clothing all white this time, his long yellow beard and hair wild and fiery. "Are you ready, my lady?" His eyes sparkled like sunlight on water. Beside him hovered a slight and vigorous spirit in red, a tiny figure with long red hair. The Red Reiver: my own sprite. I knew him in my heart and mind and soul. He was, in fact, a part of me, in me and beside me, a spirit to protect me in my sojourns into this other world.

"I am ready, Thomas."

Thomas lifted his chest and looked down at me. "But lady, my name be William."

I stepped back. "William?" I stepped further back to the door, or what passed for a door, that hole in the mud wall.

"Aye," he roared, standing taller and taller. "Thomas be the king of the Fairies, but I am greater and grander."

I had thought to meet with Thomas the Rhymer, he who lives with the fairies and courts the fairy queen with his silver harp. I lowered my head and peered at him through my lashes. "And why should I go with you?" I demanded. Was there something here to bargain for?

"I can give you power."

I felt the Red Reiver spritely and close. He nodded vigorously and hopped up and down.

"Power?" I said. "I *have* the power. I know the power of the sea, and the crow and the hare, the plants to heal, the charms and the cures."

"Ah." He looked down from his great height with the merriest of smiles, his face aglow with light and honey. "But with me, you will fly. You will eat and drink your fill; you will learn to spite your enemies. You'll be invisible; you will be able to strike and kill who you will." His smile was a fiery glint. "All this and more."

I had hoped for Thomas, but perhaps this William was greater. I could journey with him and have all manner of power. I could spite my enemies.

"Come," beckoned William, fast astride his black stallion.

And now I saw that my own white steed awaited. I sprang upon the horse calling, "Horse and hattock, ho! Ho and away!" And now I was aloft, and my body alive, every part, with the flight and the thrill and the speed. I was no longer hungry, and pain was unheard of, unknown, unimagined. My body was light—light as air. And now I was large, so great that I was part of everything, and everything a part of me. "Horse and hattock, ho!" I called again, and we flew through the night, over farmtown and field, over dunes and machair and mountains.

I could swoop without effort, and even through clouds, see all below. We soared, almost to the Cairngorms, over Ben Rinnes, its mountaintop painted white with snow. Now fading and misting, now clearing, but yes: a dingle, a fire, a camp. Men and horses, stomping and shouting and bucking.

"No time to stop," William called, and on we went, above the mountains and west, all the way to Darnaway Castle. In through the chimney and into the Great Hall, the seat of the Earl of Moray, the grandest hall in all of Morayshire and perhaps all of Scotland.

Here were noblemen and ladies in the finest of dress, gowns in silks and velvets, diamonds in their hair and on their fingers. They stood in the dusky hall in torchlight and candlelight, their satin and jewels glittering in the shadows. With glances and whispers, they stared at me. "Who is she?"

No longer the ragged peasant, one who was ignored and dismissed, now I was seen—and not only seen, but honored. The noble people looked at me in awe. I was their queen. I wore a shimmering gown of diaphanous silver, the most dazzling one of all. The people bowed to me, and I felt my power. Here was Elspeth Nychie, whom William called "Bessie Bold;" and now Lilias Dunlop, "Able and Stout." Here were Bessie Wilson and so many others from the farmtown, all dressed as fine ladies, though none as fine as Isobel the Cunning Woman.

The room flickered and thrilled with the presence of William: lusty William, so full of secret delight that when he passed and touched me with the softest graze, I warmed and quivered to my very root. This was a feeling Hugh Gilbert could never cause, let alone imagine.

William had transformed again. He was now clad all in black. A long black doublet, black breeches and boots, his hair and beard and eyes . . . all black. We were in the kitchen now, and he opened his arms and waved his hands over everything. "Eat! Drink!" I didn't stop to wonder why he had transformed again, this time from light to dark. I was hungry, and I ate.

Meats and breads, cheeses, cakes, and fruits on delicate plates, and wine in crystal glasses. We feasted until we were full and could eat no more. We laughed and danced to the pipes and sang until dawn had nearly come, right there in the castle kitchen.

In an instant, a flash of the eye, we were back on our steeds and flying. Through the sky and back to my bed I flew, a woman of power. I, who knew words and rhymes, the thread and straw and clay, the fruit of the corn, the sheaves of rye, and knew what use to make of them. And now I knew more . . . so much more.

MARGARET

CHAPTER 10

When the English soldiers had come, the young lieutenant seemed so enthusiastic and intent upon finding Henrietta. But how would he know where to look for her? Would he take his troops with him? Would they get caught in another battle?

After two days, Margaret could wait no more. She saddled Miranda and raced down to the strand, across the estuary and into Nairn and the English headquarters. Situated on the King's Steps Road, the building stood tall and stately. Except for the old castle, this was the grandest building in town. The English had commandeered it from Hugh Campbell's family, the hereditary sheriffs of Morayshire who'd been none too pleased about being displaced to one of their other homes. Of course, this was to show the Scots who was really in charge.

Margaret arrived in a flurry of skirts, her curls escaping from her cap. She jumped down and tied her reins to a post.

A soldier in full red coat over blue breeches stood guarding the door. He raised his eyebrows.

"I must see the major," she demanded.

The soldier's lips started to lift in a smile, and he shifted his weight. A leather belt was crossed over his chest to support the rifle protruding from behind his back. "And who might be asking?"

Margaret stood tall. "I am the Lady Margaret Hay, daughter of the Laird of Park and Lochloy, and I must see Major Walker on urgent business."

The soldier looked confused. His face became stern, and he studied her as if considering. His brown hair was cut straight beneath the ear, and he had heavy brows and a dark complexion. "Wait here, my lady," he said with a bow, turning and opening the heavy door behind him.

Margaret stood in the courtyard in the morning sun. The air was sharp and gusty with damp sea winds. On the road, women walked by carrying baskets or buckets as they headed to the center of the village.

Finally, the guard returned. Behind him was Major Walker, whose long black curls flowed over his shoulders from beneath a wide-brimmed hat. His small eyes looked down at her. "Good day, Lady Margaret. Has your father sent you?"

Margaret tucked back a strand of hair and hesitated. "No." Under her skirts, she tapped her foot discreetly and looked up at him. "But we are all so distressed about the Lady Henrietta. I have come to inquire about the search. Is there any news?" She turned her head, searching the windows and door, hoping the young lieutenant would emerge.

"I told your father that we will notify him at the completion of our mission."

"But where have you searched?" Margaret pleaded. "Have you found anything yet?"

"This is a military operation, young lady, and we do not discuss strategy with outsiders."

Outsiders? How dare he call *her* an outsider, when he and his countrymen had invaded her country? "But is the young lieutenant searching, as he'd said?" She'd perceived a spirit of adventure in the young lieutenant and had felt sure he would go out looking.

"Lieutenant Massie has been dispatched to more important business."

"What? Are you saying that you are no longer searching for Henrietta Rose?"

Major Walker was holding a large ring of keys, and he shook them as he glared, looking down his pointed nose at her. "Please give my regards to your father," he snapped, turning and marching back into the building.

Margaret spun on her heels, mounted Miranda, and galloped back toward the castle. Her father had been right. These English only pretended to care about the local people. They were not going to continue searching.

At the estuary, she slowed down. The tide had risen since she'd come across, and she now had to find a shallow spot. Miranda lifted her hooves and splashed, but now the water was deeper, and Margaret led her back and forth into the shallower spots where the reeds grew. They started across, but soon, Miranda's hooves sank deeper, and the water came up past the horse's knees. Deeper still, and Miranda was swimming. Margaret's shoes and gown were submerged, and her legs began to freeze. The North Sea never warmed up much, and it was still May, barely past the time of ice.

Margaret laughed. The cold was temporary, and she knew that Miranda liked to swim. Soon, they came up on the other bank. Her skirts would dry in the sun, and she'd think about her shoes later.

She started off at a gallop along the strand, but then slowed to a walk. What about Mister Harry? Perhaps he could help to find Henrietta. Margaret would go to Auldearn.

She turned and rode back to the estuary. Staying on this side, she headed south along the river away from the sea and east onto the Auldearn Road. The sun was high, and the sky as blue and sharp as Aunt Grissel's porcelain teacups. Margaret was alone on the open road.

As she came closer to the village, the Boath dovecote, a fat cylinder of stone like a giant loaf of bread, burbled and fluttered with sounds of doves.

A cloud passed over the sun, and the cold seeped up from her legs so that she was shivering again by the time she glimpsed the Auldearn Kirk high on its hill. She quickened her pace and raced up the steep hill to the kirkyard at its summit. Would Mister Harry be here? Perhaps she should have stopped at the manse first. She halted in front of the kirk and paused to think.

A sound, a low sound, was coming from within. Singing? No, not likely in this place.

Margaret dismounted and tied the reins to the post. The sound was a voice, low and plaintive, like a moaning or a keening. Hesitantly, she walked up to the door and knocked. Still shivering, she became aware of her gown, soaking wet at the bottom half.

The door opened with a sudden creaking, and there stood Mister Harry.

"I heard—"

Mister Harry's red face was screwed up into a frown, but when he saw Margaret, he smiled. "Lady Margaret," he said. "Please come in."

She stood where she was. "But what was that sound?" She picked up her skirts and swished them around, trying to dry them and hoping the wetness would not be too visible.

Mister Harry stared and pointed at her gown. "What's this then, lass?" he asked, answering her question with a question.

"I had to cross the estuary at high tide, Mister Harry. I have been in such a jumble-gut since my dear friend was captured by the MacDonalds, and the English are not helping at all."

Mister Harry winced. "Lady Margaret. Where did you learn such language?"

She swished harder, pacing back and forth. Jumble-gut? Well, she'd heard it somewhere, but why would he care so much about language at a time like this? "Mister Harry, you must help me find Henrietta."

He smiled again. "Of course, my dear. Mister Hugh's daughter. It has been much on my mind, as well. How can I help?"

"You could use your influence with the English to insist they continue the search. I have just been to their headquarters and learned that they have abandoned the search for Henrietta! Such callousness is hard to believe."

Mister Harry lifted an eyebrow. "My prayers are sent up daily for all in the parish here in Auldearn—for Lady Henrietta, Mister Hugh, and Lady Anne, especially in these weeks."

"And the English?"

"Ah, 'tis a different thing entirely. The English do not honor our kirk and have made that known in so many ways. My influence with them is very small, I fear."

Margaret had squeezed her cloak up into a ball and was clutching and worrying it in her hands as she fought back tears.

Mister Harry's face softened. "But dear lass, I will try. I will talk to the English governor myself and plead the case. I am, indeed, distressed about this situation. Mister Hugh's daughter must be returned. And I will double my prayers."

"Thank you, thank you, Mister Harry. And I thank you too for your prayers and hope the Lord will hear them."

"The Lord hears all prayers." Mister Harry went back into the kirk, and now that moaning sound came again. It must be Mister Harry. Perhaps this was his way of practicing the repentance of which Mistress Collace had spoken.

At home, Margaret couldn't sit still. She paced back and forth from room to room in the castle, unable to concentrate on her lessons or the needlework of which she had been so proud.

Would Mister Harry help? Would he contact the English government? Perhaps she should try another avenue.

CHAPTER 11

Under a gray dome of sky, with the brown earth of early spring, a wet light, and the feel of the sea in the air, Margaret walked between castle and farmtown. Inshoch Castle, high on the hill with its stone keep and towers, dominated the land, while in the farmtown, the houses were low, made of mud and thatched with heather or peat. The people were too poor even to thatch with straw. They needed the straw to feed the animals.

Margaret had never before come to this place, even though it was so close to the castle. Some time ago her, father had forbidden it, but she'd paid scarce attention because the place had sounded so unsavory. Why would she want to go there? The farmtown was just part of the landscape, like the barns, the fields, and the loch.

She stepped along the sandy path, entering a new land—a foreign country almost. The farmtown was a place of darkness and poverty, and yes, it was unsavory, but she would leave no stone unturned to bring back Henrietta.

Could Isobel's magic help? Margaret herself was a Christian woman, but there was something mysterious and powerful about Isobel.

At the loch, a flock of eiders floated in silence and turtles sunned on a log.

Margaret crested the knoll, stepping over it and into the little hamlet. The wind rose, whipping her skirts as it scurried and lashed the sand up around her. Beyond the machair and over the dunes, the waves crashed . . . the constant sound of this place.

Wattle and daub huts formed a crescent around the yard, where a few scrawny cows stood motionless with little to chew. A man, stooped beneath his load of peat, walked across the yard.

She remembered Father's words. "Those poor wretches," he'd said, shaking his head. "You are not to go near them."

"But why?" she'd asked. He looked at Mother, who turned away. Neither of them answered. *If the wretches are poor,* she thought, *should we not help? It's what we read in our Bible each night: the love, the charity of the Lord to give to the poor. It's what the minister preaches, too.*

Margaret walked slowly down the slope. Now the man with the burdensome load was upon her. It was Jack the Smith, the one-eyed man she'd seen in kirk. "Good morning, Jack."

Jack the Smith glanced up with a mulish look in his one eye—a look of defiance. He was ignorant, she thought. Father had given him many a chance, and still, he reeked of resentment, wouldn't answer when spoken to, and was even caught stealing a piglet. He should be hung, Father had said, but Mother put up a fuss and insisted that Jack could be redeemed. He was a human being, after all. So, Jack confessed, and Father relented.

And Father resented. *We are a people of resentment,* Margaret thought. *We live in an endless cycle of wrongs done and wrongs avenged, a wheel that never stops turning.*

"We are too lenient," Father had grumbled. "But most distressing are those women, who consort with the fairies and even the devil." When he spoke of them, there had been a look in his eyes like anger, but more like fear. Like a stallion who rears when startled and has to run from the terror. "When will these ungodly creatures rise up from the mud?" he'd said. "They don't even listen to the minister of a Sunday."

Margaret looked back, suddenly fearful. Inshoch Castle was far back, however. Surely, no one could see her here.

The "ungodly creatures" had risen up in anger that day when Mister Forbes preached against the fairies. The day the woman threw her shoe. Margaret chuckled at the memory, though it was a dry chuckle. Of course, the woman, too, would be punished, and the cycle of revenge would go on.

"The fairies," Bessie had said, "dinna like to be preached against. They can do you mischief if you do not treat them with respect. If you don't want them to steal your corn or milk, you must put out something to propitiate them, a bowl of porridge or the like, and leave it overnight. They will eat their fill, but in the morning, you won't know it, because the food is still there. The fairies live and work as we do and have their homes under the ground in little green hills, though *we* canna see them. Except for the people with *an da shealladh. They* can see the fairies." Like Isobel Gowdie. What else could Isobel see?

Jack the Smith passed in a cloud of unwashed cloth and man, and the stench was almost unbearable. Margaret averted her face as his one beady brown eye looked up at her with defiance, resentment, and something else—as if she were prey, a wild animal he meant to pounce upon given half a chance. Something to devour. It was the same look she had seen once in the eye of Mister Harry. It had been just a glance as she'd left the kirk, and she'd dismissed it, blaming her own skittishness. The other day, Mister Harry had been kind and gracious. Truly a man of God.

Now, here was Isobel Gowdie, a wisp of a woman coming out of a hovel where smoke escaped from holes in the roof and places where windows should be. She tossed some scraps from a bowl and glanced toward Margaret as chickens squawked and pecked.

Margaret proceeded across the dooryard, holding up her skirt and stepping over droppings and the chickens that fluttered around her feet. "Mistress Gowdie," she called.

Isobel looked up with an air of suspicion, but then a smile transformed her face, which changed from pinched and drawn to wide and bright. A pretty woman, really she was, with her blonde hair drawn up into a braided bun and her vivid blue eyes, though clearly the weather had beaten her into an older look. Voices of children came from the hovel behind her, and a thin line of smoke streamed out of the roof.

"Lady Margaret," she said in a voice quite mellifluous and pleasant, with a lilt and rhythm to it. Again, Margaret's impression of her was transformed, and she felt something magnetic, something that drew her toward Isobel. Could this be a part of the magic? Isobel beckoned her to follow and stepped through the door.

The room was so dark and smoky, Margaret couldn't see a thing at first. She stumbled along the mud floor toward the fire, which smoldered and filled the room with smoke. A child of three, and another, six perhaps—two scrawny girls—sat on the floor piling sticks into houses. They looked up with the blank stare of poverty.

This place was forbidden to her. But why? Did her father not want her to see the deprivation, the poverty, the bone-thinness of mother and children, the clothes that found no soap throughout the winter? Isobel kept her plaid wrapped tight, as did Margaret in this chilly place. The children were also wrapped up, though their noses were red. There was but one chair, where Isobel gestured for Margaret to sit. She remembered that in this bleak village, most of the furniture was gone—burned for warmth when firewood was scarce.

Margaret took some cheese from her basket and handed it to Isobel. At least she'd thought to bring something. Isobel accepted it with a look of awe. "I thank you Mistress." She bowed her head, saying, "In the name of the Father, Son, and Holy Ghost." Immediately Isobel broke it and gave it to the bairns, who ate as if they'd never eaten before. Now Margaret saw why her father had called them "poor wretches."

"And what can I do for you, my Lady?" Isobel asked with a gleam in her eye, as if she already knew the answer. She was standing at the table carding, drawing the comb across a fuzzy ball of wool, over and over. Such a slow process these people went through, with no spinning wheels—all hand carding, each laborious section, one by one. The carding was something Margaret hadn't done and had no wish to. Spinning at the wheel and weaving at the loom were her tasks, and the making of the plaids; the tighter the weave, the better. She'd been weaving since she was five.

Across the room, the animals moved in their stalls with a moo and a snort—one scrawny cow and two goats. Isobel watched Margaret.

Margaret felt in her pocket for the shell and ran her fingers over the ridges. She cleared her throat. "It's about my friend Henrietta."

"Oh, aye, the one who was caught by the MacDonalds. Is she back home, then?"

"No!" Margaret cried. "She is gone! It's been over a week now!"

"And they'll be raping her and keeping her, no doubt," Isobel said in a matter-of-fact way.

Margaret fell back onto the chair, no longer able to control the weeping. No one else had used that word. How could this woman be so heartless? "No, not Henrietta!" She made herself stop crying and sat up straight. "I know those brutes kidnap girls from the lowlands, but—"

"And keep them as prisoners and wives, which amounts to the same thing," Isobel snorted.

"But we *can't* let this happen to Henrietta!"

Isobel stared at her. The two children ran back and forth between Isobel and a dark corner of the hut. Now that her eyes had become accustomed to the darkness, Margaret could see someone in the corner. A hunched-over bundle on the dirt floor, motionless except for her hands moving. Ah, she was slowly teazing—combing a tangle of wool into separate strands.

Margaret wiped her eyes and stood up. "*You* can find her, Mistress."

"I?" And now Isobel's eyes narrowed. Her expression changed to keen alertness.

"You can use your second sight."

"*An da shealladh.*" This in a scratchy voice from the corner. In a gurgled undertone, the voice continued in Gaelic. Isobel listened.

Margaret looked from one to the other but caught only a word here or there.

"This be *mor obair,*" Isobel said, turning back to Margaret. She put down her carding, shook her hands, and began a rapid speech, half in English, half in Gaelic, about the fairies and something about other "helpers." She walked around in the tiny space, raising her arms and gesturing.

Margaret stared, spellbound. She understood very little—only the names of the saints, Brigid and Michael, and Queen Maeve.

"*Mor obair,*" Isobel shouted again and threw her hands up.

Margaret screwed up her eyebrows. This phrase must mean a great task, and perhaps Isobel was talking about money. "Henrietta's mother, the Lady Anne, will pay whatever is needed," Margaret said.

Now the "poor wretch," with her dirty plaid wrapped loose around her shoulders, stood tall and proud like a statue of Athena, and gazed with a cool eye at Margaret. Then, as if she were the lady and Margaret the peasant, she nodded her head in concession.

As she left the hut, Margaret noticed five pieces of red yarn lined up on the floor beside the entrance. Above them, hanging from the wall, were some unfamiliar dried plants. She reached out to touch the plants. "What—?"

A barrage of Gaelic exploded from the dark corner, and she quickly pulled back her hand.

"*Shee!*" Isobel addressed the corner. *Sith*, pronounced *shee*, meant peace, and obviously Isobel was trying to silence the old woman. But *sith* also meant fairy.

Margaret shivered. The herbs were certainly for medicine, but were they and the yarns also for some magic ritual? Surely, Isobel used her powers for the good—healing and helping—and not for evil. Isobel was merely a woman with extraordinary powers, Margaret thought. And she had agreed to use those powers to look for Henrietta.

As Margaret bent down to step out of the door hole, she glanced back.

Isobel's expression had changed again. The corners of her mouth were lifted, as if she knew something about Margaret that even she didn't know.

CHAPTER 12

*A*t home, she felt as though she were coming out of a dream. She had stepped into forbidden territory. And now that she'd awakened, she would direct her attention to pious matters and not to fairies and magic, however much more interesting they were. Margaret nestled into her favorite chair in the library, in a corner of the Great Hall, with its carved oak paneling and floor-to-ceiling books in red and brown leather. She opened "A Godly Dream," a poem by Elizabeth Melville.

From the drawing room came the soft voices of Lucy and Mistress Collace in their lesson, and outside the window two crows squawked above the sound of Bessie's shouts as she haggled with a peddler in the courtyard.

"Bessie is a good woman," her father had said last night at tea, "and if it be possible to save our home and lands, she'll be nothing but an asset for the Hays."

"To save our home?" Margaret had asked. "Is our home in peril?"

Mother had remonstrated. "Your father tends towards exaggeration and gloom, as you know. Our home is not at risk."

But Father still looked dark and gloomy, and she noticed for the first time that his hair was streaked with gray. "Those scoundrels," he'd moaned. "Those MacDonalds."

"But the spring planting has gone so well," Mother said. "We should be able to recover."

"If the weather stays and the Lord grants a bountiful harvest." Father had shaken his head as if he didn't believe in either of those possibilities.

Perhaps this was just Father's usual pessimism after the spring planting. He seemed to believe that optimism would be tempting fate, so he predicted dire consequences in order to prevent them.

Margaret bowed her head to the book. *"What can we do? We clogged are with sin, in filthy vice, our senseless souls are drowned: Though we resolve, we never can begin to mend our lives, but sin does still abound. When will thou come?"* She raised her eyes to the window. A blue sunny sky was visible through the new, larger window at this end of the Great Hall.

A Godly Dream was the first book by a woman published in Scotland. It was a pious poem by an exemplary woman of faith, Mistress Collace had said; and, after the Bible, it was her favorite book.

But how forlorn it was, and gloomy as well. Why couldn't Mistress Collace prefer Shakespeare?

"Elizabeth!" Father, standing in the doorway, called up the stairs to Mother.

"Into my dreame I thought there did appear . . . an angel bright with visage shining clear." This sounded like Mistress Collace's visions of Jesus. No wonder she liked it so much.

The crows screeched, and one of them flapped against the window.

"Elizabeth!" Father called again.

Suddenly, her mother appeared, in her brown dress, its voluminous sleeves and skirts flowing around her and rippling in folds over her enormous stomach. Perched on the third stone step, she looked almost like a huge bird of prey. Father started. "What is it, John?" Mother spoke in a soft and gracious voice.

Father shook his head as if to clear out all thoughts and fears—this was his dear wife, after all—and to remember the real threat, the one that came from the marauders. "Please come down."

Slowly, Lady Elizabeth descended the stairs, her dress swaying around her body. She was a beautiful woman still, and her hair was uncovered for a change. Soft brown curls framed her face, which was now, unfortunately, swollen by the effects of pregnancy. Her delicate eyebrows squeezed together into a worried look.

Father gestured for Mother to sit in one of the velvet-covered wing chairs at the fireplace.

Either they didn't see Margaret, or they were ignoring her.

"It's about the estate, my lady." Father paced back and forth as he talked. "In this recent raid, our cattle were taken as well as the corn, and with the shortage for the harvest this year, my only resort is to ask your uncle for a loan."

"Uncle Alexander? But John, we just received a loan from him in the past year. Is there no other recourse?"

Father paced faster. "I have the taxes to pay, and little or nothing with which to pay them. I'll have to confiscate from the tenants again to make up for what was stolen, but that will only tide us over for a short while. I have sent word for Alexander to come upon his return from Breda." Father looked toward the window. "I expect him today."

Lady Elizabeth rested her head on her hand and sighed.

Margaret looked around the Hall: the stone walls hung with tapestries and portraits of her ancestors, the grand fireplace, this solid foundation of her life. Were they really in danger of losing all of this?

Hoofbeats sounded from the courtyard, and Margaret ran to the window. A driver pulled up the reins, and the horses stopped with precision. Uncle Alexander, the Laird of Brodie, alighted from a finer carriage than John Hay could ever afford. With its Brodie crest, black lacquer and gold leaf, intricate carvings, and the delicate wheels that carried it with such grace, it looked as if it could glide on air.

Father had come up behind her at the window. He swallowed as if to stomach his jealousy and prepared to welcome his benefactor.

Uncle Alexander walked in with a spring in his step. In a green velvet doublet and breeches, white stockings, and shoes, he looked every bit the dignitary. He was tall, like all the Brodies, and smiled down at Mother with pleasure. It was clear that he had something on his mind. Father remained silent. "I bring news of the coronation," he announced.

Mother sprang up from her seat and her eyes filled with tears. "Oh, Uncle, to think it really is to be!"

This was a momentous time. Uncle Alexander had been appointed as a commissioner to meet with King Charles at Breda in the Netherlands and escort him back to Scotland. The young king had promised to restore the Covenant, and Scotland would be Presbyterian again.

"It is to be," he said, sitting heavily in the wing chair facing Mother. "But the commission was not an easy one."

"How do you mean, Uncle? The King is back in Scotland, is he not?"

"And he does agree to the Covenant?" Father asked.

Uncle Alexander hesitated. "Aye, he agrees to the Covenant, but not without some reluctance, I fear." His brown eyes, deep and compassionate, changed momentarily from lively to sad, and he stroked his neat beard, the dark brown flecked with gray. He had a strong resemblance to Margaret's mother Elizabeth, with her dark hair and skin of almost the same olive tone.

"Reluctance?" Elizabeth sat down with a graceful movement in spite of her bulk. "This bodes ill. Perhaps he will change his stance again?" Margaret laid her book on the seat in the corner and moved closer, taking a chair by the hearth.

"Nay, niece, I do not mean to trouble you. The king has agreed and must stick to his word."

As the fire crackled and the clock on the mantelpiece chimed the hour of four, each of them sat with the knowledge of the wrenching events of the past years. Scotland, originally Catholic, had gone through so many battles and bloodbaths in the past century that the Covenanters were constantly flung from hope to despair and back again. After the signing of the National Covenant in 1638, the Covenanters believed the fighting was over. But then came Cromwell's betrayal and the Battle of Auldearn, and once again, their hopes were dashed. Was it any wonder that Lady Elizabeth would now question the loyalty of the returning king?

Bessie entered with a tea tray and set about placing the pot and teacups, sugar and milk, scones and cakes on the table beside Elizabeth. Because of shortages in the last year, the Laird had let go of some of the servants, and Bessie had assumed the duties of the butler.

Lady Elizabeth began to pour. She didn't need to ask either Uncle Alexander or Margaret's father how they took their tea, and she knew that Margaret liked extra milk. She handed Alexander his tea. "We have had more troubles here, as well, Uncle."

He took the cup and looked up at Father. "What new troubles here, lad?"

Father, Laird of Park and almost forty, was still a lad in Uncle's eyes. He pounded his fist on the mantelpiece, his ire again aroused. "MacDonalds!" he shouted.

"They rode up in the night and stole our cattle and corn," Mother said. "And they have also taken the Rose daughter." She glanced at Margaret, then bowed her head. "The English major, this Major Walker, says they will retrieve her, but we fear—" She shook her head. "We are heartsick."

Margaret felt her shoulders tense and cried, "Do you not think she will be rescued, Mother?" She had been so disheartened after seeking out the major and Mister Harry, but after visiting Isobel, her hopes rebounded.

"And they say there is no restitution for the theft!" Father barked, as if he had no thought for Henrietta. "Seventy head of cattle, scores of sacks of corn. Leaving me with nary enough to feed the family, much less the household and farmtown."

"Indeed, I am saddened to hear of it." Uncle Brodie looked sad, but also skeptical. He no doubt knew that this last statement was an exaggeration. As did Margaret. Father had told the English major that it had been fifty head of cattle, and she knew there was plenty left in the stores.

Father hesitated, probably wondering if he had overstepped, but he plunged in anyway, apparently feeling there was no other option. "I beg to be so bold, Alexander," he said, still standing by the fire, "but a loan of five hundred would tide me over until harvest."

Uncle Alexander looked startled and glanced at his niece Elizabeth, who turned her head away in shame. "Nephew, you are most dear to me in the Lord," he said, "and I would hope you recover well. But the debt still owing to me from last year hangs heavy on my mind."

Father clenched his fists, and his face darkened. "A curse on all the sons of these MacDonalds! May their firstborn males perish, and all male infants be shriveled in their mothers' wombs. And if the Lord will not, we will exact vengeance."

Mother hung her head lower. This cursing of sons and taking of vengeance was so ingrained in the land that few questioned it, but Margaret could see that it grieved her mother dearly, especially now that she was so close to her own delivery—something Father wouldn't think of. Lady Elizabeth dared not say this aloud, dared not contradict her husband in front of her uncle.

When Uncle Alexander left in a clattering of delicate wheels and hooves, Mother and Father went their separate ways. Margaret picked up the book again: "*The joy of heaven is worth one moment's pain. Take courage, then, lift up your hearts on high: to judge the earth when Christ shall come again, Above the clouds ye shall exalted be. The throne of joy and true felicity await for you when finished is your quest.*" The words were soothing and hopeful, but it was all about the rewards after death. What about now? Would Father take up arms against the MacDonalds? Even worse, what would happen if he ran out of money?

CHAPTER 13

The evening birds sang, the distant sea undulated, and Margaret's spirit lightened—as if God were opening a window from winter into spring, giving her the message not to despair. How could she worry about money with such abundance all around: the flax flowering delicate blue in the fields, the winter oats a mass of green stalks, and from the stables and barns, the rustlings of cows and horses?

She strolled out of the castle courtyard and onto the road. A whisper of smoke floated in the air. The sheep's lowing made a steady undertone, and from a distance came the airy warbling sound of pipes. Voices. Faint singing. Something was happening in the farmtown.

She rubbed her cheek and glanced back at the castle. Just last Sunday, Mister Harry had preached on the sinfulness of pleasure. Music—any music, he'd said—led their hearts and minds astray. In kirk, they sang the Psalms, but Covenanters did not play musical instruments in worship. This was idolatry. "The Papists, and even the Episcopalians, are idolaters," he'd said, "with their 'sacred' music. But even that music is pleasure. We become immersed in it, and it takes our hearts away from God. All thoughts should lead to prayer, and all prayer should lead us closer to the love of the Lord."

Yes, to turn her heart to God was something beyond pleasure, and prayer and silence could lead to God, as Mistress Collace had said. But right now, the music from the farmtown sounded so lively and joyful. Surely, God did not require every moment for prayer and silence.

She stepped onto the dyke overlooking the farmtown, and there was the bonfire. On the next hill over, its fire blazing, black silhouettes of people ranging round. The music grew louder, and shouts and laughter filled the air.

These farm folk came to kirk, and they heard the same words from the pulpit as she, but perhaps in their world, being pious was not so important. Or perhaps piety here came in a different shape, like wine in an old vessel. Could believing in the fairies be a kind of piety?

Margaret's feet sank into the sand, and she walked between gorse bushes just beginning to bloom, bright yellow in the waning of the day. On the opposite rise, the fire sent red fingers like a blazing hand into the darkening sky. People gathered round it, holding hands and dancing, torches bobbing.

Margaret stopped. She could watch from here, and no one would notice.

Two women turned and stared at her.

Another woman walked past them and toward Margaret. Isobel Gowdie. Her light hair was uncovered and woven with yellow flowers, her feet bare, and skirts swung around bare legs. A sign of poverty, for sure, the bare feet of the peasants, but in truth, Margaret might like to go barefoot on a spring evening. She might like to wear a wreath of flowers. She might even like to dance in the ring.

"Good evening, Lady Margaret." Isobel's almond-shaped eyes were an unusual color—a vivid blue that could change to dark silver in an instant. Her expression was intense: part lively pride and part laughing, as if she knew a joke she wouldn't tell.

"Mistress Gowdie. About Henrietta—"

"Would you like to come and dance?" Isobel's smile came merry and mischievous.

To dance? Margaret hopped from one foot to the other as if stepping into a fire. "But dancing is forbidden?" she said, a statement that turned into a question. In spite of herself, she raised her voice at the end of the sentence.

"Nay, lass, not here, 'tis not. Tis *Là Bealltainn!*"

Beltane. Held on the first of May, which was today. This was one of the festivals prohibited by the kirk.

And Mistress Gowdie was wrong about dancing. The laws of the Kirk applied to everyone. Music like this was clearly forbidden and dancing even more so. Then again, Aunt Grissell Brodie played the pianoforte—beautiful strains of Bach that she said were written to be played in kirk—and no one reprimanded her for that.

"I must go back," Margaret said, turning away from the fire and the music to start in the direction of home. She should not have been here. But she turned her head again. She had to ask Isobel about Henrietta.

A slow, sweet melody whistled from the pipes, a melancholy air, and Margaret completed her turn, the plaintive tune reaching so deep into her heart that she almost began to weep. It was true that music had the power to make people feel different things, and perhaps this was why it was forbidden.

People were dancing more slowly now, dipping and bowing and circling round the fire. Did she dare go closer? She looked back toward home and could see the castle towers against the pale sky. It was not yet dark at this time so close to midsummer when the sun stayed up all night.

Isobel put her hands on her hips and cocked her head, eyebrows arched. "Tisn't wise to be out alone on *La Beltainn*."

"What?" Margaret shivered. Fire shadows were dancing, and shouts and squeals filled the air. "Why not?"

"Och! The sprites, the elves, the fairies, who knows what mischief they be about this night?"

"Mischief?" Now Isobel was beginning to sound like Bessie, and Margaret's mind set to stubbornness. She tapped her foot. She would not be frightened.

"Aye. But when we dance, they rejoice with us."

Margaret swallowed. "I *would* like to dance," she whispered.

"And the fairies will be pleased!" Isobel laughed and took her hand to lead her to the bonfire. "Everyone must dance to complete the circle."

The circle? What did that mean? Would she be entering into an evil pact?

The crowd parted as they approached, and Isobel led her into their midst. People stopped dancing and murmured in low voices. The music stopped and the people stared, weathered faces glowering at Margaret, an intruder.

She felt her face reddening; thankfully it was dark enough that they couldn't see. "Why are they staring?" she whispered. She did look different from them, she supposed, with her silk-embroidered dress and velvet cape. They probably weren't used to having someone from the castle at their gatherings.

Isobel smiled a strange sort of smile and brushed her hand in the air. "No mind," she said, taking Margaret's hand and leading her closer to the fire.

Isobel began to step and hop, step and hop, and a drum started to beat, *brum, brum, brum,* reverberating in a kind of throb with Isobel's steps, like a heartbeat from within the earth and the distant stars.

The pipe and the fiddle joined the music, and the people formed a circle, swaying and singing and stepping round and round in a ring. Margaret had never danced before, but now she found herself in step with the others, dancing round the fire, mesmerized by the flames and the music and this new way of being. As if her whole body was in the sound, and the sound in her body.

Smells of roasted mutton, fish, and apples drifted in the smoke, and a man with one eye, blackened teeth, and a dirty jerkin grinned as he stepped up and teetered in towards her, blasting her with his ale breath. Jack the Smith, the man she'd seen carrying peat—the one who had leered at her. Isobel stepped back and shoved him. "Be gone, Jack the Smith." Jack the Smith giggled and staggered away.

"Come." Isobel took Margaret's hand and led her to the far side of the fire, where a plaid was laid on the ground. She indicated by gesture that Margaret should sit on the plaid, and Isobel sat on a small boulder beside it.

The people moved around the fire as if in a trance, and Margaret felt herself being drawn into it. Entranced. She hummed and bobbed to the drumbeat.

Off to the side, men were talking and shouting. They were dressed in ragged, dirty breeches, and some were barefoot like the women. Their voices were loud and boisterous, nothing like the men she was accustomed to: her father, Mister Harry, Uncle Alexander, and even her cousin James, who was off in the army. James had been rowdy as a child, but he spoke in polite, measured tones, especially when ladies were present.

These men shouted, and much of it involved insulting one another—mostly good-natured insults, it seemed. They raised their flagons and laughed, caught up in the elation of the night. Several young men on the other side of the hill pushed and punched one another.

There was someone she recognized: sitting by himself, staring into the fire, a dark-haired man, large and handsome, but with a sullen expression that lessened his attractiveness. Hugh Gilbert, the cottar, it must be—Mistress Gowdie's husband. A little girl leaned against him, asleep with her head on his lap, one of the children she had seen in the hut.

People came to sit on the ground around Isobel now. They adjusted their plaids, wrapping them around themselves like blankets, and looked at her expectantly.

Margaret felt a warm presence beside her and looked up, puzzled, as Bessie sank down with her warm, comforting kitchen smell. Bessie took her hand.

"Did you follow me?"

Bessie bowed her head in assent, and Margaret breathed out in a whimper that came as a surprise. She hadn't realized how fearful she had been. But now with Bessie here, she was safe. She whispered, "Why are they all gathering around Mistress Gowdie?"

Bessie touched her lips with a finger, casting her eyes back toward the castle, and Margaret nodded. She understood that she was not to talk about this.

Bessie had warned Margaret about Isobel Gowdie, but now, away from the castle, she seemed less wary. "Mistress Gowdie is the cunning woman," she said in a low voice.

The cunning woman. "Because she has the second sight? And she knows the charms?"

"Yes, but she has the stories, too. And the stories have magic."

"Stories have magic? What does that mean?"

Isobel raised her chest and straightened her back, and her voice came loud and deep. "A story of Donald and the fairies."

"As young Donald was going betwixt the towns—he had been sent to borrow a sieve—he passed the Downie Hill." Isobel's eyes glittered as she addressed the crowd, commanding full attention. "And there, he met a woman—small and round and grinning from ear to ear." She hunched over, making herself small, pushed her hands down, and grinned. "And she stood in front of the Black Door. 'Will ye come into the Brugh, lad?' she asked."

Margaret leaned close to hear Bessie's whisper. "A *brugh* is a fairy house."

"He entered and found two women baking, and others dancing." Isobel used her hands and face in a lively pantomime of her story. "'Donald MacNeill, be seated,' said the one baker. 'And think you to have a reel with the dancers before you leave.' Donald joined the dance, and immediately, he forgot about the sieve, and all else, and he lost the time."

"Aye," sighed one of the women in the audience. "'Tis the fairies."

"And 'twere not 'til a year later that he remembered himself and sought to find his family again."

Jack the Smith nodded his head and lifted his flagon.

Isobel's eyes widened as she leaned in towards the audience. "So, Donald went to search, and, coming upon a thatching house, he inquired of an old man, 'Do ye know where my family be?' The old man knew nothing, he said, but perhaps his father did. Donald was amazed. 'Is yer father alive?' he asked. The old man nodded and pointed to the house, whence Donald entered. And there he found a very wise old man sitting by the fire and twisting a straw-rope for the thatching. This man too knew nothing of Donald's people. But perhaps *his* father did, he said."

Isobel looked around and winked. A man shouted, "Ahoo!" and the women laughed. "*This* father was lying in bed, a little shrunken man, and he, in like manner, referred to *his* father. Donald looked about and found this ancestor, a wizened creature, in a purse hanging at the foot of the bed. Donald took him out and questioned him, and the creature declared, 'I did not know the people myself, but I often heard my father speaking of them.' On hearing this, poor Donald crumbled into pieces and fell down a bundle of bones."

For a long moment, the people stayed hushed. And then the laughter and shouting broke out again.

Isobel came and sat on the blanket beside Bessie and Margaret.

"What does it mean?" Margaret asked. "The man having all these fathers and grandfathers?"

Bessie shook her head and Isobel laughed, a low, throaty sound. "'Tis fair Elfane," she said, "and when you go there, you have no more understanding of time. The fairies live for a long time, and when you come back, if you can, it may be six years later, or it may be fifty, but to you, it was an instant."

Margaret frowned and shook her head. "I'm not sure I believe in the fairies." Covenanter women did not believe these fairy tales, she thought, sighing and wanting more than anything for it to be true.

"Ah, don't say that so loud," Bessie whispered, her eyes jumping back and forth and her finger to her lips. "You don't want them to hear you."

Isobel nodded. "They are here tonight."

"Where?" Margaret looked around.

"There, and there, and there." Isobel pointed to the flames. "The fairies love *Là Bealltainn.*"

Margaret looked, but saw only the fiery sparks leaping into the sky. Or was there something shimmering, something like wings or spirits dancing in those flames? She blinked.

"If they catch you," Bessie said, "they'll take you to their home, and they won't let you go."

Margaret threw a stick into the fire and watched. The flames licked the night sky with ever-changing movement and power. *This element, so necessary to our lives . . . it keeps us warm, and yet can also harm.* In that other world, where the fairies existed, was fire a part of it in a different way? Since they were spirits, human-like but without human bodies, that must mean they could move in and out of the fire as they moved in and out of time.

"But if you place a nail in the doorframe before you go in," said Isobel, "you can leave again by the door. Because they dinna like iron. And if you don't eat their food, they won't be able to keep you." She laughed. "But they do have the most delicious food, and meat and drink, cakes and ale better than all the grand houses and castles."

"You have been there?"

"Aye, lass, and they have taught me many things."

"What do they teach you?"

Bessie stood and pulled Margaret up with her. "Now we'll be off," she said, raising an eyebrow at Isobel. "Your mother will be missing you, and we don't want to meet with those lads who roam about in the moonlight." Bessie steered Margaret away from Isobel, who watched them go. "You mustn't ask any more about the fairies," she said as they walked back down the hill. "Tis a treacherous path."

"But I would like to see one, and I never have."

"Aye, that is because I set out the milk to propitiate them." Bessie turned to her, swiveling her head like an owl, her eyes as hard and unblinking as those of that feathered creature. "And if you ever do see one, you must sanctify yourself."

Margaret held her tongue. Bessie had said this before.

"*In the name of the Father, Son, and Holy Ghost!*" Bessie proclaimed as she made the sign of the cross, raising her voice to the land around, protecting them from whatever evil spirits were abroad.

The moon was full tonight, and the wind had died down. As they left the farmtown and walked up the next hill, the strains of the pipes and fiddles and Isobel's voice rolled and waved like the fading wind behind them.

Margaret turned to look back and groaned. Again, she'd forgotten to ask about Henrietta. Being with Isobel was being in a different world, and everything else had flown away.

CHAPTER 14

This time, Margaret went with some trepidation, but she was determined and told herself to remember that she was here for Henrietta, not to be drawn into Isobel's magical world. Though of course she could ask a few questions.

She had told Cook she was visiting a farmtown family with a sick child, and Cook, with her soft heart, had cut a very generous piece of meat with the injunction not to tell her parents.

The mutton, rolled in salt and rosemary, was wrapped in a cloth, and Margaret hid it discreetly beneath another cloth in her basket. She walked softly through the hall, down the tower stairs, and into the courtyard, glancing around to make sure she was unobserved. Her mother had stayed abed this morning, and now Bessie and the other maids were scurrying about in a hectic manner. Perhaps it was Mother's time, but if so, it would take some hours before the baby came. No one would be thinking of Margaret now.

She crested the dyke and came down into the farmtown yard, head held high and trying to look confident. Now it felt like she knew the area well, even though this was only the second time she'd come. The farmtown had been there all her life, but she had always obeyed her father's injunction not to go near it. Now that she was seventeen, surely, she could decide for herself.

The air was still, which was unusual in this place, buffeted as it was by sea winds, day in and day out. Thick clouds hung low in the warm air, a sign of rain to come.

The yard was almost deserted. Across the way, a person, Isobel, walked from the direction of the river with a load of peat on her back. The peat pile must have been almost as heavy as she, but Isobel lumbered steadily on, glancing briefly at Margaret before she heaved it down onto a pile in front of the hut. She straightened and smiled broadly. "Lady Margaret! Ye'll be wanting to know about the fairies."

Margaret's mouth fell open. How did Isobel know this half-thought of hers? She cleared her throat. "Well, I wanted to know if–"

"Please, come in." Isobel had a stately bearing in spite of her ragged dress and skirt stained brown with peat. No plaids were necessary on this warm day, and Margaret wore only a light cape over her cotton gown.

Stooping, she followed Isobel under the door hole and into the dark room, filled with peat smoke and colder than outside. She handed Isobel the hunk of mutton and sat on the proffered chair.

Isobel thanked her and held up the meat, saying, "In the name of the Father, Son, and Holy Ghost." Another use for these words. Of course, Isobel, like everyone in this land, was Christian. It was the law.

Isobel laid the meat on her *kist* in the corner and squatted down by the fire, poking at it and throwing on another square of peat. "I'll learn ye of the fairies and elves and the magic they bring," she said, looking up with a raised eyebrow.

Margaret hesitated. This seemed a bit abrupt. Of course, she did want to learn these things, but she hadn't planned to bring it up right away. The plight of Henrietta was the most important thing. She'd imagined the subject of magic coming in sideways, slipping in so she could learn it without acknowledging it to herself. She shook her shoulders. "My family doesn't believe in magic."

"Ah, like Mister Forbes, they think 'tis evil?"

"Yes. But I am not sure what *I* think." Margaret fidgeted with the edge of her cape.

"The magic has been here since the world began, so it matters not whither ye believe in it. The fairies are here, though most people canna' see them. They dwell in the other world, their world, the place of spirits."

Margaret looked up. "The place of spirits. Another world. Please tell me, what is it like, that spirit place?"

"'Tis the world between people and angels, where the fairies dance and fly."

Margaret closed her eyes and lifted her chin. "Is it like a dream? Or like a vision that comes out of the fog? Little wispy lights and tinkly music and such? And do they appear and disappear in the trees like in Shakespeare?"

"Aye. But they have a home they go to and from. Their home is under the Downie Hill."

"Downie Hill?"

"A smooth green hill between Lochloy and Brodie."

"Can I see them if I go there?"

"Only if they choose." Isobel pulled off her kerchief, picked up a bundle of wool and a teazing comb, and began to draw the comb through the stiff, dirty bundle. "If you can see beyond sight, you may see your own sprite, he who is always with you—to help you and teach you. He will take you there."

"And what does he look like, this sprite?"

"Ah, the sprite of each person is different, just as we are all different. Mine is so high," she said, reaching her hand out to knee height, "and he is called the Red Reiver. He is all red, lively and dancing, and he always comes with me when I ride in the night and see the fairies."

"Ride in the night?"

"Aye." Isobel clapped her hand to her mouth, clearly not willing to say more.

Margaret clutched her chest. "If I had a sprite, what would it look like?"

"'Tis part of your essence, something only you can see, though I can sometimes see those of others. Perhaps I can see yours." She stared at Margaret with a cloudy look, as if with a film over her eyes. "You must sit still as a rock."

Margaret adjusted her posture and sat very still while Isobel stared.

"She may be a little woman, blue and yellow-like."

"A little woman, blue and yellow? I used to have a doll of those colors. What else do you see? Is she young or old?"

"I don't know, and I don't know her name. Only when I am with my fairy man and the Red Reiver can I see these more clearly."

In the Bible, Jesus said he would send the Holy Spirit to be with us, and that had always been a comfort to Margaret. But a little blue and yellow woman? That could not be what he meant. She pursed her lips and frowned. *This must be heresy.* And it would remain a secret.

"The fairies are made of air and spirit," Isobel said, "and they live like we do, in some ways. They come in the night and eat of the milk and cheese and meat, whatever is in the larder. But you never know they've come, because they take only the essence, the invisible substance that be the heart of the food and leave the rest."

"But if the essence is gone out of the food, what is left?"

"The food is still there and looks the same, but the nourishment is gone out of it, and the people who eat it become pale and sickly."

"Is that why Bessie puts out the milk for them—so they take that instead, and will not take the essence of the food?"

Isobel nodded. "Then they leave off your larder and go elsewhere. And ye must say the rhyming charm, too. That way, they will be your friends, and help you when you say the healing charms."

Margaret jumped up. "And I would learn these charms! For the food and for the healing!"

Isobel laughed, leapt up beside her, and led her in a little jig around the fire, singing, "Charms and potions, fairies and elves, I'll learn ye all the beautiful magic." They both laughed and danced.

Margaret sat down abruptly. "But how did *you* learn these charms? From the fairies?"

"Nay, those my mother learned me."

Margaret looked over to the corner, where the old woman had been when she had visited last time. Again, that dark lump. "Is that your mother?"

The lump snorted as Isobel, eyes flashing, quickly answered, "Nay."

Now there was a silence that felt prohibitive of any questions about her mother.

Isobel puffed up her chest and said proudly, "I can fly where I will, as straws will fly upon a highway. Wild straws and corn straws are horse to me, and I put it betwixt my feet, and it becomes my steed. 'Horse and hattock, ho!' I say."

"You can fly like the fairies?"

Isobel stood up and gestured. "Over dunes and machair and river and mountain. And I was in the Downie Hill, and got meat there from the Queen of Fairy, more than I could eat."

Margaret clapped her hands. "The Fairy Queen! Like Titania! Oh, what does she look like?"

"The Queen of Fairy is heavily clothed in white linen, and in white and lemon clothes bedazzling."

"And where is this Downie Hill?"

"Betwixt the towns of Nairn and Auldearn is where it be. The hill opens, and you come to a large, fair room, and there the queen doth dwell."

"'Tis really true, then!" Margaret's heart was beating fast and her face flushing. "Oh, that I could see that place, that I could see the fairy queen and fly above the world!"

Isobel studied her with a sharp and ponderous look. "Perhaps you *can*."

"Oh, but how?"

"That day ye came to me on the strand. Seen ye a crow then?"

"A crow? Yes! And it brushed me with its wings." That first day she'd met Isobel, when she'd hurried home across the machair. The graze of those mighty wings, the flapping, cawing creature rising to the treetops. "How did you know?"

"I can go in the shape of a hare. I can go into a hare; I can go into a crow."

"You can?" Margaret looked around the hut, confused. Isobel was animated now and went on elaborating about her supernatural adventures. Margaret did now believe in the fairies, and perhaps she always had, like so many other people—most people, in fact. Even Mister Harry believed in them, though he thought they were evil. And she knew that a cunning woman could heal with her rhymes and charms. But change herself into an animal? "You can go into the body of a crow?"

"Perhaps I were calling ye."

Margaret slumped in her seat, head falling down in her lap. Was this real? Could Isobel have been that crow? *What would my parents say if they could see me now? And Mister Harry. Would he tie me to a stake?* A silent wail rose up inside her. *And Henrietta!* She shuddered, her mind aflutter with so many thoughts, like a murder of crows in her head, flying in different directions, fighting and colliding, feathers bursting out. She sat up and muttered, "I *did* have a strange feeling about that crow."

"Perhaps ye, too, have the *an da shealladh.*"

"But I have never seen the fairies, no matter how much I wished to."

"Have ye seen the dead?"

Margaret bowed her head. "I sometimes see my brother who died in the war." She'd tried not to talk about it, as it made her family angry to hear about Malcolm. But she knew it wasn't imagination. And if it wasn't imagination, what was it? Perhaps she had pushed that question out of her mind. Perhaps she hadn't *wanted* to know what it meant.

Isobel smiled a sudden wide, open smile. "Then you may see the fairies, as well. In that other world, the world where the fairies dwell, there is also the place of the dead."

Margaret's whole body tensed against the tears that were pushing from inside. This was too much to comprehend. Malcolm, with the fairies? No, it couldn't be possible. Malcolm was in heaven, as Mother had said, and what she'd seen must have been something out of the past, a glimpse of something that had already happened.

Was she courting danger here, wanting to see the fairies?

She shook herself to rid her mind of these thoughts. The fairies were beings of beauty and magic, and Isobel was a magical woman who could heal and help. Isobel's smile spread a magical glow around her, a charmed circle that Margaret stepped back into.

"Oh!" How could she have forgotten her real purpose in coming here? She stood up and coughed in the sudden onslaught of bitter smoke. "But Mistress Gowdie," she exclaimed, struggling through another cough. "I must ask again. With your second sight, have you seen my friend Henrietta?"

Isobel's face took on that dreamy look again, and she stared off into space. "I have seen the MacDonalds' camp, and a lass with red hair."

"Oh, yes, that is Henrietta! Where is the camp?"

"Tis on Ben Rinnes."

Margaret jumped up. Ben Rinnes was a mountain this side of the Cairngorm Mountains. "Thank you, thank you, Mistress Gowdie!" Margaret called as she ran out of the hut and away from the magic.

CHAPTER 15

A red-haired lass with the MacDonalds. It had to be Henrietta. It *must* be Henrietta. Margaret walked with a skip and a hop, then lifted her skirts and began to run. Though the sky had clouded over and the air had grown cooler, there was a lightness in her body and a new brightness in her mind. She would find the young lieutenant and tell him about Ben Rinnes, and he would bring back her friend.

She had no doubt about Isobel's vision, because when Isobel had described the camp, she, too, had sensed something: moss-covered boulders around a dingle, or hollow, on the mountainside. A hidden area, but big enough for a troop of men to sit at campfires with their horses secured behind them. To one side, a *sheiling*, or shepherd's hut, cradled into the rock face. And Henrietta, surrounded by several of those fierce-looking MacDonald men. There was the wild blond hair and dark beard–the brute who had been holding her on his horse–and the others, the black hair and beards smeared with grease from the mutton they were roasting. Mutton, no doubt, from the sheep they'd stolen from Inshoch.

She stopped in midstride. This was not Isobel's description she was recalling, but a memory. Her own memory. *I saw the place. I saw it plain as a pikestaff.*

Quick upon this realization came images, vague but insistent, things she'd attributed to her wild imagination, as her mother called it: the vision of Malcolm and the soldiers, Bessie's altercation in the village with the button peddler she had punched in the arm. When Bessie got home, Margaret had shocked her with a detailed description of the incident. And the emerald necklace that

Father had bought in Edinburgh for Mother. Margaret had seen it clearly before he'd brought it home.

This must be what Bessie had meant when she'd said Margaret had had other visions.

I must have the second sight, the an da shealladh. And what did that mean? Could she be a cunning woman, too?

As she stepped through the gate to the courtyard, she gazed up at the castle, the sturdy stone house where she'd grown up. This was her foundation. She was a Christian woman, a Covenanter. She loved the Bible stories with which she'd first learned to read: Moses leading the Israelites through the Red Sea, Jesus feeding the multitudes with a few fish, Jesus walking on water. So many miracles.

But the miracles in the Bible had occurred in the past, and Isobel's miracles were happening now: dolphins bringing in more fish, Isobel flying through the sky with the fairies and seeing Henrietta, turning herself into an animal.

Margaret twisted the cloth in the basket. There was, most likely, something wrong with this reasoning, and Father would know it. He would say that Isobel's miracles were imaginary, or that they were works of the devil. But how else could Margaret explain the crow? Or the dolphins? And everyone knew that the fairies were real, though not everyone could see them. Perhaps now, with Isobel's help, Margaret would be able to see them too.

She placed her hand on her heart. The magical little people who appeared in the air and the wood, like in *A Midsummer Night's Dream,* the fairy queen in her sparkling lemon-colored robes. She could almost see them now.

The courtyard was quiet. No doves cooing, no grooms or cottars or servants or animals about. All was still. And a strange silence seemed to emanate from the house itself. Was something amiss? Margaret walked up to the door, into the tower, and up the stone stairs. No movement, no sound. The great hall was empty.

She tiptoed into the drawing room where Mistress Collace sat with a book, and Lucy was working on a sampler. They both started and looked up with alarm when she came in. "Oh!" Lucy uttered.

Mistress Collace stood immediately and came toward her. "Lady Margaret . . ." she began, then stopped. This was odd, as Mistress seldom addressed her as Lady Margaret.

"What is it?" she asked. "What is the matter?"

"It's Mother," Lucy blurted out as if aggrieved at someone or something.

"Please sit, my dear," Mistress Collace said as she herself sat down, patting the chair beside her.

Mistress Collace began in a calm, pleasant voice. "Yes, 'tis your mother, I'm afraid."

"The baby," Margaret whispered.

"Yes, the baby. I am sorry to report that all is not well with the baby."

"He died!" Lucy shouted.

Sounds of scurrying came from the hall, and Margaret glimpsed Bessie and several of the other servants whispering and hurrying toward the stair to the front door.

"It was a boy, then."

"Yes." Mistress Collace sighed. "A very difficult birth, and he lived for but an hour."

"And Mother? Is she . . . ?"

"Your mother needs to stay abed. With much quiet and rest."

Margaret jumped up and ran from the room. "Mother!" she called, racing through the hall and up the stairs to her mother's chamber.

"Mother." She sat down on the bed. Her mother looked pale and weak under the bedclothes. The bed was so smooth and neat—as if it, too, were bereft and empty. Mother took her hand but didn't smile. It was as though Margaret had been hit with a heavy boulder, even a cannonball. She felt knocked down and emptied out at the same time. What could she say? She opened her mouth, but her eyes opened instead into an outpouring of tears. "Mother! Mother!" she pleaded. "Please get better!"

Lady Elizabeth's skin had turned a waxy white, almost gray, and she turned her head away. What had happened to Margaret's strong-willed, strong-backed mother? Was this what childbirth did to women? *Never,* she thought, *never will I marry and undergo such suffering.*

"Why?" Margaret asked Mistress Collace when she came back to the drawing room. "Why does God take so many? First Malcolm, then my grandmother, and now this baby. Grandmother was part of the world my whole life, and then she was gone."

Mistress Collace didn't answer but took her hand.

Margaret furrowed her brows. "Perhaps they are still here, in a place nearby? A place between earth and heaven, like the land of the fairies? It's what Isobel Gowdie believes."

"I see that this might be a comfort to believe," said Mistress, who thankfully did not preach against the fairies again. "But this belief comes from the Catholics. They call it purgatory. We do not believe in such a place. And, truly, to know that our loved ones are with God should be more of a comfort."

"And your babies? Does it comfort you?"

"Indeed, it does. It is hard, but we have to accept that life is temporary. All of us will die. Like the grass of the field, we are here for but a day, and then gone. That is the nature of life. We are born, like the sprout that comes out of the seed. We live for a short time, and flower so beautifully—like you right now, in the flower of youth—but then the flower creates seeds that drop into the ground and begin new life. You will marry and have your children. Some of the seeds grow into new flowers, and some of them do not. My bairns were not meant to grow and flower again. It's a hard lesson, and only the Lord knows why. Our task is simply to trust in Him."

Margaret did believe that that other world existed, in spite of Mistress Collace's beautiful words. She had seen it. And she was now convinced that she did have the second sight. How else could she have seen Henrietta in the mountains? Or Malcolm and the bloody soldiers . . . seen their wounds and the fires of battle burning behind them?

And Grandmother. When Grandmother died, Margaret had been seven. She had left Margaret her pearl necklace, but where was *she*? Margaret couldn't understand, and she kept looking for her. "She is with God, she is in Heaven," Mother had said, but that didn't make the greatest sense. Grandmother was the smell of lavender in her sitting room, the soft lap to sit on, the quiet humming when Margaret sat on the floor and played with her doll. Grandmother was a warm presence Margaret could feel. She couldn't just disappear.

After she died, Margaret took her doll into Grandmother's chamber and waited. One day, two days, a week. She was punctual and went at the same time she always had. And then, one day, it happened. She smelled the lavender, and she felt the warmth. She heard the voice: "Margaret."

And now this baby, the baby boy they had all been so hopeful for. They had hoped and waited, and he had been on the way. Now he was gone even before she could see him.

But perhaps he was not completely gone. Perhaps he was in that place of spirits, where Malcolm was, and she *would* see him.

She would talk more with Mistress Gowdie. She would learn from her. To see the fairies and their queen, and whatever else was in that netherworld. She had denied her visions, had tried to please her mother and father and teacher. Now she would let herself see.

But first she had to find the young lieutenant.

CHAPTER 16

Mother was still abed, though it had been a week since the baby had come . . . born and died all in the same day. Margaret sank dejected in the pew, while Lucy, between Margaret and Father on the inside aisle, fidgeted and squirmed.

Mister Harry was preaching about witches again, and Mistress Collace, on Margaret's other side, sat straight and tall with her velvet cloak around her shoulders. She had told Margaret that this witch talk, this "obsession" of Mister Harry's, was *his* superstition.

Once, she recalled, her mother had voiced a similar complaint to Father, but Father had defended the minister. "There is evil in this land," he'd said, "and these women plot and scheme to hurt the kirk as well as their natural masters, like your uncle and me."

"There is quite an abundance of plotting and scheming in this land," Mother replied with bitterness.

Father's eyes flashed with ire, and he lifted his arm, but then saw Margaret watching and let it drop.

Margaret turned her head. There sat Isobel in the back, with her husband and two little girls. Her pale eyes were cloudy, staring off into space as if she were watching something else entirely. All around her, the farm folk shuffled and rustled and muttered their disapproval of the minister.

Mister Gordon, the precentor, led the congregation in a hymn from the psalmody, and as Margaret began to sing, she became aware that she was no longer so passionate about this kind of singing. At Beltane, with the bonfire and the lively fiddle tunes, and the drums and whistles and the dancing, she had been immersed in the music, and now this music paled in comparison.

Mister Harry preached on and on, his voice rising and falling like a song, but one that repeated the same verse and the same three-note tune, over and over, until she thought she would die of tedium. Mistress Collace did not smile. Usually, her face lit up when she heard Mister Harry, but today, her eyes were downcast, and her shoulders sank down over her chest. Was she mourning the baby? Or was she as tired of this sermon as Margaret? Mister Harry seemed to be seeking Mistress Collace out with his eyes, but she kept hers averted.

Margaret looked around again. Two English officers stood at the back of the kirk, their red and white uniforms so neat and polished, they stood out like bright apples on a bed of brown leaves. The Covenanter soldiers had never looked so bright in their ordinary plaids and jerkins. One of the officers was the young lieutenant. But surely, these English were of the Episcopal faith. Why were they here, in the Presbyterian kirk?

The young lieutenant caught Margaret's eye and gave her a smile, as if they had a secret. She blushed and turned back around.

After kirk, she walked outside with her family. Standing under the gray, gloomy sky, she shifted from foot to foot. She was embarrassed that he had caught her looking, but she needed to tell him about the MacDonalds. As she was pondering these contradictory feelings, she heard a voice behind her.

"Good morning, Lady Margaret." The lieutenant stood tall and handsome, holding his feathered hat in one hand, his blue-gray eyes smiling at her. "Andrew Massie," he said, and bowed.

Margaret cast her hands about as if to find someone to intervene, but then shook herself and straightened up to her full height, which was barely above his shoulder. She would not allow herself to act the shy blushing maiden. She would be a woman of dignity, like Mistress Collace. "Good morning, sir," she said in a rich full voice. "I am gratified to see you here today, as I have some information. Tis regarding my friend Henrietta Rose."

"Oh? I regret we have not found her yet. We have pursued a thorough search of the region and made many inquiries."

Had the major then lied, or had this lad pursued the inquiries on his own?

"I believe I know where she might be."

The lieutenant cast his eyes up slantwise as if he found that unlikely, but then those same eyes warmed into a smile. "And where would that be?"

"Ben Rinnes."

"Ben Rinnes, one of the mountains to the south?"

"Yes."

"And how would you know this?"

"A cunning woman saw it with her second sight—the MacDonalds' encampment."

He stood in silence and gazed at her. Did he think she was mad to believe a cunning woman? "We employ military science that works in logical and rational ways," he scoffed. "The king's army does not depend upon magic."

"Hah!" Margaret stomped her foot. Perhaps her father was right about these arrogant English. But this was for Henrietta, she thought, and softened her tone. "We are all so distressed, as dear Henrietta has been gone for more than a week now. Wouldn't you want to try any possibility?" And now, truly, Margaret *was* on the verge of tears, which she knew could move a man to rescuing thoughts. But she would not allow the tears to come.

He frowned. "I will consult my superior officer," he said, and turned away.

Now the tears came. He wouldn't help, after all.

HARRY

❧

CHAPTER 17

arry Forbes loosened his ruff and stroked the front of his cassock. The people had left the kirk, and he was alone—a rare moment. Well, except for Jonet Fraser, who would stay in the stocks for the rest of the day.

If he could only get through to these people. If they could only see that he cared deeply about their eternal souls. God had called him here to this part of the world not to punish and condemn, but to lift and save. Jonet was suffering now, yes, but this would help her learn that adultery had consequences. And that faith was also about faithfulness. He would work harder to manifest the vision of Calvin, of a peaceful community, both religious and civil, living in harmony. If only he could root out these ignorant superstitions people were so attached to here in Auldearn.

Harry considered the stone walls, the low ceiling, and the humble windows of his kirk, where he had served for several years now. Had he served the Lord gladly today? Or was there within him some resentment of the Laird of Brodie? With his silk shirt and velvet jacket and shoes, Brodie had never known the struggle of survival, while Harry Forbes had had to make do with the same old black coat he'd worn for years and borrow money to augment his inadequate minister's stipend.

He bowed his head. "Ah!" he moaned. These were covetous thoughts. He tore off his ruff and struck himself in the chest with it. "Oh, Lord, let me not continue in this sin!" He clasped his head in his hands. For these covetous thoughts, he would lament and chastise himself further in his journal tonight, offering sorrow and repentance.

Harry had come to Auldearn from Aberdeenshire, where, after taking his theological degree, he had served as schoolmaster for ten years. He was intelligent and curious about the mysteries of God, and in the Laird of Brodie, he had found a like-minded soul. They agreed that man could never rid himself of sin, and that the most important practice in religious life was continual repentance for one's transgressions.

Now came a noise from outside the door. It opened, and there stood the young maid, Agnes Pierson. With her fresh face and smiling eyes, Agnes flounced her skirt, flapped her apron, and skipped up the aisle to Harry. "Mistress Forbes bids me tell thee she's gone with milk to poor Anna Reid." She laughed and held out her hand.

He touched his heart. *Oh Lord, lead me not into temptation.* He turned away. But then Agnes laughed again, a lusty, musical laugh, and Harry forgot his misgivings. He gave her his hand. So ripe was Agnes, so delightful and sweet, with her rosy cheeks and lips and her plump breasts peeking above her bodice. It was so freeing to be with the lass. Here, he didn't have to keep up the authority of the minister; he could act with abandonment and be the opposite of a solemn Man of God. He had worked so hard at that guise, and had mostly succeeded, but the effort was Herculean. Trying to be virtuous and *only* virtuous was an impossible task.

Harry smiled again, a smile of pleasure, and led her into the vestry, just a tiny nook behind the pulpit, a private space. He plucked some plaids from a chair and cast them down on the floor to make a soft bed. She stood and waited while he approached. He unlaced her stays, slowly allowing the fullness of her soft body to emerge. Then he lifted her chemise and unhooked her petticoats. She stood unmoving, as was their custom, allowing Harry to view her naked body before plunging his red and panting face between those breasts. As he stood back and gazed at her again, words from the Song of Solomon came to mind. "Thy lips are like a thread of scarlet," he proclaimed. "Thy two breasts like young roes that feed among the lilies." He stroked her breasts, and, in turn, her belly and thighs. "How fair and pleasant art thou, delectable maiden."

Agnes, naked, blushed and giggled, reaching down into his trousers. She grabbed his member and shouted, "I'll sain' the prior's wand!" and laughed raucously.

His wand. He felt himself shining with ecstasy, and straightened up, so proud of his strong, straight wand. He shuddered; but, controlling himself, whispered, "I will climb the palm tree and lay hold of its branches."

Harry threw off his clothing, and they tumbled onto the plaids. As he entered her, he sang out the words of Solomon, "Come, my beloved, let us go forth!" And with a whoop, he collapsed.

All was quiet. Harry had fallen asleep, and as he half-woke, he sensed Agnes rising and putting on her clothes. In the cold stone chamber, bereft of ornamentation as was proper in a true kirk, she walked softly sunwise around the drowsy man, swinging her arms and making a sprinkling motion as she chanted, "The seed has been sown, the seed has been moistened, to bring the seed home, nay, leave him alone."

At this, Harry opened his eyes and frowned. "What is this heathen talk, lass?"

"Only a little rhyme, a charm for the seed," she responded. She slipped out the vestry door, running through the kirk and out the front door.

A charm for the seed? Harry clutched at his throat. Was she wanting to get pregnant? But if she did, no one would suspect *him*, would they? He dressed quickly and stepped outside.

"Aiee!" Jonet Fraser screeched from her seat on the ground. "Have mercy, Mister! Let me out!"

He backed away from the stench. "Jonet Fraser, you well know your punishment for adultery is to stay there all day until the sun sets. You must use this occasion to reflect upon your sin and repent."

He walked away, down the hill, and a wince came unbidden to his face. *Surely, I am not like this adulterous whore. I am a man of God.*

Along the village road, he greeted the people with his usual cheer and empathy. Jack the Smith at the forge, Lilias Dunlop at her loom, and Elspeth Nychie, who covered her eyes with her *kertsch* so she wouldn't have to return his greeting. Elspeth sidled past him, clinging to the shadows beneath the overhanging thatch. Did they know about Agnes? Was that a leer on Elspeth's face, or was that close-lipped smirk her usual smile?

But how could I have done it again? Oh, Lord, I have sinned against thee, and I deserve naught but the fiery flames of hell. His stomach contracted in pain. He,

Harry, was a man of God, not a wanton letch. He was not an adulterer—not he, Harry Forbes. It had just been a momentary lapse.

But what if he was not one of the elect? What if he was already condemned to the fiery flames of eternal damnation? The knot in his stomach tightened, the knot of fear that was always with him. He had worked so hard to become a minister, suffering poverty, long days of study, and humiliation from those in power, and had passed grueling tests. Surely, that was enough to please the Lord.

Still, one didn't know. Like everyone, Harry was predestined, but was he already saved, or already damned? If it was the former, God would forgive his sin. Surely, he was of the elect, and all that was needed was repentance. *I repent of this deed, Lord,* he shouted within his soul. *Forgive me! Rather were I a beggar on the streets of Edinburgh than offend thee in this way!* He clenched his fists and punched himself, then doubled over in anguish.

James the Miller, who was leading his ox around the corner, stopped and stared. Well, the practice of self-castigation and repentance was common. Harry would provide an example for the people.

He felt better. Confession and repentance surely brought forgiveness. *Wash me thoroughly, and I shall be clean,* he thought, paraphrasing the words of Psalm 71: *Cleanse me, and I shall be whiter than snow.*

At the end of the village, the oak tree was starting to leaf out. It spread above him, waving in a gentle breeze. Harry wiped the perspiration off his face. The important people, after all, did not know of his sin—and if they did, certainly they would take pity. His wife, Julia, it was well known, was a burden and a trial for him, and who would not want to escape her bitter tongue? And if he occasionally had discourse with a servant girl, especially this lass Agnes, who was so willing and ready to fall, like a ripe plum from the tree, would not his friends forgive him? A man who, in so many ways, brought truth and righteousness to light, who preached with a purity of spirit few could match? He lifted his head and smiled. He straightened his ruff and walked on. In so many ways, he was upholding the Word here in this Godforsaken place.

|SOBEL

CHAPTER 18

"**B**ut I don't want to speak to the minister," I said as Hugh and I walked across the machair.

"You have been summoned, and you will go." He had dragged me out of the hut and forced me to come with him, and now he wouldn't let go of my arm. "You need to behave like a seemly wife, and not make me the laughingstock of the kirk."

"The kirk is ruled by that ugly man."

"You will not speak of a man of God in such manner."

I stood tall as I walked, even though my arm was being tugged out of its socket. Hugh could avail himself of my magic when he needed something, but he didn't want the kirk to find out. And he didn't know my real power. No one did.

My shoulder was throbbing in pain. "Leave go my arm!" I shouted, and surprisingly, after peering at me to make sure I wouldn't run, he did let go. Hugh had donned his best clothes for this occasion: breeches that were not torn, and a shirt he'd made me wash at the river. He'd even combed his long black beard, of which he was very proud. Hugh had two sets of clothes, while I had only one dress. He had shoes while I went barefoot—the common lot of us women. I was wearing my headscarf—the *kertsh*—today, at his command. When I could get away with it, I dispensed with this cumbersome thing, though my freed hair earned me the scorn of my neighbors.

We trudged up the hill, where the door of the kirk stood open. We hesitated, and I straightened up as Mister Harry came out. A tall, thin man with a little pouch of a stomach, he was no match for Hugh Gilbert in vigor, but he had words that could twist and defeat, so I knew to be cautious. I looked him right in the eye.

"Please come in, Mister Gilbert, Mistress Gowdie," he said, all pleasant and courteous-like. We followed him into the kirk, a long, empty room, stone and bleak, with no decoration of any kind. I recalled the stories my grandmother had told: of cathedrals with statues of Our Lady, painted frescoes and gold leaf, cherubs and birds, so different from this bare and lifeless room. But those beautiful kirks lived now only in the stories and prayers of the grandmothers.

In the last century, the Catholic kirks had been destroyed by spiteful Protestants, who smashed and ruined the marvelous statues and paintings. Twas well known that in his youth, the Laird of Brodie had been one of those marauders. With his lads, he'd stormed the Cathedral of Elgin, torn and demolished the holy paintings of Christ on the cross, and hacked up the fine carvings on the walls. Graven images, they called them, as if those beautiful things were sinful.

We sat in the front pew, Mister Harry in a high-backed chair in front of us. He leaned toward me and smiled, baring his teeth between plump lips. "What is the Word of God?" he barked out suddenly in a grating voice.

I answered just as quick. "The Holy Scriptures of the Old and New Testament are the Word of God."

He raised his eyebrows. This probably surprised him, but I had learned the catechism like everyone else, as we all were required to do. "And?"

I was silent. Why should I go along with this bully?

"—the only rule of faith and obedience," added Hugh.

"I wish Mistress Gowdie to answer, thank you, Hugh."

"And I know the words, as everyone does," I said.

"But you did not complete the answer, Mistress."

I remained silent.

He sighed. "I have fears for your soul, Mistress. I hear that you practice the sin of witchcraft."

I flared but contained myself. "I give rhymes and charms when the people petition, and I cure sprains and wounds and shivers and such. If that be a sin, then what do you call the doctor who bleeds a person to death?"

Hugh squirmed in his seat and prodded me with his knuckles.

"And how do your cures work? Do you cure in the name of the Lord our Christ?"

"Aye, in the name of the Trinity three, the saints and the fairy queen."

"The fairies?"

"Aye, the fairies can give us aid."

I expected a lecture and a scolding now, but Mister Harry's words took a different turn. "Mistress Gowdie, I am interested in the fairy world. Can you tell me about it?"

I opened my eyes wide and froze.

He smiled and seemed to soften. Did he really want to know?

And then I softened, too, for this was a thing I loved to tell. "The *sith* be of a middle nature between man and angel, and they have bodies light and changeable, like cloud."

Mister Harry, whose skinny body was twisted around in his chair, sat forward with his elbow on one knee, resting his chin on his hand. "And how do you see them?"

"At twilight is best, though most often, only seers like myself can do so."

"So, you are a seer? And what does that mean?"

"I can see many things in the other realm."

"What else do you see?"

Beside me, Hugh shifted in his seat and gave me a frown.

I sat up straight, for this was the place of my power. Why not say it with pride? Yes, I was proud of my power. I looked down my nose at Hugh. "I see the King and Queen of the Fairy, and they favor me with many good things: meat and drink and all fine cloths." I scrutinized Mister Harry. "Thou must have respect for their ways, for otherwise, they can do thee much harm."

"Ah, then they are agents of the devil."

I stared, seeing now how Mister Harry was truly intrigued about the other world; but he had twisted the meaning just as he twisted his body.

"It is Satan within you who leads you astray," he said, looking at Hugh. "We sorrow over the evil that has come into our parish here in Auldearn, and we must pray for Mistress. Be ever vigilant, Mister Gilbert."

Hugh bowed his head in assent. "She is a good wife, though, Mister Harry."

I looked at Hugh in surprise. He was defending me—not what I had expected.

I had lived in Auldearn all my life. As a child, I tended a little plot with my mother. Our hut was on the road just outside the village, and when Hugh

Gilbert came into town to sell his oats and corn, he passed by the house. He would pause and look at me. I looked back, but Hugh didn't speak. He came again and looked, and then I, thinking he had come for a cure or charm from my mother, the cunning woman, called out, "Speak! Speak, Hugh Gilbert; say wot you will." He smiled, but still didn't speak, and every time he came into town after that, he stopped and stared, and so I would talk to him until he smiled and said a few words. I'd tell him about the chickens, or admire his cow, or complain about the lack of milk in old Pickle-foot, my mother's thin creature. Hugh was a big man, quiet and steady-seeming, and since my father, a shoemaker, had disappeared when I was ten, this man's attention was welcome. When the marriage was arranged, I didn't mind, because Hugh was a cottar, which meant he worked the land of the laird in exchange for labor and a portion of the harvest. He was poor, but I was even poorer, with a tiny plot of land and the cunning woman's payments to subsist on.

My father had been a talker, a storyteller, with a tale for every occasion. He was charming, with a sparkle and a magic about him, imaginings and inventions for every situation. So often, he stayed out somewhere—no one knew where—and my mother would have to scrimp and save and hide the money so at least he couldn't take that when he disappeared again.

Hugh Gilbert had no charm, but he was reliable.

Mister Harry went on. "As Paul says in the letter to the Romans, 'Pray constantly, that your heart may be always turned toward God.' It is only for your eternal salvation, Mistress, that we pray. We Covenanters are privileged to have wisdom from the learned Mister Knox, and to understand the way to salvation: eternal vigilance and continual repentance. Each small thing, whether an act of pride, or jealousy, whether wanting what our neighbor has . . ."

"Our neighbor the laird has milk and meat and wine aplenty, while our children starve," I burst out.

"We have enough!" Hugh Gilbert roared and hit me on the mouth.

Mister Harry, who was frowning at me, now smiled at Hugh. "You are correct, Mister Gilbert. That was an example of covetousness. And to discipline a wandering wife is no small feat."

I stared fiercely at Mister Harry. I would wander where I would, I would fly with William, I would eat with the fairy queen, and I would guard my own power, no matter what this oily oaf said or did.

Mister Harry stood, tall and gangly in his ragged black suit. "You must double your efforts in prayer, both of you," he said in dismissal.

Hugh grabbed my arm, yanked me out of my seat, and tugged me along the aisle and out the door. "You leave off this charming and rhyming and witching," he growled. "Or ye'll end at the tollbooth or worse."

"I won't leave off, and I won't give up my powers!" I shouted, struggling to free myself from his grip.

"Your power is in the Lord," he said, "and we are a Christian family. Ye'll *triple* yer prayers now, and ye'll recite the catechism in full."

I finally pulled away from him and ran. He was stronger, but I was faster, so he didn't even try to catch me. He would catch me later. He always did.

And *I* would catch Mister Harry.

HARRY

❦

CHAPTER 19

Harry reined in his horse at the entrance to Brodie Castle. The afternoon sun was warming the rose-colored stone of the castle block, a rectangle rising high and stark in the midst of its wings and turrets.

It was a beautiful building or would have been if the west wing had not been smashed to pieces. The whole section lay in ruins, with broken stones and shards strewn around like children's blocks. A decapitated staircase climbed six steps to nowhere.

After the Battle of Auldearn in 1645, the English had knocked down walls, smashed stones, and destroyed as much as they could. When Harry came to the Auldearn kirk, the battle was ten years past, but the sight of these ruins still raised his ire. The effects of the battle were everywhere: not only here at the castle, but in the wounded and maimed survivors who populated all of Nairnshire. Not a family in his parish was without loss. Harry clenched his fists and narrowed his eyes at this testament to English brutality.

Behind him, a carriage raced into view and stopped abruptly beside him. "It doesn't help us love the English, eh, Mister Harry?" called out John Hay, the Laird of Park, doffing a tall beaver hat and wiping hair away from his face.

"Sore hard to forgive." Harry agreed.

Harry had been chosen as minister of Auldearn by Alexander, the Laird of Brodie himself, and the two enjoyed a mutual interest in theology. They read the works of John Knox and Andrew Melville as well as the latest tracts that came out of Edinburgh, and almost every week, they met here to discuss these texts and support one other in their efforts to live a godly life. Harry thought with pleasure of the mutual zeal for the Covenanting cause that had forged a bond between them.

It was here at Brodie Castle that Harry received his news of the world. The laird traveled and conversed with the most powerful men in Scotland and served as advisor to the king. This gave Harry, he felt, an insider's association with royalty.

Today John Hay, laird of Park and Brodie's nephew by marriage, was meeting with them. Short and squat with an air of belligerence, Park was another of Harry's strongest Covenanter allies. Park stepped out of the carriage as a groom came up and took the carriage and horses.

Brodie's lad, dressed in gray livery, emerged from a doorway and ushered them into the entry hall, a dark and cavernous room with walls that reached to invisible heights. Swords, scabbards, pistols, and shields, mounted in geometric patterns, gleamed and threatened from the gloom.

They followed the lad through another hallway and stepped into a light-filled drawing room, with heavy gold drapes framing massive windows that looked out on a garden of exotic trees and shrubs. Ivory-inlaid tables and elegant chairs in velvet and brocade stood ready for a crowd of thirty. From the carved ceiling hung crystal chandeliers, and at either end of the room, fires burned in enormous fireplaces.

A sudden breeze blew through the windows, and the gold drapes swayed and fluttered. *Gold for the laird's house*, Harry thought, *and cold for mine. With a stingy wife who sulks on a good day and harangues on the others.*

Alexander Brodie, in a red brocade jerkin and soft gray pantaloons, rose from his chair. "Nephew; Mister Harry." His dark hair was long and curled in the current fashion, and he seemed to tower over the other two men as they entered the room.

Harry paused beside a large, gleaming globe: the Mercator Globe. Gerardus Mercator was the most famous map and globe maker in the world, and this orb on its stand with a compass at its base was surely the finest example of his work.

Harry touched the varnished surface, running his fingers over the browns and sepias, reds and golds and greens, the lands of India and China, the new continent of America where dissidents and apostates were sent, the poles to the north and the south, and the places of ice and myth where strange beasts roamed. And then his own country, Scotland. Such a tiny part of the world, but, like the land of Israel, a land that had been chosen by God. Next to the green of Ireland and the pink of England, Scotland's orange stood small but proud.

Here, God's kingdom would shine. This was where both Knox and Melville, visionaries and prophets, had come from. They envisioned a time when the wealth and corruption of the Catholic Church, those centers of corruption and greed, the places where priests robbed the poor with false promises of heaven and exacted payment for release from purgatory, would be extinguished.

And that time had come. Scotland was no longer Catholic. But there was still so much to fight for. Harry had been called here to Auldearn to play his part in that fight. To help manifest that vision by quenching the forces of darkness.

He brushed off his worn black jerkin, shiny from too much wear, straightened his ruff, and took a seat opposite Brodie.

Brodie sank back and gazed into the fire, his long legs graceful in pristine white stockings and silver-buckled shoes. Harry tucked his own scuffed boots under his chair.

Park, who had been examining an engraved gold plate on the mantel, sat down abruptly. "What news of the king, Uncle?"

Brodie smiled. "He has signed the Covenant, and a date is set for the coronation."

"Ah." Harry smiled.

"Will it be at Scone?" asked Park.

"Nay, he was crowned at Scone, as you know, in 1651. This time he will be crowned for all of England, Ireland, and Scotland—at Westminster."

Park widened his eyes, pale and blue in a ruddy face. "A magnificent celebration," he said, with a touch of irony that was not lost on Harry.

Brodie gazed into the fire. "I am not one for pomp and ceremony, as you know, nephew. Daughter Grissel, though, is brimming with excitement. She has engaged several seamstresses to concoct her apparel."

Harry himself would have liked the pomp and ceremony, but he wouldn't mention it in this company. Brodie's daughter Grissel loved fashion, and Brodie indulged her. Since his wife had died some ten years ago, Grissel had been doubly cherished and favored.

Brodie let his head fall. "I pray that she will not accede to vanity, and I have told her so," he said, glancing up at Harry, as if reading his thoughts. "She counters me by quoting from the Song of Solomon, in which Miriam and all the women danced."

"There *is* festivity in the Bible," Harry said. "The Book of Exodus, though, in which Miriam danced for the coronation of King David, does not elaborate on her clothing."

Brodie frowned and shifted in his seat. "But this commission for the witches . . ." he began, abruptly changing the subject.

The room became silent.

"The commission at Nairn," Brodie continued. "For Jane Dunlop and Bessie Morehead. I believe you were there, Harry?"

"I was."

Brodie frowned. "I was not able to go, as I served the king. I felt in great darkness about the matter, not knowing whether these were legitimate charges."

"Ah," Harry said. Legitimate. Was Brodie not in favor of the trials?

A servant girl came forward with tea, and she served the three men. Through the open windows came fitful breezes, and between the gusts, an unnatural silence, as if the birds had retreated to their nests, though it was the middle of the day.

When the lass left the room, Brodie turned to Harry and raised an eyebrow. "What were the findings, Mister Harry?"

"They confessed at first, but then became obstinate and denied all that they had formerly confessed."

"And were the confessions forced?"

"These women," Park remonstrated loudly, "are wily and clever. Like snakes, they slither about and twist the words, and defend their actions, their herbs and potions, as if these were normal and laudatory."

Harry nodded vigorously. "They hide the truth. And only pricking with pins will reveal the devil that is in them."

"These two were pricked?" asked Brodie.

"They were, and when they fell asleep, pricked again, until the truth came out."

"How long did the pricking go on then?"

"Just three days."

"Three days and nights?"

Harry inclined his head yes.

Brodie shook his head. "I am desirous that sin might be discovered and punished," he said, "but don't you see how they will say whatever is wanted to stop this torture?"

Harry straightened and sat tall in his chair. His face, with its pliable features, changed from moment to moment, the full lips pursing and widening, eyebrows raising and shifting as he looked from Park to Brodie. "Our duty," he said in his ringing preacher's voice, "is to raise our people up from the mud of these ancient beliefs."

The servant girl came in again, bringing cakes iced with a pink sugary glaze. Harry, who had no sugar at home, eyed them hungrily and took three. He also eyed the top of the girl's breasts above her bodice and smiled with pleasure as he ate.

"Yes, we are living in a crucial time in history," Brodie continued. "These folk tales and superstitions have caused much harm in this country, with the cunning women using nonsense rhymes and putting pieces of yarn on doorsteps, telling the people these will cure their fevers and keep away bad fortune." He paused, pulling on his beard. "But we must not err on the side of undue excess."

Harry bowed his head. "It is precisely for their eternal souls that we must persevere."

"We must think of our own souls, as well," Brodie replied.

Was that a reprimand? Harry gulped down the last of his cakes. He needed to regain the higher ground. "Confession of our sin," he said, "and sincere repentance is the only way to a godly life. God knows, I need forgiveness as much as any." He sighed and looked up from lowered eyes to detect any suspicion. But these men, he was assured, didn't suspect him of misdeed. And they admired a repentant soul. Confession and repentance were the foundation of spiritual practice for the Covenanters.

"I, too," Brodie said. "Why, just the other day, I experienced great pleasure in a beautiful day. But immediately, I repented hard of this temptation away from the Lord."

Park raised an eyebrow. "Was that not rather severe, Uncle? Surely, we are blessed to enjoy God's kingdom, the lilies of the field, the tiny sparrow, and so on?"

"The devil disguises himself as pleasure," said Harry, "and in all things, we need be scrupulous that he not prevail."

"Wisely spoken, Mister Harry." Brodie nodded.

"And these witches have caused harm to *me*," Harry went on, returning to his theme.

Brodie sat up and fixed his regard on Harry. "What harm to you, Mister Harry?"

"They have plagued me with objects left at my door, and crows to come in my window."

Brodie sighed, as if he was questioning whether Harry Forbes, whom he'd chosen as minister and praised for his piety, was a bit too credulous.

Harry bristled. "With all due respect, Alexander, I perceive that there are times when even *you* do not see the threat from these women."

"And as you know," Park asserted in a loud voice, "they caused the deaths of both my father and brother."

Brodie sighed again. "And Agnes Grant was duly executed. She, too, denied all charges at first and then confessed, whether out of clear conscience or because of torture, I didn't know. And I did not investigate, to my own shame and regret."

The men were silent, remembering the burning of Agnes Grant.

Brodie turned to Harry. "And the outcome of this trial at Forres?"

"They will burn."

Brodie shook his head. "A sorry time, indeed." He spoke again. "Mister Harry, perhaps we can avoid this bloodshed, and instead, you can instruct these women in the true faith?"

"I will, and I have. Just the other day, I spoke with one of these cunning women, Mistress Isobel Gowdie. An obstinate wench who cannot be controlled by her husband, and she holds power among the people. This woman may also be a witch."

Park bowed his head. "We need more evidence, Harry."

Harry nodded. "It will be forthcoming before too long." He would get the evidence against Isobel Gowdie and rid the land of that witch—one more step out of darkness. Harry pursed his lips with a painful grimace and turned to Park. "But there is another matter to which I must speak, John."

Park started and looked up warily. "Yes?"

Harry rubbed his mangy beard and paused. "It's about what I heard from our servant girl. About Beltane."

"Ah yes, the primitive bonfire fest. What did you hear?"

"That your daughter, Lady Margaret, attended."

"What? Margaret, at Beltane?" Park jumped up. "I'll have her hide, the wench!"

ISOBEL

CHAPTER 20

What I could see: the Earth, the sand, the sea, my hands carrying a basket, my feet walking. I walked and walked along the dune, searching for the spiky averans, the aromatic valerian, the mallows and maidenhair for cough, the feathery wormwood, so bitter for the stomach, the bugloss for shivers.

The sea birds flew and swooped over the water. The water was rough and wild today, a dark bluish gray with foam in the waves. I stood at the top of the dune, where the grasses prickled at my feet and the wind made coughing, rushing, clattering sounds. A crow, with its strong wings, flew against it, landing in the dune grass. "The fairy queen," it seemed to say, though its voice was silent. "She beckons."

And now, around me in the rustling grasses: tiny flitting creatures, tips of wings that fluttered and disappeared in the air, a face peering from behind a blade of grass, a hopping toad of an elf who stared at me, then jumped into nothingness. The world alive with the visible and invisible, creatures of the wind, dancers in the grass, its rainbow colors shifting and evanescing, molting and mutating, flickering like the fairies laughing all around me. And now, the Queen of Fairy herself, a still point within the crowded, shimmering air, her hair as white as snow, a young and beautiful face, her gown the lemon of sun and the white of lightning.

"Mistress Gowdie," said the queen, holding out her hand.

The dark waves rolled in the sea, the gray clouds scudded, gulls raced and called, and I studied the queen. Should I go with her? The feast awaited, fairies attending, though I knew they were fickle, and not always to be trusted. They might try to keep me there. I might lose the time, like Thomas the Rhymer, who stayed with the queen for seven years, thinking twas but a moment. The fairies were not devils, as Mister Harry thought. They lived in another realm, and I knew the way there and back.

The fairy queen stood tall in her iridescence and glory, proud and strong as a tree or boulder. "I am seven hundred years old," she said, though her words were simply a whooshing of air. "And if you covenant with me, you will have meat and cakes and wine and everything to eat you can imagine. You'll have fine gowns, and your every desire will be satisfied." The Queen of Fairy didn't smile. She *was* power. "And you will have more power, too." Beside her, my steed appeared.

To feast again and in the house of the queen! I gathered my herbs and my basket, mounted my steed, and soared. Up and up, with a "horse and hattock ho!"

The queen would want to keep me, but I would not be caught, like Thomas. I would not stay for seven years or more, because I knew to take a nail. Fairies did not like iron, and a piece of iron would prevent them from keeping me. As I followed the queen into the Downie Hill, I fastened the nail to the door. Then, after eating my fill, I flew away, swift as a swallow. Because I was for William, and it was with him I had to go.

Now I stood on the village road with my sack and water jug. As I passed the smithy billowing smoke and heat, one-eyed Jack leapt out, as if he were watching for me, and grabbed my skirt. "My sore, mistress!" His one eye glared at me from his scarred face, and his ale breath came like a squall. I pulled back, but he pulled harder, and turning his head to reveal a wide scar running from his temple down the side of his neck. At its base, an open wound smeared with dirt was oozing blood and pus.

I had forgotten about Jack's sore and my promise, but now I had in my sack the herbs I needed.

"Where is your mistress, Jack?"

Jack smiled a crooked smile on the unscarred side of his face as he realized I would help him, and he turned his head back toward the smithy. "Alison Moore!" he shouted.

From around the corner appeared Alison Moore, a tall woman with striking black hair and eyes and a small child at her side. "What's this, then?" Alison frowned, pushing a lock of black hair beneath her white cap.

"The cunning woman is here."

"Ah, Mistress Gowdie." She smiled. "Come." She led us around the smithy to the hut in the rear. We sat on the ground around a small fire pit, the little lad quiet and wide-eyed beside his mother.

I took out of my sack the meadowsweet and burdock that I had dried and boiled and mixed together with lard. I scooped a blob of it into my hand and reached out to Jack as he sat patiently. I touched the sore, and he flinched. "Hold still," I said, and rubbed in the mixture, reciting the charm:

> *He put the blood to the blood, till all up stood;*
> *The lith to the lith till all took nith;*
> *Our Lady charmed her dearly son,*
> *With her tooth and her tongue*
> *And her ten fingers.*
> *In the name of the Father, the Son, and the Holy Ghost.*

And this shall become whole," I declared, standing up.

I would need payment.

Alison hurried into the hut and reappeared with a sack of strawberries, the first fruits of the season, and handed it to me. "And have you seen our Mister Harry on your way?"

"Nay, and why should I?" I grumbled. I had been expecting a fork or a fire tong, and now, I was wondering whether to ask for it or let it be. Jack and Alison were just as poor as I, so I just sighed.

"Off like lightning, he was," Jack said. He was holding his neck, his head lifted as if to distance the head from the sore. "Came to me for a horseshoe in such a rush and puffing that he was going to Brodie Castle to see the laird."

I cocked my head and raised an eyebrow. A long ride, that, from Auldearn to Forres and then back. Perhaps I could make some mischief for Mister Harry.

I continued my walk through the village, thinking. Lilias Dunlop, with a basket of red yarn, was coming the other way—from the dye-house, no doubt. She seemed to notice that my thoughts were far off and away and didn't interrupt.

I swung my basket and smiled absently at Maggie Burnet, the alewife, as an idea came. I passed the manse with its rotten door and scraggly garden and a beady-eyed face peering out the window. I came to the well, filled my jug, turned around, and walked back through the village, nodding vaguely at passersby. I was still thinking. How to punish Mister Harry?

When I came again to the alehouse and the big oak, I put my bucket down. Jagged white clouds scalloped in angry gray moved across the blue sky, rising and swelling, and gusty winds swept here and there. Twas a good time.

I took a long piece of cloth out of my sack and dipped it in the water. Also in my sack lay a beetle and a piece of wood like a bat. I lifted it out and wrapped the wet cloth around its end. I walked over to some small boulders beside the road, took up the beetle, and began to pound. As I pounded the boulder, I chanted:

> *I knock this rag upon this stane,*
> *To raise the wind, in the devil's name.*
> *It shall not lie until I please again.*

I noticed now that a small crowd had gathered round, and Lilias Dunlop watching in wonderment and approval.

Maggie Burnet whispered loud, "Raising the wind."

"Aye." Malcolm's voice rang with fear. "She's raising the wind."

MARGARET

CHAPTER 21

argaret stood by the window, as clouds moved faster and faster and gusts of wind swept across the fields. She gritted her teeth. Since Andrew would not, she would muster some troops herself and go to Ben Rinnes to search for Henrietta. She would commandeer the grooms and stable lads, who knew her better than anyone. Surely, they would be willing to help, and would welcome an adventure.

Lucy was sitting on the bed with the china doll she'd had since childhood, embroidering a border on the doll's silk dress. She looked up at Margaret. "What was it like? Beltane?"

"Oh, it was marvelous! A fire and stories and dancing!"

Lucy lowered her voice to a whisper. "Dancing?" Her dark hair and eyes were very much like Margaret's, to the extent that people sometimes thought they were twins, but she had a very different character. Perhaps because her sister's inquisitive nature could rouse their father to anger, Lucy sought distinction by following all the rules . . . and by pointing out every occasion that Margaret *didn't* follow them.

"Yes, dancing." Margaret glowered at her sister, daring her to tell tales.

The bubbled, wavy window glass made a beautiful light, but it was hard to see through, so Margaret opened the window wider. It shook and rattled in the wind as it creaked back and forth on the brass pulley. A blast of air shot into the room. "Oh, the wind!"

Lucy dropped her doll and ran to the window. They watched as the sand blew across the fields in a gray horizontal sheet, like an ocean wave risen from the sea.

"A typhoon!" Margaret cried. "Like in *The Tempest*!" The wind raged across the fields, scattering the delicate flowers of the new flax, ripping up plants that would have made linen for sheets and nightgowns, dresses and undergarments. It swept the fields clear and whipped their gowns.

Lucy pushed away strands of hair that flopped like seaweed into her eyes, wiped her wet face, and laughed.

Now Margaret laughed, too, and they stood in the squall and shrieked as the wind and sand raged across the fields and roared in the window.

Then Margaret frowned and pulled on Lucy's sleeve. "But the flax will be gone!" she shouted. "Another crop gone, and Father will rant and fume."

But Lucy, thrust out of her cautious conventionality, was thrilled. "See the crows tossing in the clouds!" she screamed. "It's like when we race our horses on the beach."

"And bits and pieces flying every which way," Margaret exclaimed, drawn back into the game as shards of wood, tree branches, and strands of fishing net soared past her home. "Like God is playing a game of cards and tossing them into the air."

The sisters jumped up and down and clapped, their gowns lifting and flapping in the fitful storm. Lucy's pale face was blotchy and red, and her brown eyes opened wide as she laughed. Margaret laughed again, too—though perhaps, she thought, they were laughing a bit too hard.

A whirl of sand and wind like a tunnel was hurtling towards the castle. In a moment, it spread over the shepherd's hut, the sheiling, out on the machair, enveloping them like a blanket swaddling an infant. From one instant to the next, the sheiling was there and then was gone.

Lucy hiccupped. Margaret gasped, and just as suddenly, their laughter turned to wailing.

Bessie came into the room and hurried over to them. "What is this screeching like little children?" she scolded. She reached out to close the window, but the wind was too strong, and it wouldn't shut. The three of them, buffeted and lashed, could barely stand in the sandy gusts that beat inside. Bessie pulled the girls back, away from the blast.

"What will happen?" Margaret cried. "Will the sand cover us? Will our house be gone? Will we all be buried?"

Bessie folded them into her arms. "Nay, nay, lassies, it won't come here."

"How do you know?" Lucy cried. "How can you say that when you don't know a thing?!" She ran to Margaret's bed and buried herself beneath the featherbed.

As quickly as the storm had started, it stopped. A sudden quiet descended, almost more eerie than the storm itself.

"Miranda!" Margaret shouted. "I must go to the stables." She ran to the door and Lucy jumped up from the bed, still sobbing, to follow her down the tower stairs.

HARRY

꽃

CHAPTER 22

arry looked back once more at the castle as he mounted his horse. A stark building in the gray mist, alone in the open landscape, it stood as a testament to the Brodie presence. The Brodie family had resided here since the twelfth century, when ancient King Malcolm had granted them the land, and Alexander Brodie was still the most influential laird in Moray.

It was he who had brought Harry here to begin with, and to him Harry owed great allegiance. He needed to stay in Brodie's good graces, there was no doubt. Today they had spoken of sin and repentance—a good discussion, but he winced remembering his own transgressions. No one knew about them, though. At least, he hoped not.

He straightened his shoulders. Those sins would no longer be a part of his life. He would shore up his foundations, fortify the ramparts. The west wing, with its debris, broken walls, and stones strewn across the ground, seemed to contradict his intention, but he averted his eyes, turned, and rode off into the wind.

The wind, indeed. It had gained strength, and the sky was now a tumultuous mass of gray clouds. Harry hunkered down on the horse and rode west toward Auldearn. All around him, the winds eddied, and the sand lashed, changing direction every minute. He lowered his head and squinted to keep the sand out of his eyes, but now a whirlwind circled and whipped up before him. He was heading straight into it. His only option was to stop.

A tunnel of sand rushed toward him as he tried to stand firm.

His horse began to buck and whinny.

There was no way out of this. He would have to forge ahead and race through the whirlwind. He wrapped the reins tighter around his arms and wrists, spurring his horse on. "Juno, on! Onward ho!" But Juno was terrified and refused to gallop straight into the raging sands. She bucked higher as the sand whipped closer.

Now they were in the midst of it—the sand cutting into Harry's face and through his clothes, the road invisible.

The horse reared and screamed, and then, thrashed and flogged by a greater surge, they both fell.

Harry had already hit the ground when a sudden pain seared through his leg and he realized the horse was on top of him. He was pinned down. "Juno! Off! Off me!"

She trembled and whinnied and refused to move.

It seemed an eternity before the storm died down and he was able to get the horse up and off of him. When he tried to stand, his leg screamed in agony, and a bone stuck out of his thigh. Blood was pooled around his leg on the sandy road.

He managed to take off his jacket and shirt and wrap the shirt around his leg. The pain was excruciating, but he managed to heave his body up and across the horse's back.

An hour later, dripping a trail of blood, he arrived on his own doorstep.

"Julia!" Harry cried out his wife's name.

The door was closed, and no one was about.

"Agnes!" He called for the maid, then yelled more loudly. "Agnes!"

Agnes opened the door. Loose hanks of hair were falling out of her kerchief. Her bodice was twisted and dirty, and, as usual, her whole appearance was askew. She stared at him, mouth agape.

"Well, help me, lass!" he roared.

Agnes, a strong young woman, helped him dismount on his good leg, and propped him up as they entered the house. Julia was standing in the shadows of the dark hall, watching them with an angry expression. "What ha' ye gone and done now, ye damn fool?" she growled.

"Julia, have you no mercy?" he whined. "I am injured and cannot walk."

"Put him to bed," she commanded the maid, and turned away toward the kitchen.

Agnes helped Harry into bed, then stood looking at him, hesitating. "I can call for the cunning woman," she said. "She has medicine for such a wound."

At this reference to "the cunning woman," whom he knew to be Isobel Gowdie, Harry recoiled in even greater pain. "None of that fairy magic for me, lass. You must fetch the doctor."

Agnes stared and froze, as if to contradict him, but afraid to do so.

"Go! Go now," Harry shouted as Agnes ran out of the room. These peasants had such superstitions about real physicians. Doctor Urquhart, who had studied in Edinburgh, would surely come to his aid.

MARGARET

CHAPTER 23

Father had come back from Brodie Castle in a rage. "Beltane," he'd roared. The beating had been worse this time, and then he had confined her to her chamber "forever!" he'd shouted, ranting and pacing the castle floors. Margaret had lain on her side and cried herself out.

She stood by the window. The sandstorm had transformed the landscape. The fields of flax, vast blankets of blue a mere three days ago, were now covered in sand. It was as if the strand had lifted itself up and moved inland. Instead of fields *and* strand, there was now only strand, from here to infinity.

Father really hadn't meant for her to stay in her chamber *forever*, she thought. It had been three days now, three long days, and hopefully, he had calmed down and come back to reason. He had probably been as angry about the storm as about her disobedience.

She tiptoed down the stairs through the dark tower and out the door. Treading across sand that dusted the courtyard, she hurried down to the stables, where the animals were snorting and neighing and stomping.

Miranda jerked and neighed as Margaret entered her stall. "Nay, lassie," she murmured. "Nay, nay." She took the brush from the hook and brushed and smoothed the horse's back until Miranda quietened.

"Ye need not groom the horses when we have the lads to do it." Father's bellow rang out as he came striding across the stable yard.

How did he know—? Oh, he must have seen her footprints in the sand.

"And what do ye think ye're doing out here, young lassie?"

"I had to see Miranda, Father. I knew she was so worried and sad. Lucy said that since the storm, she's been hopping and jumping as if she were on fire. She does become calm with my brushing."

His face relaxed. "Ye do know the animals, lass."

"And Miranda knows me."

Father's shoulders sank as he surveyed the damage. A buckled roof on one of the barns and several fences down, the distant fields covered with sand. He turned to face the larger barn. This one, at least, was intact.

Now came a trotting sound, and from across the courtyard: a black stallion topped by a dazzling redcoat.

"Andrew!" Margaret exclaimed under her breath. Father started and looked a question at her.

"I met him at the kirk," she explained. "Lieutenant Massie."

Father's eyes narrowed as Andrew stepped lightly down from his horse and bowed. "Andrew Massie, m'laird."

Father said nothing.

And then, as if Father's rudeness were not offensive but merely ordinary, the lieutenant bowed to Margaret. "Lady Margaret." He glanced around, surveying the sandy yard and the barns before addressing Father. "How have you weathered the storm, my laird?"

Father's eyes flashed. "Almost all my crops are ruined!" he exclaimed bitterly, as if it were the English soldiers' fault.

"Condolences, my laird." Andrew bowed again—quite graciously and with no rancor. "I have come with news that I hope will brighten your loss to some degree."

"What news, then, lad?" Father almost spat out the words, as if no news could brighten his loss.

"The Lady Henrietta has been rescued."

"Oh, you found her!" Margaret burst out and ran as if to embrace him, but then saw her father's glare. She stopped and straightened her bonnet. "Where was she? And where is she now?"

"Your minister, Mister Harry, along with Mister Hugh, the girl's father, prevailed upon the major to resume the search."

"Good man, Mister Harry," pronounced the laird.

"We did find the MacDonalds' camp on Ben Rinnes, my lady, and I apologize for my gruff reception of your suggestion."

"No matter, no matter!" Margaret shouted again. "Just tell us everything!"

Andrew hesitated, as if weighing what to say. "She *was* being held by the villains, but as our troop far outnumbered theirs, we were able to arrange a peaceful surrender of the lass. She is with her mother now at Kilrock Castle."

"Oh, oh, oh!" Margaret sighed and ran to hang up the brush. "Now you *must* release me from my confinement, Father, and let me go to Kilrock!"

Father scowled. "We will speak of this in private." He turned and marched away toward the large barn, heedless that he was leaving her alone and unescorted with a young man.

Margaret opened her mouth, but no words came.

Andrew waited.

She wrung her hands, but after a few stutters, regained her composure and spoke with dignity. "We extend much gratitude to you and your troops, Lieutenant."

She turned and ran back to the castle.

CHAPTER 24

She lifted the curtain as her carriage bumped and jostled along the road to Kilrock Castle. Henrietta Rose had been rescued, and Margaret was going with Bessie to visit her at Kilrock, home of the Rose clan.

Father had not consented, but Mother had been able to bring him round. "Henrietta needs her friends now," Mother had said, "and Margaret has great kindness in her."

The fields lay open and flat around the carriage, and soon, behind a copse of pine and elm, Cawdor Castle came into view. Seat of the Campbell family, it stood tall and proud in the sunshine. Cawdor's laird, Hugh Campbell, was one of the most powerful lairds in Morayshire.

Margaret had visited Cawdor once, when the Covenanter clans were gathered for a celebration. Much younger then, she'd wandered around the courtyard with stone walls rising toward the sky and found a tower with a winding staircase. She climbed up and came out on the parapet. Below, people looked as tiny as toy soldiers, and beyond the courtyard, the hills and fields stretched away forever. In the distance, she could see Kilrock Castle.

A man had come up behind her. A smooth-faced Campbell, no doubt, smiling a craggy smile and pointing at the crenelated parapet. "There stood a traitor," he said. Young as she had been, Margaret knew quite well about traitors. "And from this very place was pitched o'er the parapet to his death." The man grinned wider and came closer. Margaret turned and hastened back down the tower steps.

Today, she peered out the carriage window at a familiar scene. The weather was mild and warm for May, and behind the castle, the Cawdor Hills swelled gently in shades of green and gold. No sand covered the earth in this inland area. *So not all is dire in this land*, she thought, and her hope rebounded like spring sunshine. "This castle hath a pleasant seat," she recited. "The air nimbly and sweetly recommends itself unto our gentle senses.'"

Bessie crinkled her face into a smile. "'Tis a lovely poem, dear."

"It's from the play about this very castle called *Macbeth*. I found it in Aunt Grissel's library, but please don't tell Mother or Mistress Collace, as they might disapprove. It doesn't have a Christian theme."

"What kind of story is it, then?"

"A gruesome tale about the ancient kings of this land, and how they betrayed and murdered each other. How ghosts came back to haunt the living, people cursed one other, and witches cast spells."

Bessie sighed. "Not so different from our times, then."

"Oh, but, Bessie," Margaret protested, "we have our faith and our kirk now. And we Covenanters fight for truth and for God, not for greed and power."

Upon hearing her own words, Margaret paused to wonder. Was this really true? There had been so many battles and so much bloodshed in recent years— throughout her lifetime, in fact. How could people say they were fighting for truth and God when they were killing? According to the Bible, killing was a sin. It was murder. It went against God's law.

And now Henrietta. Thank the heavens she was home. But what had happened to her at the MacDonalds' camp?

They drove into the courtyard at Kilrock, and there stood the new tower. Higher than the house, the square edifice formed an ell and dominated the courtyard. Kilrock had been created by the same architect who had designed Cawdor Castle, but it was smaller. Like the Campbells, the Roses were an ancient clan, but not so rich and powerful.

Henrietta was expected to marry George Campbell, the son of Sir Hugh, Laird of Cawdor, so that the families combined would be more powerful, and Henrietta always smiled dreamily when George's name was mentioned. Would anything be changed now?

The carriage bumped along the road into Kilrock Castle, wending through fields of rye and oats. Kilrock, on level ground, unlike Inshoch, sat in soft countryside, with fields framed by spring-blooming trees. Resting above the River Nairn, the castle boasted gardens and walks with unusual trees, like the Monkey Puzzle and a strange twisted oak. As children, Margaret and Henrietta had run in and out amongst them, giving them names like "the Octopus," the "Stout Elf," and "the Tickler."

The day was sunny and bright, and as they approached, the stone walls of the castle looked almost cheerful against the green of the trees and blue of the sky. Henrietta's real home was the manse at Nairn, where her father, Hugh, was the minister; but she and her mother stayed at the castle now for extra protection.

Margaret gathered her skirts, stepped down from the carriage, and pulled her cloak around her shoulders. She had put on her finest blue satin gown with the embroidered bodice today, to honor Henrietta and show respect to the Rose family after Henrietta's ordeal. In the courtyard Margaret twirled around, letting her skirt flare out a bit. This deep shade of blue was flattering, Bessie had said, to her pale skin and dark hair. Everything should come right on such a perfect day.

Two guards came from the door and stood at attention.

Ben Buchan stepped down from the carriage. "The Lady Margaret, daughter of the Laird of Park, to see the Lady Henrietta," he announced.

From the door came two lady's maids who quickly ushered Bessie and Margaret into the castle: through the great hall with its noble portraits and aroma of baking bread, down a corridor, up a set of narrow stone steps, and into the chamber where Henrietta lay in bed. Her mother, Lady Anne, sat beside her in a chair.

Lady Anne's shoulders were hunched and tense over Henrietta, who appeared tiny and frail as she lay still under the bedclothes. She stared up to the ceiling of her bed canopy and glanced without expression at Margret and Bessie as they entered and sat in proffered chairs.

Margaret bit her lip. *What could she say?* The friend she knew was lively and sparkling . . . not this bleak-looking lump in the bed. She pulled her chair closer and took Henrietta's hand in hers. Henrietta's eyes filled with tears, and she turned her head away.

"My dear friend," Margaret said. She and Henrietta were the same age and had been friends since they were children, but they had always been protected from the fighting and violence of these gruesome times. Now the violence had come to them . . . to Henrietta.

Margaret looked at Lady Anne, whose light brown hair fell in loose locks across a worried face, so different from her usual welcoming smile. Henrietta turned and slowly sat up. Her face was almost as white as her nightdress, and her hair hung loose and limp.

Margaret swallowed. "What happened?"

Lady Anne shook her head. "She rode her horse out to the strand."

"You know my horse, Michael," Henrietta began.

"Of course—Michael, the stallion with spirit, Saint Michael the archangel," Margaret said, trying to bring some cheer into Henrietta's eyes.

Henrietta's ashen face lifted in a wan smile.

Lady Anne wrinkled her nose. Like Margaret's parents, she and Mister Hugh did not believe in saints.

"You stayed on the strand to walk in the sunset," Margaret said. When she looked at Henrietta, she couldn't stem the tears any longer. "But I'll never forgive myself for leaving you there."

Henrietta stared bleakly at the canopy ceiling. "If you had stayed, they would have captured you, too."

Lady Anne shook her head again. "You lasses are no longer children, and you have been told how dangerous these jaunts and hijinks are." Henrietta pressed her lips together and looked about to cry again.

"I had just dismounted from Michael when they swooped in," Henrietta said. She sank down under the mountain of bedding and jutted her chin out defiantly.

"MacDonalds," Margaret whispered.

"Yes, the roughest lads I've ever seen, and they smelled terrible! Like sweat and dung and clothes that had never been washed." As silent as she had been until now, Henrietta spilled the words out in a tumble. "They pulled off my snood, and my hair flew about. They rode me to your castle, where they took all the cattle and the grain, and then up the mountains to the south, where they had a kind of camp hidden in the rocks, and they—" She stopped, and her whole body squeezed together into a hump like a baby. "I can't say it."

Lady Anne sat on the bed, her head bowed, shoulders heaving as she wept silently. "At least some of the English soldiers are good Christian lads," she said, sniffing. "They found the camp and captured the villains."

"And brought Henrietta back," Margaret finished. Lady Anne nodded. Margaret wouldn't boast about her own part in this or mention the dashing lieutenant. Perhaps she would tell Henrietta later.

Bessie, who had been standing aside and listening carefully, now moved up to the bedside and took something out of her gown. "My lady, this herb is known for the easing of this kind of pain."

Lady Anne looked up with a puzzled expression.

"And there is a special charm, for this wound is one we have known in the farmtown. When the English came from the Battle of Auldearn, they took no mind of the people, and ravished our lasses as they pleased. But the wound can heal, and the soul can heal, as well."

Lady Anne sighed and stood up. "Please, say the charm, Mistress Wilson."

"I'm sorry, my lady, but my power is not so great as that cunning woman in our farmtown, a Mistress Gowdie," Bessie replied.

"Isobel Gowdie?" Margaret cried out. "I thought you disapproved of her!"

"She is a cunning woman, a wise woman, and a storyteller. She has the power to heal with her magic and her charms, but she also has the power to harm, and a cunning woman can be dangerous. But when you seek her out for healing, she is obligated to help. That is the natural law."

"I have heard that cunning women can heal when the leeches and physicians, can't," said Lady Anne. "In fact, the doctor who came to heal my husband of the ague bled him so much that he nearly died."

"That's all he knows," Bessie sneered. "Bleeding."

"I wish we had known of Mistress Gowdie then. But now," said Lady Anne said in a most authoritative manner, "we must call this cunning woman to come." She stood up with her belly protruding, as she, too, was expecting another child.

"We will bring her to you," Margaret declared, and bent over the bed to hold Henrietta in her arms. "My dearest friend." Henrietta smiled weakly, but turned her head away, again retreating into silence.

The horses were ready to gallop. They stomped and snorted as Ben Buchan brought them out from the stable. He seemed barely able to control them, but Margaret knew Mister Buchan was a skilled driver, and she had no fear as she stepped into the carriage.

Bessie's face registered consternation, but Margaret was excited and called out, "Let us see how fast they can go! I'm ready to fly!" She knew not why she was feeling such exhilaration after she'd just seen her dear friend laid so low. One shouldn't be so happy when Henrietta was ill, but perhaps it was because Henrietta was *back*, and she *would* heal.

Margaret herself was not ill; she was well and alive, and feeling the thrill of living. "Faster!" she called to Mister Buchan, laughing at the expression on Bessie's face, which was a look of amusement rather than the disapproval she had expected. And then both Bessie and Margaret began to laugh, not knowing why. The more they tried to suppress and compose themselves, the harder they laughed. The carriage rattled and bumped as it bounced along the road. The two women looked away and held their mouths, but then one of them would look back, and then the other, and a giggle turned into a laugh and then a shriek.

"Ho and *arrête!*" a command roared from outside the carriage. A flash of redcoat. The horses hurtled to a stop. The carriage jerked and halted.

Red-faced and laughing, with tendrils of hair falling over her eyes, Margaret thrust her head out the window. There, on his black steed and holding the carriage reins, sat Andrew Massie, his coat unbuttoned and posture easy, sandy hair sweeping across his face. He was completely at ease, as if he and his horse were one being, in rhythm with the sky and the undulating hills behind him. He looked at Margaret, whose hair and bonnet were in disarray, and smiled.

"Oh!" She clutched her head, humiliated to have been seen in this state. "You again!" she cried in her most outraged tone of voice, "What are you doing?" She was completely flustered, so drawn to him, but angry now. *How dare he smile?! These condescending redcoats.*

"Rescuing you from a tumble, my lady." He laughed.

"Rescuing *me*? My driver knows every inch of this road, and we were just having a bit of a frolic!" She retreated back into the carriage and folded her arms against her chest. But then she shook herself and thrust her head out the window again. He was still sitting there on his horse, a sweet smile on his face beneath his wide-brimmed hat, his leather jerkin unlaced. "But I must thank you for rescuing my friend!" she said. "She is home, thanks be to God, and recovering well." Still flustered, Margaret tried again to push back the hair that had escaped from her bonnet. "Thank you, Lieutenant Massie."

He bowed and tipped his hat, and Mister Buchan smiled at Margaret from the driver's seat. The horses snorted, impatient to be off. Margaret let out a strangled kind of giggle, then quickly pulled herself back into the cab and closed the curtain. As the carriage rolled, she dropped her head down onto her lap. "How could I behave so?" she cried. "He'll think me a flibbertigibbet!" Bessie stroked her back.

Andrew. A lovely name.

CHAPTER 25

Margaret saddled Miranda and leapt up onto the saddle—side-saddle this time, as befitted a lady. She spread her skirts decorously over her legs and boots. The groom and stable boy were mucking out the stalls and did not pause or look up when she left the barnyard.

Bessie had said that Isobel was dangerous, but how? Surely Margaret would have heard something about it. And Henrietta, too, had implied that Isobel might be evil. But Henrietta hadn't even met Isobel. Isobel was a healing woman with the intent to do good, and Bessie, though she seemed to disapprove of Isobel, had also said cunning women were obligated to help when someone asked.

Margaret would ask.

She crossed the road, barely visible under the sand, and rode onto what used to be the path. Miranda was accustomed to walking on the shingle, so it was no trouble for her. Soon, she broke into a trot, and the pair rode along the ridge toward the farmtown. They proceeded down into the farmyard, where the sand was deeper, and slowed down.

Loud, arguing voices were emanating from Isobel's hut.

"Ye've done it now!" a man was shouting. "Raised the wind to ruin us all!" A woman's high voice screeched an angry stream of Gaelic.

Margaret heard a loud thump and another voice, Isobel's this time. "Ow! Ye nasty cur! Son of an evil beast! I curse ye to be drowned at sea!"

"Ye'll not be using yer evil curses on me!" Another wallop. A black-haired head emerged from the door hole, then a long black beard. Red-faced, Hugh

Gilbert straightened to a towering height, glanced at Margaret, and stomped away.

Next, a disheveled-looking young woman burst out of the door hole and shouted, less to Margaret than to the world in general, "She done it! She raised the wind and ruined us all!" And she, too, strode away across the yard. In short order, three children came out and scattered, running in different directions.

Was that woman blaming Isobel for the sandstorm? *How strange*, Margaret thought. Were these people, as her mother had said, really "riddled with superstition?"

Margaret dismounted. Should she go into the hut? "Mistress Gowdie?" she called softly.

She heard a faint voice. "Aye, lady. Come."

Margaret tied her reins to a post, bent down, and stepped inside. She heard a moan. On the other side of the fire pit lay a heap of dress and wild blonde hair. Isobel raised her head.

Margaret knelt down beside her. "Mistress, are you hurt?"

Isobel raised her head, revealing a bruise on her cheek and a swelling that almost obscured her eye. Margaret leaned in closer, gingerly wrapping an arm around her. Isobel inclined her body into Margaret with a sigh. Such sadness, such a pity, that this extraordinary being had to be subject to a brutal husband. What could she do? Margaret stayed still, and both were quiet. She couldn't rescue this woman from her downtrodden life any more than she could change the violence and killing in the wars, but she could offer comfort.

Isobel pointed to the entryway. "My basket."

Now accustomed to the dark room, Margaret found the basket and brought it. Isobel rummaged through it and removed a small bottle. She opened it and poured something onto her hand, then rubbed her face and muttered words that Margaret could barely hear:

> The lith to the lith, till all took nith;
> Our Lady charmed her dearly Son,
> With her tooth and her tongue, and her ten fingers;
> In the name of the Father, the Son, and the Holy Ghost.

Isobel stood up now and gestured for Margaret to follow her outside. In the yard, Isobel walked up to Miranda. "A fine one, ain't ye, m'dear?" she said, stroking the horse's neck.

She turned to face Margaret, and Margaret started.

Isobel's face was clear—no swelling, no bruise, no redness.

"But," Margaret stammered, "your face—? The charm—?" She could say no more and could only gape at Isobel.

"Aye."

Margaret let out her breath. "You really are a healing woman."

"And you are a good woman, Lady Margaret." Isobel took Margaret's hand, and Margaret felt herself blushing to feel this new closeness with a woman so different from herself.

Isobel straightened and stepped back. "What brings you here today?"

"A similar matter . . . a matter of healing. But first, I must thank you for helping us find Lady Henrietta." Margaret went to her saddle, took ten pence out of the saddle bag, and handed the money to Isobel.

Isobel quickly tucked it into her bodice. "And how fares the Lady Henrietta? Is she to home?"

"Yes, she is home, but she fares poorly. Her mother, the Lady Anne, begs for your presence, that you would come with a charm to heal her."

"She was raped then, was she?"

That word again. It came like a blow, and Margaret stepped back.

"Ravished by the MacDonald lads?"

Margaret lowered her head. "No one has said so. But she *was* hurt, and in other ways, too." She didn't know for certain, as no one had spoken about the violence Henrietta had experienced. It had all been communicated in lowered eyes and shaking heads and tears, leaving Margaret to fill in the details with her "wild imagination." And of course, she had done so, seeing Henrietta stripped and beaten and violated in all kinds of ways.

"I'll go to my kist." Isobel stepped back into the hut. When she reemerged carrying her basket, she looked at Margaret through lowered lids. "This will require a special charm, and it may take some time."

"The Lady Anne will pay you well."

"And I'll call on the fairies."

"The fairies help, too?"

"Oh, aye! They add to my power."

"Power?"

"Power to heal and power to harm," Isobel said proudly.

Margaret shivered. She should not have come into this house. Her father hadn't said it recently, that she must not cross the threshold of "that poor wretch . . ." but he had, with a look of fear, told her to stay away from the farmtown. Not that he would have called it fear. He would probably have used a word like "perspicacious" or "decent" or "not according to the Lord." Her father was a pious man and wanted to keep her safe.

And who or what was Isobel Gowdie? A battered wife, or a powerful cunning woman? A healer, or one capable of doing harm?

Margaret hesitated, but had to ask. "That woman who came out of your house. She blamed you for the storm. Surely, you do not have that kind of power?"

"Oh, aye, I have power to raise the wind."

"But—how?"

"When the clouds begin to darken and move, I say the charm and strike the rock. And the fairies do help, to be sure."

Margaret was tightening her horse's girth. She stroked Miranda's neck. It sounded like Isobel had waited until a storm was rising, then said her charm . . . and took credit for it.

"But that woman is Agnes Pierson, who does tarry with the minister," Isobel said.

"Mister Harry? What do you mean by *tarry*?"

Isobel didn't answer. She turned and wrapped her plaid round her shoulders. "Now we go to Kilrock Castle. And I will cure the Lady Henrietta."

"I pray," Margaret said, "that Henrietta will regain her spirit, and not become dull and dead-looking like the MacQuarrie lass." After the battle, Cromwell's soldiers had invaded towns, plundering homes and ravishing many Covenanter women, like Jean MacQuarrie. Her mother had told Margaret about the lively Jean, who had become so gray and dismal, even suspicious of others who meant her well. Suspicious towards Margaret's father, because the Hays had not been attacked. Some people thought John Hay had provided support to the English. But of course, he would never do that. "People just want to find someone to blame," her mother had explained.

"Come." Isobel walked toward the road.

Bessie, heeding Margaret's order, had brought the carriage and was now waiting in the farmyard.

"You can take Miranda," Margaret said to Isobel, and without hesitation, Isobel turned back and jumped lightly up onto the horse. "Horse and hattock, ho!" she shouted, and took off at a gallop. How did Isobel, who had no horse, learn to ride like that?

Margaret stepped into the carriage and sat beside Bessie. At the reigns, Ben Buchan urged the horses forward, and they were off.

Margaret had never let anyone else ride Miranda. What had possessed her now? Why had she so easily loaned out her precious filly? She did want Isobel to go as quickly as possible to Henrietta, but there was something else. Isobel commanded respect—deference, even. She did have power.

When the carriage arrived at Kilrock Castle, Isobel was already waiting in the courtyard. Standing straight and proud, she seemed taller now, no poor wretch, no mistreated wife. Isobel was clearly in charge.

Lady Anne, short and bustling, appeared in the doorway and showed them immediately to Henrietta's chamber.

They stepped into the room; its stone walls unadorned. A recessed window on one side brought in some light and a vigorous fire in the fireplace made the room warm. In the middle, the four-poster bed, draped with embroidered white satin, framed the small figure beneath a featherbed. Her face flushed with fever; Henrietta glanced at Margaret then closed her eyes.

Margaret sat down beside her.

Isobel, standing at the foot of the bed with her basket, addressed Lady Anne. "How long has she been like this?"

"A week and three days." Lady Anne paced back and forth in the small room. "Ever since she came home."

Isobel reached into her basket. "Straw, clay, and an herb from the field," she said. She turned to Henrietta's maid, Jean, a young dark-haired lass who was hovering in the corner. "This must be boiled." She handed Jean the straw. "And this washed." She took out a lump of clay and a bowl. Jean wrinkled her nose and shook her hand, reluctant to take the slimy clay.

"Go on now, Jean," Lady Anne ordered.

Jean took the clay and hastened away.

When Jean came back, Isobel took the boiled straw and mixed it in the bowl with the herb, a trailing stem of green leaves, and the clay. She spat upon it and shaped it with her hands, then applied a portion to Henrietta's forehead and temples. The remainder, a sticky lump, she held high above her head and marched about the room, chanting another rhyme, while the three other women watched.

"I forbid the quaking-fevers, the sea-fevers, the land-fevers, and all the fevers that God ordained, out of the head, out of the heart, out of the back, out of the sides, out of the knees, out of the thighs, from the points of the fingers to the nibs of the toes; let all the fevers go, some to the hill, some to the heap, some to the stone, some to the stock. In St. Peter's name, St. Paul's name, and all the saints of Heaven. In the name of the Father, the Son, and the Holy Ghost!"

Isobel recited the charm twice, then again as she circled the room, stopping only when Henrietta opened her eyes.

Margaret frowned. Could a fever be charmed out of a person and transferred to a hill or a stone? But, she remembered, Jesus himself had cast demons out of a man and into a herd of swine. So why was that a holy miracle, and this would no doubt be called magic? Perhaps because Isobel was not a minister authorized to say a public prayer.

And because Isobel was a woman.

Henrietta was breathing evenly now, and her expression became placid as if she'd just stepped out of a storm-tossed boat onto dry land.

"Oh," Margaret breathed, taking her friend's hand.

Henrietta smiled.

"Lord in Heaven!" exclaimed Lady Anne. She threw herself down on Henrietta, weeping with great heaves, as Henrietta murmured, "Mother, be calm."

Lady Anne looked up and stared at Isobel in wonder.

Margaret, now standing beside the bed, found herself holding the slimy straw-and-clay lump that Isobel had handed to her after the charm.

Henrietta's red hair was pushed away from her wet forehead, and the bright redness of her cheeks had faded. A sliver of sunlight crept through the window, illuminating Lady Anne's white neck against her green velvet gown.

Isobel sank down on the Persian carpet and bowed her head. With her pale hair hanging down and her body drooping, she looked exhausted.

Margaret studied the lump of clay in her hand, and now she saw that it had a shape: an oval, no, a pear shape, almost like a woman, with two tiny mounds that could have been breasts and a nub at the top for a head. She made to hand it back to Isobel, who shook her head.

What should she do with this? She looked around then gently placed the clay figure on the window well. It would dry and Henrietta would have it as a reminder.

Margaret leaned over the bed. "Henrietta," she whispered. "How is it with you?"

Henrietta cast aside the satin featherbed and sat up. She looked at her mother, at Isobel, and then at Margaret. "I believe I feel better." Her skin had a bit more normal color now, and her eyes were brighter. She slowly drew her legs up and over the side of the bed.

"Not so fast, m'lady." Isobel rose from the floor and came over to the bedside. "Ye might be feeling better, but ye must go slow to come back to the living."

"Yes," Henrietta said in a quiet voice. "It was as if I were dead, and I now feel more alive."

Lady Anne stood and cried out, "May the Lord be praised!"

"And Saint Peter, Saint Paul, and helpers three," Isobel said, echoing some of the words from the curing. "And Queen of the Fairies, fair Maeve."

"The fairies," Henrietta cried. "I thought I saw angels, but perhaps they were the fairies."

"Around your bed, as we are now," Isobel said in her low, deep voice.

"Yes . . . how did you know?"

"I did see them, too. Queen Maeve and her sprites."

Henrietta looked confused. "But—" she protested, turning to Margaret, "I didn't see those—or if I did, I didn't know their names."

"St. Michael, St. Mary, and the Holy Three," Isobel sang, humming in a voice like a reverberating cello as she moved about the room. Bessie remained standing at the foot of the bed, as did Margaret, and watched Isobel.

Lady Anne leaned over and stroked Henrietta's arm. An air of serenity seemed to radiate around mother and daughter. Lady Anne looked up at Isobel again, and stood quickly. She thrust her hand into a fold in her gown, pulled out a small leather bag, smiled, and gave it to Isobel. "Thank you, and may the blessing of Our Lord be yours, my dear."

"My lady." Isobel bowed in a manner less like a peasant than a queen acknowledging her subjects. And then, like quicksilver, she slipped out of the room.

Bessie's face widened into a big, one-toothed smile.

"Cunning women," Bessie told Margaret on the way home, "know the fairies and the saints and all the other beings most of us can't see, and they can call on them to help with their healing."

Margaret hugged her arms. "I know that, Bessie. Mistress Gowdie was telling me about the fairies and her powers."

Bessie looked at her with alarm. "When did she tell you that?"

"Just today, in her hut, when I went to fetch her." Margaret wouldn't mention that she had been there before.

"Ach, ye mun' never go into that hut again. Didn't I warn you about that woman? You must take great care with her, as her powers can go to harm." She sighed. "But today, they went to the good. She prayed to the saints, and they brought a cure for the lass."

"Mister Harry says that praying to the saints is evil, too. It is superstitious, like worshipping idols. He says it is of the devil."

Bessie lifted one eyebrow. "And dost thou believe that what just happened was of the devil?"

Margret shook her head no. "Henrietta has been returned, and it looks as though the life has been restored in her. How can that be evil?"

Bessie didn't reply. Margaret could see that she was being prudent, not wanting to contradict the minister lest she be seen as one of "them." And indeed, Mister Harry probably *would* call this witchcraft. She thought of Jane Dunlop's witch trial. Margaret's father said the punishment was just desserts for the evil she had done, but her mother had shaken her head in sadness, saying she was horrified at "the terrible times we live in, when we return evil for evil." Margaret had heard her parents arguing long into the night.

After today's events, she knew that Isobel's magic was real. It was good, not evil, no matter what Bessie or Mistress, or even Isobel, said.

And she intended to learn more about it.

ISOBEL

CHAPTER 26

I crossed the farmtown yard to Elspeth Nychie's hut and stooped to enter. This hut was almost identical to mine, but Elspeth had a table and two chairs. Elspeth and her husband, Jacob Taylor, unlike most of the farmtown people, had been able to keep some furniture over that hard winter when everyone else had had to burn theirs for heat. Maybe they had stolen a tree from the Lochloy Wood, the laird's wood, or perhaps it had come from a neighboring farm.

Elspeth's brittle gray hair was bound up on her head today, but as usual, the strands fell out all over, making her look like she was always in a hurry with no time to fix it proper. She leaned over the table toward me. "I dreamed we danced at the Downie Hill," she said, almost in a whisper. She stood up and waved her arms in exuberant gestures. "T'were you, and me, and Lilias Dunlop and Bessie Wilson. We danced and frolicked and feasted!"

"We put the besoms in the beds," I added, "and off we flew to the fairy house to eat and to dance!"

"So, you had the same dream?"

"T'were no dream. We do fly from our beds in the night, real as can be, though none of the people can see us. They see our besom and think it our body."

Elspeth furrowed her eyebrows in a skeptical look. "In my dream, we went in the likeness of a crow and a hare. You a crow, and I a hare."

"And we went to the dye house of Alexander Cumling."

"Yes! But how—"

"And we took the yarn and cast three knots and put it in the dyeing vat."

"To make it all black!"

"We have our powers, and we made some mischief."

"We did!" We both laughed with loud guffaws, and Elspeth smacked the table.

"But I hear," she said, "that Mister Harry be plotting to bring you to the council, and there to try you as a witch."

"As he did my mother."

"Your mother, Agnes Grant."

I hunched over, remembering. "They poked her and prodded her, and when she fell asleep, they pricked her with pins. Over and over, until she cried and wailed and admitted to whatever they forced her to say. 'Did you attend Black Mass with the Devil? Do you repent?' And when she denied, they asked her again and again, for days and days, not letting her sleep at all. She was bruised and red with sores all over, and almost unconscious, until finally she confessed."

We huddled in our plaids, squeezing tight our shoulders as if to protect ourselves from the memory. "I never suffered so much, even through hunger and cold and weariness from work, as to see my mother murdered like that. I felt it in my own body, that burning."

"And Mister Harry, the examiner."

I stood up and raised my fist. "I did vow to exact revenge on Mister Harry."

Elspeth grinned wide. "You raised the wind and knocked him down, and now he is a'fever!"

I smiled with pride. "And we must make sure that there he'll stay for two months or more." I took my sack and laid on the table the things I had gathered: the flesh and guts of toads, pickles of barley, parings of fingernails and toenails, the liver of a hare, and bits of cloth, all slimy and rough and soft together, a feast for the devil. "And now, to task!"

I took my knife and hacked the ingredients into small pieces. Elspeth brought a pan of water, and I dumped the minced concoction into the water. "Now we let it steep, and tonight, we will say the charm."

In the evening, when the men and the bairns were asleep, I came back to Elspeth's hut. The concoction was now congealed, and we poured it into a sheep's bladder. Outside, we walked a little distance from the farmtown, set the sack on the ground, and together recited, "He is lying in his bed; he is lying sick and sore; let him lie intill his bed two months and three days more."

"And we shall say it thrice against the recovery of Mister Harry." Twice more, we chanted the charm.

We took the bag and set off on the road to Auldearn. We would go to the manse and say the charm over his bed. Singing as we went, and all manner of folk could see what merry friends we were, laughing beneath the gloomy night sky, but no one was on the road at this hour. When we arrived at the manse, we peered through a window. There was Mistress Forbes, sitting in the parlor in her sour loneliness, even though 'twas the middle of the night. We went 'round, but the back door was locked. We couldn't get in the house.

The next day, we set out again, over the fields and into the village, where we came across young Jane Martin, a bonny maid all pink and dimply, on her way to the manse where she served alongside Agnes Pierson.

I waylaid Jane. "Jane, we want to make some mischief for Mister Harry."

"And we need your help," Elspeth added.

Jane smiled slowly at the thought of the mischief, then frowned. "Not to raise the wind, I won't."

"Nay, Jane, not to raise the wind. We want you to smear your hands with this potion and rub it on Mister Harry, then swing the bag over him in his bed. And say this rhyme, though say it quietly: 'He is lying in his bed; he is lying sick and sore; let him lie in till his bed two months and three days more.' Ye must say it thrice o'er."

"And why should I do this?" Jane asked with fearful eyes.

"Because you know how he hurts with his words and his witch hunts. You know he is an evil man who claims to be of God. And that does make him doubly evil."

Jane looked up at the sky and swiped a lock of curly blonde hair out of her face as she considered. Her skin was flawless, soft and creamy. Elspeth and I shared a look that said, *the perfect trap for that man.*

"Yes, I know what you mean," said Jane at last. "He does swipe and grab at me whenever I pass, the lech'rous demon." She smiled again. "And I will do it!"

Mister Harry would welcome Jane into his chamber . . . that we knew. And for her to swing the bag and pretend it was a healing cure was no large task. She simply had to utter the words quietly, and the sick man would most likely not hear.

HARRY

CHAPTER 27

The doctor had finally arrived, and Agnes Pierson showed him into Harry's chamber. Harry winced as Doctor Urquhart came in carrying a large black satchel. He knew what was in that bag.

The doctor placed the bag on the floor and sat on the chair beside the bed. He looked around the room, then at Harry, and sighed.

Doctor Urquhart was a squat man who moved slowly with an air of dreaminess, as if he were thinking of anything but medicine. He was the only doctor in all of Morayshire, and rarely came to Auldearn. Though Harry knew this procedure could very well prove more painful than the injury itself, he was grateful that the doctor had come for him. No doubt this had been because he was the minister, an important person.

"Lie still and open your arm," the doctor said.

Harry lay back obediently and pushed up his sleeve.

Doctor Urquhart took a tortoiseshell case out of his pocket, opened it, and removed the thumb lancet, a two-edged knife with a sharp point. He laid the point on Harry's arm at the inside crook of the elbow and pierced the skin. A copious amount of blood immediately spurted out and into the cup the doctor held.

Harry gasped, but he was determined to endure. He was sure the treatment would alleviate his fever, shivers, and the huge red swellings on his leg.

The light was dim in Harry's chamber, with only three candles around the bedside. Heavy gray clouds outside the window made it feel like night. His wife, Julia, and Agnes Pierson stood in the shadows, watching.

When the first cup had filled with Harry's blood, the doctor took another one out of his bag.

"No!" Agnes yelped.

There came a scuffling sound and a slap. "Quiet!" Julia barked.

Doctor Urquhart punctured the skin again and held the second cup while turning toward the women. "The only cure for the fever is a vigorous bloodletting," he stated in a quiet, authoritative voice. "This removes the burning heat from the skin and lessens the pain. It will require several cups."

"Proceed, doctor," Harry whispered. He suddenly felt so depleted he thought he might faint, though fever still raged throughout his body.

Agnes ran out of the room.

Harry lost consciousness.

When Harry awakened, it was to the sound of someone murmuring. He barely made out a young woman walking around the dim room, and he could hear but a few words: "... in his bed ... sick and sore ..." She was carrying something, a bag, perhaps, and was swinging it as she swayed and chanted.

He tried to sit up, but could barely move, and when he tried to speak, the words barely emerged. "What's this, lass?" he finally managed.

She came close to his bed, and he saw that it was Jane Martin, the fairest lass in the village with her soft skin and hair, rounded curves, and blue eyes rimmed by dark lashes. When she bent over his bed and looked at him, he smiled. Such lovely breasts ... so enchanting a lass. And such a gift at his sickbed. He immediately felt a little more alive.

"'Tis for your sickness," she said, putting her hand in the bag and smearing his forehead with something greasy and foul-smelling.

This was some superstition of the peasants, he knew. And if they were trying to help him, what harm could it do? Perhaps it might even help.

Harry tried to take her hand, but he could still barely move his arm, so he smiled up at her in gratitude.

Like a deer in the forest, she vanished.

KATHARINE

CHAPTER 28

In the gray light before sunrise, Katharine entered the parlor.

It had been several weeks since the sandstorm that had devastated the land, and the farm workers were still struggling to save the crops. Walking to Inshoch Castle, Katharine had tried to give them some encouragement. She'd recognized the first man she met on the road and had stopped to speak to him. Hugh Gilbert was a silent sort who doffed his hat and bowed when he saw her. He'd said that almost all the flax and half of the oat crop had been lost.

The curtains drooped and sighed in the draft. She sat down in the chair by the fire and stirred the embers, knowing that this wouldn't heat the room, but that she'd soon feel a warmth within herself. She knelt on the floor. This kneeling in the quiet before dawn, before her husband John Ross awakened, was precious time. She could turn all her thoughts to the Lord, knowing that his presence was with her.

Perhaps, in another time and place, she would have been suited to the monastic life. In a nunnery, she could have devoted her days to prayer and supplication. Several hundred years ago, perhaps, before these places became so corrupt, and the popes so full of greed and lust.

A loud knock on the door interrupted her thoughts. Katharine made for the hallway, only to be accosted by the stolid presence of Mistress Forbes, who had let herself in.

Julia Forbes, in a tall hat with wide brim that rendered her short, compact presence and angry glare all the more menacing, stepped forcefully into the room. "Whore of Babylon!" She shouted, reached out, and pushed Katherine back against the banister.

"What–?" Katharine clutched her heart.

"I know what you've done and where you've been!" Mistress Forbes's face, with its short nose and gaunt cheeks, was like a snarling dog, and there were tears in her tiny eyes. She appeared barely able to keep herself from bawling hysterically.

"What's this? What's this?" John Ross bellowed as he came down the stairs, buttoning his shirt over a hairy chest.

Katherine took hold of the banister to keep herself from falling over. She blinked and stammered, "I don't know, John."

"Well, what have you done?" he demanded.

"I have done nothing." Katharine could barely speak, and her voice came out in a hoarse whisper. "I don't know."

"Why is the minister's wife here accusing you if you've done nothing?"

"Aye, she knows what she's done, all right," rejoined Mistress Forbes with a smirk. Now that she had an ally in John Ross, she was more composed. "Improper relations with my husband, is what."

"What?" Katharine cried. "No, no, not at all!" Where had this wild accusation come from?

John, more riled now than Mistress Forbes, raised his hand and smacked Katherine on the cheek. And now Katherine was crying, clinging to the banister.

Mistress Forbes shoved her again and turned to leave. "You'd best be away from here altogether," she said. "Be gone from this place." She shut the door behind her.

John looked to hit her again, but Katherine held up her hands in a plea. "No, John, she is wrong. Nothing improper with the minister. All I've done is take counsel and guidance from him."

"And should I believe such a story? Perhaps you *should* be gone from here." With that, he climbed back upstairs.

Katherine went to her room and looked in the mirror. A red swelling was forming on her cheek. *The Lord does not give you more than you can bear.* That was what she had always believed. But now?

She went back to the parlor and her prayers but could not regain peace. Julia Forbes could bring great shame upon Katherine's head with this accusation, and people would believe her. What could she do? Perhaps this was a sign that the Lord was calling her to leave Morayshire. Katherine would consult Alexander, Laird of Brodie.

MARGARET

CHAPTER 29

"**I**sobel Gowdie must be a true cunning woman," Henrietta said. She stooped to rake her fingers in the wet sand, pulled up a cockle, and held it high. "Aha! We'll have these for soup tonight!" She placed it in her leather satchel and stooped again to rake.

"Isobel Gowdie truly *is* a cunning woman," Margaret agreed, wrinkling her nose at the cockles. Sometimes her cook prepared these, but only when they were low on other supplies, and she herself had no fondness for cockles.

The two young women had hitched their horses to a post, taken off their shoes and stockings, and were now walking along the strand beneath the high-tide line.

"I was so afflicted, so downcast, I feared I would never mend. And now look at me!" Henrietta skipped and twirled around, her petticoat flipping gaily beneath her dress.

Margaret watched and smiled, then resumed gazing out to sea.

"But what causes you such quietude?" Henrietta asked.

"I am watching for Titania and Oberon." Margaret brushed back the hair that had escaped from her cap. "I'm trying to think of a charm that will bring them in."

"A charm?" Henrietta lowered her voice and came closer. "But that sounds like magic."

"I believe 'tis more like a prayer. Or perhaps a prayer in combination with a wish. Mistress Gowdie used one to talk with the dolphins. And they understood her! Or perhaps 'tis a call, like the farmers call the cows, with a rhyme in the name of the Father, Son, and Holy Ghost."

Henrietta looked hard at her friend, then laughed, putting her satchel down in the sand. "Yes! We can devise a rhyming prayer." She raised her hands to her mouth in a cupping motion and called, "All the dolphins in the sea, come to Margaret and me."

The waves rolled, and the sea shimmered calm and blue.

Margaret stepped up and shouted even more loudly, "Saint Michael, Saint Mary and Trinity Three, bring Oberon and Titania to me!"

The sound of the waves, the smell of the sea, but no dolphins.

Margaret kicked the sand and looked up at Henrietta's innocent face: her delicate nose, the blonde eyebrows and lightly waving red-gold hair. "I went to the Beltane feast," she said.

Henrietta started. "No, my lady!" The pair often called each other "my lady" in jest or affection, but this time, it seemed Henrietta was using it to tamp down a sense of fear that had arisen. "And what was it like?"

"Mistress Gowdie was magnificent. She led me round the fire, and we danced! I danced! And then she told a story of the fairies. She *knows* the fairies, Henrietta. She visits them and dines with them!"

"The fairies? Did you believe it?"

"I wasn't sure, but I do now."

"But we are taught the higher truth of Christ's presence, not that of the fairies."

"Why couldn't both be true? And why are we not allowed to dance? The dancing was glorious!" Margaret lifted her arms and kicked her feet, twirling so that her skirts flew up.

"Yes! Dancing *is* glorious." Henrietta took friend's hand, and they skipped along until Henrietta stopped them both short. Her face seemed to freeze.

"What is it?" Margaret asked.

Henrietta didn't answer. She stood still, her face paler than pale, her body trembling. The strands of hair that had come out of her cap hung like limp seaweed across her eyes, and she didn't wipe them away.

"Henrietta?"

Finally, Henrietta turned to face Margaret, but her gaze was still far away.

Margaret's shoulders sank. "Were you back on that mountain just now?"

Henrietta bowed her head, her body stilled now. "There were so many of them."

139

Margaret hesitated. "What did they do?"

Tears welled up in her clear light eyes as Henrietta sank down on the sand, curling up her body and shaking her head back and forth.

Margaret sat beside her and put her arm around her friend.

Henrietta's shoulders stopped shaking and she seemed to calm down but remained silent.

"But then you were rescued."

"Yes, and I praise God for those English soldiers. How did they find me, I wonder?"

Margaret took a deep breath and gave a satisfied smile. "Again, 'twas Isobel Gowdie."

"Isobel Gowdie? What can you mean?"

"I went to visit her and implored her to use her second sight. And she did! She *saw* you with her second sight, right on Ben Rinnes, and then I told the lieutenant what Mistress Gowdie had said, and Mister Harry stepped in, and the next thing I knew, you were found."

Henrietta's eyebrows knit together in an expression of fear. "Mister Harry and Mistress Gowdie?"

"Oh, he didn't know I had consulted her. Margaret looked hard at Henrietta and her red-gold tresses blowing about. "Isobel Gowdie saw you there, on the mountain. And I believe that *I* saw you, too. I think *I* have the second sight, Henrietta."

Henrietta raised her eyebrows.

"I didn't believe it at first, either, but now I know 'tis true."

They walked silently along the sandbar, Henrietta stooping to rake and pick cockles again.

"That lieutenant is the most handsome soldier." Margaret smiled dreamily.

At this, Henrietta smiled, and her spirits seemed to lift. "The spring doth come at last, and hearts turn to love."

"Love? I do not think so far ahead as that," Margaret said, frowning. "But when can I ever see him? My father forbids any association with the English."

"Dancing," Henrietta said out of the blue.

"Dancing?"

"You can come to the ball!"

"The ball?"

"Yes! The ball at Darnaway to celebrate the coronation. Father disapproves, but Mother thinks it would be good for me, to liven my spirits. And there will be no Royalists there. Just the English officers. Your young man may well attend!"

"A ball! To think of it! But my parents would never allow such a thing. You know what the Covenanters think of dancing. Besides, I don't know how to dance."

Henrietta smiled smugly. "You'll come stay with me for a while, to help me regain my strength." She winked. "And I will teach you how to dance. Such fun we'll have. We'll do the allemande, the sarabande, and the gavotte. And we'll go to the ball!"

They untethered their horses and mounted, waving goodbye as they rode off in different directions. *How can Henrietta change so quickly from happy to sad and then back again?* Margaret wondered. And to think of a ball. Would it really be possible?

CHAPTER 30

"The venison was delicious, Cook," Lady Elizabeth said as Cook circled the table. Cook was a small, thin woman with a turned-up nose that caused her to look constantly cheerful, even though she rarely was. She was serving whim wham, a custard made of cream and eggs, Margaret's favorite pudding.

"Thank you, m'lady," Cook said as she disappeared into the kitchen.

Everyone immediately took a spoon to the pudding—even wee John, who ate so little that Lady Elizabeth worried and even became frantic at times. Wee John was a tiny, frail boy of five, and most of the time, he was unable to come downstairs to the table, much less go out and play like other children. Margaret didn't know what illness he had, only that it kept him sick and in bed most of the time.

Mother looked down the table at Father. "Grissel was here this afternoon. And she has invited us to the coronation and ball."

"Oh!" Lucy cried and clapped her hands.

"The coronation! Westminster Abbey!" Margaret exclaimed. "Oh yes, Mother, I have for so long wanted to go to London! And to a ball! Just think of the gowns, the lords and ladies, the dancing, and—"

"Quiet!" the laird roared. "You know quite well that dancing is a sin. There will be no dancing, and no trotting off to London with Grissel Brodie!"

Lady Elizabeth glanced at Margaret, holding a finger to her lips. Sometimes, she could bring her husband round.

"But," Lucy interjected, "couldn't we go to the coronation, Father, just the ceremony?"

"To see the king," Mother said, "and to participate in history, John. Such an opportunity may never come again for our family."

"Do you not understand, Elizabeth? We have suffered a raid and a sandstorm, and our stores are dangerously low, worse than after the raid. Even with the stores from the farmtown, I'll have to borrow again. We cannot afford the gowns, the trip, and the wastefulness of that decadent city. I said no, and I mean no!" He threw down his serviette, stood up, and stalked out of the room.

After some silence, Mother looked at the girls with regret. "I'm afraid we'll have to accept that, lassies."

"Do you think, though," Margaret inquired, "that Father would accept a compromise? Henrietta has invited me to a coronation ball here in Nairn with the English soldiers."

"Ah, the English. Nay, I'm sorry, lassie, but you know what your father thinks of the English. To say nothing of dancing." Mother gave Margaret a sympathetic look as she leaned over the table and took her hand. *Well,* Margaret thought, *perhaps Henrietta's idea had some merit.*

Lucy narrowed her eyes at Margaret as if she knew that Margaret was scheming for a way to go the ball. Margaret glared at her, a silent threat not to tell.

After the meal, Margaret slipped outside again and gazed over the lands to the east toward Darnaway Castle, where the coronation ball would take place. As much as it sounded heretical, she did NOT believe that dancing was a sin. And she knew that Aunt Grissel agreed with her, though she may not have said it in plain English. Grissel had told Margaret stories of the dances and balls she had been to in Edinburgh and London, and even in Paris. So why should Margaret not go to the ball with Henrietta?

The music of the pipes, fiddles, and drums of the farm folk, and the harpsichord Aunt Grissel played, all so lively and sweet—none of that could be a sin. Grissel had taught her to play a little and sing to accompany her. Music was Margaret's greatest joy. Music was for the soul, as Mister Shakespeare wrote.

I must, then, be a heretic, Margaret thought, for she would abjure her Covenanter belief in this. Perhaps not just in part, but in whole. Perhaps she would renounce the Covenanting kirk and Mister Harry. Perhaps she would choose the music and the songs of Isobel, and the fairies flitting in the flowers.

She laughed and gazed across the land to the east, toward Darnaway, as the western sun lit the fields and woods. Of course, she would not renounce her faith. Now she knew that Isobel's magic was real, and certainly, it would do no harm to learn a bit more about it.

CHAPTER 31

Margaret hesitated as she approached the hut. Isobel had invited her to visit today but hadn't said what time. Perhaps it didn't matter, since the peasants had no clocks or timepieces, so she wouldn't be expected at any particular time.

It was midmorning, another day of oppressive clouds and wind and seagulls screeching back and forth, busy at their sky-soaring and squabbling over fish.

Yesterday, she'd had her lacemaking lesson along with the usual homily from Mistress Collace—this one on a passage from Romans. The early Christians, Mistress had said, suffered much at the hands of the Romans, like the Covenanters suffered from the Royalists and the English. However, they clung to their faith and followed Paul's instructions to love and care for one another, even through the murders of their friends. Margaret wasn't sure what the point was, but perhaps it had to do with the death of her brother Malcolm, and Mistress's own lost children. She found it difficult to see the Auldearn Kirk as a place where people would join in caring for one another, as in the Roman kirk. Most of the farm folk hated Mister Harry and went to kirk only because they were forced to do so by the law.

Margaret stood in the farmyard, still layered with sand. The chickens didn't seem to mind it. They scratched around her, fluffy yellow chicks following a mother hen this way and that, pecking at whatever was available. No sound came from Isobel's hut except for a few animal snorts and knocking of hooves on wood.

Isobel's home was squat and poor, but today, there was something charming about it. What was it? Margaret raised an eyebrow, studying the front of the hut. The roof! The roof was thatched with heather, and the heather was blooming. It formed a field of lacy pink flowers on top of the hut, like a soft hat.

In the door hole appeared a face, and with it, a bright smile. "Lady Margaret!" Isobel called, stepping out to greet her. Her dress seemed a little cleaner today, and her hair was neatly pulled behind a cap. She beckoned. "Come inside."

Margaret bent low and stepped through the door hole into what was beginning to feel very familiar: the smoke, the darkness, the feeble peat fire. And now she saw other people . . . two women.

"D'ye ken Elspeth Nychie?" Isobel pointed to the gray-haired woman who greeted Margaret with a sudden embrace. Margaret looked around with confusion. To be embraced by a peasant? This was a different world, with different rules.

"And this be Jane Martin," Isobel continued. Jane was a young girl of not more than sixteen, a pretty lass with light blonde hair and fair skin who, as opposed to Elspeth, gave Margaret a timid smile and a curtsy.

Isobel indicated the chair, and Margaret sat as the others squatted down on the dirt floor around the fire. "Art thou ready to learn the magic of fair Elfane?" Isobel asked.

"Oh, yes," Margaret replied, then gulped. Was she, really? She was here now, and there was no sense in hesitating. "I want to learn everything, Mistress Gowdie."

"Ye may call me Isobel."

"Isobel. I want to know how you call the dolphins and how you go to the fairy places, and how you change your body into a hare or a crow."

Isobel and Elspeth exchanged a look. "But first ye must learn about the Earth and the seasons," Isobel said.

"I already know about the Earth and the seasons."

"Not in the way of magic, ye don't. For this is not a thing ye can know in kirk or castle. Tis a thing can only be known in feeling the Earth beneath your feet every day, in walking the ground and the sand, hearing the waves all day, listening to the crows as they perch and talk, and sitting with the hare as she comes close. To know all the animals and plants that be living with us."

"But how can I do that? I do walk and listen, but I do not live as you do. I wear shoes and read and learn from books."

"Aye, but I have seen you with your horse."

"Yes, I talk to Miranda. And I try to listen to her, to what she needs."

"So. And you did listen to the crow."

"The crow?"

"The crow 'round the path when thou first came to me."

"I heard and saw it."

Isobel nodded.

All was dim inside the hut, dark as night, with only the little fire for light, but when Elspeth Nychie smiled a broad smile, Margaret saw that, amazingly, for a woman of her age and status, she had all of her teeth.

"And now ye must learn," said Elspeth, "to listen to the wind and the rain, and the trees in the forest, even each plant in the field. Each one has a spirit if ye be still enough to know it."

Alert in her whole body, Margaret felt her skin tingling. "Are the spirits the same as the fairies?"

"Aye, the fairies be there," said Isobel. "They need quiet waiting and listening."

"And singing," added Jane.

"Singing?"

"They love music, and so we sing all the songs for each thing." Elspeth spoke in a rich, clear voice, as if she, too, had the magic to spin meaning and beauty out of words. Was she also a storyteller?

"Songs for the cows, songs for the fish, songs for the trees and each flower," Isobel said, and her voice, as she spoke, took on a lilt like a song.

"For each day and each time of day," Elspeth added.

Jane stood and began to sway and dance slowly around the fire, singing,

I will kindle my fire this morning,
In the presence of the holy angels of Heaven,
In the presence of Ariel of the loveliest form,
In the presence of Uriel of the myriad charms,
Without malice, without jealousy, without envy,
Without fear, without terror of anyone under the sun,
But the Holy Son of God to shield me.

Jane coughed and fanned the smoke away from her face as she sat down again, smiling sweetly at Margaret. "A prayer for the morning."

"A prayer," Margaret said. "With angels."

"Angels and fairies. They know themselves, each to each," Elspeth said as she poked the fire.

Isobel, however, was not smiling like everyone else. Perhaps because she was the cunning woman, though it was curious that anyone would not smile at such a lovely song and dance. Isobel's face looked more worried than serene. "'Tis enough for now," she said.

Walking back home on the farm path, Margaret felt something new within her. She felt the ground beneath her feet, the air that buffeted her dress, the grayness of the clouds, the sounds—wind, birds, distant waves—all in a new way, in her body. As if she belonged here, not just as a member of the Hay clan. As if she were not separate and above the Earth, but a part of it. The song came back and lifted out of her like a mist from the sea: "*I will kindle my fire this morning in the presence of the holy angels of Heaven, in the presence of Ariel of the loveliest form . . .*" She remembered all the words and the tune and sang the whole song.

On the roadside ahead appeared an old woman. As Margaret came closer, she noticed that the woman was not a peasant, as she'd assumed, but a well-dressed woman of some rank. The woman stood back from the road in a patch of yellow gorse, and she was still, very still. She wore a faded velvet gown and pearl necklace. Like the pearl necklace Grandmother used to wear, the one Margaret had inherited.

She approached to greet the old woman, but then stopped. It *was* Grandmother. "Grandmother!" Margaret exclaimed, excited and happy, not pausing to reflect that her grandmother had died four years ago. She wanted to run up and touch her.

Grandmother stood silent, immobile, still as stone. Margaret hesitated. "Are you really there, Grandmother?" she whispered.

The woman didn't move or smile, but Margaret felt her presence, a presence filled with love. There was no sound, but she felt something, a message, as if Grandmother was warning her of some danger on the road ahead, but at the same time promising protection. *This road will not be easy, but I will be with you. I will guide you.*

Margaret walked closer, but when she approached, the woman had disappeared.

She was alone on the path, the wind gusting and frisking around her. As she continued on, she watched the road, scrutinizing the way ahead and everything around her: open fields changing from dark to light under the racing clouds, the flax and rye swishing and bending in the wind, the treetops of Lochloy Wood swaying, and she, walking the path and holding her bonnet and her skirts.

This was an ordinary day on the Moray coast, and there was no danger.

The castle was enveloped in gloom. Margaret felt it the moment she stepped into the tower and began to climb the stairs. In the great hall, Lucy sat reading, and she glanced up when Margaret approached. She took a chair beside her sister, who remained silent, eyebrows pursed. "What is it?" Margaret asked.

"Ah." Lucy shook her head. "Mother."

"Oh! Is she—?"

"No, not—" Lucy's brown eyes were sad. "Just the cough again, and she stays abed. I have been sitting with her, and Bessie has brought tea and warm blankets. Father wants to call Doctor Urquhart, but Mother refuses," she sobbed.

Margaret took Lucy's hand. Her little sister was more like an older sister, in some ways. She tried so hard to care for everyone, even their mother. "Mother is right, Lucy. The doctor will only bleed her, and, according to Lady Anne, he almost killed Mister Hugh that way." She took a deep breath. "I know what to do," she said, and sprang up from the chair.

"Nothing rash, please, dear sister," Lucy pleaded, the familiar mother hen taking care of her sister, as well.

"Not at all," Margaret called as she raced to the stairs and back down the tower.

Isobel was sitting on a stump in front of the hut, weaving a half-finished basket. Her lips formed into a grim smile as she worked, snaking the willow shoots in and out, lacing, winding, and turning. She looked up as Margaret approached. "Back so soon, Lady?"

"We need a healing, Isobel! 'Tis my mother." She sat down in the sand at Isobel's feet. "She coughs and coughs, and we fear she has the consumption."

"Aye, there's a charm ye can learn."

"But *you* have the power!" Margaret protested.

"Nay, ye do have the gift, and this is not a difficult one." Isobel smiled. "I can learn you."

Margaret's shoulders dropped. "Yes, I do want to learn, but—"

"And you may learn to be a cunning woman as well." Isobel wove the willow basket with a quick hand, in and out, over and around.

"Oh." She, Margaret, a cunning woman? She felt a sudden elation, but then a shiver of fear. What would that mean?

"Here is what you do, but it must be once on a Thursday and then two Sundays." Isobel spoke quickly, and Margaret struggled to come back to Earth and concentrate.

"First, you take two sprigs of hyssop, and boil them in wine. Lady Elizabeth must drink that, and then, when she is lying down, you take a bowl of water, dip in your fingers, and sprinkle it o'er her body. As you do, say this charm:

> *Let me tread on thee, tightness,*
> *As the swan treads on the shore,*
> *Tightness of the back,*
> *Tightness of the chest,*
> *Tightness of the throat,*
> *To strip from thee the foul disease,*
> *From the top of thy head to thy sole,*
> *To thy two thighs beyond,*
> *By the might of God and His powers together.*

Margaret repeated the instruction and the words.

"And then you must say it again, twice more."

Margaret said the charm a few more times until she had learned it. She jumped up. "Oh, thank you, Isobel!" she cried, mounting her horse.

When she arrived home, Margaret went out to the kitchen garden and picked the green hyssop stems, then into the kitchen, where Cook boiled them in wine for her. She skipped up to her mother's chamber. "Mother, I have a special cure for you from the cunning woman."

Lady Elizabeth, wan and weak, gave her a skeptical look. "You know we don't go in for that, Margaret."

"I know, but this is just some hyssop in wine, and a prayer. Shouldn't we try it?"

Her mother shrugged feebly. "I suppose it will do no harm." She drank the wine that Margaret offered, and Margaret repeated the charm three times, as Isobel had instructed. When she finished, her mother's eyes closed, and she tiptoed out of the room.

Margaret followed the instructions and waited until Thursday to repeat the ritual. Before the following Thursday, Lady Elizabeth was up and about, taking charge of the household again. She thanked Margaret for her care but denied that the charm had cured her. Nevertheless, Margaret was thrilled, and determined to go to Isobel for more lessons.

Perhaps she *could* be a cunning woman.

KATHARINE

CHAPTER 32

"I am going to meet the king!" gushed Grissel Brodie. The people around the table stopped eating and looked up in astonishment. "I will accompany my father to London for the coronation." Grissel was a tall woman, dark of hair and complexion like her cousin Elizabeth and her father, Alexander, the laird. While the laird was quiet and soft-spoken, Grissel was always in motion, always tucking in the corkscrew curls that flew around and out of her cap. "Father, you escorted the King back from Breda. Tell, me, what is he like?"

Katharine sat at table with the family in the dining room of Brodie Castle. Alexander had given a long and heartfelt prayer of grace, and a young maid was now serving the soup. The fragrance of herbs and mutton filled the room.

A crystal chandelier with at least thirty burning candles made the silver gleam and the faces shine as twilight fell outside the windows. Grissel's two lads fidgeted beside her, and across the table, the laird's son, James, and his wife watched calmly. The family seemed peaceful, she thought; a community in harmony, so different from the atmosphere in Katharine's own home, where John Ross erupted in angry tirades at every meal. He was away on business now, though what kind of business, she had no idea. The incident with Mistress Forbes burned heavily in her heart.

The lads slurped their soup, each trying to outdo the other in volume. Grissel ignored them, no doubt accustomed to their antics.

The laird looked from Grissel to the lads. "This is not an alehouse," he said. The lads became silent, and he turned to Grissel. "The king is a young man, just turned thirty, tall and commanding in presence. He is overjoyed at the Restoration, as are we."

Grissel clapped her hands.

"And what are his sympathies?" Katharine asked. "Will he remain true to the Covenant?"

"He says as much."

James, a thoughtful young man, stroked his beard. "But when he agreed to the Solemn League and Covenant back in fifty, it was under duress. Signing that was the condition we set to allow him back in the country."

"Yes," the laird reflected, "it did take some measure of persuasion. He was just a lad then, and I believe that now, he has begun to see the wisdom of the Covenant. This month, he issued the Declaration of Breda, a worthy document that promises tolerance and liberty of conscience for all religions."

"But," James argued, "that gives him license to favor the Anglicans if he decides to change his course again."

Katharine looked from son to father: two tall, intelligent men, though Alexander was more seasoned and settled, a man of wise compassion and solemn countenance.

Grissel burst out, "Are we bringing back Charles as king, but not sure of his allegiance?"

"This is the Restoration," said the laird. "And everyone, especially the king, knows that this means the restoration of Presbyterian Scotland. It is not to be taken lightly. We must trust the king to keep his word."

"I will remind him of his word and his duty!" Grissel exclaimed.

Katharine smiled to herself. She was proud of the tradition of Scottish women to speak their minds. They were of strong stock, and not prone to accommodating or compromising their principles. Grissel would, she was sure, hold the king to account.

Just as suddenly, Katharine's smile faded, and she sighed. Her husband was not, like Alexander, a man of integrity. Did she accommodate him too much? Compromise her own principles? Perhaps Alexander could shed some light on this, in addition to the other matter.

After dinner, as the company dispersed, the laird ushered Katharine through the great hall and into one of the chambers. She took the chair he indicated beside the fire, and he sat opposite, poking the fire with a set of tongs. The drawing room looked out on the gardens of Brodie Castle, glowing now in the light of this June evening.

Katharine turned her gaze from the window and back to Brodie. "I fear that I must leave this place," she said.

He started and raised his eyebrows. "This is a great surprise."

"I have been accused and threatened—sorely and falsely accused of an immorality."

"Immorality? You are a woman above reproach, Katharine. You are greatly treasured by my niece for the teaching of her daughters, and I highly value our discourse as well your contribution to the Covenanter cause. Who dares to make such an accusation?"

Katharine studied the pattern on the carpet, then raised her eyes to the tall windows and flowering fruit trees. "I am loath to tell tales," she said, "but I am so aggrieved and shamed." Her cheeks and arms were hot and red just at the telling of it, but she had to go on. Katharine hung her head. "'Tis Mister Harry's wife."

"Ah!" The laird raised his arms in a gesture of helplessness. "And now I see, to my own despair." He looked so downcast that she thought he might weep, but he lifted his head and looked at her. "When I first met that woman, I found much ignorance—even invincible ignorance—in the family. I desired to groan under it, and their incapacity to God."

"But Mister Harry is so earnest and pious."

He shook his head. "Mister Harry is, indeed, an educated theologian, and I know not how he lives with such a woman."

She remained quiet. Alexander himself had chosen Mister Harry to be minister here in Auldearn. Dare she tell him what Harry had done?

He studied her carefully, looking hard at her face, and suddenly, his eyes widened in an expression of shock. "Did Mister Harry," he asked, as if reading her thoughts, "commit an indiscretion?"

She bowed her head slightly in assent. "And Mistress Forbes, in her ignorance, as you say, believed that I reciprocated. She pushed me and accused me in front of my husband. *He* then punished me, as well." She rubbed her cheek where he had struck her. Hopefully, the bruise was not visible now. Of course, one didn't talk about such things, but she felt such despair in this moment, it hardly mattered what she said.

"What perfidy!" Alexander cried out. "Against you, a lady of Christ!"

Katharine had suffered so much death and loss, but always, the Lord had showed her the value of her own life and encouraged her to go on in her mission. Now, she had been struck down by someone from the family the Lord had called to be here, and also by her husband, the man with whom she had made her sacred covenant. Scorned and viewed as worthless. Perhaps she *was* worthless, at least in this place. She hung her head again, and almost whispered, "Perhaps this is the Lord's chastisement, his way to call me away from this place."

"Do you mean to leave Auldearn? Or John Ross, your husband?"

"I am thinking to go south again. Alone. But I am perplexed, Alexander, and solicitous to know my duty."

"Ah, such suffering is more than we should bear. Perhaps you know the talk about your husband?"

So, he knew about the whoring. Others, too, must know of this. Katharine inclined her head in assent and felt her arms tingle with the humiliation. Perhaps the shame alone would send her back to Edinburgh. "I know that leaving one's husband is not what the Lord requires, and I have been in prayer about it. I have not heard His answer."

"Your lot with a wicked husband is a hard one," he said. "And one I would not wish on anyone, much less a woman with such high principles and such a pure heart. One could say this is no marriage. It may be the better to part from him, but I am loath to advise you."

"Perhaps you might confer with Mister Thomas Hogg when you travel to Kiltearn?" she asked. Thomas Hogg, minister at Kiltearn, was Katharine's most trusted correspondent and advisor.

"Mister Thomas is widely admired by all the Covenanters for his wisdom and discernment. I will consult with him, and I will pray for light from Heaven."

The next day, as Katharine donned her cloak and set out in Brodie's carriage to return home, she felt assured that both Alexander and Thomas would confer with compassion about her decision. In truth, she already knew what her decision would be, but it was wise to garner support from these influential men, who often consulted her in kind for advice. Both Alexander and Thomas were men of morality and above reproach. Thomas, especially, stood above most other men in passion, eloquence, and erudition. Why couldn't she have married someone like that?

MARGARET

CHAPTER 33

"The red velvet!" Margaret jumped and clapped when the seamstress, Lilias Dunlop, held up the bolt of deep red cloth. Henrietta's plan had worked. Margaret was staying now with the Rose family at Castle Kilrock, and she and Henrietta were preparing for the ball. Henrietta's chamber was strewn with silks and satins, and on the bed lay the fabrics from which they would choose for their gowns.

Margaret smiled with delight when she looked at the red velvet. It would set off her dark hair to perfection.

"And *I* love the blue satin," Henrietta said.

Lilias picked out the two fabrics from the pile and lay them side by side on the bed. "You will shine like pretty birds just beginning to fly," she said. Lilias herself always wore an array of colors like a rainbow. She used remnants from her work to sew her own clothes. Today, she wore a red gown, yellow apron, and blue kerchief, all trimmed with lace—lively colors that complemented her cheerful demeanor. "And I have a picture of the newest style from the Lady of Cawdor."

"Oh, yes, what they are wearing in London!" Margaret exclaimed. "That is what I wish. Like a splendid lady in the queen's court."

Lilias showed the two young women a drawing of the dress. The bodice was similar to what they were wearing now, but this new style had a longer V at the waist and a higher neckline rimmed in lace.

"So much more modest than the low necks that show half your bosom," Lady Anne said.

They hadn't been permitted to wear that style, anyway, Margaret thought. It was only the peasants and servants whose necklines plunged so low. "But look at the sleeves," she gushed. "Billowing silk below the shoulder . . . so much nicer than the puffy shoulders we have been wearing."

Henrietta brought her hands to her heart. "Your young lieutenant will be awestruck."

Margaret blushed and looked quickly at Lady Anne. "He is not *my* young lieutenant, Henrietta. I barely know him."

"And would this be one of the English?" Lady Anne asked.

"Yes, Mother, he is the young man who rescued me from the MacDonalds. He and his troops. And he has been courting Margaret."

"Oh, no!" Margaret exclaimed. "Not courting. Please, Lady Anne, do not talk to my father about this. He is opposed to the English."

"Have no fear," Lady Anne replied with a smile. "Your secret is secure."

"The soldiers are so handsome and genteel," Henrietta protested. "I could not even think of them when I came home in their charge—I was that undone. But lately, I have noticed them in the village." She held up the blue satin cloth beneath her chin and peered into the looking glass. Above it, her skin glowed, soft and creamy, framed by delicate ginger hair in wavy tendrils. She began to dance. "But none so handsome as George," she sang, swaying back and forth.

"The young laird of Cawdor," Lady Anne added with a smile.

Henrietta stopped at the looking glass again. "My father doesn't approve of balls, either," she said. "I don't know why he has allowed this one."

"Your father wants to please you," replied Lady Anne. "But he does wish you to act with propriety. We *are* Covenanters, though perhaps not so strict as Margaret's family."

"Who are, perhaps, too strict," Margaret huffed. Lilias looked sharply at her, just for an instant, then continued tidying and packing the fabrics into a sack.

As the day of the ball drew near, Margaret found herself fearful of discovery. What if one of the servants traveled to Auldearn and told the servants there? What if her father came for a visit when she was trying on her gown for the sixth or seventh time—or, worse, when she and Henrietta were setting out for the ball in their carriage? Margaret wrote letters daily to her mother, who, if she suspected the secret, did not mention it.

The days passed without incident, and she enjoyed spending time with her friend. At times, Henrietta lapsed into silence, and sometimes, she cried quietly. Margaret knew that Henrietta was remembering her captivity. Quickly, she would recover her spirits and smile as if nothing was wrong.

The pair strolled down to the River Nairn at the bottom of the garden to watch the water flow. They raced their horses on the strand. They took nets and managed to catch salmon at the estuary, watched the seabirds gather and vie for territory, and took off their shoes to wade in water that was still ice cold, though now it was June, and the air was warmer.

They studied with Henrietta's father, Mister Hugh, who was Minister at Nairn. Margaret felt grateful that with him, she could read some poetry, not just the Bible and the Westminster Confession. Mister Hugh loved poetry, and he was pleased to find that Margaret, unlike Henrietta, also loved it . . . especially Shakespeare. She was thrilled when he introduced her to the sonnets.

One mild, temperate day, Margaret and Henrietta were sitting on a bench in the garden overlooking the river. Above them, a plum tree was beginning to form its fruit, and a woodlark trilled from its branches. Margaret read aloud. "'*How oft when thou, my music, music play'st, upon that blessed wood whose motion sounds, with thy sweet fingers.*' Oh, such wonderful things Shakespeare writes about music and nature and love."

"'*And all of nature rejoices.*'" Henrietta quoted a verse from the Bible. "At the ball, you shall dance with Andrew, and I with George."

"The handsome George."

"Oh, yes. You know, we are engaged. Well, almost engaged. George is a fine young man, tall and curly-haired, though his complexion is ruddy. We have been promised to each other since birth, almost."

"Has he come courting?"

"Yes. He came once with his men, and we had a lovely feast." Henrietta became still and cast her eyes skyward. "Of course, he hasn't formally asked for my hand yet." Suddenly, her expression clouded over, and she bowed her head. She sat very still, as if frozen.

Margaret reached out, touched her friend's shoulder, and waited. Still no movement.

Suddenly, Henrietta's face brightened again, and she jumped up. "But speaking of love . . . 'tis time to learn the sarabande!" She began to dance around the grassy garden. "Step, step, plié," she sang, lifting her arms up and down in a swinging motion.

She proffered her hand, and Margaret rose and took it. They stepped and pliéd and waved their arms up and down.

"Not so fast," Henrietta said, slowly lifting her arms again. "'Tis like the arms are floating." Margaret slowed down and copied her, and they raised their arms in graceful motions as they danced around the garden to the song of the woodlark.

In the great hall of Darnaway Castle, the ball was in progress. Built in the 1300s by King Robert the Bruce to hold one thousand warriors, the hall was the largest and most magnificent in Morayshire. Margaret looked up at the hammer-beam roof, so high that the ceiling seemed to reach up to heaven. Those massive dark trusses and arches, she thought, were like heavy claws reaching down over the assembled people, and they would surely impede one's flight to the angels.

Lieutenant Andrew Massie bowed low. Margaret giggled, then stomped her foot to rebuke herself. How could she giggle at a time like this? Andrew looked resplendent in his dress uniform: the red coat with its brass buttons shined, and the white pantaloons, white stockings, and black shoes with silver buckles. His hair, though, was straight and floppy as usual, in contrast with the other officers, who sported flowing curls.

"My lady," he said, rising from a bow and extending his hand. "May I have this dance?" Did Margaret detect a hint of amusement in his eyes, as if he recognized the silliness of this formal ballroom with its shine and glitter? As if he'd prefer to be out riding his horse? She realized that she, too, would rather have been outside.

But Andrew seemed at ease in this setting, as if he'd been doing this all his life. Margaret took a breath and followed him onto the dance floor, where they formed one side of a square with three other couples. Luckily, this was the sarabande, the dance she had practiced most with Henrietta, and as the music began, Margaret remembered the steps and moved through the dance as relaxed as she could be in this intimidating room.

Andrew kept his eyes on her. Her red velvet gown fit perfectly. Both Henrietta and Lady Anne had cooed and exclaimed at how lovely Margaret looked, with the garnet color against her pale skin and dark hair. Her curls were pulled back into a black-beaded net, and everything was punctuated by enormous teardrop pearl earrings that had belonged to her grandmother. They served as a heartening reminder of seeing her on the road. *She will guide me*, Margaret thought, and immediately felt more confident and clearheaded.

Margaret basked in Andrew's smiles as they danced, aware of the other couples stepping, floating their arms, and moving in and out of the square, and the people on the sides of the room watching. Light flickered from candles in the silver and crystal wall sconces, lending a glow and mystery to everything. Resplendent in their finest satins, silks, and lace, ladies fanned themselves in the unusually warm evening. Everyone chatted and inspected one another, though the room was so vast that many were too far away to recognize.

Suddenly, Margaret stumbled. There was Aunt Grissel. In a gold satin gown, Grissel stood near an arched doorway with a group of ladies and men. Margaret glanced again, and this time, Grissel was looking directly at her. What to do? She would know that Margaret was not supposed to be here, and Margaret would have to entreat her to keep this secret.

When the dance ended, Margaret hastened away from Andrew without a word, leaving him with his mouth open. She went to the doorway where she'd seen Grissel, but she was no longer there. Margaret walked around the great hall and peeked into the adjoining rooms but found not a trace of Grissel. She had to find her before Grissel spoke to her mother or father. She made her way back to the arched doorway, approaching a small, stout lady who had been standing beside Grissel. "Beg pardon, madame," she said. "Have you seen the Lady Grissel of Brodie?"

"Ah, Grissel left in some haste," the woman replied. "She had illness at home."

Andrew appeared behind her. "Lady Margaret, is there something I can do to assist you?"

She looked up at him. In his characteristic stance, erect but relaxed and almost careless, his eyes remained steady on her, and he looked ready to jump into battle if necessary. "Perhaps there is," she answered.

She glanced around the room again. Henrietta was standing to the side, looking forlorn and not dancing at all. She was watching a tall, ruddy-faced gentleman dance with a young, giddy-looking blonde woman. *That must be*

George Campbell, Margaret thought. Why was he not dancing with Henrietta? Henrietta stared at George, then despondently cast her gaze toward the distant ceiling. Lady Anne, who was nearby talking with some other ladies, watched her daughter with a worried look.

Margaret sighed and glanced back at Andrew. Could she confide in this man? She took her fan out of her bodice and fanned herself while she thought. *Fans are useful for other things besides cooling*, she reflected. "Lieutenant," she began.

"Please call me Andrew."

Margaret blushed, and fanned more furiously. "Andrew, then. There is something you *can* do. I must reach my Aunt Grissel, the Lady of Brodie, on an urgent matter, and it appears she has departed."

Oh, what joy! What thrills! Riding through the night behind a gallant lad, under the stars and over the fields, the wind blowing cold and her cloak wrapped around her shoulders. Holding Andrew. Feeling his strong back warm against her as he raced the horse in the smoothest gallop she'd ever felt. She could have ridden like this forever.

Brodie Castle was nearby, and they could get there and back in close to an hour. Lady Anne would not miss her.

Across the fields of Darnaway they flew, then through the Darnaway Wood, the earl's hunting ground. It was a dark forest even in daytime, but now, the massive beech and oak groves created an inky black space where Margaret could not see a thing. Andrew slowed down as the horse leapt across the Muckle Burn, then burst out again at speed on the road to Brodie. Now they were within sight of Brodie Castle, which loomed stark and black under a sliver of moon and millions of stars.

The sound of hooves ahead, and a carriage came into sight. Gilt-painted scrolls and flourishes shimmered in the starlight. "The Brodie carriage!" she shouted.

Andrew pulled the horse alongside and grabbed the reins of the two horses pulling the carriage.

"What ho!" the coachman cried.

"Tis Margaret!" she called. "Do not be alarmed."

They stopped beside the carriage carrying Aunt Grissel.

"Margaret?" Grissel leaned out with a puzzled expression, glancing wide-eyed from Margaret to Andrew. "What—?"

"Can I sit with you a moment, Aunt?"

"Of course."

Margaret dismounted and climbed into the carriage beside Grissel while Andrew waited. The scents of lavender, musk, and wool filled the carriage—the smells of her aunt. Their gowns rubbed together, Margaret's red velvet against Grissel's rustling gold satin.

Grissel raised her eyebrows and pursed her lips as Margaret smoothed out her gown. "What matters your gown, now that you've mussed it on the horse?"

"Aunt Grissel, I must entreat you not to tell Mother that you saw me at the ball. You know that dancing is forbidden."

Grissel started to laugh, then checked herself as she saw Margaret's distress. "Don't you know that half of Moray saw you at the ball? What makes you think it will be a secret now?"

"But the Covenanters were not there. And I saw only the Earl of Moray and one of the Campbells. They haven't seen me since I was a lass, so I don't think they knew me, and the hall was dark, with so many people."

"Mmm. Perhaps. You do look like a splendid lady in that red gown! And who is the young man there?"

Margaret leaned out toward Andrew. "Andrew, this is my aunt, Lady Grissel of Brodie."

Andrew bowed. Grissel raised an eyebrow at Margaret.

"But you mustn't tell about him, either . . . please, Grissel! You know what Father thinks of the English."

Grissel's face squeezed into a skeptical expression, but she nodded reluctantly. "Now I must get back to my William, who is ailing."

"And we must go back to the ball!"

Grissel pointed a finger at Margaret. "Young lady, I advise you not to go back. There are many who will scheme to weaken your father if they see you."

Margaret tossed her head. "If so, they have already seen me." She would not be daunted. Margaret climbed out of the carriage, and Andrew, who had dismounted, helped her up into the saddle, where she again sat sidesaddle and spread her skirts in a decorous manner. He leapt up in front, and with another bow to Grissel, gently clucked to the horse. Away they flew, back to Darnaway.

CHAPTER 34

Hoofbeats charging into the courtyard. A familiar gallop. Margaret ran to the window and peered out.

There was a flash of red, a wide-brimmed hat, and now a vigorous knocking on the door.

Bessie darted through the hall and down the tower stairs.

"I come to see the laird." Andrew's clear voice (a pleasing tenor,) echoed from the tower stairway, and he emerged into the great hall behind Bessie. She ambled away to fetch the laird, who soon came out of the library as Margaret stood unobserved in a corner.

When he saw Andrew, Father stopped short.

"My laird," Andrew began. "I beg an audience."

"What matter brings you here?" the laird snapped. He stood straight and strong, his presence commanding, though he was a foot shorter than Andrew. "Is there a disturbance with the Royalists?"

"No, m'laird, no disturbance. Another matter entirely."

Father studied Andrew as if debating whether to grant him an audience, then led him into the drawing room and closed the door. Margret crept up and put her ear to the wooden paneling. She could hear voices, but they were so muffled, she couldn't understand the words—except for one from her father: "Impossible!"

What was impossible?

Finally, the door opened, and she hurried away before they came out. Father ushered Andrew to the tower doorway, but Andrew had seen Margaret in the shadows and gave her a quick smile before disappearing down the stairway.

"An English soldier, John?" Mother stood at the foot of the stairs into the hall.

Father cleared his throat. "Apparently, this young man wishes to court Margaret."

"Oh!" Margaret stepped back. Courting?

"But, of course, I rejected that proposal out of hand."

"No, Father!" she cried and began to run towards him, but then stopped. Why did she say no? She didn't want to marry, did she?

Mother stepped into the hall.

Father frowned. "You know I have spoken with the Duke of Gordon about one of his sons—"

Margaret gasped. Not one of those Gordon boys. They had teased and laughed at her on too many occasions.

"Did you inquire about this lad's family, John?" Mother continued in her steady voice.

"Of course not. He is English! "

"Perhaps we should consult Uncle Alexander."

"Brodie? But why?"

Lady Elizabeth raised an eyebrow. "If the family is respectable and has means, this may be to our advantage." She winked at Margaret.

Margaret took another step back and stumbled over a chip in the stone floor. Courtship. She knew that marriage was her fate but hadn't thought so far ahead with Andrew. She'd just met him, and they'd had only the one evening together at the ball, though what a glorious evening it had been.

A great elation, like a delicious bubble, arose in her chest. To ride the countryside with Andrew again! To fly across the land with the wind whipping her face. To see his smile and hear his laughter.

But marriage? That meant childbirth and pain and drudgery. She wanted to read, study, go to court, and converse with educated people, not stay home and have babies. Babies who died.

CHAPTER 35

S he had to tell Henrietta. Henrietta was still at Kilrock, which was farther away than Nairn, but Margaret persuaded her mother to let her take Miranda rather than the carriage. It was a longer ride for the horse, but Margaret knew when to stop or walk when Miranda was tired, and when to spur her into a gallop. She and Miranda had a rhythm. They were like one body, one being, as they flew along the road. On Miranda, Margaret was like an African warrior woman—the women Grissel had told her about who rode and fought more fiercely than the men.

They had power. Women didn't usually have much power.

Isobel could call the dolphins and heal the sick. She had healed Henrietta and taught Margaret a healing charm. In kirk, Lady Anne now looked to Isobel with awe and respect, just like the plain folk. Isobel had power.

Mistress Collace had power, too. She had education, intelligence, and influence in the kirk. Mistress Collace was respected by Mister Harry, Uncle Alexander, and even Father. The two women Margaret most admired were both independent and powerful.

She turned down the drive to Kilrock and galloped between the fields. Castle Kilrock, with its smooth gray stone and pinkish tint in the sun, was a comforting sight, as welcoming as Lady Anne herself.

Margaret's peaceful mood, however, was soon disrupted. Henrietta's maid, Jean, a slight lass with dark eyebrows, came out of the door, recognized Margaret, and shrieked.

Lady Anne, now almost as wide as she was tall, appeared behind her. "What is this racket, lass?"

The girl stared at Margaret, then back at Lady Anne. "Lady Henrietta said—she said she would see no one. No one!" She glared defiantly at Margaret.

Why would Jean try to protect Henrietta from her?

"Up the stairs with you, lass, and back to the kitchen." Lady Anne pointed the way, and the girl scampered inside.

Margaret dismounted, and a groom came to take Miranda.

"Don't mind her," said Lady Anne. "Henrietta will be grateful to see you, Margaret. Come." Lady Anne led her in the door and scurried through the great hall.

"Lady Anne," Margaret called from behind, stopping before an ancestral portrait. "Why did Henrietta not wish to see anyone?"

"Ah, you can ask her that, Margaret," she said, shaking her head and commencing the walk to Henrietta's chamber.

Henrietta was in bed again.

"Henrietta!" Margaret called and rushed to the bedside. "I thought you had recovered. You taught me to dance, and we went to the ball!"

Henrietta turned her face away.

Lady Anne sat down on the other side of the bed. "We have had another misfortune," she said, hanging her head.

"Misfortune? What happened?" Margaret cried.

Henrietta shook her head and looked back at Margaret. "George."

"Did something happen to George?"

The room was silent. Margaret, confused, looked from mother to daughter.

Henrietta's voice came out like a sigh or whisper. "You can tell, Mother."

Lady Anne straightened in her chair, resting her hands on her pregnant stomach. "George's father, the Laird of Cawdor, has withdrawn the offer of marriage."

"What? But, how can he? How *dare* he?"

A low voice came from the bed. "I am a fallen woman."

"No, Henrietta! What happened to you was not your fault!" Margaret stood up and wrung her hands. "This is impossible! George and Henrietta are in love. What does George say about it?"

"George has said nothing."

"Angus, the MacDonald laird," Lady Anne sneered, "has publicly pronounced that Henrietta is now wife of his son, James. He threatens to come and claim her."

"But they can't do that!"

"They can, but we won't let them."

Henrietta sank down further in the bedclothes, covered her face, and shouted, "I would die before I go with those brutes!"

Lady Anne sighed. "'Tis why we stay here at Kilrock with our troops, such as they are, rather than back in Nairn with Mister Hugh."

"And the English?"

"They have pledged to watch for these villains, but—" Lady Anne shrugged.

Margaret knew about those empty promises.

On the journey back to Inshoch, she lay down on Miranda's back. She hadn't even thought to mention Andrew, and now the world seemed as black as it had bright when she arrived.

What a sorry place this was, this country of Scotland. A land of savages. The Royalists kidnapped and raped, the Protestants murdering innocent women in the name of God, and both sides raging and killing.

That charming English village came into her mind's eye. Warm houses surrounded by flowers, gentle people bowing and smiling, no one scowling or cursing . . .

CHAPTER 36

Isobel was sitting on the grass when Margaret dismounted. Rising from the open fields, the symmetrical mound looked like it had been carefully placed in the land, and its grass, a bright and verdant green, was more vivid than anything else around it.

"Good morning, Isobel. Is this the Downie Hill? They said 'twas between Inshoch and Brodie, and a lad pointed me to this place."

"Aye, 'tis here, the Downie Hill."

Margaret removed her cape, laying it across the saddle as Miranda searched out a spot where the grass was higher and began to graze.

She sank down on the grass beside Isobel. There *was* something different . . . some special kind of quiet here on this level summit. The place was different from all that surrounded it, as if the wind itself was hushed in this one spot.

She spread out her skirts. The deep green of the cloth seemed to blend in with the grass.

"Thy gown, 'tis a color the fairy queen will favor," Isobel pronounced.

"Oh, will the fairy queen appear today?"

"Ye do have the gift, but the sight does not come when bidden. Tis a matter of waiting."

Margaret sighed. "My friend Henrietta is ailing again, and we are so sad." Her shoulders slumped as she whispered, as if the shame were hers to bear, as well. "Her betrothed, the young laird of Cawdor, has rejected her."

Isobel snorted.

"Do you have a charm to change someone's mind?"

"Twould be a curse. A curse on the laird, on his cattle and sheep, on his house and hold, on his—"

"No! No evil curses, please. I only wanted to help Henrietta and restore her to health again. I thought your magic was good magic, for healing and helping, not cursing."

"Magic is neither good nor evil."

The two women sat in silence.

Margaret waited, but it appeared that Isobel would not offer an alternative for Henrietta.

Isobel pointed to the ground. "This be the elf house. The elves are here today."

"Elves?"

Isobel opened her hand and showed a small triangular-shaped stone.

"Ah," said Margaret. "A thunderstone. My Uncle Alexander has some of these. They come out of the sky with the thunder and lightning."

"Nay, these are elf arrows. I have been inside. And I have seen them whyting and dighting these. The elves are always busy." She handed the stone to Margaret.

Margaret examined the stone. Indeed, this was what her uncle had called a thunderstone, but she didn't want to argue, and gave it back to Isobel. Margaret stood up, stepped down from the summit, and walked around the mound, touching the sides and stroking the fine grass turf. "How do you get inside?"

"I go in the night with William, my fairy man, and Red Reiver, who doth keep me from harm." Isobel stroked her fingers on the stone, turning it over and over. "And betimes, if ye're passing by, ye can see the small man who stands guard. He is all green-like, an elf. And oft'times, the elf bulls be here as well, routing and skirling, and they will affright ye."

Margaret started and pulled back her hand. "But I am affrighted now! I thought this was the home of the fairy queen."

"It *is* her home, too. She is the ruler of all the fairies and elves. And the king of fairy, too, who is a brave man, well-favored and broad-faced, all clothed in blue."

"But there is no door," Margaret observed. "How do you get in? I had hoped to see the fairy queen."

Isobel smiled up at the cloudless sky. "When I leave my bed to go with William, I take a windle-straw, or beanstalks, and put them betwixt my feet, and say thrice, 'Horse and hattock, horse and go, Horse and pellatris, ho! ho!' And immediately, we fly away wherever we will."

A light breeze lifted strands of Margaret's hair as she gazed out over the fields. "It sounds like a lovely dream."

"Nay, 'tis not a dream. We fly in the other world . . . the world that is always present, just not seen by the most humans."

Margaret twisted a shiny dark curl that had fallen below her cap and looked at Isobel, who was rubbing her pockmarked cheek. "I know I have seen things in that world, because, as you say, I probably have the *an da shealladh*. But flying in the night? This is not something I can imagine."

"Then ye must come to the coven, and we will learn ye."

"The coven?"

"We who have power." Isobel looked up at the sky, then back at Margaret. "But this must never come to the ears of the minister."

"A secret." Margret frowned. Would she go to Isobel's coven, a group of people who had power, who flew in the night in the other world? She wanted to see the fairies and learn magic, but this sounded so strange.

She stood up to leave.

Isobel opened her hand. Grasping the elf arrow, she gave it to Margaret. "What—"

"For the Lady Henrietta, for protection."

Margaret gasped and took the proffered stone. "This is an honor, I'm sure—that you would entrust this stone to me, and to Henrietta."

"But thou must be careful, as it can cause deadly harm."

"Deadly harm? These?" Margaret jumped and immediately handed the stone back to Isobel. "But how?"

"We have no bow to shoot with, but spring them from the nails of our thumbs. Sometimes, we will miss, but if they touch, be it beast, or man, or woman, they will kill, though they have a coat of armor upon them."

"I don't see how that little stone could kill someone."

"'Tis magic." Isobel gave the stone back to Margaret, who hurriedly put it in her pocket.

"She must say the words, as well."

"The words?"

"When we shoot these arrows, we say, 'I shoot you, man, in the devil's name. You shall not ever go hame.' And this shall be always true. There shall not be one bit of him left alive." Isobel stared at Margaret, her eyes intense and challenging.

Margaret's stomach was churning, and she cast her eyes about as if to find something familiar to focus upon. She was in a place where the footing was unsure, where she might stumble and fall at any moment. How could she give this stone to Henrietta? "But Isobel," she stammered. "In the devil's name? I thought your charms were like prayers. In the name of the saints, the Trinity, and so on?"

Isobel waved her hand, dismissing this as unimportant. "Different charms require different names. This one needs the help of the devil."

|SOBEL

CHAPTER 37

I scooped up an armful of straw from the corner and hefted it into the byre—some for the cows and some for the goats. Humped in the far corner sat Hugh's mother, who rarely spoke, but watched everything as she carded the wool. The bairns ran outside as soon as they had finished their porridge.

Why was I helping Lady Margaret? She was sincere and sweet-natured. She had the *an da shealladh*, though she didn't yet know the power of it. She was eager to learn, and she could learn. She was strong-willed enough to defy Mister Harry, if called upon. And I needed her on my side. Margaret need never know about the curses on Mister Harry. Had I gone too far with the elf arrow?

I poked the fire and stepped outside into a day that was unusually warm for mid-May. I removed my plaid and lay it on the hitching post. No one was about in the farmtown yard. The men were out in the fields, what was left of them—raking sand away from the crops that remained. The flax was ruined, but there was still hope for the barley and oats, which had been planted on higher slopes.

Hugh, when he'd left this morning, had grumbled a prediction. "Hardly any harvest will come," he said, pointing his finger at me. "And this be *your* fault."

They all blamed me for the sandstorm. I'd only wanted to blow Mister Harry down, not cause a disaster. I gazed out into the distance, where the edge of the dune met sky. The wind was coming softly now.

Was I sorry? Yes, I was sad about the crops, though I did not cause that damage. And, in spite of Hugh's dire predictions, we did have some stores for the winter.

I was glad, though, that I had laid Mister Harry low. He had killed my mother, after all, and now he was trying to catch me, too. I smiled a grim smile. Mister Harry was still abed and would stay there if I could help it.

I took a load of straw from the rick and made my way toward the cattle yard behind the houses. It was Hugh Gilbert's responsibility to care for the cattle in the farmtown barns, and mine to take them their daily straw.

But now a commotion arose from the direction of the castle, and the sound of stomping hooves carried into the barnyard. Here was the laird himself, John Hay, with several men leading four draft horses yoked to two large sledges.

The men drove into the yard and began loading sacks of oats and barley from the storehouse onto the sledges.

"What do ye think yer doing?" I shouted.

The laird said something to one of the men, young Able Watson, a sinewy, ruddy youth, who sauntered over and stared at me in a scornful way. "These are needed now for the laird," he said, "as he'll have to sell it all to make up for the raid and the crop failure."

"But these are for the farmtown!" I cried. "The cattle will starve, and the bairns will be starvin' now, too. What else do we have but the corn to feed them all winter?" There was fish, of course, but as Able knew perfectly well, there'd be nothing now to trade the fishermen for it.

Able didn't answer, as he had already turned back to his task. I watched, mouth agape, as the men cleared out the barns and loaded the sledges as full as possible. They left a small portion, but not near enough to go round.

Our stores for the winter. After the sandstorm, there wouldn't be much of a crop, and now it would be so much less, not nearly enough to feed everyone— to say nothing of selling at market.

I glowered as the workhorses turned and dragged the sledges back to the farmyard and onto the road. The men gave not a backward glance.

As they rounded the bend, I raised my fist and cried, "*Marasg ort!*" Go to hell!

But I could do better than that.

CHAPTER 38

I walked across the fields and under the clouds of white and gray that filled the sky and dipped below the horizon, darkening in the north and obscuring the light over the sea. The sun peered from behind their great white shapes, piles of new wool dropped into sky. Over the hillocks and dunes and under the sky I walked. No trees here . . . all were long gone, used years ago to build the houses, all except in the Lochloy Wood, the laird's own wood.

The laird, John Hay . . . so "kind" he was. Such fame for generosity and protection. But we who lived in the farmtown, with barely a scrap from the fields, we tilled and plowed and planted and harvested. He'd taken it—almost all of it now—leaving a pittance so the bairns would barely survive. The one baby dead this past year, and Maria needing the meat and cheese and fruit that graced the laird's table.

I climbed the great Nachran, the last dune before the sea, and stood on top. The ocean was mighty and wild today, with waves swelling far out on the horizon. They crashed together, sending sprays of white this way and that. Gulls screeched and dived, pushed and pulled hither and yon by the wind.

The wind knocked and grabbed me, flapping my plaid and bonnet, whipping my face with sand and salt so that I could barely stand. If I could lay the wind to rest, I would. But my power was to raise the wind, not lay it.

The fairies were dancing 'round, agitated and thrilled in the tumult, and I was called to a song for dawn:

Who brought'st me up from last night,
To the gladsome light of this day,
To win everlasting life for my soul,

All to the end and three times ending with Father, Son, and Holy Ghost.

Today, the fairies' color was blue. Blue and purple and green and shades between, these wind-tossed beings that flitted in the tall grass, flitted and laughed and teased and hid.

And here was my own, my William, with the wicked grin and the pointy cap and ears, beckoning with a finger.

I would go with William. I'd punish the laird as he had punished my people.

William would give me gowns of silk and velvet, shoes, and feasts of cakes and wine and meat . . . all I could eat. And power.

He beckoned again to me, to me alone, and I leapt onto my steed, Red Reiver beside me. With a "Horse and hattock, ho!" we flew, into the sky and over the sleeping lands below until we arrived at the Downie Hill. In front of it stooped a tiny man all in green, and behind him an open door. He ushered us into the room beneath the mound, where crouched fifteen elf-lads, hollow and hump-backed. They hammered and chiseled, bent over their tasks with industry.

They were whyting and dighting the elf-arrows, just as I'd told Lady Margaret. William picked up two of the finished arrows and gave them to me. "And when you shoot them at someone just so," he said, flicking his finger and thumbnail, and repeating the command I already knew, "you say, 'I shoot you in the devil's name,' and the person shall not go home that night. There will be not one bit of him left alive. And when you make your covenant with me, I will give you greater power."

Now I knew for sure that William was the devil and 'twas wrong to go with him, but the laird had to be punished for his evil deeds, and Mister Harry, too. How else could that happen? I had no other power, no troops at my command, no way to avenge the wrongs that had been done to me, to my mother, and to all who lived in the farmtown.

I would go with William.

We flew east and into the night, above the fields and cattle, over the firth and the farmtown, over Inshoch Castle, and toward the Auldearn kirk.

In a field, a farmer was laboring at his plow. I flicked an arrow at him, but it fell short and missed the target. There another man. I aimed and flicked again, with a snap of finger to thumb. "I shoot you in the devil's name," I cried. The arrow hit home, and immediately the man fell down dead beside his plow.

"Oh!" I gasped, for this was William Bower, a kind man who had given a toy to wee Maria. But *my* William laughed and cheered me on, and immediately, I forgot my remorse in the thrill of being with this brave and mighty being.

I did not pause to wonder why now twas night nor why farmers were out in the night but followed William.

"Tis the wild hunt!" he cried, "And you, the huntress!"

I swelled with pride . . . a huntress in the night, as I followed him under the stars and clouds, and we alit beside the Auldearn kirk.

The kirk stood dark and cold, a ghostly gray in the light of the stars. William was now clad all in black. His feet were cloven hooves. He had a tail, and he was black all over . . . black as night. "Now you are my lady," he said, "and I will give you all your heart's desires when you make your covenant with me."

Inside the kirk was a bitter chill, and a sour smell lingered in the air. The light of one candle showed several faces around the altar: Elspeth and Agnes and Lilias, and even some men among them. This was the coven, and these were the people who knew the charms and the stories, who fed the fairies and said the rhymes.

"I am the devil," said William, leading me to the altar. "And now, you must renounce your baptism." Around me, solemn faces, watching and waiting as if they, too, had undergone this ritual and were expecting me to join them.

By now I was sore affrighted, for the devil had grown larger and larger, and he emitted such great power. Would he do me harm?

Lilias stood with her head bowed, bruises and scratches all over her body. I knew, without a word being said, that the devil had done it. He was a hard taskmaster and demanded obedience and submission. Lilias was a rebellious sort, and not inclined to submit.

I took a step. William the Devil smiled, a broad and handsome smile, the smile that had won my heart—though this time, his eyes shot fiery sparks. He reached for my hand.

I took another step. What did it mean? His promises of meat and wine and all sorts of food to fill the belly—and more, much more. If I refused now, it would all stop: the night flying, the dancing and feasting with the fairies, the powers he had given, and more he had yet to give. Besides, and this I knew in my depths—I had no choice.

It was sinful to traffic with the devil, but what had the r
ised? No food for the starving, no magic to heal or strength to f
wronged us. Rewards only after death—and, in the meantime, the judgment
of God.

I had to survive. I needed the magic, the power to heal the sick, to garner
the best fruits of corn and cow and sea, to live, to thrive, both I and my family,
in *this* life. I needed power to get back at that sniveling snake of a man, Harry
Forbes. And the laird, as well.

Perhaps my mother had not gone this far, but *I* would, and I would avenge
her cruel murder at the hands of Mister Harry.

I took the devil's hand.

I rose up from the bed, Hugh Gilbert still snoring loudly beside me,
removed the besom with its rough wooden handle, and placed it back in the
corner.

The devil. I had made a covenant with the devil. Had I done wrong?

When I took his hand, it was cold as ice, and the freezing coursed within
me and all through my body as I walked with him to the altar. Everyone stood
solemnly round the altar. The devil appeared huge and black and cold, looming
in the reader's desk, a black book in his hand.

I did as he said, for I'd seen the welts on Lilias. "Yes, I renounce my baptism," I said, and "I covenant with thee, and all betwixt the sole of my foot and
the crown of my head, I give freely up and over to thee."

He marked me on the shoulder, and with his mouth, he sucked out my
blood, spat it into his hand, and sprinkled it upon my head and face, saying, "I
baptize ye, Janet, to myself, in my own name." A new name. Now, in this other
realm, I was Janet.

"Janet, we seal this pledge with our bodies," he said and shed his clothes
in a flash. There he stood, mickle black and large, his member exceedingly
great and long. He came into me like a horse to a mare, filling me with delight
and dread, and cold as ice. All the people 'round in the circle . . . and I had no
shame. "And ye shall have no other gods but me," he bellowed, and I cowered
and bowed before him.

And then he went into the shape of a mighty deer, and, like the steed, he
flew.

My mother had told me about the devil and the black mass, but she had not believed it. Twas all the invention of ministers, she said. Cunning women were healers, not devil worshippers. She'd been firm on this point: no self-respecting cunning woman would go in for that.

CHAPTER 39

I did go in for it. I made my covenant, and now I would have more power: power to punish those who thought themselves invincible. I could shoot them with elf-arrows, stick them with pins, roast them, and do all manner of evil to them. I had no guilt, no shame. The devil had given me power, and I would use it.

I hummed and sang and greeted my neighbors as I walked through the village. Here came Lilias with her basket of yarns, but no red marks from the devil on her cheek. Why not? Ah, 'twas only in that other realm that these things could be seen.

Here was Jack the Smith with a load of nails. He waylaid me to examine his sore. "The sore is almost healed," I said, and he smiled his one-eyed smile as he resumed his journey.

Now came Elspeth walking a goat to market, and we exchanged a look. "Tonight," I said. The devil had given me power, and I would use it.

Hugh Gilbert was snoring in one corner, and his mother lay sleeping with the children in the other. I had said the charm for sleep and given them ale with valerian and hyssop.

Elspeth and I chanted together as Jane Martin, all pink and dewy, stood watching. "*In the devil's name, we pour in this water among this meal, for long duyning and ill heal. We put it in the fire, that it may be burnt both stick and stour. It shall be burnt with our will. As any stickle upon a kill.*"

"We must repeat it thrice o'er, as the devil has taught me," I said.

"But," Jane winced, "the devil?"

"The devil has taught me this."

"But is it not a sinful thing?"

"This is a sacred trust, and with this, we have power. We have no money, we have no troops, our grain and cattle have been taken, and we could starve. What do we have to fight back with except the power of the devil?"

Jane stood up and gave a little hop from one foot to the other, wiping her hands on her apron. "Would we not come before the kirk and such?"

I glared at Jane. "If anyone tells."

"Not I!" Jane exclaimed.

"Mister Harry called the fairies devils, so William the Fairy Man took heed and became the devil."

Jane shuddered. "Then the devil can save us from the laird?"

"He will punish the laird."

"Now we must sit and say the charm," Elspeth commanded.

Jane sat, and we repeated the charm three times as I poured water from the jar and Elspeth stirred the clay that had been sifted into meal.

Jane looked around the hut towards Hugh, his mother, and the bairns. "What if they wake up?"

"Isobel has assured us that they will not," Elspeth said, exchanging a glance with me.

When the clay began to congeal, I scooped up a lump in my hands and worked it into a ball, then began to shape it. I chanted, "Little hands, little lips, little arms folded at his side."

Elspeth stood straight and tall, her face stern. "It will lack no part of the child."

"This is the *corp creadh*," I sang triumphantly as I finished the figure of the child. "The image of all the male children of the Laird of Park."

We all fell silent as I gently laid the clay figure in the fire. Solemnly, I proclaimed, "In the devil's name, it will roast 'til it be red as a coal."

Jane shuddered.

Grim faces flushed, we leaned forward and watched the little body roast. I took two sticks and lifted it out of the fire. "Till it be broken," I intoned, "twill be the death of all the male children that the Laird of Park will ever get."

"But how might it be broken?" Jane asked.

"Cast it over a kirk, and it will not break, until it be broken with an axe or some such thing. And if it be not broken, it will last one hundred years."

"Now we must roast it again every other day," Elspeth said.

"That all the male bairns *and* the laird will sicken and die."

"That never again will the lairds steal from their tenants and servants."

"As there will be none left alive."

Outside the hut, a figure turned from the window hole and crept away into the night. In the sand, her bare feet made no sound. It was almost midnight, and though the stars were multitudinous as the generations of Abraham, her dark clothes made her almost invisible. *She* had not been invited to the gathering. Isobel hardly looked at her when they washed their clothes at the river or passed in the village, and though she had asked and pleaded, Isobel wouldn't tell her about magic or teach her the charms.

But now she knew.

MARGARET

CHAPTER 40

"The lad is of a stellar family." Alexander Brodie had come at Lady Elizabeth's request, and they sat in the drawing room.

Margaret smiled at her mother, silent thanks for her intervention. She still didn't want to get arried, though she knew she would have to sooner or later. At least Andrew was far better than the man Father had favored, William Gordon. The son of the duke, he was wealthy enough, but the one time Margaret had met him—when her family dined at the castle in Fochabers—William had spent almost an hour complaining about his sheep. A tiresome man.

"But English, Alexander, English!!" bellowed John Hay. "How could anything good come of this?"

"Not English in the way you imagine, John. His family is of the Covenanter persuasion. In fact, his uncle, Edward Massie, is one of the leaders of the Covenanter movement in England. Massie was with me at Breda and helped me escort King Charles back to the English shore."

At this, Father was quiet.

And so, it happened that Alexander, Margaret's great uncle, provided the impetus her father needed to allow the courtship. The Massies were a genteel family, Uncle said, long established in Chesire and staunch defenders of the Presbyterian cause. And it didn't hurt, Mother emphasized, that the Massie family was quite wealthy, holding vast tracts of farmland in Chesire.

Father, who had been lamenting loud and long about his debt, was then persuaded to welcome Andrew as a suitor.

Andrew now came calling on a regular basis. Almost every Sunday after kirk, he appeared for the midday dinner. Margaret feared that he would view their diet as provincial, so she persuaded Aunt Grissel's cook to teach the Hay Cook some recipes from London. With Grissel's direction, Cook made two new recipes for mutton, a haddock with a sauce of cherries and onions, and a salmon with potatoes and kale, which, to everyone's surprise, turned out to be delicious. Most people considered kale something only to be eaten when little else was available—and even then, only by the peasants or the animals—but now, Mother declared it suitable for the Hay family. And the new puddings were delightful, though Father bewailed the expense of so much sugar.

After dinner, Andrew and Margaret usually took a walk outside. Margaret loved to hear his deep voice with its soft English inflection, and see his face change from somber to merry in an instant. Andrew, in turn, paid her the utmost attention, holding out his hand for her as she stepped over a rock, then gazing at her with an admiring smile that caused him to trip over that same rock, causing them both to laugh. By now, the insouciance Margaret had first observed in him had evaporated like the morning mist.

Andrew told her about his home in Chesire—a manor house rather than a castle, with thousands of acres, all varieties of dairy cows, and rolling farmlands that were not too different from the Morayshire terrain. The climate was milder and the growing season longer in Chesire, and it sounded to Margaret like a softer, more civilized place—like Andrew himself, whose gentle manner and ease of being had reshaped her image of a gentleman.

Margaret floated through the days. The joy in her heart lifted her into a new dimension, like the magic world she had imagined she would find with Isobel. She had been disturbed by Isobel's use of charms calling on the devil and was troubled still when she looked at the "elf arrow" she kept hidden in a drawer. Could that little stone cause deadly harm? She didn't really think so, but neither did she know what to do with it. Surely, Henrietta wouldn't want it. Margaret didn't want to think about it. Caught up in the whirl of courtship, she put it out of her mind.

With Andrew, even in winter, when the nights were long, the days were dark, and the fires never seemed warm enough, everything vibrated with life.

Margaret woke in the morning, heard the birds, and felt the light from the window, which made everything sharper and clearer than ever before. She breathed in the air, new and clean and fragrant, the same air that Andrew breathed.

They sat by the fire or rode to visit Aunt Grissel at Brodie Castle, where they sang with her at the harpsichord and played blind man's bluff and leap-frog with the lads, running around the castle grounds. Andrew taught the lads stoolball and other May games from England, and they all joined in. He talked of marriage, but Margaret put him off . . . for what could have been better than this world of laughter and joy? She wanted it never to end.

Now was spring once again, and Margaret and Andrew were strolling around the gardens at Brodie. The lads had gone off on their horses for some adventure. At their feet, flowers were starting to bloom again, yellow and white and orange, the colors of sunshine. Andrew took Margaret's hand. She felt him, skin to skin, his strength and attentiveness. This, too, was a natural part of their new life, and it warmed her from within.

"A kiss?" he asked, standing close and looking into her eyes, their warmth heating into a fire that drew her closer. Margaret's body leaned into his without a thought. They shared a gentle kiss. His lips were soft, and both of them lingered in the embrace. She wanted to stay enfolded in his arms, feeling his strong body against hers and this new warmth that flared from within.

Bessie had laughed when Margaret told her she wouldn't marry. "You'll see," she'd said, "when you want more than anything to be with him." Was this what Bessie had meant?

She'd thought she could enjoy her time with Andrew without the part that led to the marriage bed, but now she was confused. How could she live without him? She *would* want to feel him close beside her every night, his warmth and love and strength.

Andrew smiled as if to confirm what Bessie had said.

Even the death of another boy baby did not dull Margaret's happiness for too long. This time, the baby lived for a week—a tiny thing Margaret had fallen in love with immediately. When he died, she was overcome with sorrow. His name was Thomas. In truth, Margaret had steeled herself against hope that he would live at all, and so she was able to continue with her own life very quickly. She was becoming callous, she thought . . . or perhaps just accepting, like Mistress Collace, that death was a part of life.

Then wee John died. A double blow. No one had expected him to live, it was true; but he was a brother she had known and cared for, and her happy mood was dampened.

This winter was a time of mourning for the Hay family. Her mother's cough became worse, and Margaret again administered the charm with the wine and hyssop, but it didn't appear to help as it had the first time.

As the days grew warmer and longer, Andrew became a more regular presence, and at the same time Margaret went out more on Miranda.

She began to stop at Isobel's hut to ask her more about magic. Margaret avoided talk of the devil, as she hadn't yet sorted out for herself what that meant, but she still wanted to see the fairies.

Isobel said that the fairies would come when they wanted to, not when people searched them out. Instead, she taught Margaret about valerian and carmile for sleep, averans, wormwood, and many other healing herbs. Margaret was learning more charms, too: a charm for bruises, a charm to ward off the evil eye, a charm for a toothache. Many of them involved transferring the sickness to a stone or an animal, like a cat, and she was not sure about those. Was it right to infect an innocent animal? But then she remembered Jesus exorcising the demons into the herd of pigs.

One night after dinner, Andrew approached her father and formally asked for Margaret's hand in marriage. When Father accepted, she was surprised that she felt so pleased. She no longer worried about the dreary lot of women in marriage. This marriage, *her* marriage, would be different.

On another bright evening in early spring, Margaret and Andrew walked from the courtyard to the stables and mounted their horses. He tried to help her onto Miranda, but she waved his arm away and leapt up onto the saddle. She raced ahead at a gallop and reached the estuary first.

Andrew didn't seem offended. "You ride like the wind," he laughed in admiration. "And your father permits it?"

"It is one thing my father does permit; indeed, he encourages it. He says we Scots women need to be strong."

"Ah, yes, the wild women of Scotland. The young ladies in London trot about town in their carriages or ride sidesaddle looking decorous."

"I would love to go to London, but I would hate that kind of riding. If I couldn't gallop on Miranda, I would waste and wither."

"*Age cannot wither her, nor custom stale her infinite variety,*'" Andrew quoted. "What is that from?"

"*Antony and Cleopatra*. Shakespeare. It's a famous love story."

"One that I have not read. Does it have a happy ending?"

"Not at all. It's a tragedy, and Cleopatra is a woman of sorrow and secrets."

Secrets. Margaret turned and guided Miranda at a walk across the sandbar. Here, the sand stretched out for miles before one reached the sea, wide and flat like a great desert.

No one knew about Margaret's visits with Isobel. She had hoped to confide in Henrietta, but on second thought, decided against it. Henrietta was languishing at Kilrock, her name and reputation tarnished. Margaret visited often, bringing gifts and herbs. Henrietta would cheer up some, but then lapse back into her dreary sadness. It seemed futile and fruitless to tell her about Isobel, of whom Henrietta had disapproved to begin with. She would have been scandalized by Margaret's relationship with her.

What would Andrew think? Margaret slowed Miranda down and stared out at the horizon. Should she tell him? They were so close now, and their betrothal would be announced soon. Husbands and wives should not have secrets from each other. She'd read that, she thought, in the Bible.

Andrew learned over and searched her face. "My lady, is this a sudden turn to melancholy?" His mouth, rimmed by brown mustache and beard, was smiling, and his clear eyes watched her with compassion.

She took a deep breath. "What do you think of the cunning women, Andrew?"

"Magic and fairies and all that?"

"And second sight. You remember the cunning woman who saw where Henrietta was?"

He rubbed his beard. "I believe she got that information by other means."

"Other means? How could Isobel have known the MacDonalds were on Ben Rinnes?"

"This woman is quite well known in Morayshire, as are the MacDonalds, and we believe she simply asked her compatriots."

"You do not believe in the extraordinary power of cunning women?"

"I believe that she has the power of influence *and* that of cunning."

"But not magic?"

"Why believe in magic when we know the extraordinary power of our Lord?"

Margaret dropped her head. Andrew was beginning to sound like Mistress Collace. He didn't believe magic was real. She could not confide in him about Isobel or about her own second sight.

She walked Miranda to the water. Andrew followed, and they led both horses into the gentle waves. The horses pranced and splashed, lifting their legs high, trotting along the water's edge. Just offshore, two humps emerged, soft gray skins gleaming, leaping, and twisting in the sun.

"Oberon! Titania!" Margaret raised her arms. The dolphins lifted their heads and looked right at her. They seemed to be smiling and came closer. Margaret began to sing as Andrew watched in astonishment. In her clear, airy tone, she sang:

> *His voice doth rule the waters all,*
> *Even as himself doth please:*
> *He doth prepare the thundercaps,*
> *And governs all the seas.*
> *The voice of God is of great force,*
> *And wondrous excellent:*
> *It is most mighty in effect,*
> *And much magnificent.*

The dolphins jumped, dived, and came closer. They squeaked and trilled as Margaret sang louder, like a pure, high bell. The dolphins danced.

CHAPTER 41

I scattered crumbs for the chickens and watched the bairns.

Maria, bright of eye and browned by the sun and weather, her dress half on and half off, a torn and ragged thing, sat on the ground. She threw sticks into a circle she had inscribed in the sand. She was seven. The two little ones, five and three, sat watching me with full attention, as Robert, who was also seven and lived across the farmtown yard, stood behind the circle chewing seaweed.

The day was windy and raw, and the children shivered in the gusts of cold air; but they were used to the cold, so none of them thought to run into their homes. Robert chewed and watched as Maria led the game.

"This stick is the king," she said, "and this is the laird. And the princess has to go 'round the backside of the king and the laird and run all the way 'round before they can catch her. Robert, you can be the king, and little Charles, you the laird." She took a deep breath and looked at her playmates with a sigh. "*I* am the princess."

"Me, too!" said Martha, the wee one. "I wan' be a princess, too."

"There is only one princess, and it be me."

I knelt down beside them. "Can I play, too, Maria?"

"Aw, you a big person," Maria huffed. She was losing control of her game, and the princess was not pleased.

I took another stick and tapped the princess three times. "And that is for the Father, Son, and Holy Ghost. And will mean that you will play with love and care for your little sister." And then I made the stick hop, hop, hop and dance around the circle. "Now catch me if you can," I said in a low spooky voice.

Martha giggled and made her fingers run to the stick. I grabbed them and shook three times.

Maria took her stick and chased mine, and soon, William was chasing, too. We were all laughing. When Hugh Gilbert came across the open yard, he stopped and glared.

Maria saw his face, jumped up, and ran away toward the sea, her blonde hair wisping every which way in the wind. She was so fast; we hardly saw her before she reached the top of the dune and scooted over it.

Hugh shouted at me. "What have ye thought, lass, to waste yer time playing? What of the teazing and carding, what of the cow with the lame foot? What of the washing that sits in the house?" His face became a fiery frown as he walked up to me. The other children scattered, Robert running after Maria and the two little ones to chase the chickens by the hut.

I stood up and faced him squarely, hands on hips. "I'll play when I like, and I'll go with the fairies when you don't like."

He scowled and raised his fist. "And ye'll do your work or feel the fist."

I stepped back to avoid the blow. To divert his attention, I asked, "Ye'll go to market now for the beef?"

"Aye." He hesitated, fist in the air, then lowered it and walked toward the cattle yard behind the house.

I bent low and entered the house, heading straight across the room to my kist, where I stored the herbs and potions. I opened it, rummaging through until I found what I was looking for.

When Hugh came back, leading the cow, I was ready. He stopped and let me approach. I took the feather, sheer gray tinged with blue—a swallow's feather, it had to be—and attached it to the head of the beast with a piece of yarn. The delicate feather was barely visible against the brown of the cow's coat. And now I recited in a singsong voice:

> *I put out this beef in the devil's name,*
> *that mickle silver and good price come hame.*

And again:

> *I put out this beef in the devil's name,*
> *that mickle silver and good price come hame.*

And then again, as it had to be thrice for the charm to work.

Some charms called on the Holy Trinity, some on the saints, and others the fairies. This one needed the help of the devil.

And though my husband disapproved—he was always lecturing me, thinking he be like Mister Harry, no doubt—he allowed it, because he knew the magic worked.

He strode off with the cow, confident that now he would get a good sale.

I went into the house, banked the fire, and gathered the clothes for washing. I stepped out and started to walk to the river, but now I heard the sound of hoofbeats. I stopped and looked. Over the dyke came three horsemen.

Who could this be? There was a stirring in my heart, and I heard a faint voice. It must have been my mother, whispering or calling in the wind, but the words I did not know. Something cold and fearsome came into me, and I was sore affrighted.

The three horsemen came. Three solemn faces: one red and puffy, yellow hair fuzzed around pale cold eyes; one black-haired with unsure expression; and lastly, the sheriff, tall, mickle red-haired Sir Hugh Campbell. All were fierce dressed in plaids with scabbards. They stopped and dismounted, never taking their eyes off of me.

"Mistress Gowdie, you must come with us," said Sir Hugh.

"And why must I?" I tried for my voice of power, but only a feeble sound came out. I knew the answer.

"I arrest you in the name of the king. You are charged with the crime of witchcraft."

I looked around and around. Was there anywhere to run, to hide? My Maria with big eyes was peeking from around the corner. Nowhere—but I dropped my bundle and bolted. I ran toward the sea. Up and to the top of the dune, with hoofbeats close behind . . . and then a rope around me. The yellow-haired one jumped down, grabbed me in a rough manner, and tied my hands together. He remounted, holding the end of the rope. I was forced to walk behind, half-dragged down the side of the dune and across the yard. We left the farmtown and continued in procession toward Auldearn, where Isobel Gowdie would be on display, led to the tollbooth.

KATHARINE

CHAPTER 42

Katharine sat quietly in a side pew. She was not in favor of this display. Mister Harry, though she still admired his preaching, was now almost repulsive to her. She had heard reports of his tryst with a servant woman and didn't doubt its truth. Of course, no one would dare to bring *him* up before the session, much less sentence him to the stocks.

The kirk was dark, though a few beams of light streamed in through the tiny windows in the stone walls. Candles and lamps illuminated the dignitaries in the front pews. Mister Harry was at the pulpit, with Jonet Fraser, a wide, blowsy-looking woman in several extra layers of clothing, standing between them. Onlookers from the congregation were scattered throughout the other pews, though in the gloomy half-light, they were discernible only by the sounds of shuffling, coughing, and heavy breathing.

"Mistress Jonet Fraser, what charge do you bring?"

Wasn't this the woman who had been in the stocks for adultery and drunkenness? She must be trying to win back Mister Harry's good graces.

A man's voice roared out of the darkness. "How could ye believe that drunken whore?"

"We'll thank you for silence, Jacob Taylor," Mister Harry admonished, "or you'll be outside forthwith."

Grunts of protest came from the invisible congregation, and something slammed on a pew. A woman's voice was heard, in quiet but distinct tones. "She's a liar."

"Mistress Fraser, go on," Mister Harry said.

Jonet Fraser straightened up, took a wide-legged stance, and placed her hands on her hips. Though her apron was stained, her hair was tucked into her cap, a sign that she had made some effort to look proper. "Like I told you, Mister Harry, I heard Mistress Isobel Gowdie saying charms in her home. And I went to peek in the window."

"And what did you see?"

"I seen her kneading the clay and making shapes of the laird's bairns." She looked defiantly at the elders, in particular John Hay. Everyone knew he was the laird to whom she referred. She glanced behind herself, toward the dark congregation.

"Making graven images of the laird's children?" Mister Harry countered.

"Aye, and she were saying curses and roasting the little bairns in the fire."

The room broke out in more shouting and commotion.

Katharine shuddered. If Isobel Gowdie had been making clay figures, roasting them, and cursing the laird's children, this was, indeed, a serious offense. These rituals were just superstitions and mutterings, but if people believed them—and Katharine knew that John Hay did—then the curses might have some effect.

The elders and dignitaries sat stiff and quiet in the front pews: John Hay, Alexander Brodie, Hugh Rose, the minister at Nairn, and five other men from the Moray region. Alexander's head was bowed.

Katharine had talked with Alexander before this meeting. He'd shaken his head over and over and sighed. "That woman has put herself in this position," he said, "and I do not see what can save her now."

"But we must *help* these women," she said, "not punish them more."

"Yes," he agreed. "The poor wretches. But it's too late for this one, I fear."

"Jonet Fraser, thou flea-bitten toad!" shouted a woman's voice. "Speak on yerself, ye fat strumpet!"

Jonet raised her fist at the unseen woman. "I'll tell on thee, too, Lilias Dunlop!"

At this, a barrage of shoes flew across the room, hitting Hugh Rose and John Hay as well as Jonet, who picked it up and threw it back.

Alexander, Laird of Brodie, stood and faced the congregation. "This is the house of the Lord," he pronounced in a deep voice. "And we will listen in silence to these proceedings. It is a heavy matter, indeed, that comes before the magistrates. Judgment will come from this commission, not the congregation. The law of the kirk is the law of the land." He sat down, and the room quieted.

Isobel Gowdie was led to the front of the kirk to stand facing Jonet Fraser. "After I tried to help thee, Jonet," she said, "when thou wert in the stocks?"

"But ye didn't help me, did ye? Just a trick like yer other tricks, Isobel Gowdie."

"Enough!" Harry shouted. "Now, Mistress Gowdie, you have been accused of witchcraft. How do you answer this charge?"

Isobel was silent.

"Speak up, wench!" called one of the elders.

Silence.

Alexander Brodie stood again and faced Isobel. "Did you create the *corp creadh* and pronounce curses on the family of Hay?"

Isobel nodded and lowered her head.

A collective gasp arose from the congregation.

"And did you also roast them in the fire for the purpose of causing sickness and death to the male members of the Hay family?"

She glanced up through lowered lids at John Hay, who wore a stunned expression.

Katharine's jaw dropped. She covered her mouth with her hand. Perhaps this woman *was* a witch. Or had she simply been capitalizing on dire conditions that already existed to assert her power? Everyone knew that the young Hay lad had been sickly and frail and unlikely to live, but everyone also believed in these charms and curses.

Jonet Fraser, arms crossed in front of herself, stared triumphantly at Isobel. "And she were not alone, m'lairds."

Hugh Rose, a large man with a compassionate expression, stood up and addressed Isobel. "And who else participated in this *maleficium?*"

"And that I know, as well," shouted Jonet. "Elspeth Nychie and Jane Martin, both were there. And they spoke the words, too."

A howl arose from the congregation.

"A coven." Mister Hugh looked around the room. "And who else is in your coven?"

Isobel remained silent, her head bowed, her eyes observing the congregation.

Alexander looked at Isobel with an expression of pity. He shook his head and waited until the crowd quieted down. "Mistress Gowdie must stay in the tollbooth," he pronounced in a quiet voice. "Mister Harry will seek to counsel this misguided soul to confession and repentance."

MARGARET

CHAPTER 43

"What?" Margaret gasped, spoon midway between her bowl and her mouth. They were at dinner, and Bessie had just served the soup, a creamy mixture of fish and onions.

"They caught another witch," Lucy repeated. "Isobel Gowdie."

"Isobel? But she is not a witch. She is a cunning woman." Margaret put down her spoon.

"Isobel Gowdie is a witch, and she has been plotting to harm our family," her father pronounced.

"*Harm?* You must be mistaken, Father. I know this woman, and she does good." She braced her shoulders, forcing herself to deny her doubts.

Father put his hands on the table and glared at her. "How do you know this woman?"

"I visited her at her home." Margaret looked up warily. "With her second sight, she found Henrietta at the MacDonalds' camp. And when Andrew brought her back, Isobel cured her wounds and despair."

"And you have had discourse with this wretched creature?"

"Yes, Father, and she is not a wretched creature. She has the gift of second sight, and her healing charms have helped many throughout Morayshire."

Father pounded his fist on the table. "You were forbidden to go to the farmtown, Margaret. Forbidden! And you have disobeyed me again. Those people are mulish and ignorant, and this woman is evil. She consorts with the devil."

Well, Margaret thought, Isobel did invoke the devil for one of her charms. But she wouldn't tell that to her father.

Mother bowed her head over her bowl. Before Father could go on, she spoke. "She has put a curse on your father and brothers."

"A curse?"

Father remained silent, staring down at his soup.

"That could not be true, Father?"

Head down, he hissed, "She will burn at the stake, and may she burn in hell."

For once, Mother did not protest this type of condemnation. "But the trial has just begun," she said, "and the testimony came from someone else. They will question her more until she confesses. Perhaps she will repent."

Margaret's soup sat in front of her, untouched. "Why did I not know of this trial?"

"You have been off in the clouds with your lover," Lucy said, waving her spoon in the air.

The family at table sat illuminated in the soft twilight from the two windows. The sounds of clanking pots emanated from the kitchen. Lucy was the only one eating her soup. Bessie hovered in the corner of the room.

"Isobel Gowdie is the daughter of Agnes Grant," Father spat. "That evil witch who killed my father, your grandfather, and my brother William. Agnes Grant was tried, confessed, and found guilty."

"What happened to her?"

"She burned. The only way to destroy that wickedness is to burn it away."

Mother stiffened and looked at her husband. "Your father and brother died, but it was at the time of the plague."

"I have told you repeatedly, Elizabeth," Father shouted. "It was not the plague. It was that witch who killed my family. And now, her daughter intends to kill the rest of us. They will destroy us, wipe out the line of Hay, unless *she* is destroyed."

Margaret ran from the room, across the great hall, and up the tower steps to her chamber. *They must be wrong*, she thought. Isobel, cursing her father and brothers? How could she? Isobel, whom she trusted, and who had shown Margaret her own gift of second sight? Grandmother had come to her on the road, giving her the promise in her heart.

But Isobel! Margaret's tears wet her gown as well as the bedcovers. *She is my friend! She is my teacher. A teacher of magic who has "learned" me so many of the magical rhymes and chants. The charms heal . . . like the one for Henrietta. The hyssop and wine, and the charm, cured Mother's consumption, at least the first time. Magic is for good. Magic is not for evil.*

Everyone, Lucy said, now knew of Isobel's curse against the Hay family. Isobel had not confessed, but another woman had *seen* Isobel making the clay images and *heard* the curses she uttered. Curses against Margaret's father and brothers! To make them die! And the brothers had died . . . both wee John and baby Alexander. Had Isobel caused that?

What was Margaret to do now? She knew now that there was more to God's kingdom than what the Covenanters believed. Music and dancing were good, and the Earth and its plants and animals held many secrets, power to be discovered and used. Power for the good, for healing, and for spreading love, even the love of Jesus. Saints and angels and fairies, the dead . . . there was such a vast universe of life within and around, worlds within worlds, if only people could learn to see.

All this she had learned from Isobel.

Isobel *had* talked of cursing, she recalled. Isobel would have cursed the Campbells to avenge Henrietta. Margaret had dismissed that idea and put it out of her mind, but perhaps she should have paid more attention.

And now Isobel had tried to destroy Margaret's family. To murder, yes, *murder*, her own father and brothers. How could she have done that? And *why?*

Margaret knelt beside the bed. She must ponder and pray.

The prayers wouldn't come. She got up and walked, back and forth, as the thoughts raced through her head.

She could no longer accept the Covenanter way, no matter how much she loved Mistress Collace. There were too many other truths, and the world was much bigger than that . . . but she could no longer trust Isobel, either. That woman had turned on her family like Cromwell turned on the Covenanters. She would have them bloodied and slain, like Cromwell had done. Perhaps she *was* a witch.

Margaret's stomach clenched into nausea. She would be ill. She *was* ill, so heartsick she knew not what to do. She could not confide in anyone—not even Andrew. He had never believed in Isobel at all.

Margaret dropped down on her bed. She would stay in her chamber. She would languish, like Henrietta.

KATHARINE

CHAPTER 44

"I am grateful for your understanding, Alexander, and for your wise influence in this land." Katharine was strolling in the garden with the laird. The green of the grass shone brightly, and the fruit trees were beginning to flower on this April day.

Brodie hung his head. "A land of sorrow and trouble."

"Yes, a sorry place. The fighting is endless, and not just between nations, but within our own country: Scots fighting Scots, brother against brother. And death, it seems, is our constant companion."

"As you, dear lady, know so well, having suffered the loss of your children."

"Ah, yes." She spread an arm toward the flowering trees. "This beauty, this spring light, seems to mock our attempts to find God's truth. His light remains hidden in the depths of these dark times."

They entered the *parterre* garden, a geometric design of pathways lined with yew hedges and flowerbeds. Sparrows hopped and twittered in a bed of pale-yellow tulips.

"And yet when I seek the Lord, even within this sorrowful place," Katharine continued, "my losses become my strength." She stopped at a bench flanked by yew shrubs, and they both sat down. Katharine picked a needle from the yew and rubbed it in her fingers, releasing the pungent scent. She looked up at the laird's face, a kind and thoughtful countenance. "You have returned from Kiltearn, Alexander. And have you spoken with Mister Thomas Hogg?"

"Ah, a grave matter." He cleared his throat. "Mister Thomas understands the difficulty of your unfortunate marriage, and extends his sympathy as concerns your desire to go south again. However, he bids me ask you consider that you are needed here in Auldearn."

She nodded. "I did feel that God was calling me to go south, but now I see it was my melancholy speaking. The Lord is showing me that there is more work for me here."

"Lady Elizabeth is still ailing and has great need of you—for herself and also her daughters."

"She is a good woman. And she has promised to build me a house on the estate, so I need not dwell in that place of darkness."

Alexander's face softened into a look of pity.

Katharine looked up into a blue sky filled with white, puffy clouds. "I feel called, as well, to seek His light in another way. I am sorely troubled by the matter of the witch trial."

"Let us pray that the Lord will send us gifts of wisdom and zeal for finding out the crafty workings of the devil. Mister Harry has been appointed to question her further."

"And what advice would you give Mister Harry?"

"I would neither press her to tell nor hinder her but exhort her to do nothing in ignorance or to any sinister end."

"Yet she is accused of just that ignorance, and just those sinister ends—making images and incantations to harm the Laird of Park and his children. I know that these practices come from mere superstition, but so many believe in these powers."

He sighed. "Yes, even the Laird of Park, my nephew. He believes she has the power to kill him, and he would have her to the stake already."

Katharine raised her voice. "But I was there, at the arraignment! And 'tis clear to me that this poor woman has no such power. As I have said to Mister Harry, the way to alleviate these ignorant beliefs is to teach these women to read. If they do not know or understand the Bible, how can they see what the Lord requires?"

Alexander smiled at her. "Your passion is admirable, Katharine. And you are right that ignorance is at the heart of these superstitions. But peasants, reading? That is hard to imagine."

"I find Mister Harry not so sensible of this as he could be."

"No, Harry is certain that she is an agent of Satan. And he may be correct. But let God manifest Himself in bringing wickedness to light."

In the carriage on the way to Inshoch, Katharine considered the conversation. Alexander, so earnest and thoughtful, had depth of character, and he seemed convinced that this woman was guilty. He was right, she supposed. Isobel Gowdie did practice *maleficium*, or black magic. But had anyone actually been harmed by these charms and incantations? Perhaps the answer would be revealed in the continuing trial. Or perhaps this was not a question they would ask.

The puffy clouds were moving fast. The sky cleared, and Katharine felt a clearing in her mind.

She could see it now. Harry Forbes had, in some way, strayed from the path. She'd felt such discomfort at his improper advances that day . . . and then his wife's fury. It suggested that he had acted on that impulse with others. Mistress Forbes had been mistaken in blaming her, but there must have been a reason for her suspicion. Harry was a man of passion, and passion could so easily go astray. Now, it seemed, he was directing all of it into convicting the witch.

Inshoch Castle lay quiet in the bright sun. The only sounds were doves cooing in the courtyard and the muffled voices of Bessie and the cook in the kitchen. Lady Elizabeth, still ailing from her failed pregnancy and consumption, stayed in her chamber.

In the drawing room, Lucy was working on her needlepoint. When Katharine entered, she looked up. "Margaret is keeping to her chamber," she said with a pout.

Katharine frowned and sat down. "It has been over a week."

"She won't come down and won't talk to anyone. She won't even see Andrew."

Katharine rose from her seat and stood behind Lucy, examining the needlepoint. "I see that you are doing well, Lucy. Simply redo this knot," she said, pointing to a spot in the design, "and it will be perfect."

Katharine walked away, though the great hall to the tower staircase. At Margaret's chamber, she knocked.

No answer.

"Margaret," she called. "Tis I, Mistress Collace."

After a few minutes, she heard something on the other side of the door. Slowly, with loud creaking, the door opened, and Margaret stood in front of it, her dark curls and faded blue gown in disarray, her expression blank.

Katharine reached out, and Margaret allowed herself to be held. She sighed and lay her head on Katharine's shoulder.

"All is lost," Margaret whispered.

Katharine's cheek was wet. If her first child had lived, she would be almost Margaret's age now. Lady Elizabeth was so ill, perhaps she didn't even know of Margaret's distress. Perhaps Katharine could give a mother's comfort to the lass. "What is it, my dear?"

They went into the chamber. Margaret sat on the bed, and Katharine on the chair beside her. "They tell me you have not come out of your chamber for a week, Margaret. What causes you this despair?"

Margaret looked at Katharine, her eyes wary and defiant. "I *do* believe in magic."

"Magic?"

"I know that Isobel saw the fairies and talked to them, and that they helped her. And she healed Henrietta and did other marvelous things. But—" Her lips twisted as she tried to hold back the tears. Margaret threw herself face down on the bed and wept.

"You have had more intercourse with this woman?"

"Yes! I have seen her and talked to her and *seen* her magic! But it was good! I thought it was *good* magic!" Margaret's shoulders shook as she sobbed into the coverlet.

Katharine sighed. "And now this."

"My father! My little brother!" she wailed. "And the baby who died. Perhaps it was she who caused it!"

Katharine laid her hand on Margaret's heaving back. "No, no, dear lassie. Tis not magic that causes sickness and death."

|SOBEL

CHAPTER 45

The tollbooth was a mickle cold place. They led me up the tower stairs with none but a slit of a window to see the sky, and then to this room with no light at all.

I sat on the floor, stone like the walls and cold as the devil's wand. No chair, no fire for heat. No windows. No peat, no pots or mats, no kist for my stores, nothing to spin or weave or card or knead. Nothing to do with these hands that have never been idle.

I was allowed one delivery of food a day, and either Elspeth or Agnes brought it. They were not allowed to see me, and they probably brought more than what came to me—just a hunk of bread. Dry, mealy bread. There was a bucket to pee and shite in, but no one emptied it. When I asked, they laughed at me and told me to "turn it into a cat."

The first night, I shivered on the stone floor, with nothing to cover me except my thin, ragged plaid. In spite of this, I started drifting off to sleep. William, my fairy man, was just beginning to appear when I heard a clanging, kicking, and cursing. The door opened, and a beefy man with curly brown hair and beard and a dirty jerkin appeared—a new guard. He didn't look at me as he brought a stool, placed it beside me, and sat down. This man was not from Auldearn, or I would have known him.

"I was almost asleep," I protested, and started to rise.

He pushed me down with vicious strength. "Stay," he commanded, and took from his sack a large pin the size of a knitting needle. "What evil magic hast thou done against the Laird of Hay and his bairns?"

I stared at the floor.

"Did ye pronounce a curse and make a clay image?"

I remained silent.

He grabbed my arm so I couldn't get away, though of course there was nowhere to get to anyway. He pulled up my skirt and pricked me in the thigh, jabbing in the pin three times.

"Leave me alone, ye son of a whore!" I screamed.

He jabbed again and again until I stopped struggling and collapsed in pain and silence.

He stood up, took the stool, and left the room, locking the barred door with a loud jangling of keys.

I moaned. My leg was bleeding from the puncture wounds. I stanched it with my skirt, but the pain was now so much worse than the cold. I could only sit and hold my bunched-up skirt over my thigh.

This was what they did to my mother.

And now the tears came. Where was William the Fairy Man? Could he not come and carry me away? I tried to concentrate, to go into that place of trance, but the pain was too great, and my sorrow overtook me until I could cry no more.

Then I remembered a charm. I placed my hand over my wound and whispered, "*For pang, for swelling, for hurt, for wound, Christ went out at early morn, put blood to blood and flesh to flesh, juice to juice and vein to vein. May he heal this, too, with fair Mary and his powers together.*" I had no herbs or salve to accompany the charm, and whether or not it worked, I could not tell.

Finally, I fell back, but as soon as I fell asleep, the loud clanking and clanging woke me again. The pricker. He placed his stool beside me and commenced to repeat the questioning and pricking. I was about to confess just to make the pricking stop, but then he left.

When they brought the bread in the morning, I was almost too worn out to eat.

This treatment was repeated on the second day, but this time, the pricker took me outside the tollbooth, where a crowd had gathered. He stripped off my clothes until I was naked and forced me to stay standing, though I felt I would fall down with weakness and shame. He took a rough blade and shaved my head and whole body.

People spat and jeered, but I remained silent.

"Now we'll see what power ye have!" screamed Jonet Fraser. "Devil's whore!"

The pricker rubbed his hands over my whole body, then held up the giant pin to show the people. "To find the devil's mark," he declared. "This be the way to find the devil's mark and prove that she is a witch. Where the pin produces no blood or pain, this be the mark of the devil, and will be proof she is no mere mortal, but the devil's own."

He began to stick the pin in, jabbing my legs and arms, buttocks, stomach, and breasts. At each prick, I recoiled and gasped. The blood spurted out, running down my body in rivulets.

I felt myself rising above my body, and now I saw myself from above. That miserable, wasted body, so pitiful in its nakedness and shame.

I would fly with William. I would call out, *"Horse and hattock, ho!"* I would fly away from this horrible place to the land of the fairies.

But William did not come. I could not rise up to leave the yard, only enough to hover a few feet above my body where at least I did not feel anything.

At the next prick to my back, I did not flinch.

"No blood!" shouted the pricker.

The devil's mark!" the people cried.

"And there you have the proof," the pricker said with a grin. He wiped the pin and put it away in his bag as he let me go. I sank down onto the ground.

The next day, Mister Harry came to the tollbooth.

I sat up, skirts stained with dried blood, my hair dirty and askew. Mister Harry was still limping and wincing, and this brought my first smile. It had been almost two years, but the charm against him had worked. He was still in pain.

Harry sat on the stool, fidgeting on the small seat. He lifted his bad leg and crossed it over the other, revealing socks so full of holes, they looked like fishnets. He tugged on his mangy beard and leaned over me with a look of pity. "I see your suffering, Mistress, and I have great regret that it has come to this."

How dare he feign sympathy? I glared at him.

"And yet the Lord desires only that you come to him with a clean heart. To know the comfort of his love, the fruits of salvation."

The stones were icy beneath me, and Harry's words brought a deeper chill. He talked about comfort and fruits, but it was all a lie. These pleasures did not come from the Lord or the kirk. William brought them to me . . . only William. With him, I had earthly *and* unearthly delights.

"To be forgiven, we must confess our sins. And to repent will bring you great joy." Mister Harry's words came out in a blast of sour breath.

I cringed and inched away from him.

"Mistress Gowdie, did you curse the laird, John Hay, and his sons?"

If only the curse on Mister Harry had worked more completely. It was I who had caused him to lie in his bed sick and sore for several months . . . a span of freedom from his hateful preaching. Would that he was still sick and sore! Or that my elf arrow had hit the target!

I had been flying through the sky on a night ride with William when I saw Mister Harry walking through the village. He was walking in daylight, though we were riding at night. No matter . . . for in that other world, night and day can happen together. As we flew through the sky under the stars, William gave me two elf arrows, and I flicked one at Harry. But I missed.

"Mistress Gowdie, you must answer the question."

"You killed my mother." I spat.

Mister Harry started. In the course of a minute, his face transformed into several different expressions. He raised his eyebrows in surprise, wet his lips, and grimaced like a hissing cat. "Agnes Grant, with her maleficent magic, did harm and kill David Hay, the former Laird of Park, as well as his son, William. She confessed to the crime."

"And that be," I snarled, "only because you put her on the rack. You pricked her awake all night. You tortured her until she could say only what you wanted to hear."

"Agnes Grant was a stubborn woman with no respect for the kirk or our Lord in Heaven. She could not face her Maker unless she confessed and repented. And you must do the same."

I had no intention of confessing, even though I, unlike my mother, *was* guilty of trying to harm the laird's family. I kept silent.

Mister Harry asked me the same questions over and over until at last, he sighed and stood up. "Such looseness and ignorance, lying, and contempt of God I have rarely seen. I am sorely afflicted for your soul, Mistress, and I will pray for you." He raised a hand and voice. "Lord, I am sorry and afflicted that such evil has come among us. That this miserable creature before me refuses to cling to You and your son, Jesus, and has concocted such wickedness in our land. Move her to confess her evil deeds and repent, as forgiveness is Yours. We know You offer it freely when supplicated." He droned on in a tedious manner, and I shut my mind to it.

When he was done, I narrowed my eyes at him. "And perhaps I know something of the wickedness in *your* house, Mister Harry."

He flinched and went red all over. He knew of what I spoke. I did not need to say the name of Agnes Pierson.

Finally, Mister Harry left, and I lay down again. Now I could conserve my strength, and perhaps even sleep.

But sleep was not to be.

The pricker came again.

And Mister Harry came again. But this time he had a different scheme.

I was lying on the floor, so weary, so cold, so hungry. Pain in my thighs, my arms, my side, and two festering sores on my back–all the places I was pricked.

Mister Harry sat on the stool, opened a sack, and brought out a loaf of bread and a large hunk of cheese.

Of course, I ate it. I ate it all right there as he watched, careful not to eat too quickly, as I knew the effects of a large meal on a starving body. When I was done, I heaved a sigh.

"And now, I would like to hear about your travels with the fairies," Harry said with a pleasant smile.

I stared at him. "Is it a confession you want, then?"

"Not a confession, as yet. I and the other members of the commission are greatly interested in your story. I understand that you have great power. And that you see the fairies."

I smiled. Yes, I had power. And now they acknowledged it. But would I tell them?

"We wish to know of your magic and charms."

I inhaled, and my whole body seemed to swell with pride, though the movement caused me pain all over. The lairds and ministers wanted to hear *me*. Now they would know me as a woman of power, and they would know how small *they* were. I would tell about the powers that went beyond their world. "I will speak of my gift."

"Will you speak to the commission about this?"

"Aye. It is time. And you will hear of a land that is not visible to you. Only the ones who are chosen, such as I, can move between the worlds and use the powers of that other realm, the powers given to us."

He led me out and into the larger room of the tollbooth. Here sat the others: the minister of Nairn, Hugh Rose, the Laird of Park and Lochloy, John Hay, the Laird of Brodie, and six others, local lairds and dignitaries. The men's faces were smug and perplexed. The notary, John Innes, sat at a desk to the side with his pen and book.

Fortified now by the cheese and bread, I stood tall.

The notary spoke: "At Auldearn, on the thirteenth day of April 1662, in presence of me, John Innes, and witnesses named herein, the said Isobel Gowdie, appearing penitent for her heinous sins of witchcraft, without any compulsion, now proceedeth in her confession."

Mister Hugh, a portly man with a kind face, was the first to speak. He rose from his seat. "Mistress Gowdie, please tell us your tale."

MARGARET

CHAPTER 46

"Margaret." Someone was calling her name. She was walking on the strand, sand between her toes, skirts pulled high and tucked into her pantaloons. It was midmorning, and the strand was empty now. The fishermen were out to sea, the farmers at work in the fields. Margaret looked up and down the shoreline and behind herself to the dunes, but there was no one about. Where had the voice come from? It was low and lilting, like the rocking of waves on a balmy day or the undercurrent of the wind.

Was it a voice or was it the wind? It sounded like Isobel's voice. Like her singing. Margaret sat down on the sand with a plop. That voice *was* Isobel's.

On the day Mistress Collace came, after Margaret had calmed down, the two had talked. "What was the magic you saw?" she had asked.

With eyes half closed and her body slumping down in despair, Margaret spoke. Isobel had betrayed her. She'd cursed Margaret's family, so what difference would it make now for her to tell?

She told Mistress about the beautiful land of the fairies as she imagined it, her thrill at hearing about William and the nightriding, and her hopes of seeing the fairy queen. The real, yes, *real* magic she had seen when Isobel healed her own bruises with a charm, when she had *seen* Henrietta at the MacDonalds' camp, when Henrietta had arisen from her sickbed, renewed and lively. "I know you believe that magic is evil," Margaret said, "but how could it be a sin to help people and restore them to health?"

Mistress had remained silent for so long after this that Margaret had become fearful. Would she condemn her? Would she report Margaret as a witch?

A heavy rain beat on the window, and Mistress Collace stood and walked over to it before coming back and sitting beside Margaret on the bed. "Magic is sinful," she said, "but all of this—communing with the fairies, riding through the sky, even thinking that charms and rhymes can heal or harm—don't you see how these ideas are fantasies and illusions?"

Margaret frowned. "Then how would you explain the fact that the magic *did* work?"

"When a person heals, it is the life force within them, the love of God that surges like a light in all of us."

"Yes! And that is what I thought, too! The charms are prayers!"

"No, the charms are empty words. The way they use the name of the Lord or the saints, these are remnants of Catholic beliefs. The Catholics also believe that words and rhymes are magic."

Margaret stood up and started pacing back and forth. Was this true? Could the charms really be just empty words? Everything in her resisted this idea. "But I believe," she said, "that words *do* have power. When I hear psalms and poetry, and when you quote the Bible, these words give me strength. Inspiration. They make me feel better."

Mistress Collace smiled. "You are a clever lass. The Bible gives me strength, too. It is, after all, The Word. But we do not use it to get what *we* want, either for good or ill. We refer to it to find God's wisdom, so that we can come to Him in our hearts."

"Do you not, then, believe that curses cause sickness and death?"

"We cannot make these things happen with words or rhymes. Your father and brothers will not die because of them. All of us will die, but only the Lord knows the manner or time."

Margaret stopped her pacing and stood at the window. The rain was letting up, and now, with the sun coming through the window, the drops on the glass created patterns of light: blue, green, purple, yellow, an undulating design. She turned. "And what about the flying in the night with her fairy man, and the fairy home under the Downie Hill?"

"These are her dreams and illusions, don't you see? In her wretched life, the poor woman would escape to fairyland, where life is beautiful. And so, she imagines this place."

"Yes." Margaret sat down again. She had almost been able to see that marvelous place in her imagination, but try as she might, her second sight hadn't worked. Were these places really just in Isobel's imagination?

"And rather than burning," Mistress added, "this sad creature deserves our pity . . . only our pity and forgiveness."

After Mistress Collace left, the rain stopped and the wind died down. Margaret opened the window. A whisper of a breeze drifted in, and outside, a seabird was floating beneath a cloud, calling a plaintive song. Forgiveness. Could she forgive Isobel? Isobel had betrayed her trust and tried to kill Margaret's father. No—she could not forgive such a wicked act.

Now, as she stood by the water, the sky over the Firth was clear, and she could see all the way to the cliffs of Inverness.

Had she really heard the voice? Perhaps she'd imagined it. She'd been thinking so much of what Mistress had said: about Isobel and the trial, her imprisonment, her "delusion." She envisioned Isobel in the tollbooth, forced into that dark and clammy place—she who had lived with the earth beneath her feet and the sky above, with cows mooing and goats jumping, she who loved the trees and the birds and the dolphins.

A groan escaped from Margaret's chest. Her father was on the commission. He would vote against Isobel. Isobel *would* burn at the stake.

"Margaret." That voice again . . . wild and desperate, now almost a screech like a gull, but human. *It must be Isobel.* But, where was she? There was no one here. No one down the strand or on the dunes or the machair. No one at the water.

Behind her perched a crow. Isobel had claimed she could "go into a crow." Could the crow be Isobel? No, the voice had come from the sea, from the gentle susurration of the waves. In this place where the wind coursed across the strand and whipped in from the water, where gales would start and stop and change direction, where storms howled and buffeted, where skirts flapped and twisted, today held an unusual quiet. Except for that one voice, everything was still. The sky, the wind, the birds, the crow. As if God had placed a finger on his lips and said *hush.*

Margaret gathered her skirts and ran. She scurried up the dune and back along the path toward home.

She would see Isobel. She would ask and beg and wheedle, if necessary. She would go to the tollbooth.

CHAPTER 47

"**N**o one is permitted to see the prisoner except her confessor, Mister Harry," said Uncle Alexander.

"But, Uncle, I *must* see her."

They were standing on the road outside the tollbooth. Margaret knew that visiting a prisoner was forbidden, but she also knew that Uncle Alexander could arrange it for her, if anyone could.

"No, it simply isn't done."

"Uncle, she has spoken to me. She's told me about her fairy beliefs and her adventures. I believe I have been a friend to her."

He raised an eyebrow and looked down at her. "You *do* know what she is accused of?"

"Yes, but I have talked with Mistress Collace, my tutor, and she has helped me see that Isobel is deluded." Well, perhaps *some* of Isobel's adventures were delusions, but the magic, Margaret knew, was real.

"Mistress Collace?"

"Yes, and she has turned my heart to pity, not hate."

Uncle Alexander shook his head. "It is a good thing, to feel in one's heart for one of God's creatures. But this one has had discourse with the fairies, and with the devil. This wickedness must be extinguished." He shook his head again. "I am sorry, Margaret, but there is no hope for Isobel Gowdie."

Margaret glared at him and raised her voice. "In that case, all the more reason for me to see her and bring what solace I can!"

Alexander studied her, almost as if seeing her for the first time. No longer his niece's little girl, she was a young woman now, and quite certain of her convictions. Perhaps he saw something of his daughter Grissel in her—a woman who did not hesitate to speak her mind, even to powerful men. He turned his head to face the tollbooth in the solitary gloom behind him. "I will speak to the sheriff."

Margaret climbed the tower steps. Pity was not the only thing she felt. As she stomped and huffed, her eyes grew wet with anger. How could Isobel have done this to her? How could she have used her magic against Margaret's father? Behind her, the jailer jangled his keys and followed her up the steps.

The stairway was dark, with a trace of light coming from each window as they passed. And the smell! Margaret covered her nose with her handkerchief. It was rank and sour . . . a hundred years of desolation and fear. As she approached Isobel's cell, the stench grew stronger: feces, urine, and sweat combined. Margaret was glad she had to sit outside the door. The jailer, a frightening man with a dirty leather jerkin, disappeared back down the tower stairs.

Margaret looked through the grate guarding the door. At first, she could see nothing in the room except the gray stone of walls and floor, uneven, chipped, and dirty. Then something moved in the corner: a creature in rags, with clumps of hair sticking out from a bald head, like an etching she had seen of a monster. No wonder they thought this woman was evil.

When Isobel saw Margaret, she raised herself up and limped to the door— hobbling, barely able to move, vacant eyes staring without comprehension. Reaching the door, she dropped instantly back onto the floor. Isobel's bald head was covered with sores, bloodstains spotted her skirt, and she was so weak and emaciated that Margaret hardly recognized the strong, earthy woman she had known. Her heart ached at the sight, and her anger began to melt.

"Thou hast heard me callin', Lady Margaret."

"What?" Margaret sank down and sat on the floor, where the reek was not so strong. "I did hear you, Isobel." She coughed and covered her mouth. "But I thought—"

"I was able to go in the shape of a crow," Isobel replied in a faint voice that rang hollow from weakness. "But now, I have lost my powers."

"What have they done to you?" Margaret cried out.

"They tried to make me confess, and I would not. But now I am ready."

"To confess? To witchcraft?"

"I have done many evil deeds that I am sorry for."

Margaret let out a breath, and with it, her anger dissipated entirely. Who was this person, this creature wilted on the floor on the other side of the bars? "Then it is true? You have used black magic?" Even though she knew of her wicked intent, Margaret still thought of Isobel as a cunning woman, a healer. This picture of her as evil, as maleficent, was too hard to grasp.

"When I was out with the fairy man, there was a man I killed, and I am sore afflicted with sorrow about it."

"Killed? But how?"

"I killed him with the elf arrow. There were many of us, Elspeth Nychie and Jacob Taylor, Agnes Pierson, Lilias Dunlop and many more, all in my coven. And as the devil gave us the elf arrows, we shot and killed people."

Margaret thought of the stone Isobel had given her, the one she still thought of as a thunderstone. But no one could kill a person by flicking a stone off a thumbnail.

"And we did covenant with the devil," Isobel continued.

"The devil? Not William, your fairy man?"

"William *is* the devil, as Mister Harry said."

So, Mister Harry had given her the idea that her fairy man was the devil. Of course, Mister Harry believed that all fairies were devils. Probably, Isobel had heard his preaching on this so many times that she had come to believe it. "And do you now believe that all the fairies are devils?"

"Nay. The fairies are neither good nor bad. Sometimes, they are both. But they can catch you and tempt you, like William did, and then you can never escape." Isobel exhaled, sagging down a little more, as if she could hardly sit. "And I am sorry to you, too, Lady, for the curses I made on your father and brothers."

"But why, Isobel? Why did you do it?"

Isobel shook her head sadly. "We suffered such loss in the raid."

"When my father took the cattle and grain?"

"Aye. And the devil taught me the charms and the words, so I could have power, too."

"Power to kill?"

Isobel nodded and lowered her head.

They sat in silence, both women slumped on the floor. It was all so confusing. "But Isobel," Margaret said, remembering Mistress Collace's words, "my father and brother are alive. Your curse did not kill them. Perhaps you have been imagining the fairies and such?"

Isobel quivered, wobbling her head. Margaret reached her hand through the bars, and Isobel slowly extended hers to take it.

Why hadn't she brought her something to eat? The woman was feeble, and obviously hungry.

"She is so frail and thin," Margaret said to Uncle Alexander. "They are not feeding her, Uncle. And no one empties the chamber pot. You must do something."

"Not feeding her? This must not continue. The woman needs strength to stand at trial." He turned back toward the tollbooth. "I will arrange it."

Margaret's life was turning again, this time in another direction. What she knew and understood to be true now seemed as shaky as a boulder teetering on the edge of a mountainside. She had seen magic and the way it healed. She had heard the crow, and seen both her brother Malcolm and her grandmother, even though they were dead. She had even heard Isobel's voice calling her. These things were not evil. They were a part of the world that most people didn't know or see. They didn't conflict with Margaret's Christian beliefs, but now everyone, including Isobel, was convinced that all of it was of the devil—and that Isobel had consorted with him. Could that be true, as well? Or was Mistress Collace correct that it was all delusion?

CHAPTER 48

E very inch of the kirk was filled. People were packed into every pew, crowded along the side aisles, and standing in the back. Most of the commissioners were in the front pew, while Mister Harry and Uncle Alexander sat on a dais facing them.

Margaret sat beside Mistress Collace in the family pew. Being in kirk for a witch trial . . . how different it felt, how unreal. She knew there had been other trials in this place, when people were tried for working on Sunday or adultery. But to be in this place of worship for the purpose of condemning someone to death? That was wrong. How could she bear to live in such a place as this?

Margaret trembled, clutching the edge of her cape. Isobel, who had been so full of life and strength in her own milieu, the world of nature, of earth and sky, now stood fragile and alone in a chamber of hostility. Uncle Alexander must have arranged better care, though, because she did look cleaner and stronger.

The men sat like pillars of stone: Henrietta's father, Mister Hugh, Uncle Alexander, and Margaret's own father. These were the same men she had once known as kind and protective, all of that in another lifetime. Faces blank or twisted in deceit, they sat there looking important. They were ready to put Isobel to death. How could Margaret bear it? Her head fell down over her chest.

She rubbed and twisted the wool in her fingers. She was cast down, lost like the pilgrim in the book by Elizabeth Melville.

Margaret sat up. The people around her were talking and laughing as if it were any Sunday before kirk. Was Andrew here? She didn't see him.

There was Henrietta on the other side of the room. She was sitting beside her mother, Lady Anne, and looking at Margaret. Henrietta mouthed the words *I'm sorry*. Margaret felt such joy, and sadness too, at the sight of that pale face and the wispy red hair slipping out from under her bonnet. Margaret lowered her head again. She hadn't visited her friend in so long. If anyone should be sorry, it was she. Henrietta was living in exile, and now she was offering sympathy to Margaret.

The room was filled with noise and chaos. People argued and shouted, standing up and shoving, pushing to get a seat. In their midst, Margaret's family was quiet. Mother had rested for some days and had now declared that her cough was almost gone.

It was all so strange, like something Shakespeare could have written—but worse, because this was real. Isobel, who had always sat quietly in the back of the kirk with her family, was now the center of attention, forced to stand between the commissioners and Mister Harry. The crowd yelled, jostled, and shouted insults at her and each other, while Isobel, motionless, gazed out the window. She stood, forlorn but dignified, like a lone tree on the machair buffeted by wind and weather.

But now Isobel's body began to bend, as if the tree could no longer withstand the wind, and she buckled over. As she began to fall, Mister Hugh rushed to catch her and help her stand, and the commissioners argued amongst themselves until someone brought her a chair. Isobel sank into it as she sat down. People in the pews stood up to look at her. Her every move was significant, a thing to marvel at or scorn.

Mister Harry stood and cleared his throat. The room had quieted, but still echoed with muttering as he began the opening prayer. It lasted ten long minutes, during which time the rustling, voices, and shoving grew louder and louder.

Finally, the prayer ended, and the notary, Mister Innes, rose from his seat. "At Auldearn, on the third day of May 1662," he proclaimed in a quiet voice, "at the hour of two or three in the afternoon, in presence of John Innes, notary public, Master Harry Forbes, minister of the gospel, John Hay of Park and Lochloy, Alexander Brodie of Brodie, and diverse other witnesses, a confession and declaration was spoken forth of the mouth of Isobel Gowdie, spouse to Hugh Gilbert . . ."

Silence. The congregation, the commissioners, and Isobel all remained silent, as if the stone walls surrounding them had already absorbed this woman into death and the history embedded here.

Mister Harry spoke. "Isobel Gowdie, you have confessed to intercourse with the devil. Speak now before this congregation of your sin."

Isobel rose from her seat. She stood tall and lifted her chest, seeming to gain new strength. Eyes flashing, she addressed the crowd. "I first met with the devil betwixt the towns of Drumdevan and the Heads, and there, he spoke to me and appointed me to meet with him in the Kirk of Auldearn, which I did in the nighttime."

"Ooh! Ah!" Sounds of shock and disbelief erupted from the congregation, contrasting with Isobel's calm, almost merry voice.

"And what did you do there?"

"And there," she continued, "I denied my baptism and put one of my hands to the crown of my head and the other hand to the sole of my foot and renounced all betwixt my two hands over to the devil."

Margaret caught her breath. Mistress Collace took her hand and squeezed it.

"And what did the devil do?

"The devil cut my shoulder, sucked my blood, and spat it in his hand. He sprinkled it on my head, and said, "I baptize ye, Janet, in my own name."

Isobel stood firm, smiling grimly at Mister Harry.

Mister Harry coughed. "You have confessed to these heinous sins with the devil. And now you must tell, as you have admitted to me in private, of your carnal copulation with this vile creature."

Isobel glared at Mister Harry, raising her voice. "He had carnal copulation with me then, and frequently thereafter."

"And what did he look like?"

"He was a large, hairy man, and cold. I found his nature as cold within me as spring water. And he lay all heavy upon us in my coven and had carnal dealings with us like a stallion among mares. His member is exceedingly great and long. No man's member is so long and big."

There were more gasps and exclamations of shock, but the people remained still, spellbound throughout this recitation. Was Isobel talking about a real man she had met, or was this a product of her imagination? Or had she really met the devil?

"Sometimes, he wore boots, and sometimes shoes; but still, his feet were forked and cloven. He was sometimes with us as a deer or roe."

Mister Hugh rose heavily from his seat. "And who else was with you in your coven?"

Isobel looked around the room and smiled, her body alert. "There are thirteen persons in each coven, and each of us has a spirit to wait upon us. There is one called Swane, who waits upon Maggie Burnet in Auldearn—"

"The alewife!" came a shout from the crowd.

"Nay!" a woman's shrill voice cried.

"Hush!" another voice commanded.

Isobel continued. "He is a young devil clothed in grass green, and the said Maggie Burnet has the nickname of Pickle Nearest the Wind. The next spirit is called Rorie, and he is clothed all in yellow, and he waits on Bessie Wilson in Auldearn."

Margaret's mouth fell open. Bessie, who was sitting at the end of the pew, went red and shook her fist. "Liar!" she shouted.

Margaret's mother, Lady Elizabeth Brodie, then stood up and called out, "Fairy tales, m'lairds. Do not believe these tales!"

Margaret was hard pressed to take it in. It was all happening so fast—Isobel talking about carnal copulation with the devil, Bessie accused of being in a coven, her mother shouting out loud in the kirk.

"Silence!" Mister Harry shouted as Mister Gordon, the beadle, marched down the aisle and threatened both Bessie and Mother with the mace.

"Please continue, Mistress Gowdie," said Mister Harry in a quiet voice.

"How many are there in your coven?" Mister Hugh asked.

"There are thirteen persons in my coven." Isobel went on to name seven other women, including Mister Harry's servant girl, Agnes Pierson; Jane Martin, whom she called the "maiden" of the coven; Elspeth Nychie; Lilias Dunlop, the seamstress; and one man, Jacob Taylor. She gave the names of all of their spirits: The Roaring Lion, Mak Hector, the Thief of Hell, and Robert the Jacks in addition to her own spirit, Red Reiver. Each coven member had a fanciful nickname. Jane Martin's was Over the Dyke with It, and Bessie Wilson was called Through the Cornyard.

By this time, the crowd was in uproar. As Isobel went on to name other people and nearby covens, it was all Mister Gordon could do to keep the noise down to a level at which she could be heard.

"She'll name the whole of Auldearn!" someone shouted. "The whole of Moray!"

Uncle Alexander rose and faced the congregation. "We will hear the confession," he declared, "or those who create disturbance will leave the kirk." The shouts died down to murmurs as he turned back to Isobel. "And what is the magic," he said with a wince, "that you perform with your devils?"

Isobel turned and addressed the congregation, most of whom made up her usual audience in the farmtown. "Jacob Taylor and Elspeth Nychie, his wife Lilias Dunlop, and I myself met in the kirk yard of Nairn, and we raised an unchristened child out of its grave; and at the end of Bradley's cornfield land, just opposite to the mill of Nairn, we took said child, with the nails of our fingers and toes, pickles of all sorts of grain and blades of kale, and hacked them all very small, mixed together . . ."

"No!" cried one woman, as two others wept noisily.

". . . and did put a part thereof among the muckheaps, and thereby took away the fruit of his grains, and we parted it among two of our covens."

"Have you done this before?" asked one of the men.

"When we take grains at Lammas, we take but about two sheaves, when the grains are full; or two stalks of kale, and that gives us the fruit of the cornland or kale yard, where they grow. And it may be, we keep it until Yule or Pasche, then divide it amongst us."

"And what other harm have you done?" Mister Harry asked.

Isobel stooped over, sinking back into the chair and loosening her hair from the cap. Her body hung down heavily and she swayed from side to side, pulling at her hair. "Alas!" she wailed. "I deserve not to be sitting here, for I have done so many evil deeds, especially the killing of men. I deserve to be riven upon with iron harrows and worse, if that could be devised."

Mistress Collace's head bowed over her lap, and Margaret held her hand tightly. Now they would surely execute this woman. Such sorrow, such deep sadness and misery, such loss. There had been so much death in this place—Mistress's children one by one, and now to hear of Isobel digging up a baby from the grave and using it like an ingredient in her potions. Margaret sat stunned by all that Isobel had said. A gray fog surrounded her and the whole congregation as if they, too, were dead, without feeling or thought, wandering ghosts in an endless dungeon.

CHAPTER 49

The sun was still bright in the sky as the Hay family sat down for the evening meal at eight. Through the open windows came the sounds of people working in the fields.

To think that life could go on as usual after such desolation! Margaret was reeling on the inside at the image of Isobel stooped and wailing, and the thoughts of what she had done. Margaret could not reconcile any of this with the picture she had held for so long of Isobel surrounded by light and music.

Mistress Collace sat at table with them, as did Andrew, who glanced at Margaret with smiling eyes. He had not attended the trial, and she was comforted by his attention in the midst of her misery . . . but this same attention was also disturbing. He was eager to get married, as was she, but not yet! Margaret didn't want to think of leaving home, of moving with him to England—and then the marriage bed, which would become the birthing bed, and then, inevitably, a place of pain and death. Did she really want to stay in this land of fear and vengeance and murder?? According to Andrew, England was more civilized, and Chesire a beautiful land. Could Margaret leave all she'd known here—her home and family?

They were talking about the witch trial, a subject that was surely on the mind of every person in Auldearn and Nairn.

"There is no question that this woman is guilty of witchcraft," John Hay asserted.

"But," Lady Elizabeth protested, "what evidence is there that she has done actual harm?"

"What harm?" he thundered. "The witch has raised the wind and caused Mister Harry to fall and break a leg, as well the sandstorm that ruined the crops. She cast a spell to keep Harry from healing. She has put a curse on *this family*. She has made a covenant with the devil. All confessed by her."

"She did talk at length about her bizarre deeds," Elizabeth replied in a more measured voice. "Turning herself into a hare and being chased by a dog, flying through the night with the devil, raising the wind with a charm, killing people in the fields. And condemning *our* Bessie as one of her coven. Really, John, how can we credit such tales with belief?"

"This woman cursed the males of the Hay family. Do you believe 'twas an accident that our recently-born son died in one week?"

Everyone froze. Mother glared at Father.

"That curse came *after* the baby died, Father." Margaret's voice was barely audible, her head hung down.

"I find her tales quite fascinating," Andrew interjected.

Father frowned at him.

"I have read records of other witch confessions," Andrew went on. "And her testimony follows a known tradition. The stories of a covenant with the devil, and so on—these have all been reported in similar stories by other witches." Bessie leaned over to take his plate, stepped back, and paused behind him to listen. "But this woman adds such embellishments," he continued with a wave of his hand, "and in poetic language."

"It *was* fanciful stuff," Mother said. "It reminded me of Shakespeare . . . like the witches in *Macbeth*."

Margaret looked up. "I thought you disapproved of Shakespeare, Mother."

"I disapprove of your reading Shakespeare before you complete your religious education. But to complete your education as a woman, you will read it. He is the foremost author of our century."

"Shakespeare took some of Macbeth's story from the history books," Andrew added. "From King James's tome on witchcraft, in fact. King James believed that a witch raised the wind and caused a storm to destroy his ship at sea. Shakespeare tells the same story in *Macbeth*."

Mistress Collace, who had been unusually quiet, now spoke in a contemplative tone. "Then much of what this woman says and practices has been said and done before. Yet she does not read, nor do her associates, so how could they learn such things?"

"Her mother was a witch, an evil woman who caused the death of my father and brother," Father said, glancing up at his wife—who, he knew, did not believe this.

"The tradition of fairies, elves, and witches goes far back in this land." Mother sighed. "The peasants do believe it all, and I'm sure these magical practices are passed from one generation to the next. But with the Reformation, and now the Restoration, we hope to bring greater light and love into their lives."

"I do agree, Lady Elizabeth," Mistress Collace replied. "Would that we could teach them, *show* them, a finer understanding, the higher truths of our Lord."

"I see that we are not in accord on this matter," said Father, "but be advised that the leaders in the kirk and in the region know, as do I, that the only way to eradicate this wickedness is to destroy it."

After dinner, Margaret and Andrew walked the castle grounds. Her feet took her naturally to the path toward the sea, and so they strolled between the fields of flax, now blooming again as if the terrible sandstorm of the past year had never happened.

Andrew took her hand. "When shall we be married, my love?"

"Oh!" Margaret was surprised by his bold declaration. "I don't think I am ready to set a date yet, Andrew. There is so much that remains unsettled in my mind."

"Unsettled? In your affections for me?"

"Oh, no, not that. It's only that I have been so troubled by this trial."

"You have feelings for the witch?"

Feelings? She gazed down over the fields, the farmtown invisible now except for a few distant wisps of smoke, the sea beyond. Andrew had scoffed at her sympathy with Isobel, and he clearly thought that fairies were only superstition. She looked up at him, his face so open and caring. But he did love her. And she loved him. She could trust Andrew with the truth. "I know you do not believe it, but I am convinced that she has extraordinary powers. She found Henrietta, and afterward, she used charms and rituals to cure Henrietta of her wounds. And yes, I visited her in the tollbooth, and I felt such compassion for her suffering."

"Do you believe in her magic?"

"Some of it. The songs to mark the hours and days, the rhymes for the plants and the animals. These things are real, Andrew, and a comfort to the soul in ways that our kirk is not. They find the spirit in nature and link our spirits with the Earth. What Mother said about this being a long tradition is correct, no doubt; but the tradition is not all bad. It's a way for people to make sense of life, and God within it."

"Well said!" Andrew exclaimed. "Though it is not something to be shouted from the rooftops."

"No. But if we are to be married, you should know my deepest thoughts, and I yours."

Andrew turned and took Margaret's other hand, smiling into her eyes. "There is no one with whom I would rather converse."

She looked into his sweet face and felt a familiar warmth in her body. *All will be well*, she thought.

They walked along the ridge that skirted the farmtown. Below, in the farm-yard, children were playing, and a woman came out of one of the huts. She watched the children, then lifted a square of peat from a stack and carried it back inside. Ahead of them, the sea roiled and churned.

"But what about the other side of that tradition?" he asked. "The witching?"

Margaret sighed. "This is what burdens my soul. The things Isobel said, about the devils and spirits and the evil she caused."

"She is a very imaginative woman. In another class of society, in another time and place, perhaps, Isobel Gowdie would be a poet."

"Yes. I think that is part of her charm. She is a storyteller in the farmtown. But Mistress Collace convinced me that much of her own story is imagined. It must be, because some of the elements don't make sense. I don't believe she has the power to kill people with her magic arrows."

"No. But most of Auldearn *does* believe that."

"Including my father." Margaret sank down onto the sand. "How can I think of marriage when they are going to murder Isobel? My father is going to burn her at the stake!"

"Simply for inventing stories."

"Not only the stories. She performed the rituals, said the curses, and wished evil upon my family, and that is a great wound to me. There is no evidence that her curses caused harm. The sandstorm came, but she couldn't have created that. Mister Harry fell from his horse and lay in bed, but her potions didn't keep him sick. My little brother was ill and died, but that had been expected since his birth. But they all believe that she is the cause. *She* believes it."

Andrew sat down beside Margaret and picked a flax flower. "In England, witch trials have all but died out. There are so many questions, and questionable executions. Women tortured and forced to confess. The educated people have come to understand that belief in fairies and magic and witches is superstition. This superstition was held by the common people, but also by the ruling class that executed them. Now that the magistrates and judges are more educated, they see no need for witch hunts."

"England."

"It's where I would like to take you."

The two sat in silence, gazing out over the farmtown toward the horizon and the sea. Andrew's presence was ardent and tender and sparked within Margaret deep affection and excitement. Even though he didn't believe exactly as she did, there was something exactly right about being with Andrew. If he left Morayshire without her, there would be nothing but dreary emptiness here.

HARRY

CHAPTER 50

Alexander Brodie cleared his throat. "Let us begin our deliberations."

After her confession, Isobel had been taken back to the tollbooth. The men were now sitting in a circle formed by chairs and the front pew. They had eaten a meal at the alehouse provided by Maggie Burnet, one of the women Isobel had named as part of her coven. Maggie, in her white cap and smudged apron, had bustled around them, insisting that she was innocent. "Thou knowest me, m'lairds," she proclaimed. "The alewife I am, and never a witch!" They had eaten hastily and come back to the kirk.

Harry sighed. "'Tis a troubling task, gentlemen, to understand the workings of the devil. I know that some believe I am too zealous in my pursuit of evil and my desire to bring salvation to Auldearn, but it is my hope to save just one more lost soul." He studied the faces around him, not sure whether the others were on his side.

Hugh Rose wiped his high forehead and balding pate, then raised a finger. "Isobel Gowdie has told us many a tale and many accounts of her *good* deeds. She claims to have a cure for a baby who has been bewitched: transferring the evil spell to a dog or cat. She claims to heal bruises and sores with her magic. And, I must say, I admire the poetry of her speech."

"Admire?" Harry almost spat out the word. "Is there anything to admire in this creature?" Of course, there was something *he* had admired, at least before her time in the tollbooth—but he would not reveal that here.

"All of this *is* magic, of course," continued Mister Hugh, "and not the work of the Lord. The remainder of her confession tells of her numerous evil deeds. These things are so wicked, so staggering in their wickedness, that they are hard to comprehend." He shook his head.

"Her relations with the devil are the most troubling of all," Alexander Brodie remarked. "To think that she would renounce her baptism in our Lord Jesus Christ and submit to baptism with this demon."

"But these tales are so fantastical," commented Alex Dunbar, the schoolmaster in Auldearn, a tall man with red hair and beard. "This meeting with the devil in the kirk, and the devil sucking her blood and having carnal copulation with her . . . how can this be believed?"

George Phinney, an official from Kirkmichael, leaned forward in his seat. Phinney was the broadest man in the room, and his bright red doublet emphasized his bulk. "Is she imagining this, or is there a *man* she met in the kirk, someone large and hairy whom she took to be the devil? Perhaps she committed adultery, and means to cast blame on the devil?"

"That explanation holds water," said Dunbar. He cocked his head and cast a glance at the men around the circle.

"But then, would she add all the other adventures simply to justify this one action?" Mister Hugh asked. "No; it is clear to me that this woman has, indeed, dealt in black magic. Whether in a real or a symbolic way, she has trafficked with the devil and the demons of hell."

"Symbolic?" Mister Harry cried. "Do you not see, then, Hugh, how very real this evil is? I myself have felt proof of this. When I was abed with fever and swellings, these women came to witch me, and made me suffer greatly."

Brodie nodded, but remained silent. Did Brodie believe him or not?

Harry winced. He himself served as titular head of the commission, but Brodie's vote would carry the most weight.

"There are so many details to her story, and she seems to add more and more as she speaks." Dunbar spread his arms. "It's as though she is inventing things as she goes along."

George Phinney rubbed his mustache. "Undoubtedly, the woman is mad."

John Innes cleared his throat. Innes was a lawyer and scholar, and as notary, he was fastidious in his recording of Isobel's words. "I have read numerous accounts of these trials, and it is remarkable how these witches repeat the same stories of their doings: the Black Mass, the rebaptism, night flights, destroying the crops . . . all that we have heard here, and almost in the same words. But this woman adds fascinating detail that has never been heard before."

"Would this not, then, be the proof of her guilt?" asked Mister Hugh.

"Or proof of her imagination and inventiveness?" Dunbar added.

"She herself admits her guilt and expresses sincere repentance," Brodie observed.

Harry smiled, knowing, as they all did, that confession and repentance were not a means of absolving guilt, and would serve only to satisfy her executioners that her soul was prepared to meet God.

Brodie raised an eyebrow. "Can you read us one of those statements, John?"

Innes riffled through his book and found the page. "'Alas!'" he quoted, "'I deserve not to be sitting here, for I have done so many evil deeds, especially the killing of men. I deserve to be riven upon with iron harrows and worse, if it could be devised.'"

"But I say!" exclaimed Dunbar. "This 'killing of men.' What on earth could that mean? There was one man she named, William Bower, a miller in Moynes. I knew Bower. He was already dying of consumption. How could Mistress Gowdie claim responsibility, while flying through the night or otherwise? To me, this indicates that much of her testimony is fabrication, perhaps due to morbid and unrealistic guilt."

"Some do believe, "Brodie said, "that this woman is mad—a case of possession by the devil. And she certainly has given us testimony that she was coerced. It may be that her dealings with the devil were involuntary?" He glanced at Harry, then at Innes. "Can you read something which points to that, John?"

As Innes searched through his book, Brodie and Phinney lit their pipes. Harry crossed his legs and jiggled his foot at a feverish pace. Had he been too zealous?

"Ah, here is one example," Innes said. "She tells how the devil subjugated the women into subservience with beatings. 'He would be beating and scourging us all up and down with cards (the wooden implements used for carding wool) and other sharp scourges, and we would be crying, *Pity! Pity! Mercy! Mercy, our Lord,* but he would have neither pity nor mercy. When he would be angry at us. He would grin at us like a dog, as if he would swallow us up.' And in another place, she says, 'He made us believe there was no other God but him.'"

Mister Hugh bowed his head, shaking it from side to side. "Twisting the words of the Ten Commandments."

"It is as I thought," said Brodie. "The women were subjugated, enslaved almost, to this demon, whether in their imaginations or otherwise."

"The theory of possession is persuasive to me," Dunbar declared.

"But, if she was possessed," countered Harry, "then all the more reason for her execution. A madwoman possessed by the devil, and one who has much influence on her countrymen, is certainly a danger to our society."

"And to our religion," Hugh added. "Our faith is based upon righteousness and truth."

"We are commissioned by the Lord himself to eradicate iniquity," Harry continued. "And we must seek out the other witches in the coven."

"But," Dunbar protested, "is this not madness in itself? She has named so many—at least fifteen other women, and two men. Do we try all of them, as well?"

"And does not this long list of names also speak to the fact of her madness?" Phinney asked.

Harry raised his hand to interrupt the discussion. "Gentlemen," he said, "Isobel Gowdie has confessed to witchcraft, and she is aware of the gravity of her sin. It is not only biblical, but also the law of the land, that a witch must be condemned to death."

John Hay, the Laird of Park, had been silent up to this point, but now he spoke. "And we do know that this woman's mother was also a witch. Agnes Grant's evil curses killed my father and my brother. There can be no doubt that these curses carry the power of the devil to destroy."

"We must examine her once more," pronounced Brodie, "before our final verdict."

Harry sighed again. He had not expected such differing opinions from these men.

MARGARET

CHAPTER 51

Margaret and her mother stepped down from the carriage into a crowd of people around the kirk. Isobel's fame had spread throughout the countryside, and the kirk was now filled with not only the Auldearn congregation, but also lairds and gentry as well as farmers, merchants, and craftsmen from all parts of Moray. The lower classes, the peasants and laborers, had been turned back from the door in favor of more important people, and had to stand outside. As they passed through the kirkyard, children ran about and the people shouted and laughed, eating the bannocks and dried fish they had brought, drinking from flagons of ale, and generally enjoying a festive atmosphere.

Lilias Dunlop, who was carrying a large basket, and buxom Agnes Pierson stood a few paces from the others. Some of the farmtown folk huddled and muttered to one another, glancing at Lilias and Agnes and directing slurs in their direction. "Poisonous toad!" hissed Jonet Fraser. "Eel-skinned witch!"

"No more a witch than thee, Jonet Fraser!" shouted Agnes. "Thou flap-mouthed traitor!"

Inside the kirk, everyone sat in their pew. When John Innes stood, the crowd fell silent. He lifted his book and read, "At Auldearn, on the twenty-seventh day of May 1662, Master Harry Forbes, minister at Auldearn; Mr. Alex Dunbar, schoolmaster and clerk of the session of Auldearn; George Phinney of Kirkmichael; John Hay of Auldearn; and Alexander Brodie of Forres witnessed the confession of Isobel Gowdie, spouse to Hugh Gilbert of Lochloy. On said day, Isobel professed repentance for her former sins of witchcraft, and confessed she had been overlong in the devil's service. Without any compulsion, she proceeded in her confession, in manner following . . ."

Isobel, who had been imprisoned in the tollbooth for over a month, stood in front of the congregation and raised her head. Her dress hung limp on her gaunt body, and her eyes, magnified in her sunken face, stared into some mysterious place beyond the ceiling. "I acknowledge, to my great grief and shame, that fifteen years hence, I denied Father, Son, and Holy Ghost, in the Kirk of Auldearn, and gave over my body and soul to the devil."

Margaret was again sitting between Mistress Collace and her mother. *Fifteen years? How could that be? That must have been part of her fantasy world, as Mistress Collace said.*

The kirk was quieter this time, a crowd of rapt, staring faces, ears straining to hear every word.

Isobel then repeated, almost word for word, her other statements, but now elaborated in greater detail. She spoke of her coven falling to their knees with their hair loose, bowing to the devil, who had taught them many terrible things. She had seemed so weak when she came in, but now she stood up tall and spoke clearly. How had she rallied this strength and power?

The congregation watched her, mesmerized, so similar to the circle that had surrounded her at Beltane, when her stories had filled the people around the fire with awe. Could it be that she had slipped back into her position as storyteller, as performer, and was inventing this story as she told it? Could she now be lifting herself out of this place by saying these words? Would saying the words make them true?

"He marked me on the shoulder and sucked out my blood and spit it in his hand. He sprinkled it on my head and baptized me as Janet, in his own name. After that, he had carnal copulation with me in the New Wards of Inshoch; and many times thereafter, at our pleasure."

Mister Harry stood. "What pleasure could you have in copulation with the devil?"

"He would lie with us in the presence of all the multitude, and we would never refuse him. He would come in the shape of a deer, or any other shape. The youngest and swiftest women would have very great pleasure in carnal copulation with him, yea, much more than with their own husbands; and they would have exceedingly great delight of it with him, as much as he could have to them, and never think shame in it. He is abler that way than any man can be. Alas! That I could compare him to any man!"

Margaret held her head in her hands as the congregation sat in silence, the commissioners shifting uncomfortably in their seats. This was an expansion on Isobel's previous description of her relations with the devil. But why was Mister Harry smiling?

After a period of silence, Uncle Alexander rose. "What are the names of the others in your coven?"

"The names of the coven are these: Bessie Wilson in Auldearn, Elspeth Nychie, there, Jane Martin the maiden, Margaret Hay in Auldearn—"

"Margaret Hay!" someone shouted. "Aah!" The crowd erupted in outcries, and Mother let out a wail. Father stood up from his seat in the front pew, his face so red he looked about to explode. "How dare you!" he roared and raised his fist, as if about to attack Isobel. George Phinney restrained him while Brodie led him back to his seat.

Margaret was speechless and sat frozen to the pew. Everyone in the kirk turned to look at her, and now the side aisles were packed with people gawking. Mistress Collace took her hand.

Uncle Alexander Brodie turned to face the congregation, Mister Gordon the beadle beside him holding the mace. "We will hear the rest of the confession," he announced, and the crowd gradually quieted down. Margaret choked and gasped for breath while Mistress put her arm around her. The people thought she was a witch!

Isobel, who had stood motionless throughout the uproar, spoke again, and again seemed eager to talk and tell her story in spite of the consequences that might follow. She didn't even look at Margaret. It was as if she had no idea how what she had just said might affect her.

In rapid order, she named Maggie Burnet, Agnes Pearson, and many others, and again, the nicknames the devil had bestowed upon them; but this time, instead of "spirits," she called the helpers "devils that waited upon us." She described how she had seen the elves making the elf arrows, and how the devil had taught the coven to shoot people with them. Each member of the coven had shot and killed fauns, hares, or people, and she herself had shot at Harry Forbes and John Hay, though she said she had missed. Margaret heard all of this as if from a distance, somewhere outside the frozen place her head was in.

Alex Dunbar held up his hand. "Mistress Gowdie," he interrupted. "In your last confession, you called the helpers 'spirits,' but now you call them 'devils.' What is the meaning of this change?"

Isobel looked at Mister Harry, who was still smiling, and lowered her head. "Twas Mister Harry made me see," she murmured, "that the spirits are truly devils."

Margaret barely heard this last bit of confession, so shaken was she with sobs. Mistress Collace reached over her and tapped her mother on the arm. "I will take her out," she whispered. Mother nodded, and Margaret rose with Mistress, who led her out of the kirk, past hostile stares and muffled exclamations of "Devil's whore!" and "Witch!" At the doorway, someone spat upon her.

KATHARINE

❧

CHAPTER 52

Katharine paced back and forth in the drawing room while Lucy sat on the horsehair sofa and watched. Margaret had flung off her cap, shaken her hair loose, and run up the stairs, wailing. They heard her door slam shut.

Lady Elizabeth came into the room. "She will not answer my knock."

"Yes, Lady Elizabeth," Katharine replied. "I have tried several times, but to no avail."

"Will they put her on trial, too?" Lucy asked. Lucy had been at the spinning wheel, and had rushed to the drawing room when Katharine came in.

"Oh, no!" Lady Elizabeth dropped into the nearest chair and held her head in her hands. "This could not be true. Our Margaret, accused of witchcraft? How could this happen? Mistress Collace, do you know how this could be?"

"I knew that Margaret met this Isobel Gowdie, and that she believed this woman helped the Lady Henrietta." Katharine sat down and brought her hands together in her lap. "She was interested in magic, and we had several discussions that I thought were instructive. I explained about the ignorance of believing in magic charms, and the evil in it."

Lucy clenched her hands together. "I heard Margaret reciting a charm," she burst out.

Both women looked up sharply. "A charm?" Lady Elizabeth asked.

"Yes, reciting the names of the saints: Saint Brigid, Saint Michael, Saint Brendan, and—"

"And she spoke a charm for me when I was ill," said her mother. "Harmless enough, I thought at the time, but now . . ."

Katharine noticed that mother and daughter were now staring at the doorway.

Margaret was standing there, her tear-stained face glowering. "You would have me to the stake, as well?" she sobbed. "My own family! Thinking me a witch!"

"Nay, nay, dear Lassie," Katharine murmured, approaching Margaret and reaching to cradle her in her arms. "How could anyone believe that?"

Margaret

CHAPTER 53

From the tower stairs came the sound of Bessie's voice, and then she was in the room, beaming at Margaret. "Lieutenant Massie to see the Lady Margaret." Bessie stepped aside as Andrew entered.

Andrew's face was pale, and his body tense. He looked intently at the group of silent women, then bowed to Margaret's mother. "May I speak with Lady Margaret, my lady?"

"Yes, of course, Andrew," she answered, waving the two of them away with her hand.

Margaret looked up from the chair where she had dropped, wiped her eyes, and smiled wanly. Andrew would be a comfort and provide some steadiness in this world gone awry.

The pair stepped out of the castle and into a soft rain. Everything was a blur of mist and fog. Margaret pulled up the hood of her cloak, and Andrew walked with his head down, a wide-brimmed hat hiding his face.

Margaret clutched at the neck of her cloak and bent over to see Andrew's face, but his countenance was grim and forbidding. She stumbled. What did that mean?

He quickened his pace, and she had to run to keep up. "Where are you going?"

"To the barn."

"But why?"

He didn't answer.

When they got to the barn, Andrew marched inside. Ceiling timbers arced high above them to the apex of the roof. A groom at the far end watched them come in, then turned back to his work. In the stalls, horses snorted and moved about, and the damp air intensified the smells of the animals and seasoned wood. Miranda whinnied when she saw Margaret. All of these were smells and sounds that Margaret loved, that usually made her feel warm and comforted. Today, they barely registered.

Andrew turned around. "Why did you not tell me about this coven?"

"Coven?" Margaret shrank back toward Miranda. "But how—do you think—?" She gasped. "Do you think I am a witch?"

"I certainly do not know, do I? Isobel Gowdie thinks you are, and she has named you as a member of her coven. Are you?"

"Andrew! How could you think that of me?"

"What should I think? You have talked about magic, and a witch claims you as one of them. I must know the whole truth. I won't be married to a witch."

Margaret thrust out her chin. "I am not a witch, Andrew, and if you do not trust me or believe me, then I agree! We should not be married. Marriage has to be based on trust. For you even to suspect me of this evil wounds me deeply."

"Margaret, can you not see how this looks?" Andrew paced back and forth, holding the side of his head. In the stall behind Margaret, Miranda gave an agitated whinny and stomped her hooves.

Margaret glared at him. "The other day, you said witchcraft was all superstition, and that in England, people are too educated to believe in it. And now you fear that *I* am a witch?"

"Just tell me, please—what was your involvement with this woman?"

"I visited her a few times. But—" Margaret turned into Miranda's stall, patted her horse, and scratched under her ear. She laid her face down on the warm neck. "If only you could imagine what this confession has done to *me*, Andrew. They may bring me up for a trial. They may actually think, as you do, that I am a witch." She kept her face down.

"I do not really think you are a witch," Andrew admitted quietly.

"I don't know why she named me as being her coven. Perhaps because I wanted to learn about the fairies? And she taught me some charms. Good charms, with healing herbs and prayers. One I used to heal Mother of her cough."

"Charms. That is what they call their magical incantations. And you recited these charms. But you think they are like prayers?"

"Yes. And like poetry. They are what the cunning women use for healing a wound or a sickness." Margaret let go of Miranda but felt weighed down, heavy with the import of this talk. "And I thought Isobel was a cunning woman. She *is* a cunning woman. I didn't know about all the other." She looked up at him. "And the charms . . . Mistress Collace says they come from a Catholic tradition, prayers mixed in with magical beliefs, and so it is all evil."

"It *is* evil when used to hurt or kill."

"Yes." Margaret lowered her head. "I see that now, though I still believe that the healing part is good."

"No matter whether or not anyone believes that these evil charms work, or whether she actually flew on straws and trafficked with the fairies," he said, his voice softening, "they will condemn her for her language and these rituals."

"I am so confused now, Andrew. Mister Harry and my father do believe that the charms can sicken and kill, though Mistress says that though they are evil, that, too, is superstition."

He shifted from foot to foot. "Some of what she said is so horrific as to chill the blood. This digging up of an unchristened baby and chopping it up; the curses against your father and brothers, the charms against Mister Harry."

"Enough to terrify me before even hearing my own name."

"Why did you not tell me of this association earlier?"

"Because I knew you sneered at magic, and I thought you would scorn me for it."

"I do disdain it, and I do believe it is all superstition, even the so-called 'good' magic. My esteem of your judgment has suffered."

Margaret buried her face in Miranda's mane.

After Andrew left, she clung to Miranda, crying deep, heaving sobs into her neck. Miranda stood patiently, giving a few little snorts of sympathy. Margaret hadn't been sure of wanting to marry Andrew at first, but now that she'd come around, *he'd* suddenly changed, gone cold and rejecting. He'd lost esteem for her. What did that mean? Did it mean he didn't love her anymore? That he was withdrawing his offer of marriage? How could she bear it? A life without Andrew, and now perhaps even prison? Or perhaps worse?

Margaret did the only thing that made any sense to her right now. She saddled Miranda and rode slowly out of the barn. Lying down on the horse's back as they ambled away from the castle, wandering this way and that, she felt the desolation of a world with no sunshine, no birds, no hope. She had lost everything.

When she sat up, Margaret saw that Miranda had been heading east toward Nairn. They had reached the estuary. Of course. Miranda knew where to take her.

At the manse, a servant girl holding a small child answered the door. As the baby babbled, Henrietta came up behind her, and the servant girl went back into the house.

The two friends stood in silence; Henrietta's countenance solemn as she gazed at Margaret. "You were named in the coven."

At that, Margaret crumpled. "Oh. Oh, Henrietta!" she cried.

"Come in," said Henrietta, putting her arm around Margaret and leading her into the drawing room. The interior was dark now at the end of the day, and as Margaret sank down onto a chair, Henrietta went about lighting the candles in the wall sconces, then sat to face her.

Margaret tore off her cap and grasped her hair. "You don't believe it, do you, dear friend?"

Henrietta hesitated, perhaps a moment too long, before saying, "No, of course not."

"But so many do, Henrietta. I was spat upon! And now I will be tried, as well."

"But if you are innocent, you have nothing to fear."

"Oh, my dear, you of all people should know the wrongness of that."

Henrietta softened then and sighed. "Yes, I know that innocence is often not a factor."

"George has not come back?"

"George will never come back. His father has forbidden the courtship and has put it about that I am already married to that MacDonald villain."

"Did they ever come to Kilrock to claim you?"

"No, and the English did help with that. Your young lieutenant was able to threaten them with something worse unless they stayed in their mountain lair. Mother and I have been here in Nairn for these past months."

Margaret hung her head. "I am sorry, Henrietta, that I have been so caught up in my own affairs that I have not visited you before this."

"The young lieutenant?" Henrietta smiled. "Courtship, I understand?"

"Ah!" Margaret yanked at her long curls. "All is lost, Henrietta! He, too, has abandoned me. He believes that I am a witch."

Miranda found their way home in the dark, and when Margaret stepped in the door, the castle was quiet. What did it matter now if she stayed out after dark? Soon, she would be with Isobel at the stake.

HARRY

CHAPTER 54

"Shall we call up these other people, the women and men named in the coven?" asked Mister Hugh. Harry remained silent as the commissioners looked at John Hay, Laird of Park.

"Spite and libel!" Park exclaimed. "This woman is filled with bitterness toward me and my family, and this is why she seeks to implicate my daughter."

It had been a month since the last trial. Harry had just expounded upon the guilt of the prisoner. He had given a speech—more like a sermon, though somewhat shorter than the full hour that was the custom for homilies. He'd defended his belief that fairies and devils were real and present, threats to all people and perhaps more so to the pious. Isobel Gowdie, he said, had aligned herself with the devil to kill both him and the Laird of Park, as she herself had confessed.

And Mister Hugh had brought up the question of the other coven members.

"We must complete this trial first," John Innes said, "and then attend to the matter of the others accused."

"She even spoke of robbing the grave of an unchristened child, and using the body in her charms and potions," Harry expostulated. "Outrageous!"

"Yes, that is, indeed, a crime," Brodie said, "though not a sacrilege, as the child was not christened. But still, an unnatural and brutal act."

"Unimaginable!" Harry exclaimed. "And trying in various ways to cause *my* death, the death of one anointed of the Lord. She mixed her potions and spells and sent her minions to administer them to me. She flew with the devil and shot to kill me."

"Surely," interjected George Phinney, "you do not believe this woman flew through the air, able to kill with little stones?"

"'Tis absolute madness," cried Dunbar. "Do we execute a person for madness?"

Alexander Brodie sat silent as the debate continued. Dunbar and Phinney held to their rational disbelief of Isobel's tales, but both Harry and John Hay were equally convinced that they were true. It was true that Isobel's mother, Agnes Grant, had confessed to cursing and bewitching John's father and brother, though Harry knew Brodie remained uneasy with the methods of that interrogation. It was also true that both of the Hay male babies had died.

"I cannot deny the effectiveness of some of the curses," Brodie said. "People curse their neighbors for revenge—to stop a cow's milk, or to ruin a harvest. These things happen, but then the neighbor will utter his own curse and terrorize back. And on and on. There is so much venom and vengeance in this country. So much wickedness." Brodie bowed his body and shook his head. "Will it ever be possible to change those ways, to create the new and equitable society that Calvin envisioned? Will the way of Christ, of forgiveness and compassion, ever take hold? Or is it simply human nature to attack and defend, attack and defend, *ad infinitum?*"

It was a time of sadness for them all, Harry thought, as they all knew the truth and wisdom of Brodie's words.

Brodie stood. "Perhaps this woman *is* mad, but there is no question that she has some kind of power, and perhaps even a connection with another dimension of life."

"Aye," Mister Hugh agreed, "and in that dimension, she has covenanted with the devil to seek the death of Mister Harry and the Laird of Park."

"She is guilty of the crime of witchcraft," Harry pronounced to a round of *ayes.*

Brodie rose from his seat. "All who name Isobel Gowdie guilty of witchcraft, please stand."

Everyone stood except George Phinney and Alex Dunbar. Phinney looked around the group, then he reluctantly stood, too.

Brodie directed his gaze at Harry. "Prepare the prisoner for her death."

|SOBEL

CHAPTER 55

I took a small stone and etched another line on the wall. This was the twenty-fifth day of my imprisonment, I knew, because I had scratched one mark for each day. With the pricker coming at all hours to wake me and keep me awake, I was losing track of time, and only by the light from the window could I tell the difference between night and day. I had not had one night of sleep since I had been in this foul place.

At the window a gray drizzle through which daylight barely showed. Rain and more rain. It was dreary out there, but even more so in here. If only I could be out there, I would walk in that glorious wetness, be drenched and soaked, and feel the mud beneath my feet. So happy would I be that I would dance.

But now I could barely walk, much less dance.

I hefted my body away from the stinking pot with its three days-worth of shit and piss. Since I'd been here, with barely enough food and water to keep me alive, my pitiful droppings had become more potent and now smelled even worse.

Those men, the judges, they thought my confession was too proud, and so it was. I was proud of my powers, my flights and my feasts, and all my times with William. Who else could fly in the night with such a great laird? Who else received the powers of life and death? They were all jealous, not only Jonet Fraser and her like, but Mister Harry and the men.

But where was my William now?

He hadn't come to lift me up, to fly away and to dance. He hadn't come since the first time I talked to Mister Harry. I lay with eyes closed and conjured the sight of that brave and yellow-haired man, but never he came. Even the mickle black and cloven-footed one, the devil I pledged my life to, the one who had given me powers beyond thinking. He never came.

I could no longer see my fairy man, my William, the devil, my master. I could not fly on my steed. Nor could I visit the Queen of Fairy, nor the humped-back elves in the Downie Hill.

They would tie me to the stake and burn me, just as they had done my mother. And I would never see my children again.

I lay on the cold stone and wept.

My powers were gone.

But now came other visions. Creatures of fire, twisting and contorting into colors and shapes never imagined. They floated and swooped with bizarre grimaces, with voices like clanking of chains and screams of death, they came, snapping their fangs and clawing at my hair and face.

"Stop!" I cried. "Leave me be, you fiends!" I wailed and tore my hair. I thrashed and shouted, but my shouts lacked strength and the demons snarled and came closer, breathing their foul breath at me. "Go away! Be gone from here!"

I heard a laugh. The jailer, spying through the bars, was laughing at me.

I had opened my heart to the devil. I had killed a man. I had caused this. All of this. Through my own actions, I had raised these monsters and ghosts, and I couldn't go back. I deserved this torment.

My powers were gone.

Miserable creature that I was, I moaned and wept.

KATHARINE

❧

CHAPTER 56

Katharine sat across from Alexander Brodie in the great hall of Brodie Castle. Rain battered the windows like horse's hooves on a road, and the fireplace between them threw a faint warmth into the chill air.

Fingers steepled beneath his chin, Alexander was staring at the floor. "I have been long in prayer and contemplation on this matter, Katharine. And I have asked you here, dear lady, because I am sorely afflicted about this trial, and am under great indisposition of mind."

"'Tis indeed a troubling time, Alexander. This woman's testimonies and her deeds . . . who can know what she actually did?"

"Yes, and the commission was also torn, some believing in her deeds whilst others believe it all to be fabrication or madness. I felt caught betwixt and have turned to the Lord for an answer. I am led to seek your wisdom in this matter."

"Is not the matter then decided, Alexander? The execution date is set?"

He hung his head almost to his knees. "Yes, but I am loath to allow it to continue. I would seek your counsel."

"If there is a way to stop it—?" she asked, her gaze shifting to the rain-beaten window.

"Perhaps there is, if the decision be wrong with God."

"I mean not to criticize the wisdom of the lairds and ministers," Katharine said, hesitating, "but to me, this is the wrong decision. Mistress Gowdie does not traffic in reality, nor does she traffic with God. Her head and heart are with the fairies, and her thoughts take her to these imaginary places. She has been convinced that these places are the abode of the devil, and now she is smitten with guilt and despair."

"Then you do not believe that she has actually been with the devil? That she has committed these terrible deeds?"

"I believe she is a woman of sorrow and misery, with evil intent. In that sense, she has been with the devil. But I do not countenance relying upon force or violence against the enemy. It is not the enemy, but the Lord we must answer to."

"She has been brought low and expressed sorrow and repentance."

"And perhaps it is this way the Lord will bring her to him."

"If you will go to her, Katharine, I will stay the execution for a few days and convene another meeting with the commission."

"Tisn't right," the jailer said. "The witch is not to have visitors." He gave Katharine a foul look but opened the cell door, ceding to the Laird's authority. Behind her he grunted and muttered as his bulky body lumbered down the staircase.

Katharine sat on the stool as Isobel looked up warily from her spot on the floor. Such a rank smell filled this filthy room, lit by a single sliver of light from a candle the jailer had given her. She could barely see Isobel. "I am Katharine Collace."

"I know who you are, and I know that you are a friend to Mister Harry."

"I am friend to the anointed of the Lord. Yet I do not go in with everything said by Mister Harry."

"For me, it matters not who is a friend, nor who comes here. For soon, I will be in Hell." Isobel sighed and lay down on the floor.

"I see that your suffering is immeasurable," Katharine said.

Isobel looked up with curiosity.

"And it is at times of greatest affliction, even nigh to death, that the Lord is waiting for us."

Isobel shrugged.

"Perhaps you have never felt near to the Lord, but perhaps He is waiting for you now."

"My sins are so great; the Lord will have none of me."

"When we feel so far from God, then it is that God is most near."

Isobel looked puzzled.

"When I was in my greatest misery after my fifth child died, I was sure the Lord had abandoned me. In despair, I turned to prayer. That was when the Lord showed me his face."

"Would that I—"

"Ah, but you can, my dear. The Lord is waiting for you."

Katharine sat on the floor with Isobel and took her hand. "To desire a place of beauty and love is no sin, but you did not find that place with the fairies and the devils. You found only more pain and misery. When you find the true Christ, He binds you to him through love, not evil deeds. His beauty is much greater, and your ecstasy complete."

"But what I have done is so evil. I have killed and caused sickness and death." Isobel shook her head slowly. "I can never be forgiven."

"You must give all of that pain in your heart to God. That shame and guilt. This is the Covenanter way. Not to run away, but to see the tempest of misery and trust that it is only by forging through that peace will be found."

After Mistress Collace left, I felt a great peace. Such relief and tranquility I had not felt since my sojourn with William, before he revealed himself as the devil. Mistress Collace had prayed with me, and as she described the presence of Jesus, I actually saw Him sitting in front of me, the marks of the nails on his hands and feet, his hair flowing and eyes soft in a way I could barely imagine. Mistress kept praying, but I heard none of the words. Christ reached out His hand to me, and I took it.

As I lay down on the cold stone to sleep, I saw angels, too, all around Jesus, as numerous as the fairies in the grass. Angels and saints, for there were the saints: Brigid and Michael, Gabriel and Brendan.

And there, below the angels, in the green grass, sparkling and flitting back and forth, were the fairies. With them was a slender woman heavily clothed in white linen, her colors white and lemon. She was smiling at me. The Queen of Fairy.

MARGARET

CHAPTER 57

Thumping and clacking, the horses' hooves hammered in the courtyard. Lady Elizabeth ran down the tower steps to the door, flinging it open.

It was Sunday morning.

John Hay and Alexander Brodie stepped out of the carriage as Lucy and Margaret came from behind their mother. The two men, weak and ashen, shambled towards them.

"All night!" Mother cried. "You were in the kirk all night?"

Uncle looked at her with weary eyes. "We were, niece."

"But why? What happened?"

"We were hard pressed to find agreement on this matter."

"Agreement that had already transpired," Father said in a bitter voice as he sneered at Uncle Alexander and moved a step away.

"There were clouds over us," Uncle said with a sigh. "Mistress Collace did see them, and I was convicted by the Lord to seek again, to consider again, whether this decision should hold. We spent much time in prayer."

Mother regarded their faces, one after the other. Uncle Alexander now seemed older than his sixty years, and Father's sagging jowls drooped to an even greater degree.

Father hung his head and shook it back and forth. Uncle glanced at him. "Not everyone was in accord; we found that impossible."

"Was there a new decision, then?" asked Margaret.

"We believe the Lord was telling us not to commit one sin in order to expunge another."

"The witch goes free," Father sneered again.

Margaret dropped down onto the stoop as a great sigh issued from her whole body. Isobel would live.

"There was the problem of all the others she named." Uncle Alexander looked at Father, then back to Mother. "We saw that so many dozens of people could not all be guilty. Especially our Margaret."

"Ah." Margaret sank farther back.

"And our Bessie," Mother added.

"And we ceded to the opinion that there was so much fantasy in this confession that it could not be believed." He directed his gaze to Margaret, his expression unreadable. There was compassion in his look, but at the same time, a distance that hadn't been there before, as if he could no longer accept her with the love she had always expected from him. In his eyes, she had associated herself with evil, and he wouldn't soon forget. Nor would the others. When she'd left the church, they spat on her. They called her "witch" and "devil's whore." Who knew what else they had muttered and sniffed as she leaned on Mistress Collace, weeping and weeping?.

Margaret hunched over, forehead on her knees, and wept again. She cried out all the fear, horror, and despair, all mixed together. Isobel had been under a dark cloud of evil and hatred, and that cloud had descended on Margaret, as well. Isobel, this woman she had come to admire and yes, even love, this strange and beautiful soul. But now the cloud was lifted, and Isobel was free.

Margaret raised her head. But still. Isobel had named *her*, Margaret, as a witch. Why? Had Isobel been so tormented, almost beyond endurance, that she had named almost everyone she knew as her coven? *Coven*. Margaret had never even heard that word before.

She shivered in a sudden drop in temperature but had no inclination to go back into the castle. In her world, her religion, were so many dreary and joyless things. So much cruelty and hypocrisy. The Covenanters preached about love and charity but then turned around and murdered the women who sang and healed and cured. Margaret had sought something more, something of beauty, and she hadn't wanted to think that Isobel's world, too, could have another, darker side. Or that Isobel would feel so wronged–for the raid, for the execution of her mother– that she would want to use her magic to kill Margaret's father and Mister Harry.

A gust of wind whipped at her skirt and she held it down. Margaret could see now that she hadn't paid enough attention to Isobel's reality. The cold, the threadbare plaids, the smoke and dark in the hut, the hunger. Even Isobel's children, who were so ragged and bone thin. Margaret had brought a piece of cheese, a leg of mutton, yes, but she hadn't attended, really, to Isobel's suffering.

The wind was picking up and the sky was darkening, with clouds moving across the sun.

There had been clouds blocking her vision. That was it. Even when Isobel said a charm in the devil's name, Margaret hadn't seen.

A verse from the bible came to mind: *For now, we see through a glass, darkly; but then face to face: now I know in part; but then shall I know even as also I am known.* The Apostle, it seemed, was telling her that we can never see clearly, not until we get to heaven. And what we know is only a part.

But now Margaret could see more. The darkness of the glass was clearing, at least in part. She could see now that Isobel had power to do good and power to do evil, and she had done some of both. And her Covenanter people. They strove to do good, to understand God's laws, but they, too, had failed in enormous ways. People were not all good or all bad; most of them were some combination.

Everyone had departed—Uncle Alexander in his carriage, and Mother, Father, and Lucy into the castle, while Margaret stayed in the courtyard, lying on the stoop and studying the clouds: great masses of gray and white hovering above the bog and the lands to the west and south.

To the south lay England. She could have had a life with Andrew. If only she had been more discreet; if only she hadn't been so curious. Mister Harry had been right, she thought. About curiosity. Her curiosity had condemned her, but it was also her longing for something magical, something more beautiful than the dreary life of the castle.

What would happen to Isobel now?

Margaret walked around to the north side of the castle and gazed out toward the sea. Would Isobel go back to the farmtown? What kind of reception would she receive there? Would she be shunned by her neighbors, or would she resume her position as a cunning woman?

The wind blew from the west across the machair and the fields, and the sound was a constant roaring, so loud she didn't hear Andrew approach.

Suddenly, he was in front of her, coat flapping, hair blowing away from his face.

They stood and looked into each other's eyes.

"Please, come out of the wind," he said.

She led him to a sheltered spot between the north tower and the back of the great hall, and they sat huddled in the corner.

They sat in silence, looking out and away to the sea.

At last Andrew spoke. "I have been thinking and reflecting, and I see that my words were harsh and hasty."

"About your esteem of me?"

"My admiration and esteem of you are very great. I see now that you were searching for something beyond what we know. Your spirit, your curiosity, and imagination—these are the things I love about you. Perhaps you were a bit naïve about this woman . . ."

"Isobel taught me to see," Margaret replied. "Perhaps not the fairies, but the music in the world. To feel a shoot of hyssop and smell its essence. To see the soul of life in a bird or a hare. To understand the dolphins' voices. To hear the song of the sea."

He smiled. "I think you are a poet."

"A poet? I?"

"Perhaps you will write some of this."

Margaret had to pause. This was a new thought. Like Elizabeth Melville, she could write poetry. Hers would be about beauty. The beauty of nature, the things Isobel had taught her.

Andrew took her two hands in his. "I am just a soldier . . . but a soldier who loves poetry. And I love you. Will you forgive me?"

Margaret felt a sob welling up. He embraced her and she yielded, softening into his strong arms. Beneath the castle walls, with the wind bellowing around them, she felt something beyond this moment, something deep and eternal.

CHAPTER 58

When Isobel was let out of the tollbooth, Margaret was waiting, with Andrew beside her. The door opened slowly. Isobel, in her rags now washed clean, stepped into the light. The light was hazy and overcast, but it seemed to dazzle her. She blinked and looked around, then pulled her bonnet down to shade her eyes.

A few people lingered at the side of the road, silent, watching. There were no shouts of welcome, no rush of greetings or hugs. Stillness and suspicion permeated the murky light. Isobel's husband Hugh Gilbert stood to the side, in the shadow of the tollbooth, but did not approach her.

Margaret stepped forward. Andrew took her arm and gave her a questioning look.

"Isobel is my friend," she said. He nodded

She began to walk across the tollbooth yard.

The yard had never seemed so wide. Margaret took another step. "Isobel," she called.

Isobel saw her and almost smiled.

They walked toward one another.

⟨AUTHOR'S NOTES

Bitter Magic began with curiosity about the Covenanters. I was looking through a book my grandfather wrote about the Presbyterian ministers in our family history and saw that in the 17th century many of these ministers were "Covenanters." What were Covenanters? I wondered.

In 1638, thousands of Scots, incensed by King Charles I's attempt to suppress Presbyterianism, rallied at Greyfriars Church in Edinburgh to sign the "Solemn League and Covenant." This document declared the religious independence of Scotland from the English king and his bishops, and its signers were labeled "Covenanters." They became a military as well as a religious/political (inseparable terms) force, and as the Scottish Reformation grew, the Scots and English, Catholics and Protestants, vied for power in bloody battles.

These Covenanters were passionate in their fight for religious freedom and self-rule, but in the late 1600s, they were also caught up in the witch craze. Although they were rebelling against the Catholic religion, they embraced the aspect of Catholic theology that labeled some women "witches"—demons in human form that had to be obliterated.

At this time, most people were living rural agrarian lives, and most adhered to the ancient customs and traditions that drew on their connections to the earth, its seasons, plants, and animals, as did other agrarian cultures throughout the world. In Scotland, the Catholic Church had to some extent incorporated these traditions, but to the new Protestants, these beliefs were superstitious or heretical, and the leaders, most often women, were targeted as witches.

Here were two different ways of knowing–the rational, as manifest in ideals of freedom and justice, vs. the intuitive, with connection to earth, body awareness, and healing–that collided in a pivotal time in history. Not coincidentally it was a time when male power was supplanting female.

I became fascinated with this conflict; I could see the roots of it in our own time, and in particular, in my own spiritual life.

As a child of the seventies and a staunch feminist, I had been inspired by the Earth-based spirituality of Starhawk, the Wiccan author. Then, as my spiritual path evolved, in the eighties I went to theological seminary.

In seminary I thrilled to the genius and clarity of the Presbyterian theology that had inspired the creators of the U.S. Constitution. This was rational, western theology at its best, I thought. But the body-centered intuitive way of knowing was missing from it, and this was where feminist theology came in. In the seventies and eighties feminist theologians were enthusiastically reclaiming intuition as knowledge. Feminist theology begins with lived experience, women's connection to the earth and the body, rather than the rational mind. I was inspired by the Christian mystics like Julian of Norwich and Hildegard of Bingen, whose theologies had been marginalized by the church, but who, like yogic philosophers, Native Americans, and Wiccans, understood the Divine to be embodied in nature.

I identified with both ways of knowing: western theology that delights in the knowledge of the mind; and the grounded discernment of the mystics.

When I discovered the story of Isobel Gowdie in the heart of Covenanter territory, I was hooked. Here, at a turning point in history, were these two different worldviews in a battle for authority, two different roots of my own history. I dug into the research.

Coming from a liberal twenty-first century perspective, I struggled to understand the Covenanters. We now tend to see those Reformation Christians, because of the witch craze, as ignorant and evil. And we assume that the "witches" were good, herbalists and healers. But maybe, I thought, there was more to it on both sides.

Some of the Covenanters, like Harry Forbes, did indeed fit the stereotype: they lived in fear and justified horrible crimes against innocent people. But others, like Katharine Collace and Alexander Brodie, were earnest, caring, educated individuals who struggled to comprehend their world and their faith.

The cunning women had more than one dimension, too. Like Isobel, they did heal and uplift their communities, but they could also resort to vengeance and harm against their neighbors.

I also struggled to understand Isobel's tales of flying with the fairies and visiting the Queen in her underground abode. What did she mean when she claimed to travel in that "otherworld"? I never got an answer to that question, but studying the research about psychics, shamans, astral travel, and trance experience was a fascinating journey.

Throughout history, there have been people who have had (or claimed to have had) supernatural powers and the ability to communicate with the dead. Shamans, sorcerers, necromancers, and witches have been alternately revered and feared. In 1590, when King James VI of Scotland and I of England accused over seventy people of using witchcraft to cause a storm that destroyed his fleet, the fears and the persecutions mushroomed. Many of the people accused by James were tortured to confess, and some were executed. James then published the treatise *Daemonologie* to prove that magicians, sorcerers, and witches were demons in human form, and a perilous threat to Christianity. In 1604, he made witchcraft a felony punishable by death.

Thus, at a time when the majority of people believed in an otherworld of fairies, charms, and rituals, ensued an era of fear and persecution. The esteemed folk doctors and healers, mostly women, were now accused and devalued as witches.

The seventeenth century was also a time of great change in Europe. Scotland was moving into reduced dependence on agriculture and greater emphasis on trade. Ideas were flowing more freely, and the Age of Reason was beginning. The Scottish Reformation, while it brought many benefits to society, also ushered in the idea that religion and theology should be based upon reason. Traditional folk beliefs that depended on intuition, extrasensory perception, and belief in a deep connection to the Earth and nature were all deemed superstition. They had to be abolished. And, since the leaders of traditional belief systems were most often female, women were judged to be, if not witches, at least irrational. Only men, who were deemed rational, could be trusted as rulers, leaders, and ministers.

By 1735, when the witchcraft law was finally repealed, almost 4,000 people, mostly women, in Scotland alone had been accused, and roughly sixty-seven percent of them had been executed for witchcraft.

CHARACTERS

Most of the characters in this book were real people. I have tried to remain true to their life situations while incorporating them into a work of historical fiction, which is always a blend of fact and imagination.

ISOBEL GOWDIE

In April and May of 1662, the four confessions of Isobel Gowdie were recorded by John Innes, notary, in Auldearn, Scotland. Scholars believe that Isobel was probably convicted and executed, but there is no record of this, and I have used that lack of knowledge to put a different spin on the verdict.

Most of Isobel's charms and rhymes in *Bitter Magic* came directly from her confessions, as did her accounts of flying with the fairies, rituals for healing, black magic, and her intercourse with the devil, though I modernized some of the language.

Isobel did claim that she could "raise the wind." There was no catastrophic sandstorm in 1662, but in 1684, further up the coast, there was a similar storm that buried estates and changed the landscape, and many people believed that witches had caused it.

Isobel's confessions followed, to some extent, a well-known formula in witch confessions: the black mass, coven meetings, intercourse with the devil, and more. We don't have records of her interrogators' questions, but they probably knew and could have articulated those formulae for her to repeat. But some scholars believe that Isobel was not, in fact, tortured or forced to confess; her confessions digressed from the formula, and were so fantastical and imaginative that questions multiplied. Had the things she related really happened? Was she a shaman? A visionary? A psychic/astral traveler? Psychotic? A witch? Read Emma Wilby's fascinating study in *The Visions of Isobel Gowdie* for an analysis of theories from then and now. I put some of these into the mouths of her trial commissioners.

Women who had some power in the community, the "cunning women," were healers and herbalists. They also often had a strong sense of social justice. Raids on tenants' stores by oppressive landlords were common, and cunning women did sometimes use the only power they had to fight back: black magic. I think of Isobel's revenge rituals as, among other things, a pre-feminist fight for justice.

HUGH GILBERT
Isobel's husband's real name was John Gilbert. I changed his name, since there were so many other men named John in the story. His character, their spousal relationship, and their children were my inventions.

JOHN HAY
The Laird of Park and Lochloy was married to Alexander Brodie's niece, and did have two daughters. In historical documents, he is portrayed as continually in debt, often borrowing money to stay afloat. Tensions were high between Hay and his tenants—particularly Isobel, whom he believed (and as she confessed) was out to kill him. He also believed that Agnes Grant had caused the death of his father and brother. Agnes Grant (who was not, in reality, Isobel's mother) was tortured and executed as a witch.

MARGARET HAY
The real names of John Hay's daughters were not recorded. Margaret is my invention, as is Lucy.

ELIZABETH BRODIE
John Hay's wife was the niece of Alexander Brodie. I could find no record of her first name, so I called her Elizabeth.

KATHARINE COLLACE
Katharine was a real person and earnest Covenanter who served as a tutor to John Hay's two daughters. Katharine did lose nine children to death, and, as she expressed in her diary, struggled with wrenching feelings of despair and distance from God. She also found the courage to go on through faith and comfort in her mystical experiences of Christ. In her diary, she voices regret about her marriage to John Ross and her admiration for her mentor, Thomas

Hog (or Hogg). Katharine hints that Harry Forbes "took a liberty" with her. Other sources report that Harry's wife told Katharine to leave the area. There is no evidence that Katharine was involved in the trial of Isobel Gowdie.

ALEXANDER BRODIE

The Laird of Brodie, also an ardent Covenanter, was one of the commissioners who escorted King Charles II from Breda in the Netherlands to Scotland for his coronation. In his diary, he expresses respect and friendship for Katharine Collace. Like her, he practiced the spiritual disciplines of confession, self-degradation, and repentance, a ritual practice among the Covenanters. Brodie also writes of his disgust at the ungodliness of Harry Forbes's family. Brodie was a powerful and respected laird in the community, and he did have a daughter named Grissel. It is true that, in his youth, Brodie joined a gang of fanatic anti-papist youth who vandalized the Elgin Cathedral in an effort to destroy "graven images."

HARRY FORBES

"Mister Harry" was minister of the Auldearn Church from 1655 to 1663. He had very little money, struggled with solvency, and was a fervent Covenanter and witch hunter who targeted Isobel. He was, indeed, "sick in bed" for a time. His illness didn't result from falling off a horse, but Isobel did perform the ritual curse to keep him "sick and sore." Like many of the ministers of his time, Mister Harry was resented and disliked by his parishioners because of his strict moral code. At the same time, he was known to be having an adulterous affair with a servant girl.

JULIA

Harry's wife, whose real name is unknown, apparently knew about his affair(s) with the servant and suspected Katharine of this as well. She did command Katharine to leave the area.

ANDREW MASSIE

Andrew is my invention. Edward Massie was an ardent Covenanter who helped escort King Charles II back from Scotland and could have had a nephew Andrew's age. Many of the occupying English soldiers courted local Scottish girls.

HUGH ROSE

Hugh was the minister at Nairn and served on Isobel's witch trial commission.

HENRIETTA ROSE

Hugh Rose had a family, but Henrietta is my invention.

ISOBEL'S COVEN

In her confessions, Isobel mentions Elspeth Nychie, who taught her witch-craft—and many other names, some of whom I used in this story (including the "maid," Jane Martin).

TRIAL COMMISSIONERS

Most of the named commissioners in *Bitter Magic* were those of real people on Isobel's commission, though what they said and believed was my invention.

PLACES

INSHOCH CASTLE

Inshoch was the seat of the Hay family, the Lairds of Park and Lochloy. Toward the end of the 1600s, the Hays lost the castle due to overwhelming debt, and it passed into the hands of Alexander Brodie. Apparently, it has not been inhabited since that time. It is now in ruin, but you can still see the castle shape and one of the towers in the ruins. Inshoch sits on land now owned by James and Doreen Campbell. When I was performing my research in the Moray area, I visited these ruins. James and Doreen graciously welcomed me to the site, served me tea, and provided me with a great deal of castle history and lore about Isobel, who was known in the area as "the witch of Auldearn." You can find the story of this visit, with photos, in my blog under "The Kindness of Strangers" (nancykilgore.com).

KILROCK CASTLE

In reality, the name is Kilravock (pronounced Kilrock). Kilravock has been owned and occupied by the Rose family since the 1500s. The castle is now owned by a Christian trust established in 1971 by Elizabeth Rose, the 25th Baroness.

BRODIE CASTLE

The historic home of the influential Brodie family, this well-preserved castle is now owned by the National Trust for Scotland.

DARNAWAY CASTLE

Darnaway, one of the grandest castles in this region of Scotland, is the seat of the Earls of Moray. Someone like Margaret probably did attend a ball in its great hall. Built in the 1500s, it is the one remaining original section of Darnaway. The castle has remained in the same family for centuries and is still a private residence owned by John Stuart, the 21st Earl of Moray.

CAWDOR CASTLE

Cawdor is the legendary home of Shakespeare's Thane of Cawdor in *Macbeth*. Shakespeare adjusted the facts to fit his story (when the real Macbeth reigned, Cawdor wasn't built yet), as have I. Cawdor Castle, where some members of the Campbell family still live, is administered by the National Trust of Scotland.

DOWNIE HILL

Downie Hill is a real place and in the same area Isobel indicated in *Bitter Magic*. It is now known as one of the many Iron Age dun forts dotting the Scottish landscape. When I visited the area, I had a lot of fun searching for Isobel's fairy mound, that even some of the locals had not heard of. When I finally found it, accompanied by my friend Morag, we traipsed up the bracken-covered hill in the middle of a wood (the Downie Wood, of course) and discovered a real sense of deep and magical peace, though we didn't see any fairies. *In Search of Isobel*, a story about this adventure, was published in *The Bottle Imp* by the Association of Scottish Literary Studies. https://www.thebottleimp.org.uk/2018/12/in-search-of-isobel/.

THE FARMTOWN (OR FERMTOUN)

This is where Isobel and the other farmworkers lived, on the estate of the Laird of Park and Lochloy. Its ruins are thought to be near Loch Loy.

OLD SCOTS LANGUAGE TERMS

An da shealladh – second sight, (in/of two sights)

burn – small river or fresh water

corp creadh – human figures of clay or wax used for ritual magic

duyning – fading or wasting away

kill or *kil* – riverbed (in the context of Isobel's confession); little chapel

lith – limb or joint

machair – grassy plain where cattle graze

mickle(or muckle) – large

nith – ill will, envy, hatred, enmity, abject, abhorrent

stickle – little stick

stour – dust

wighting and dighting – making ready (fashioning) and weighing

FOR FURTHER READING

Black, Ronald, ed. *The Gaelic Otherworld: John Gregorson Campbell's Superstitions of the Highlands and Islands of Scotland and Witchcraft and Second Sight in the Highlands and Islands*, 1900 and 1902. Edited by Ronald Black. Edinburgh, Scotland: Birlinn Limited, 2014.

A classic compendium of folklore and the supernatural by a nineteenth-century scholar.

Brodie, Alexander of Brodie and Brodie, James of Brodie. *The Diary of Alexander Brodie of Brodie and of His Son, James Brodie of Brodie, MDCLXXX–MDCLXXXV.* Aberdeen, Scotland: Printed for the Spalding Club, 1863. Reprinted Middletown, DE, 2016.

This 560-page journal was transcribed from the handwritten and printed in 1740. In it, Brodie mentions his daily activities and encounters, but it is primarily a spiritual journal in the 17th-century style: a pious examination of one's acts and flaws, including prayers and pleas to God. He refers to Isobel Gowdie as "Park's witch."

Brodie-Innes, J.W. *The Devil's Mistress.* London: 1915. Electronic edition published by Black Heath Editions, 2014.

The author was a descendant of some of the main characters in his (and my) story of Isobel, but his Isobel was a red-haired, middle-class sex siren—a turn-of-the-century romantic male rendering. Brodie-Innes was involved in the occult movement of his time, and his version of Isobel's story is fun to read.

Carmichael, Alexander. *Carmina Gadelica: Hymns and Incantations*, 1899. https://www.sacred-texts.com/neu/celt/cg1/.

A contemporary of John Gregorson Campbell, Carmichael traveled the islands and highlands of Scotland collecting folklore, rhymes, stories, songs, and prayers, the melodies woven into the daily lives of the people.

Collace, Katharine. "Memoirs or Spiritual Exercises of Mistress Ross. Written with her own hand." In *Women's Life Writing in Early Modern Scotland: Writing the Evangelical Self, c.1670-c.1730*, edited by David George Mullan. Hants, England: Ashgate Publishing Limited, 2003.
    Like Alexander Brodie, Katharine Collace writes of her anguish over her many losses, turning from and then back to her faith, her interactions with people, and her work in the beleaguered Covenanter movement. Like Brodie's writing, the diary is written as a spiritual exercise.

Goodare, Julian, Lauren Martin, Joyce Miller, and Louise Yeoman. *The Survey of Scottish Witchcraft, 1563-1736*. Edinburgh, Scotland: University of Edinburgh, January 2003. http://witches.shca.ed.ac.uk/
    A massive study including a database compiling facts about witches accused and executed, genders (of whom 80+ percent were women,) marital status, geographical context, and dates and locations in Scotland.

Kirk, Robert. *The Secret Commonwealth of Elves, Fauns and Fairies*, with an introduction by Andrew Lang (2nd edition). New York: 2008. A delightful little book written in 1691 by a Presbyterian minister who studied and sympathized with the beliefs of his parishioners. He describes second sight, the different levels of seers, the otherworld of spirits, and the fairy kingdom with thoroughness and a sense of awe and respect for this complex belief system.

Melville, Elizabeth. *Ane Godlie Dreame*. A Calvinist dream-vision poem. Edinburgh: Robert Charteris, 1603. https://digital.nls.uk/selected-wee-windaes-books/archive/125652021 - ?c=0&m=0&s=0&cv=21&xywh=0,-586,5965, 5383. This poem is the earliest known published work by a Scottish woman.

Wilby, Emma. *Cunning Folk and Familiar Spirits: Shamanistic Visionary Traditions in Early Modern British Witchcraft and Magic*. Sussex Academic Press, U.K, 2006.
    Exploring similarities in British witchcraft with shamanism in tribal societies throughout the world.

Wilby, Emma. *The Visions of Isobel Gowdie: Magic, Witchcraft and Dark Shamanism in Seventeenth-Century Scotland.* East Sussex, U.K.: Sussex Academic Press, 2013.

An important study of Isobel's life and trial that compares her experiences to international accounts and theories of shamans, visionaries, night flights, fairies, witches, and the otherworld. This book contains the complete confessions of Isobel Gowdie in the original Scots language.

$\mathcal{A}$CKNOWLEDGMENTS

Many thanks to Emma Wilby, whose stupendous research in *The Visions of Isobel Gowdie* provided the foundation for my understanding of Isobel's life, stories, experiences, and the community she was in.

I am grateful to the people in the Moray region in Scotland who graciously welcomed and helped me with the research for this story: Andrew Coombs, whose Lochloy House sits in the midst of Isobel's territory, for the generous gift of his guest cottage during my stay in the area as well as his knowledge of local history. It was wonderful to walk through the Lochloy Wood, to feel and smell the air in the very place where Isobel lived her magical and tragic life; John Stuart, 21st Earl of Moray, and Grant Kerr, castle keeper, for access to and information about Darnaway Castle and its great hall, built in the 1500s; James and Doreen Campbell, owners of the land where Inshoch Castle sits; Morag Paterson, who caught my enthusiasm for Isobel and gamely joined me in the search for Downie Hill.

Thanks to my doulas in the birthing of this novel: sister writers Anne Bergeron, Rebecca Buchanan, Miranda Moody, and Tania Aebi. For feedback and encouragement, I thank the writers of the Burlington Writers Workshop, the Writers in Paradise Workshop, and the Spanocchia Writers Workshop. I am grateful to Laura Lippman, who helped with the novel's direction, plot, and points of view. Many thanks to my pastoral psychotherapist writing group, Ron Baard, Laura Delaplain, and John Karl, whose ongoing support, wisdom, and inspiration has sustained me throughout.

For time apart to focus exclusively on writing, I thank Virginia Center for Creative Arts, Silver Bay YMCA of the Adirondacks Ministry Program, and the Turkey Land Cove Foundation.

Last but not least, thanks to my husband, Jess, for unstinting and continual support of my writing, including his creation of the map of old Moray.

ABOUT THE AUTHOR

NANCY HAYES KILGORE is the author of two other novels, *Wild Mountain* (Green Writers Press, 2017) and *Sea Level* (RCWMS, 2011). Her writing has won a Pushcart Prize nomination, the Vermont Writers Prize, and a ForeWord Reviews Book of the Year Award. She holds Master of Divinity and Doctor of Ministry degrees and is a graduate of the Radcliffe Writing Seminars. She is a psychotherapist and former parish pastor who coaches writers and leads workshops on creative writing and spirituality.

As in *Bitter Magic,* Nancy's other books express reverence for the natural world while exploring clashes in beliefs and values in people and their communities. *Sea Level,* set in an isolated seacoast town, is about a church in conflict and two women searching for spiritual truth; *Wild Mountain,* set in a Vermont mountain town in conflict over gay marriage, is an adult love story.

CPSIA information can be obtained
at www.ICGtesting.com
Printed in the USA
LVHW031601030821
694341LV00005B/587